PENGUIN BOOKS

PURPOSES OF LOVE

Mary Renault was educated at Clifton High School, Bristol and St Hugh's College, Oxford. Having completed her nursing training in 1937, she returned to nursing in 1939 until the end of the war. In 1948 she went to live in South Africa. Her other publications include *Kind are Her Answers*, *The Friendly Young Ladies*, *Return to Night*, *North Face*, *The Charioteer*, *The Last of the Wine*, *The King Must Die*, *The Bull from the Sea*, *The Lion and the Gateway* (for children), *The Mask of Apollo*, *The Nature of Alexander* and *The Praise Singer*. *Fire From Heaven*, the first volume of her acclaimed Alexander trilogy, won the Silver Pen Award in 1971 and was followed in 1972 by *The Persian Boy*. The third volume is *Funeral Games* and the three books are published in Penguin in individual volumes and have also been published together as *The Alexander Trilogy*.

Mary Renault was made a Fellow of the Royal Society of Literature in 1959. She died on 13 December 1983. *Purposes of Love* was her first novel, originally published in 1939.

Mary Renault

—

Purposes of Love

Penguin Books

Penguin Books Ltd, Harmondsworth, Middlesex, England
Viking Penguin Inc., 40 West 23rd Street, New York, New York 10010, U.S.A.
Penguin Books Australia Ltd, Ringwood, Victoria, Australia
Penguin Books Canada Limited, 2801 John Street, Markham, Ontario, Canada L3R 1B4
Penguin Books (N.Z.) Ltd, 182–190 Wairau Road, Auckland 10, New Zealand

First published by Longmans 1939
Revised edition published 1968
Published in Penguin Books 1986

Printed and bound in Great Britain by
Cox & Wyman Ltd, Reading

To
J.M.
for Thoughts

— 1 —

At a white-tiled table a young girl was sitting, sucking a bullseye and sewing a shroud. Her hands moved in and out of a pool of red-shaded lamplight, glowing in their passage first crimson and then white. She was nineteen, pretty, undersized and Welsh; hideously dressed in striped cotton, a square-bibbed apron that reached her high collar, black shoes and stockings and a stiff white cap.

Nightfall had simplified the ward, picking out highlights and resolving them into pattern, drowning detail, subduing movement, fixing for a moment the symmetry for which, all day, everyone fought errant nature.

Over some of the cots that lined the walls lamps were burning, muffled in red. Under one of them, the child who presently would wear the shroud was lying with a pinched, waxy face, breathing jerkily through a half-open mouth. An apparatus of glass and rubber tubing was running salt and water into her veins to eke out the exhausted blood. It was all that could now be done. Sister, going through her stock that afternoon, had noticed that all her shrouds were too short, and had put out the necessary materials in the sewing-basket. The little nurse stitched doggedly away, thinking of a film she had seen that afternoon, of the boy who had taken her, and of what she would wear when she met him again. She had made plenty of shrouds; the first few had made her feel creepy, but they were just like the rest of the mending and darning now.

Under the green-shaded lamp at the Sister's table the staff-nurse was writing the day report, glancing up at the patients now and then to refresh her mind with ideas. She was hoping that Joan would not die before her parents arrived from the next county. Joan was unconscious; and when the mother

I

came there would be nothing for her to do but to sit, heavy with sleeplessness, staring into that severe and distant face until, after a monotonous eternity, she cried with relief when the screens were closed and she was led away. Still, it looked bad to put in the report, "Relatives not present". It was seven o'clock, the time when one began to look at a dying patient and wonder whether they would last till the night-nurses came on duty. A death meant about an hour's steady and unpleasant work, and forms in triplicate.

There was a whimpering from a cot in the corner. A fat little boy, admitted that day, was sitting up with a damp sheet rucked under him, clutching the cot-bars, his eyes round and bright like a trapped animal's between his fists. He had slept in his mother's bed every night, till tonight, of his two years, and would probably have felt no more alien in a Brazilian forest.

"Do get that child straight before the night people come," said the staff-nurse. "He looks awful. Wet, I expect."

The probationer laid aside her sewing and wearily collected a clean sheet, soap and water, spirit and powder. She was tired, but reflected that in an adult ward she would not have been sitting at all. Even here, where there was so much sewing, it was tacitly understood that one selected the smallest and most uncomfortable chair, and appeared to sit reluctantly. The chairs used by the day-nurses had been designed in the 'eighties for straight-backed Victorian children. To relax was unprofessional. There were two full-sized basket chairs, but only the night-nurses used them in the secret and sacred watch after the Night Sister's midnight round.

Presently she put her screens back in the corner and, opening the glass doors at the end of the ward, tossed the sheet through on to the balcony tiles.

"One more. Sorry."

"It's all right. I haven't counted yet."

Vivian Lingard stooped in a pool of blurred light from the windows, sorting laundry and entering the numbers on a long printed list. She had come to the babies' squares, and was

2

counting them by the moist plops as they fell. Two children in cots, muffled to the ears, breathed rhythmically on either side. If she put the light on they would wake, but there was time tonight to work in the dark.

Vivian propped the list against the wall and wrote, "Squares, 15", and rubbed her back, which was aching. Beyond the wrought-iron balcony railings was a huge ragged pool of luminous sky, the space round which the hospital was built. The black surrounding skyline, owing something to every decade for a century and a half, was as irregular as a Dolomite range and less consistent; Victorian-Gothic crenellations here, a decent Georgian pediment there; then a new block of the 1930s, an austere functional cube. From them all came the same unwinking stare of red eyes, except where a great beam, like a stage lime, picked out grass and leaves in unnatural aniline colour; the theatre was at work.

Above it all, looking vague and supernumerary, a half-moon drifted across the clouds. Vivian blinked at it, lifting a hand to shut the theatre light away, and trying to remember how moonlight looked over the high moors at home. It made her think—as many other things did—about her brother, the only person she used to allow to accompany her there. She realised that she was very tired, and would have rubbed her eyes; but her hands were so dirty that instinctively she drew them back again.

A man's feet sounded on the iron balcony stairs. The house surgeon, no doubt, come to see if the intravenous apparatus was working. She bent to tie up the laundry bundle.

"Excuse me. Does Nurse Lingard——"

"Jan!"

Unbelievably he was there, standing behind her in the reddened light from the ward.

"Well, I'm damned." Not only now, but always, Jan's voice seemed freshly warmed by some pleasant discovery. "I never thought that efficient backside could belong to you."

"But I was thinking about you!" She stared at him, unconsciously rubbing the palms of her hands, which felt sticky,

3

against the sides of her apron, incredulously smiling. For Jan to be present on a wish, instead of half a continent or so away, was like a delightful reversal of nature. He had got very tanned, though it was so early in the year; she always noticed how this made his hair, which should have been the same colour as her own, look much fairer. "I was thinking of you," she said delighted, "only a moment ago."

"Were you?" He slanted his head, looking not at her uniform which he had never seen before but at her face; seemed to form some conclusion, and came over to kiss her. Her starched waistband amused him; he drummed a little tune on it with his fingers. "How extraordinary you smell."

"It's dirt, mostly," she said, but did not move. It was always pleasant to be touched by Jan; as if, from being much in the sun, he could give out a little, as the sea does, when it was absent. As soon as he put his arm around her she had forgotten she was tired. He was sniffing her shoulder in interested analysis.

"Carbolic, isn't it, partly? I like it. Most individual."

"Individual?" -She laughed under her breath; his presence was so inevitable already as to be commonplace. "Really, Jan, I didn't know your experience was so limited. Do you mean to tell me you've never made love to a nurse?"

"Well," Jan apologised, "I haven't been ill, you know, since we had measles, and it was a bit early then. By the way, does it matter my being here?"

Vivian looked round in sudden panic. "Of course it does. You can't come here, I'm on duty. I was so surprised to see you, I didn't think."

"Oh, very well, see you later." He moved towards the stairs with that light contented acquiescence which she had always thought must be so intolerable to the people who fell in love with him. Even Vivian, after all these years, was not wholly immune.

"If Nurse Page sees you," she said to keep him a moment longer, "she'll think you're a man come to see me."

"Better let her come and take a look."

4

Jan—he was twenty-nine—was the elder of them by three years, but from their teens onwards strangers had often taken them for twins. They themselves, more conscious of their differences as close relatives are, still found this amusing. They took for granted their light beech-brown hair, clear brown skins shaped closely to the bone, grey eyes, thick soft eyebrows nearly meeting in the middle; their springy uprightness, their long thin hands and feet: and remained unaware of a hundred tricks of voice and manner, some family stock, some individual to the one but picked up by the other. These things seemed trivial to them, their inner contrasts enormous and, to their accustomed eyes, colouring the outside too.

In the last few years the resemblance had lessened. Vivian had shed an early boyish gawkiness; and Jan, toughening under climatic and other influences, lost an air of rather fine-drawn aestheticism which had misled a good many people to their confusion. At some unnoticed stage of the process he had acquired an arresting kind of beauty which Vivian found teasing, because she possessed most of its raw materials herself. It was a style, though, that went better on a man; typical, she often thought, of Jan to get the best of the bargain so early and unawares.

There were other differences. Jan was a few inches taller, and there was a hazel fleck in his eyes which turned them by some lights from grey to green. In repose Vivian's mouth shut straight and rather seriously, while Jan's had that slight, remote and somewhat disquieting smile often found on the statuary of archaic Greece.

As he stood in the weak shaft of light at the iron stairhead, poised, as he was always poised, ready to go, she considered him afresh. He has everything, she thought, and seems to need nothing. It's curious that I shouldn't detest him. Most sisters would. And she wished, wondering how many other people had wished it, that she loved him less.

"Come up here," she said, "against the wall. You can't be seen then."

"All right." He moved over accommodatingly, sat down

5

on the bale of laundry and propped his back against the wall, stretching out his nailed shoes. "Come on." He patted the hummock beside him, smiling up at her.

"No thanks," said Vivian, withdrawing. "Neither would you if you knew what was inside."

Jan arranged himself more comfortably. "What is dirt? Merely, as someone said, Russell I expect unless I thought of it myself, unwanted irrelevance. You can sit on my knee if you're so fussy." He took a handful of the seat of her dress and pulled her down with a thud.

"Jan, you're insane. Someone will come out and they'll never believe us." But she settled herself, a stream of dim childish recollections lulling her into pleasant security. His jacket smelt of peat-smoke, petrol, tobacco and dry summer earth.

"How do you come to be down here, anyway?" she asked curiously. "Not to see me."

"Of course. Partly." A sleepy noise came from one of the cots, and they lowered their voices.

"Is Alan with you?"

"Alan?" he murmured in vague surprise. "No. Alan's in Italy somewhere. I think."

"Short innings," was Vivian's only comment.

"He's writing," said Jan sharply. "He's damned good, too."

"I expect so," Vivian agreed, confirmed in her opinion by this punctilious loyalty. Alan had struck her, during a brief meeting, as dangerously tenacious.

"How did Scotland go?" she asked.

"Oh, very well. The new pendulum's a great improvement. More stable, and gives finer shades of accuracy. Shall I tell you about it?"

"Not here, we won't have time. Did you write anything?"

"Only the work. I don't know what we did all the time. Talked, I shouldn't wonder. Oh, yes." He grinned retrospectively. "And Mic tried to photograph birds."

"Mic?" she asked with tepid curiosity. If she found out who he was she would never remember; she had long ceased

6

trying to keep track of what, fresh from *Comus*, she had once annoyed Jan by calling his Rout.

"Yes," he said. "You must meet Mic, you'll probably like him."

"Shall I?" She smiled, concealing a certain lack of enthusiasm. Her encounters with the Rout had not, so far, been very felicitous. Alan, cold with jealousy, had hated her unobtrusively; Thora had appeared in her room, weeping, at three in the morning and stayed till five; and Nigel, during a fortnight's visit that seemed to last for months, had whiled away Jan's lengthening absences by engaging her in long nostalgic conversations, which he opened by telling her how like Jan she was.

"No, I meant it," said Jan. "He's here."

"Where?" She peered, alarmed, into the shadows. "He mustn't be here, get him away quickly."

"Don't be fat-headed," said Jan, reverting to the schoolroom. "I mean I'm staying with him. He's starting a job here. We've been looking at digs, but Mic's sensitive to the macabre and decided to take an unfurnished flat. I'm helping him fix it. Filthy place, but it'll be all right when we've done it up."

"Why don't you have it done?"

"Because Mic's only got three pounds sixteen and fivepence."

"It sounds a bit bleak." She found herself, to her own surprise, concealing an unavowed hostility. "Where will you sleep, on the floor?"

"No," Jan explained in good faith. "The floors aren't stained yet. We've slept at a pub so far."

So far? And he had only just come to see her. She asked, with polite interest, "Are you staying with him long?"

"No," said Jan slowly. "I shall be leaving as soon as we've fixed the flat." He added, quickly casual, "Going down to Cornwall to hunt for tin."

"Hope you find some," said Vivian; foolishly, since whatever minerals happened to be present would afford him equal interest. But she had been, for a moment, abstracted. A certain regretful finality in his voice had informed her that Mic was on his way to join Alan and the rest in the limbo of Jan's unfinished symphonies. She rested her head against his friendly unyielding shoulder, wondering again what it was that, mixed with his hardness, made him so ineluctably dear. She thought of Alan with his smooth wit and angry eyes; of Thora and of the dark brilliant woman she had only seen once, of whom Jan would never talk at all; her compassion tinged with contempt, because they should have known that Jan was not for them or for anyone. As for herself, she thought, life had freed her from possessiveness. She might have reflected with more truth that Jan had trained her to suppress it.

"But what about you?" he asked her suddenly. You're the one whose impressions are interesting. I want to know."

"There isn't time now." She doubted whether there ever would be time. "We'll be meeting tomorrow."

"It's changed you." He tilted her face in his hand towards the light.

"It's the uniform."

A thin whimpering, blurred with sleep, began in the nearest cot. She got up from his knees and slid her hand between the sheets.

"Wet?" inquired Jan, interested

She nodded. "Where did you find out about babies, Jan?"

"Don't be evil-minded. I remembered you."

"Well, you *will* have to go now." She patted the keening child with encouraging noises; a little awkwardly, for she had not been on the children's ward long. Jan was watching her with private enjoyment.

"All right, come to the pub tomorrow. When are you free?"

"Ten-thirty. But we're sacked if we're seen in a pub."

"Great heaven. Well, I'll wait for you outside here."

"No, don't. They might change my off-duty to two or half-past five, you can never be sure. (S-sh, good girl, Nurse

8

is coming.) I'll meet you at eleven at Dilling's, it's a coffee shop, anyone will tell you." If they met outside it meant eating her next meal in hospital to an accompaniment of, "Was that your brother meeting you this morning, Lingard? He *is* like you, isn't he? I said to Walker as soon as I saw you out together, That must be Lingard's brother, you could tell it anywhere. He looks very clever. I expect he *reads* a lot, like you." And, hopefully, "I expect it's rather *boring* for him when you're on duty, isn't it?"

Dilling's was dowdy and comfortable, had no wireless, and was not much patronised by the hospital staff.

"Dilling's. Eleven," he said. She did not urge him to write it down; he never forgot things he intended to remember. "I'll bring Mic along, shall I? I think it would do him good."

"Do if you like," said Vivian; a defence-mechanism, which practice had made nearly automatic, concealing the fact that she was hurt. But the invitation stopped short of warmth.

"No? Good, we leave Mic to do his house-painting. We can talk better by ourselves."

The intrusion of Mic was wafted away. For a moment Vivian clung obstinately to her receding indignation; but, as usual, it turned to mist in her hands. Jan leaned over the edge of the cot, and absently stroked the baby's stomach with the back of a bent forefinger. Its crying sank at once to an unconvinced whimper. He went on stroking with a half-smile; but his eyes were not smiling and his thoughts seemed on other things.

"When you meet Mic—if you do—" he said slowly, "be easy on him." He surrendered his finger, without looking, to the child's sleepy clutch. The whimper became a faint hiccup, then silence. "He's had a very——"

But Vivian's eye had been caught by the balcony door.

"I believe Page saw you then. She's still looking. Suppose I tell her who you are? She might give us another few minutes presently, when I've changed the child."

"What? Oh, no, leave it. Too much fuss. See you tomorrow."

He was gone. At the top of the iron stairs he smiled over his shoulder and disappeared; and the baby, after an instant of shocked silence, broke into a wail shrill with outrage, astonishment, and loss. Vivian picked it up. It slobbered indignantly into her neck, its fat year-old face creased with grief under a bandage that sat, like a lopsided turban, over one ear. She rocked its damp softness for a moment in her arms, its cries blending with Thora's dimly-remembered sobbing at the back of her mind.

On the threshold of the ward Page met her, peering out.

"Whatever was Mr. Herbert doing out there all that time? I particularly wanted to speak to him. Has he *gone?*"

"It wasn't Mr. Herbert. It was my brother looking for me. He's just arrived from Scotland. Stupid of him to come here, but people don't realise, you know. I told him I was on duty and sent him away."

The staff-nurse's eyes had lost their narrow look, and quickened with interest.

"What a shame. You needn't have sent him off like that, kid." (She was two years younger than Vivian, but all juniors were "kid" to her unbent moods.) "He could have stopped a minute, and had a look at the ward." A pity, she reflected. You could let Lingard have little things; she was a good kid and didn't take advantage. Besides, her brother would be sure to be a nice type of boy, probably an undergrad. Undergraduates came next after housemen in the scale of achievement.

— 2 —

Vivian woke early, before the maids came trampling along the corridors, thumping the doors, and popping a shrill head through each like a cuckoo out of a clock.

"Twenty-to-seven-nurse."

"Thank you," said Vivian. The sun was shining, and she wondered for a moment why this was making her so pleased. Then she remembered that she was meeting Jan. She lay and looked at the light leaping on a favourite bowl of thick green glass; liking even her room, a square cream-coloured box eight feet by seven and identical, down to the seams in the lino, with a hundred others, the bed, chest and chair disposed in positions ordained by regulation and unalterable. The tenant was allowed to display not more than six objects of her own; Vivian, with some difficulty, had succeeded in getting her row of books counted as one instead of seventeen.

At breakfast she shared a table with the other nine members of her training set, half listening to what they said, which in six months had become familiar, even soothing, as the National Anthem.

"Well, you know what the round is on Malplaquet when you're on alone. And then she ticked me off for not having started the washings, and she hadn't done a thing herself except play up to all the housemen. . . . Sister's day off, I remember because we were having a cup of tea behind the kitchen door. . . . And they found it simply full of fluid, six pints they got. . . ."

The noise died down as if a door had been shut on it. The Sister who was taking breakfast had risen to call the roll. Vivian answered to her name mechanically, seeing in her mind the coffee-shop and Jan sitting at a window-table

11

which, for no particular reason, she had assigned to him. The roll came to an end.

"Nurse Cope to Crecy. Nurse Fowler to Harfleur. Nurse Kimball to Verdun. Nurse Lingard to Verdun." The Sister sat down; the rattle of voices began again.

"I say, fancy. Were you due to change your ward, Lingard?"

"No," said Vivian stolidly.

"Does it mess up your off-duty?"

"I was meeting my brother."

"Oh, bad *luck*."

As if she had staked on the wrong colour at roulette, Vivian thought. Indeed, making any sort of engagement outside the hospital was very similar in principle. Her mind felt heavy and dull; she could see Jan looking out of the window and, after a long time, at his watch. She had, too, a silly vision of the hospital spinning round like a wheel and nurses rolling round it to fall, feebly struggling, into fortuitous holes. There was no way of getting at Jan. She had forgotten, in any case, to ask where he was staying.

Following the usual procedure—notice of moves was never given, so hers was a predicament happening to someone nearly every day—she sought out one of the Verdun probationers.

"What duty will I be taking, do you know?"

"You're extra. Heavy take-in this week. Extra beds both sides and right down the middle."

"Oh," said Vivian. "Thanks." It meant that she was not on the ward schedule and would be sent off each day when the Sister happened to think of it.

"Made arrangements?" said the Verdun probationer. "Bad luck."

The Home Sister went out, releasing them. Through the scraping of chairs she could hear Colonna Kimball, two tables away, swearing. She was the other nurse who had been read out for Verdun, a second-year whose path Vivian had not crossed so far. Her vocabulary seemed richer than the one in standard use, and Vivian noticed that a rather precious public-school accent lent it the effect of higher explosive charge.

Verdun was the newest women's surgical ward, a dazzling open stretch of light and symmetry and porcelain and chromium. Even with its extra beds it looked spacious and orderly; but custom had, for Vivian, invested the Victorian muddle of Crecy with a kind of shabby cosiness, and she felt chilly and jumpy like a cat in a new house. She imagined Jan watching her fuss as one might the scuttlings of a worried ant in a formicarium; pulled herself together, and began on the line of beds, stripping them, because she was extra, for the others to make.

"Beds again," said the first old woman she came to, drawing her knees up under the loose blanket. She rubbed her skinny arms, sore from daily injections. "Seems to me life's nothing but beds and stabbing." Vivian made a standard soothing answer, and went on quickly because she had thought of something that made her laugh.

"What are you thinking?" said the voice of Kimball behind her.

"Casanova."

"No, *no*. Cellini. Cellini definitely."

"Well, yes." Vivian folded the next quilt over a chair.

"Casanova's such a windbag. Before he's got to the point I'm always asl——"

"Do get *on*," said the staff-nurse. "What do you think we're having an extra nurse for?"

When the beds were made Sister Verdun arrived to read prayers. She was a little fretted woman with an anxious bun, entering with a sense of grievance on middle-age. Rising from her knees, she began at once to run poking about the ward like a hen after maize, finding this and that undone and not waiting for the offender to appear, but making a clucking pursuit into passage, bathroom or sluice. She had the patients' letters in her hand, and, as she darted about, stopped occasionally to distribute one and to say something with eager, brittle geniality. Vivian, dusting, pictured her twenty years back; a popular, skittish little nurse, nervous of responsibility but goaded up the ladder by an inferiority complex and the impossibility of standing still.

One of the probationers, fresh, round and smiling, was making a patient laugh as she flicked round the bed. Vivian saw the Sister's face swing round like a sharp little compass needle. She began moving down the ward towards them; but the probationer had pushed the bed back and passed on to the next.

Presently Colonna went up to the desk to ask about some treatment or other. When she had gone Vivian, who was dusting a light-bracket close by, heard Sister Verdun say to the staff-nurse, "I hoped she was only temporary. Don't like her. Can't make these girls out who cut their hair off to look like boys. I've seen her out. *She'll* never make a nurse. Too many outside interests."

Half an hour later, when Vivian was cleaning up the bathroom, the staff-nurse came in to say, "Sister says you can have an evening."

"Thank you," said Vivian unemotionally.

"You lucky devil," said the little round probationer. "I was dying for an evening, and I've got a morning."

"I'd rather have a morning too." Vivian looked round; the staff-nurse had not gone. "Do you think Sister would let us change?"

"Sister never changes off-duty time. She bit my head off last time I asked her so I'm not going to again." The staff-nurse went out. Vivian spent the morning doing blanket baths.

As she was putting round the knives and forks for dinner, Kimball intercepted her in a corner and asked, "Did Sister let you take your call?"

"What call?"

"Someone rang up for you twenty minutes ago. A man's voice. I had to tell Sister because I knew she'd heard the bell."

"It must have been my brother. I was to have met him this morning."

"Oh, bad luck."

14

"Silly of him to ring me up on the ward."

"She might have told you he did, though."

"Yes," said Vivian without excitement. She had long ago realised that any personal life had to be lived in the hospital's teeth, and continual protest made the effort more tiring.

"Is there anything you want to know, Nurse Lingard?" Sister had come in from the linen room. "If there's anything about the patients' diets you don't understand, ask me, not a second-year nurse."

Extra beds told most on the probationers, whose routine included every patient while the seniors' treatments did not; but somehow, always by the skin of their teeth, they got it through nearly to time. When, sticky and aching, Vivian got down to tea at a quarter to six, she found a note in her pigeon-hole.

"I'm sorry I rang you up," Jan wrote. "And I'm afraid you are too by now. I'll be with Mic at 20a High Street all day, painting floors, if you can get out. If you're not there in the afternoon I'll expect you at half-past five." Vivian looked at the clock, shrugged her shoulders, and finished her cup of tea.

"Doing anything?" Kimball, ignoring a table occupied by members of her own year, slipped in beside her.

"My brother wants me to go round this evening."

"Oh. Well, I'm glad you won't miss him. What is he, by the way?"

"A geodesist."

The nurse on the other side of Vivian said, "What religion's that?"

"It's a science," Vivian explained. "Measuring the specific gravity of minerals under the earth's surface." To Colonna she remarked, "I don't know quite why he chose it, there are two or three other things he might have done. I think because it takes him to the back of beyond, and he can stay there indefinitely getting the instrument repaired. It always breaks down in the good places because of rough transport."

"Is he much like you?"

"He's supposed to be."

"He must be an unusual young man." Kimball went over to make toast.

Except that her feet hurt her, Vivian felt less tired walking through the town than beforehand, sitting on her bed trying to collect the energy for unstrapping and unpinning and un-hooking her uniform. (It was the stockings, though, that for some reason always seemed the last straw.) Now, in a brilliant March night, fine after rain, the stars were hanging low with a liquid glitter. The wind, like a clear astringent water, washed her mind coat by coat from the accumulated grime of small discomforts and fatigues and indignations. She no longer felt, as she had felt once or twice in the day, incapable of meeting Jan.

Number 20a, was a first floor flat over a draper's shop with its own faded green front door. She knocked, heard nothing, and knocked again.

A voice, not Jan's, said, "Push it, my dear, it isn't locked."

Vivian opened it, and went up some bare wooden stairs. At the top, in an open doorway, a young man was crawling about with a tin of floor-stain and a brush, shifting a piece of sacking under his knees. He straightened, rubbing his lumbar spine, and she saw that he was just about middle height, lightly made, and not in any way remarkable; he had one of those pleasant, thin, non-committal faces which might belong to half a dozen kinds of personality, and about which one un-consciously reserves judgement till one has seen the person smile or speak. The most definite thing about him was the darkness of his soft untidy hair and of his eyes, which, because their lashes were so thick and long, would have looked thought-ful whatever was going on behind them.

"I'm sorry," he said composedly. "I thought you were Jan. You're his sister, of course." His brown eyes were still and direct on her face, but he did not seem to stare; it was a re-ticent regard, curiously free from masculine challenge or assessment. Before she had time to say anything, he remarked, "You're very unlike him, really, aren't you? But of course, I see what he meant. Do come in. I've left some islands

16

leading to the window-seat, if you wouldn't mind walking on them."

Vivian thanked him, and picked her way by the light of a naked electric bulb.

"You're Mic," she said, "aren't you? I'm afraid that's the only part I know."

"Well it's all you'll need." He might as easily have been discussing the varnish. "But Freeborn's the rest."

"Is Jan anywhere about?" The flat looked very small and gave forth no sound but their own.

"He went to meet you. I knew he'd miss, of course, but he had repressed claustrophobia of long standing so it seemed unkind to tell him so. These places do look small when they're empty. Have a cigarette." He looked at his hands. "That is, if you wouldn't mind taking them out of my pocket. This side. I'm sorry; I really will wash."

"No, don't. It will dry patchy if you stop." But he wiped his hands on the sacking apron and disappeared. When he came back the dark patches shone up brilliantly against a background of pink.

"Success very modified," he apologised. "It reminds me of something. A rather clean pig?"

"No, I think a fox-terrier's stomach. It's the same kind of markings. Jan will have waited at the wrong door, of course. There are four."

"I told him which was the nurses'."

"I used the main entrance, so that explains it." She wondered which nurse he was in the habit of waiting for; hearing, with a sudden flat of irritation, the voice of fat Collins saying, "Ever so nice. What I call a thoughtful boy. You should see the books he reads"; and wondered how long Jan would be.

"You see," he said, "I've had to find my way about a good deal in the last few days, for interviews and so on. I start on Monday."

"Do you?" What could he be doing? None of the house-men were due to leave. She had the impression that he had known about her first assumption and preferred to remove it.

"What's your job then? Are you a doctor?" It was nearly impossible to know one of the housemen without becoming involved in every kind of silliness and embarrassment, and she had no conviction that in this case it would be worth the fuss.

"No. A pathologist. Or rather, a pathological assistant, here." He spoke with the uninviting flatness of one who dislikes a subject and is determined to run it out as soon as possible.

"How exciting," she said vaguely. She had never got nearer to the Pathological Laboratory than leaving a decently-draped specimen-glass outside the door.

He gave her a quick expressionless look from under his thick lashes. "It's convenient, at the moment," he said. His tone not only closed the subject, it sat on the lid.

Vivian thought, This is worse than Alan: I wish Jan would come. She turned in the window, and looked out. It was uncurtained, and a street-lamp glared on a level with her eyes.

As she moved, it seemed to her that he gave a little start followed by stillness, as if he were staring at something he had just seen. She would have turned back to the room, but suddenly felt this fixity to be directed to herself, and stayed where she was.

"It isn't particularly exciting, really." He was speaking quite differently, with a cool naturalness that seemed, somehow, to have been startled out of him. "You spend most of the time, I gather, doing about half a dozen simple routine tests. I intended of course to do research, as one does."

"Really," said Vivian as non-committally as she could. The flat spoke for itself; even in this early bareness, it was beginning to take on the mannerisms of educated poverty—the streaky stained floor, whose string rugs were already present to her mind's eye; the amateurish paintwork, in cheeky but successful colour-combinations; the aura of half-dry distemper from the walls; a little oil-stove in a corner giving out more smell than warmth. She could imagine Jan (who would stay indefinitely anywhere where the roof did not leak nor the food give him ptomaine poisoning) helping with it unseriously, as he would have helped a child to play trains; and felt a sudden ill-defined resentment against him.

It took her a moment to think her way back again.

"What kind of research?"

"Cancer, chiefly, I think."

It happened that Vivian, on the strength of her negligible experience, had acquired a bee in her bonnet about cancer. She thought the cause was psychological, and told him so.

Mic laughed. His laugh was something of a shock; brief and brilliant and quite transforming. He had a trick of laughing not, like other people, to himself, but straight into your eyes, which from the midst of so much guardedness was both attractive and disconcerting. It necessitated, for Vivian, some readjustments.

With something between a stretch and a spring he got from his sacking mat to the window-seat, and curled up on some book-boxes beside her. From this vantage he looked at her reflectively and suddenly laughed again, to himself this time.

"Well?" she asked.

"Nothing. Only the weirdness of your likeness to Jan."

"I thought you said we weren't."

"It's just sometimes. Things you say and look wipe it out completely. But when you turned round to the window just now, for instance, it might have been Jan in the room. It's grotesque."

"Is it?"

"Don't be cross. It's hard to express."

"I'm not of course."

"But it's. . . . Do you know that *conte* of Gautier's about a man who took possesion of another man's body for purposes of his own?"

"No."

"Anyway, its rather like that. You can't both be right; one of you must have cheated, and I don't know which, but I think it's you. One feels you've got no right to go about the world casually stripping Jan of his aggressive detachment."

"Aggressive," said Vivian half to herself, turning it over.

"I'm sorry," he said abruptly. "That was a purely personal reaction, and I think not true."

"It's all right. I was just interested. In any case, you probably know him better than I do." She said this not because she believed it to be true, but because now that she had got under his guard she found that she had not wanted to. "Relatives are the last people, as a rule."

"Relative is not a term that suits you, somehow," he said.

Vivian did not know the right answer to this, if there was one; so she peered into the open part of the book-box and said, "What are all these?"

"I don't know. Shop in that one, and God-knows-what in this." He moved himself to the edge of the box to let her explore. It was an odd jumble, she thought, for a scientist; Froissart, Baudelaire, Lawrence (both T.E. and D.H.), Morgan and Huxley, the *Chanson de Roland* and *Don Juan*. She found herself with the Hamilton *Memoirs* in one hand and the *Symposium* in the other, and laughed.

"House-moving makes strange bedfellows," said Mic.

"Compared with the Restoration people," said Vivian idly, "how full of purpose the Greeks were, even in their sins. Nothing, however intrinsically pleasant, without a reason, even though they each had to find a different one." She stopped because, though she had been looking at the book in her hand, she had been sure that Mic's eyes, under their unnecessary lashes, had slanted round at her. But he was searching for something in the packing-case. She went on, rather more quickly, "There wasn't a soul in the *Symposium* who could have sat through an evening with De Gramont except possibly Alcibiades, and he'd have been yawning long before the end."

"Yes," said Mic. "I suppose so." But his attention seemed to have wandered. Vivian looked up and saw Jan, smiling, in the open door. She wondered that she had not heard him on the carpetless stairs.

"Don't stop," he said. She noticed that he had remembered

to put one foot on the unvarnished place, and then unconsciously shifted his weight on to the other, which was planted
firmly on a wet board. "Which of you was wanting an evening
with Alcibiades?"

"Neither of us," said Mic, uncurling himself, "very much.
We were just remarking that Socrates had the right idea.
Look where you're walking, blast you."

"Sorry," said Jan.

— 3 —

Vivian raised the bathroom window carefully, listening for footsteps in the passage beyond. The night air had been crystal clear, and the waves of steam and bath-salts and human wetness felt like folds of blanket in the darkness. She took off her outdoor things and hung them over the rail, meaning to come back for them later. Merely to be out of one's room after ten was a minor crime compared with being out of doors. She had just fininshed when a handful of warm water struck her face.

She looked round. A strip of moonlight, shafted with wreathing steam, fell on a corner of the bath, to which it gave an unreal metallic whiteness. Against this she now perceived what seemed curves of a darker metal. Someone was laughing in the surrounding gloom.

"Enjoyed yourself?" whispered Colonna Kimball.

"I'm terribly sorry."

"It was funny. I watched you outside deciding which— ssh!"

In the passage sounded the loud tread of legitimate feet, a tapping on doors and the click of electric switches; the Night Sister, putting out lights. The noise came nearer, rebounding from the narrow thin walls of the passage.

"Who's that in the bathroom?"

A wet hand gripped Vivian's wrist.

"Who's there?"

Colonna had drawn breath when a dutiful voice from the next bathroom said, "Nurse Price, Sister. I've got late leave." The feet went hollowly on.

"Had fun?" said Colonna. She had one hand behind her head, and floated herself on the other elbow.

"Lovely." Vivian rested a knee on the edge of the bath. Her escape did not impress her much. She was still in a mood not contained within the hospital frame, and did not reflect that a second-year, having a bath in the dark after hours, had caught her climbing in at a window. The gloom of the place had thinned to her dark-accustomed eyes, and the lightly-muscled shape blurred with shadows of water pleased her as coolly as the birch outside. She had never seen Colonna before out of her obliterating uniform. Her hair was fair and thickly curling and cut like a Greek's.

"A penny?" Her voice floated with the steam in the moonlight, vague and faintly warm.

The most relevant answer Vivian could fish up was, "My brother's brought me a dancing faun."

"Show me." Colonna turned over, silver runnels glittering down her side.

"I left it behind. I thought I'd break it climbing in." She had thought too that Mic liked it and that it made the flat look less bare, and that its newness would be something to look forward to tomorrow. She was beginning to be very sleepy; but Colonna's unexpected beauty gave her a remote delight. Her lips moved, uncertainly quoting Marlowe.

"What?"

"Something you reminded me of in *Edward the Second*, but I can't remember it properly." She rubbed her eyes. "'Sometimes a lovely boy in Dian's shape,'—something-or-other about his 'wreathed arms . . .'"

There was a moment of darkness where Colonna's eyelids had been. Then they came down again; the water closed over her throat.

"You run along to bed, my beautiful. This bath's getting cold."

"Sleep well," said Vivian. She let herself out. Colonna drifted back into the night's perspective, a metal fountain-girl in the lead of a garden pool.

The moon was bright enough to undress by, and to see about the room. The glass bowl shone with a submerged glimmer. She put off till tomorrow morning deciding what would have to go to make way for the faun.

"One of us can leave it at the Lodge for you," Jan had suggested. Mic had looked up and said in his most neutral voice, "Will it be safe there?"

"Probably not. All kinds of things get slammed down. I'd better come here for it, I expect."

"I would." He added, "I'll have the pictures up by then."

Jan had brought her back. He looked puzzled when she steered him away from the main entrance.

"It's late. I'll have to get in at a window."

"Why? When ought you to have been in?"

"Ten, and it's a quarter to eleven now."

They stood in the shadow of the wall, a spot generally used by the wardmaids and their young men.

"You puzzle me," said Jan. "I wonder what you get out of this."

"Get? Has no one ever told you nursing's a vocation?"

"Don't be absurd. You've as much vocation for nursing as I have for punching cows."

"Well, I suppose I like to think I'm satisfying my personal needs in a way that isn't entirely useless to the community."

"Of course. But what personal needs?"

Vivian wondered, as she undressed, what she would have said if it had not seemed needless to tell Jan anything. But she was too sleepy for definitions. Jan's voice was getting disjointed in her mind's ear. "Not money for instance. Or a career. Or even sensation. . . . Some sort of discipline. . . . The monastic rhythm. . . . Yet you don't submit to it."

Vivian slipped into bed. Her reply mingled in her head with the fantasies of approaching dreams.

"Life's an uncertain medium, I suppose. The effects you arrange in it don't always come off." Her mind floated into absurdities; her body relaxed and grew warm.

The door had opened. In hospital this could mean many things, all requiring wakefulness; and Vivian woke. She could just see a tall shape, fair hair, and the gleam of a man's dress-

24

ing-gown in some extravagant brocade. Colonna stood beside her bed, in the manner of one whose presence needs no explanation.

"Hullo," Vivian whispered.

The bed creaked beside her.

"Here I am, lovely thing. Did you think I wouldn't come?"

Vivian's hand touched her hair that was silky and smelt sweet like a child's. She stroked it, recalling, with infinite remoteness, the Sunday evening counsels of a careful housemistress. Her emotions, it was true, were unstirred; but she was flattered as one is by the caresses of a fine and fastidious cat, say a Siamese. It seemed boorish to offer no saucer of milk. Vivian grieved at her own unprovidedness, burying her fingers deeper in the curls behind Colonna's ears.

What next? Call on the hills, presumably, to cover her. But in her dream-entangled mind the dancing faun was still sliding between rain-washed stars. "Do you know De La Mare's *Silver*?" she said. Her eye had been caught by the green glass bowl, and it seemed the only thing with real existence in the room.

"No." Colonna slid an arm round her waist, bringing with it a faint scent of fern. "How does it go?"

Vivian said it, sleep and the sound together making her voice streamlike and slow.

Colonna's arm slackened almost at once. Before the poem was over she was looking up at the window, her hand behind her head. When it was finished she said, lazily, "I wonder why I thought I wanted to make love to you. I don't, at least not physically. There's something rare about you. I don't know what I want."

Vivian did not feel relieved, because she was transported already into the world she had evoked. Reinforced by Colonna's belief she felt as rare as mist, and would not have been astonished to find herself levitated an inch or two above the bed.

The night had grown windy, and the stars seemed to be cruising at speed between lazily drifting wreaths of cloud.

They lay side by side and watched; the rhythm was hypnotic and lovely, spinning round them a thickening web of silence. Colonna's drowsy weight and faint fragrance were companionable and undemanding. When, later, she stretched and kissed Vivian and went away, Vivian realised that they had both been sleeping and that the cocks were beginning to crow.

In a moment of lazy thought as she curled up to sleep again, Vivian reflected how half-baked a virtue was inflexible consistency, a kind of small-town shrewdness of the hick perpetually nervous of letting himself be taken in. In every civilised personality there ought to be a green-room and a looking-glass at which to remove make-up and change it for the next act. She was on a large stage, dressed as Hamlet, explaining this to Horatio in very subtle blank verse. Horatio was Mic. He responded with a long speech of the eloquence of dreams, so moving that her throat ached and she slept without stirring till the morning.

– 4 –

M ATRON announced the number of the hymn.
It was a wet morning. In sunshine, the Victorian
glass of the chapel windows had a tawdry but cheerful glitter, like that of a kaleidoscope; against a dull sky they
looked heavy and slimy, like grocers' oleographs.

The nurses sat in tight rows, arranged in strict order of
seniority. Their shoulders were dragged back by the straps of
their aprons, their heads were kept stiffly upright by the
effort of balancing their high starched caps. Sisters, sitting at
the back, found chapel-time very convenient for reviewing
these caps, and noting aberrations for future criticism.

The chapel was of the Pusey-Newman period, and had not
a square foot of plain surface anywhere. Checkers and scal-
lopings, studs and foliations and convolutions, wrought iron
and turned brass and glazed tiles, repelled the eye with shocks
so various as to produce, in the end, the effect of monotony.
The frescoed walls were hung with large oil paintings illus-
trating the Miracles of Healing, both medical and surgical
cases being treated, but the clinical methods varying very
little.

Chapel was compulsory. As they sang the hymn for Ember Days (it seemed mysteriously always to be an Ember Day
in the hospital chapel), Vivian counted, to pass the time, six
Methodists, two Baptists, four agnostics, and a militant Marx-
ian atheist lending their spiritual force to the chant.

A few rows up she could see Colonna, half a head above
the crowd. She looked as flat and inanimate as the sheeted
patients in the wallpaintings; a clean-looking girl with a good
profile, too tall to wear a uniform very well. Her cap was
badly made up, and had pins showing which ought to have
been concealed.

"Let us pray."

They scraped and wriggled to their knees, taking care of their clean aprons, while Matron read the hospital prayer. The words, unheard as the ticking of a familiar clock—they assented to them every day of their lives—made a dim background to their multitudinous private thoughts and expectations for the day.

". . . To the physicians, surgeons and nurses wisdom, skill, sympathy and patience . . . and shed Thy blessing on all those who strive to do Thy will and forward Thy purposes of love. For the sake of Jesus Christ our Lord. Amen."

"Amen," they agreed. The sound had a dead plump, like that of a suet pudding dropped on a wooden floor.

Vivian recalled that, in her new days, she had extracted a quaint period flavour, a kind of pathos sometimes, from all this. She tried now, vaguely, to recapture it; but the woolly texture of everyone else's boredom devitalized her efforts; she found herself escaping like the rest into expectation and remembrance. Jan was calling at the Lodge for a note; there would be no mistake about meeting him today. She wondered what Mic's pictures would be like. A Van Gogh reproduction, probably, and etchings of some sort.

Three more casualties, she found, had reached Verdun in the night. She got a severe reprimand from Sister for breaking off her dusting to address an envelope for a girl with a broken arm.

Jan had arranged to meet her outside the Lodge; but she found him sitting on the porter's desk, doing his crossword puzzle for him.

"Well," he remarked, sliding off, "if five down comes to me later in the day I'll ring you up about it. Hullo, Vivian. Walk?"

"Yes, it's the right day." It was blowing, gleamy weather, light swift clouds and sharp slivers of sun. The hospital was on the outskirts of the town, and they were in green country almost at once. Jan was, as usual, enjoying himself, and delighted to be where he was. The spring sun picked out the patches on his jacket, let in where the straps of rucksacks, cameras and scientific apparatus had worn it through; and in the hard brilliant light the green stains on his flannels became visible even to Vivian.

"Jan," she inquired, "have you *got* any clothes except the ones you're wearing?"

"Oh, yes. Somewhere." He was watching a swift wheeling after flies. "In Cambridge, I think. You don't mind, do you?"

"Of course not. Just academic interest."

"I hate clothes that you know are there."

"You should wear our uniform," said Vivian, enviously.

People whom Jan had upset often put down his shabbiness to a particularly arrogant self-confidence. Certainly there was nothing dim or apologetic about it, and it only seemed to make his looks more conspicuous; in very dilapidated states he was—perhaps because his linen was inconsistently clean— almost comically suggestive of the prince thinly disguised as a swineherd in Act I. But Vivian acquitted him of realising this. On the rare occasions when she really wanted to call him to order, she had a secret method which consisted simply in employing the word "picturesque". It annoyed him a good deal and produced an unfailing, though transient, effect.

They had not walked together since she started her training, and she could not at first think what was different till she found that it was her aching feet. They had become an almost unnoticed background to life, except for a rather vivid moment when she first put them down in the morning. But her stride, too long for good deportment, still went with Jan's very well.

They made for some Scotch firs which were the highest point on the immediate skyline, while he talked to her about Scotland, the new pendulum, and people who had amused him since they met. She knew he would not open last night's conversation without her leave. Jan treated other people's fences with all the punctilio he demanded for his own.

Round about the firs the turf was short, spongy and hummocked by the rabbits of eternal years. The tiny grass was sprinkled with flowers to scale, of pinhead size. Vivian spread her raincoat for them to sit on.

"What's that for?" asked Jan.

"For you, and you can sit on it and shut up. This grass is soaking. You'll get acute rheumatism and it'll leave you with a heart and then you won't be able to climb hills at all. What will you do then?"

"Shoot myself, what do you think?" Jan sat down on a corner of the mackintosh, looked round him for a few minutes, and lay back to watch the fir-branches weaving with their sea-sound against the sky. His hands were clasped behind his head, and his shoulders were settled comfortably into the glittering grass. Vivian swallowed what she had been about to say, took off her own shoes and stockings and worked her toes in among the grass-roots, dislodging sharp wet smells. The pain went from across her soles. Jan was looking with a half-smile, remotely expectant, at a space of blue in the treetops that changed its shape as the wind shifted. Neither of them spoke for five minutes or so.

Vivian picked up a little bullet of rabbit-dung from between her toes, flicked it down the hillside, and said, "All the same, Jan, I think I shall carry on."

Jan rolled over on his elbow, his eyes focusing down to her slowly as a cat's do. "Why not? You may as well complete the reaction, whatever it's going to be."

"You're right. It's not being what I thought. But it wasn't the monastic rhythm I came for. I can get that at home; too much of it. It's so long since you lived there, you wouldn't remember. I was prepared for the discipline and the routine, of course. But I came here really as a sort of test."

"M-m?" said Jan. He tasted a blade of grass critically and spat it out again. "Not that you were capable of holding down the work, surely? You must have known that."

"No, not that. As a matter of fact I rated my practical capacities a good deal higher than I've found them. You've got the usual lay idea about nursing, I see. When people have

30

disabused themselves of the belief that it consists entirely of stroking foreheads, they always conclude that it consists entirely of emptying slops. Actually, it's a highly technical skill, and I've always been a bit clumsy with my hands, you know. That's just one of the things I didn't bargain for."

"This is interesting," said Jan. "Go on."

"Well I suppose my real reason for coming here was to find out whether my personality really existed or if I was just making it up."

Jan looked round at her. "My dear girl," he said, "don't make me laugh."

"You know what Anstice used to say——"

"No?" He turned his face up to hers, vivid with interest. "A friend of yours? Tell me about her."

"Jan! You practically lived with her for a week in Germany last year."

"Oh. Oh, of course. Not practically, angel. Pure theory, I swear to you. My God, yes."

"Why did you really take her all that way up the Rhine with us, Jan? It *was* because her elbows were double-jointed, wasn't it?"

"Certainly not. I can look deeper than a woman's elbows, I hope. She believed in the Great Pyramid, as well." He lifted his wet shoulders from the grass, shrugged them in vague discomfort, and deposited them in her lap. "Well, go on about you."

"She used always to be talking about my detachment."

"So she did. I could never make out why it annoyed you so much."

"I used to imagine I was concealing that. It was because I liked saying that to myself, and when she said it I knew it wasn't true."

"It's true within limits, I think."

"Exactly. And I haven't the least idea what the limits are. All these years at home I've spent wrapping myself up in a sort of spurious tranquillity. Without dust and heat, you know. I enjoyed it, too. I used to think it was the result of

31

having arrived somewhere. Then one day it occurred to me that it was the result of not having started out."

"You're severe with yourself," he said, thoughtfully.

"Why not? So are you, on your own lines."

Jan's head moved a little on her knee, but he said nothing. Vivian pulled a leaf, twisted it in her fingers, and said slowly, "You see, what Anstice thought about me was so much what I used to think about Father—before."

Jan looked away. "A little severe on him, too, perhaps," he said in a hard voice. "Aren't you?"

"I dare say." She tore the leaf down the middle and threw the pieces away. "I haven't the right to be severe on anyone. I've experienced nothing myself, except at second-hand. No one would think ——" She stopped.

"You mean," said Jan distantly, "that Mother died in her dressing-room at Wyndham's with people weeping over her in about half the European languages. Quite."

'Oh, well, that's—nothing to do with it, really." She found she had been moving a hand towards him, and took it quickly back again. "Anyhow, the point is that I was right. I know that now. The detached person was something built up, like a face for the films, except that I was my own audience. Now I have to start again. It's interesting, though it's uncomfortable."

"I see. I thought something of the kind might be happening, but I don't think I was quite prepared for your knowing so much about it. Do you like Mic?"

"I haven't the least idea," said Vivian, whose train of thought this sudden swerve had jolted. "He's hardly the sort of man you can summarise when you've met him once, is he?"

"No," said Jan, with an emphasis born of his own thoughts "he isn't. I mean, he's another person who's too good at seeing through himself."

"That wouldn't surprise me."

"One of the few people I know who doesn't regard his own limitations as the coping-stones of a completed personality."

32

Vivian laughed to herself. "He'd never make a nurse."

Jan had not listened. His brows were drawn together in a thick soft bar. "It's the only thing one can respect, of course," he said. "It's a pity."

"What is?"

"Nothing, really. It's a pity your lousy hospital can't pay him more, they're getting a good brain dirt cheap. Go on telling me."

"It's hard to put over to anyone outside. I don't think I can."

"Do the physical horrors upset you?"

"No. One faints, or retches, or whatever one does, the first time, and that's that. It's the purely childish things that get under my skin. The social survivals. Like being forced to wear a hat when you go out."

"Are you forced to? Good Lord. I wondered why you did."

"Because Florence Nightingale did. Nursing began as a reform movement, you know. Like the Church of England. It's curious how they tend to reach a certain point and then petrify. Thank God, at least we have an advancing technique to keep abreast of. We're one up on the C. of E. that way."

"You know," said Jan, "you rather disconcert me. I've learned to shed a certain amount of lumber, I suppose, but I should think twice before I committed myself to a thing like this. I suppose, to be even with you, I ought to join the Army."

"I hardly think——" began Vivian seriously: but imagination suddenly stirred, and she laughed so much that Jan complained of sea-sickness and got up.

"What about collecting the faun?" he reminded her.

On the way back they talked books, in reaction perhaps from a conversation, for them, more than usually personal. Vivian had not had time lately for much reading, but between them they had supplied enough ideas to take them as far as the High Street without noticing. As they tramped up Mic's echoing stairs they were flinging at one another far-fetched

33

parallels between Huxley and Voltaire. They were on their most common ground, all their resemblances displayed, their contrasts submerged; falling unconsciously into the same phrases, gestures, inflections of voice. Mic, who had been painting in the bedroom, came out, said "Hullo," smiled, and seemed to flicker down like a fire in a shaft of sun.

The floors were finished and dry, and there were a few packing cases to sit about on.

"You've hung the pictures," Vivian said.

"Yes." It was his politest monochrome. "I did it in the morning. Do you like them?"

"Very much," said Vivian with truth. They turned out to be, after all, a set of costume designs for the Casse-Noisette Suite; very pleasant and new to her. Over the mantelpiece there was a photograph of Dolin in "Hymn to the Sun". It loosened Vivian's tongue a little; she was excited by ballet, but rarely had an opportunity of seeing it. Mic replied very civilly to all her questions, revealing preferences and aversions similar apparently to her own; but the contact was sparkless, and they soon left the subject, which was, in any case, a little lost on Jan. He never went to ballet. Music was one of his fundamentals, and to disturb one's perception of it with visual interferences was, to him, an incomprehensible blasphemy, though he never said so.

The faun was standing under Dolin, looking much at home.

"Thank you for looking after him."

"I liked having him," said Mic nicely. It was all very pastel and under-emphasised, even her own feeling of meanness, as if she were taking something that really belonged to him.

"Bed come yet?" inquired Jan.

"Only the mattress."

"We'll sit on that, and watch you paint. These boxes have too many damned splinters."

"I'll have to go soon," Vivian said. She had another hour, but was not enjoying herself.

"My dear chap," Jan urged her, "talk sense. You haven't

34

had any tea. Mic, my sweet, finish your sunset-effects and we'll go and find some."

"I don't think I'll have time, thanks. But"—he turned to Vivian—"do stay and have a cigarette before you go. It seems all there is in the place to offer you."

"Thank you," said Vivian. Cheered by the prospect of detaching Jan, and unwilling to advertise the feeling, she sat down on the mattress, which was certainly an improvement on the packing-cases. The only other furniture in the room was a new whitewood chest of drawers, and a battered trunk in the window.

"I'll unpack for you while you finish." Jan pulled out a drawer, sniffed the new wood with enjoyment, and threw back the lid of the trunk, displaying the very orderly arrangements inside. "Save time."

"You'll do nothing of the kind." said Mic over his shoulder. He was stroking a fine line of water-green, with great speed and accuracy, along a stone-coloured panel. He had slim long-boned hands which had a fluency of their own and seemed, somehow, to evince an independent enjoyment of their skill. To Vivian, their vitality only served to underline the uncommunicativeness of his face. "Those are things I need, and I'd like to find them again. I know your unpacking."

"Why the hell you don't keep a card-index for your socks and pants," said Jan, rummaging, "I can't think. Excessive neatness is a psychological disease. It comes of not having made enough mud-pies when you were little. Broadly speaking. These are the bird-photographs, aren't they? Mind if Vivian looks at them?"

"Of course not." Mic flicked his brush to a point. "You know none of them are any good."

"If you mean they don't contain anything recognisable as a bird. But as landscape-studies some of them are lovely. You knew that too, that's why you stopped bothering to get the birds in focus." He produced a smile which he reserved for people he liked when they were being difficult. Vivian saw

Mic's unresponsive face thaw a little; but his smile disconcerted her more than his reserve, it was so unlike his laugh of yesterday, and accompanied, it seemed to her, by so much weariness. He put down his painting things, came over, and tipped the contents of the folder into her lap.

"But these are beautiful," she said. "Why did you bother with the birds? They do look rather like bits of paper floating about, but they don't matter."

"They never let you get up to them."

"Shouldn't try," said Jan, firmly. "'He who catches joy as it flies ——'"

"Kisses, not catches," said Vivian. "Don't be illiterate." She shuffled the photographs together, and picked up the folder. It contained one more, which Mic, as he emptied it, must have overlooked. She slid out her hand, and exclaimed applaudingly.

"This is the best I've seen of him. It's got just that— how did you manage it? I can never keep him still long enough."

"Which?" said Mic, idly. He had been looking out of the window. "Oh, that. That's a misfire. It was trying to be a gannet till Jan came lurching across the lens."

"Sorry," Jan said. "Didn't know you were taking it."

Mic balanced the print on his thumb and forefinger and flipped it across to Vivian. "Any use to you? They'll all get thrown out some time in the moving, I expect. There isn't room in a place this size to harbour junk."

"Oh, thanks, if you don't want it." Vivian tossed it aside with the hurried naturalness of an actor concealing a muffed cue. Before she spoke she slid a secret glance at the folder to be sure that the negatives were there, and caught Mic's eye as she did it. They both looked away quickly.

Jan, in delighted concentration, was stirring the green paint with a piece of stick.

"It makes patterns," he explained.

Damn him, thought Vivian, resentment suddenly possessing her: it's a perpetual insult that anyone should ask for so little assistance in being happy. Thou shalt enjoy the Lord thy God, and thy neighbour as thyself. Why do we tolerate it? She turned unconsciously towards Mic, as if in search of an answer; but his attention was elsewhere.

It makes all the classic forms," murmured Jan to himself and anyone concerned. "But it's too thin for anything romantic."

· I wonder, Vivian thought, why that profile should look so sensational on him and matter so little to me. He was hunkered on the floor with no more attention to dignity than a savage over a cookpot, yet contrived somehow to retain the serious grace of a young Marcellus taking auspices.

"Look." He twirled the stuff into an ascending spiral. "There's a lyric of Catullus exactly that shape. No, it's gone." The viscous mass had settled, leaving only a few concentric rings. "Landor," he said. "One of those terse quantrains. See, Mic?"

"You and your patterns." Mic got up. "Get yourself a microscope. You've a vicious taste for illusive syntheses."

"Of course they're elusive. So's everything worth bothering with." Jan rose, pulling Vivian with him. "God, I am hungry. Come on, dears, tea." Collecting them each in a casual arm, he steered for the door.

Mic removed himself, with a jerk so sharp that Vivian felt it from the other side.

"Use your wits, Jan," he snapped. "I can't eat in public in this state. I'm not coming; I told you."

"We'll wait while you change," said Jan. He looked sobered but spoke, to Vivian's surprise, very nicely. He was not tolerant of irritability as a rule.

"You'll excuse me, won't you, Vivian?" Mic picked up his paintpot again. "I do rather want to finish this while the light holds."

"Of course. It's going to be very effective. Good-bye."

"We shall meet in the hospital some time, I expect."

"I expect so. No, don't bother to come to the door."

Jan had found some brown paper and proceeded in his own

fashion to pack the faun. As he fiddled with the string Vivian saw that he was occupied with thoughts of his own. There was a cloud on his face, more like remorse than anything she could remember seeing there before.

They had crumpets for tea and talked of a great many things, but not of Mic.

— 5 —

THE neat pink theatre-nurse said, as she scraped out the jam-dish, that she preferred to work for Mr. Scot-Hallard. He was quick, she said; too quick, added her little black eyes as they swept the tea-table, for any of you.

It saved no time to speak of, suggested stout Collins as she rang irritably for more jam, when he threw a tray of instruments on the floor. But this did not happen, said the theatre-nurse—snicking it in like a scalpel—when he was given the right ones.

Vivian listened unmoved. These subcutaneous hostilities were as normal as their breath, evolutionary weapons with which the strong manœuvred for precedence, and the weak fought off the slur of inferiority. Her own contribution was to the effect that Sir Bethel was nice, and it was restful to hear please in the theatre sometimes.

Colonna Kimball put her elbows on the table and—seeming to toss her personality across it like a bright paper streamer—said that Sir Bethel was the perfect knight, a lamb among the ladies and a lion in battle. She, personally, would rather be disembowelled by a lion, provided it brought a good anaesthetist, than by Little Beth; it would be over more quickly.

The theatre-nurse, who was four months senior to Colonna, explained that one appreciated Sir Bethel's technique when one had more experience of theatre work, and engaged herself in conversation with an equal. Colonna turned to Vivian, who was sitting beside her.

"Why do you say things! Which would you prefer for anyone belonging to you, Beth or Scott-Hallard?"

"Scott-Hallard, of course," Vivian surrendered wearily. "He's a first-class operating machine. But I like Beth." Sir

39

Bethel was the oldest and gentlest of the honorary staff. She had seen the patients who returned to the wards shocked and collapsed after his long fiddling operations; but she had seen them on the wards, warmed and made hopeful by the old man's loving courtesy, while Scot-Hallard would have run them over like an index file. She could not sharpen her wits, as everyone else did, on Little Beth.

"I think you foster lame dogs to get confidence." Colonna, when the time was not auspicious for courting, was always ready to break a lance on the object of desire. "It's a subtle form of inferiority complex."

"I expect it is." said Vivian placidly. "I distrust power because I'm unfitted for it." (She should have said efficiency, she supposed, but power came easier, thinking of Scot-Hallard's broad head and great square hands.) "By the time I'm middle-aged no doubt I'll have inflated my fears into a philosophy."

"Or accepted power. That's more likely if you go on in hospitals."

"I shan't do that," said Vivian with certainty.

The general conversation, she found, had branched off meanwhile into a new channel. "Ever so interesting to talk to," the theatre-nurse was saying. "When I took up the things for biopsy we had quite a chat. More like a varsity boy, I thought, than the type you generally get in the Path. Lab. here."

"Not much life about him, though." Her friend took another bun.

"He may be a bit quiet. But that's often the way with a boy that thinks and reads a lot."

"He looks a pansy, I think." Fat Collins patted a galvanised wave back into her cap.

"We all know what your type is, Collins."

"Go on Frere, you think you know a lot."

"Know, you'd be surprised what ——"

Vivian out in the passage, dropped the swing door on the mounting crescendo.

"Are you overworking, or what?" Colonna overtook her.

"You of all people. Collins can't help being a nymphomaniac, it's just a matter of hormones."

"I'm due back on the ward."

"No you're not, for seven minutes. Don't blackleg. Come to my room while I change. I'm on at five-thirty too." Colonna had been off duty, and was in mufti. She wore, as she always did, man-tailored clothes of a cut that would have looked flamboyant on a man, but which she succeeded somehow in subduing to her personality. Her suit and suède brogues were pale grey, her shirt navy, and her tie bright scarlet. While she removed them with the speed acquired in hospital she contrived to make love to Vivian tacitly, expertly, and with finesse that made it the merest running commentary to the conversation. In the intervals that allowed of thought, Vivian decided that she enjoyed Colonna not altogether in spite of this, but because she eluded classification. Colonna, by all laws of literature, ought to have been plain, heavy, humourlessly passionate and misunderstood, pursuing in recurrent torments of jealousy the reluctant, the inexperienced and the young. She ought to have behaved like someone with a guilty secret. But Colonna, it appeared, accepted her own eccentricities much as she did the colour of her hair, though as a source of more amusement. She was, as Vivian knew quite well, vain, selfish, and without social conscience; a shameless and deliberate *poseuse*; dressed like Byron in the evenings and like a chorus boy during the day; and was, in fact, by the standards of almost any society impossible. But she enjoyed life, did what she set out to do gracefully and well, had a sense of humour, and, whatever other liberties she took, knew how to refrain from handling one's personality. It was the last virtue which, today, made her company a pleasure which Vivian did not feel like refusing.

As she plodded through the evening's routine, the high-powered lights of Verdun looked yellow and dingy, the patients seemed dreary and querulous, the staff dim saltless spirits, Sister a lost soul. Yet when she had said good-bye to Jan that morning, she had not experienced any poignant emotion. It was impossible in his presence; he had life in too light and loose a hold. He never attached people to himself nor supported them, so that when he departed there was no tearing of adhesions nor shock of altered equilibrium. But slowly, when he was gone, the light faded out of the web of things, and one only realised then whence the light had come. The mischief of Jan was that when he had removed his vitality he left his standards behind.

Sister came bustling up, a labelled test-tube in her hand.

"Nurse Lingard, take this blood. Take it straight to the pathological department, and tell them it's Mr. Henniker's specimen for grouping. Mr. Henniker has arranged for someone to stay on and do it. I don't know who it is but *find* him, and tell him Mr. Henniker may want to do a transfusion *tonight*, so will he do it at *once*, please. And don't be too long." Sister never omitted this valediction, even when she sent a nurse to Matron to report the breakage of a thermometer.

The Pathological Laboratory was the remotest place in the hospital, approached by several hundred yards of passage, two staircases, and some prison-like folding doors. The last floor was in darkness, and Vivian, who had only been there once before, could not find the switch. She groped her way along the passage, while from the shelves at either side of her came the sweetish smell of aberrant organs bottled in spirit. Rounding a corner, she saw a chink of yellow light from a door, and quickened her pace; caught her foot in an upturned edge of matting, and pitched forward. The test-tube fell from her hand, and she heard it break.

The fall, assisted by the darkness and the weirdness of the place, jolted her for a moment into a nightmare-like terror, in which she expected to feel some pursuing shadow leap on her back. Then someone snapped the passage light on, and, returning to her senses, she bethought her that she would have to creep back to Verdun and ask Sister to take another specimen. She thought, too, of the wretched patient who would have to be pricked for it a second time. It was, she reflected, the perfect climax for the evening.

While the light was still making her blink someone, moving rather neatly and lightly, picked her up and steadied her to her feet. She screwed up her eyes at the glare and at some changed familiarity. It was Mic, in a white coat which made him look curiously older and a little severe.

"I do hope ——" he began stiffly. "Good Lord. It's you."

"Thank you," said Vivian, still a little dazed. He was holding one of her hands in both of his, and her mind registered an impression that this was comforting before anything else. Then he turned it over, and she realised that it was splashed with blood and he was searching it, with impersonal thoroughness, for a cut.

"It isn't mine," she explained, "unfortunately. Look what's on the floor.

"The blood-group from Verdun, I suppose," he said without looking. "But these things splinter sometimes. Seems all right." He let her go, adding as an afterthought, "Got any in your knees do you think?"

"No, thanks. You've been waiting late for this, haven't you? I'm sorry."

"It's entirely my fault for not seeing the passage lights were on. Evans must have turned them off after him. He never thinks of anything unless it's been mentioned in *Das Kapital*. I'm glad you're not hurt."

"Not a bit," repeated Vivian, her resources supplying nothing more. They looked at one another, beneath their awkwardness a reminiscent caution braced for hostility.

"I'll get this repeated as soon as I can," she said. "I hope you won't have to wait long."

Just as she had been thinking what a hard defensive mouth he had, she had found herself returning his sudden smile.

"It's all right. As a matter of fact, I wangle these after-hours jobs when I can. It's almost one's only chance of doing any serious work."

He had acquired, she reflected, a good deal of unobtrusive confidence for someone who had only been a day or two in a new job: more than she herself had managed in seven months.

43

"Look here"—he stooped down suddenly to one of the splashes on the floor—"there's no need to take another. I've plenty on this splinter. I only need enough to make a slide."

"Doesn't it have to be sterile?" asked Vivian doubtfully, clinging to the first of her calling's ten commandments.

He laughed a little. "No, why? It isn't a bacterial test." With his hand on the laboratory door he paused to say, "Look, there's a seat there. Don't go."

Vivian sat down on the bench, in a space between specimen-racks and piles of reports. The ward was busy that night and she had not a shadow of excuse for staying except that she felt unhappy, inferior and tired and wanted to escape for a minute or two. There had been something grateful and sheltering about Mic's quietness, his air of not being much impressed with the importance of anything, and acceptance of herself as something slightly more interesting, in degree rather than in kind, than the test-tube she carried. Suddenly remembering the theatre-nurse, she got up to go; but at the same moment Mic reappeared, with a slip of paper in his hand, and propped his knee on the bench beside her.

"See Jan off?" he asked.

Their glances met. He was not smiling, but it was as if he had unstrapped a weapon and dropped it on the bench between them. She was instantly filled with a reasonless sense of comfort and relief. His dark incurious eyes held, along with their reserve, a kind of weary humour so like a thought of her own that she lost, momentarily, the sense of contact with another personality. She could have told him everything she had been thinking that evening, except that there seemed no need.

"No," she said. "I was on duty too."

"It doesn't make much odds, does it?"

He spoke without emphasis, casually even. She reflected that this was the first of the Rout who had no grievance and did not protest.

"Not much," she answered. "I shouldn't have gone to the station in any case; he hates it."

"I know." He smiled faintly. "I thought you might be the exception, though."

"Jan doesn't make any."

He looked at her quickly, as if acknowledging something; a weapon of hers, perhaps, laid down also.

"Oh, well," he said, "stations do reduce almost anything to ultimate atomic futility."

"I know. One gets a kind of aphasia which makes it impossible to say anything except 'Don't forget to write to me.' It's a fact that I once said that to Jan."

"A good one, certainly. What did Jan say?"

"He just looked wondering." She added, half to herself because his quiet made this possible, "Jan never allows fag-ends. I don't know if that's as uncommon as I think it is."

"It depends. It isn't rare as a principle, I dare say. I mean, no doubt a good many people try to plan their lives on that line. More dignified, and so on. But Jan's peculiar in that he doesn't seem to expend any thought or will-power on it. Chucking away fag-ends is a reflex with him."

"Yes," Vivian considered. "I suppose, by now, it is."

She looked up at him, as he stood half-propped by one arm against the wall beside her; but he was looking past her down the corridor, occupied with his thoughts.

"A genius for letting go," he said. "It's the most envied form of genius, I suppose. Certainly the most spectacular. 'They rightly do inherit heaven's graces . . .' The ancients would have surnamed him Fortunatus, don't you think?"

She had been watching his almost expressionless face, and listening to his voice, a light, pleasant voice, flexible and without mannerisms, as dispassionate as if he had been discussing the contents of the test-tube she had brought. Suddenly she got to her feet—leaning as he was, it brought her eyes on a level with his—and said to her own astonishment, "Do you hate him sometimes?"

"Sometimes," said Mic, looking her in the face without a change of voice or expression, "I think it's better to think so."

45

There was a kind of unseen jerk, as if they had come to the edge of a parapet before they expected. Then Mic swung himself off the bench and said, quickly and conventionally, "He'll like Cornwall. The digs are good, too, I've stayed there."

"Jan likes it anywhere."

"I know. It's depressing, isn't it?"

"I must go," said Vivian in sudden panic. "Sister will kill me. And well she may."

"Tell her it's Group 4. That will cheer her up." He had been holding, she realised, the report form in his hand.

"Have you done it already?" she asked foolishly.

"Oh yes. I did it straight away, it doesn't take long. Don't worry about the lights, I'll switch them off after you." She had turned to go when he said, "Why not change your apron before the Sister sees you?"

"I'd better, I suppose. May as well be hung for a sheep as a lamb."

"They're showing some new sculpture at the Art Gallery this week. Shall we go together some time?"

Vivian hesitated. Her imagination played dimly on the sculpture, very vividly on the hard floor of the gallery under her aching feet.

"That is," Mic said, "if you don't get too tired on the wards for any more standing about."

"No, I'd like to. I'm afraid it can only be short notice, though, because I'm not getting proper off-duty at present."

"That's all right. Any evening. Or Saturday." With one of his unnoticeable movements he disappeared behind the folding doors.

As she went down the stairs she had a sudden terrifying conviction that she had been away from the ward for hours. It was cut off from her as if by some huge lapse of time. She pulled out the big watch from the pocket of her bodice; she had been gone, she found, about twelve minutes.

"Nurse Lingard, where *have* you been? I never heard of such a thing, when I want you to wait for the result I'll let you know. The man is capable of walking down to the ward with

46

it, I suppose. If the rest of my nurses were as unreliable as this, how do you suppose I could carry on? Go and collect the mouthwash bowls, everything's behind."

Sister trotted off, her face red, her body angular, every muscle contracted, taut as an uncoiled crane. Vivian noted her ugliness with satisfaction, and the satisfaction with disgust.

At bedtime that night Colonna brought in some China tea. When she sat down on the bed it became gracefully evident that her stiff dragon-encrusted dressing-gown was all she was wearing; and a wave of grey hopeless irritability made Vivian aware for the first time how much she had been looking forward to going to sleep. But the tea was delicious, a liquid fragrance. She drank it thankfully, feeling ashamed of herself because she was turning over, simultaneously, expedients for dislodging Colonna as quickly as possible. As it happened, none of them were needed.

"You look bloody tired," Colonna said as she put the cup down. "Sister on duty, I suppose. Get straight into bed, I'll tidy up."

She helped Vivian undress like a mother, folded her things, tucked her in, handed her night-cream and cleansing tissues. Vivian submitted with gratitude. She had been taken unawares before by these sudden illuminations of kindness and perception; apart from their own pleasantness, they were part of the variegation which made Colonna interesting to her and, in spite of everything, worth while.

"I was wondering this evening," she said as she brushed her hair, "whether one has the right to attach any value to oneself whatever apart from one's function in the community. What do you think?"

"Aren't you a Communist?" asked Colonna in faint surprise.

"No; at least, not philosophically. It doesn't seem to me a a sufficiently final thing to lose oneself in as they insist you should. I suppose in practice I could muck in with it; in a lot of ways it can't be so very different from this."

"I thought you would be one. Nearly all my friends are,

47

and hate personality worse than cancer. Other people's particularly. But sometimes we reach a gentleman's agreement that I'm Wrong but Romantic. . . . I came here tonight with the worst intentions, did you know?"

"Of course. But I like you so much more like this. Do you mind terribly?"

"No, I think I'm glad if I could only make up my mind to it. It's funny how I won't let you alone, we've so much that would spoil. But—I don't know—I'm not in love with anyone at the moment, and you're rather beautiful in a clean hammered way that's refreshing after all these plush peaches. And you take it all for granted so restfully, instead of popping your eyes and saying oo-er. Making love to you is pleasant and graceful—and innocent, it seems to me, though I suppose I I wouldn't know; because we're happy and don't struggle to possess one another." She paused; the rare planes of meditation, replacing those of motion, made her face seem strange. "Some day, perhaps, we shall look back to this and want it. To be living in the moment, with a light lover who couldn't hurt us: to be free."

"Don't," said Vivian. "I felt then as if something were walking on my grave." She pulled the eiderdown, with a shiver, up to her chin.

"Don't you want a lover?" asked Colonna with dispassionate curiosity.

"No." Vivian's mouth shut straight. "I'm not ready to cope with it. I haven't learned yet to run myself alone."

"Who has?"

Jan has, thought Vivian. But she said, "I don't know yet what I am. I must be something before I can be part of anything else. Love only uses part of you, and it changes that part and makes it seem much more than the whole. If you haven't seen yourself first and where you're going—even if it were only for one clear moment—you might get lost. Utterly lost; lost for ever, perhaps." Her eyes, fixed on the window, seemed to reflect the dark outside it. "No. Show me a lover in ten years' time."

48

"You're posing," remarked Colonna with the interested appreciation of the fellow-craftsman.

Vivian considered this for what it was worth. "If I am," she concluded equably, "it's probably half true. Most poses are. They show your aims though not necessarily your achievements."

"Utterly lost," said Colonna meditatively; and laughed. "A damp, blasted, female way to be in love." She stretched herself, five feet ten of handsome arrogance. "I'm always going to be like the Kitchen Cat in Kipling. "She is my Cookie, but I am not her cat.""

Vivian wanted suddenly, protectively, to silence her.

THERE was a new charge-nurse on Verdun, a small, olive-skinned, wiry girl with dark hair, blue-brown eyelids, and a brittle, mask-like animation like that of some Frenchwoman. When she was left in charge, though the work got done faster than usual, she was curiously little in evidence, so little that Vivian had hardly noticed her by the evening of the first day, till someone said to her in the sitting-room. "You're lucky to have Valentine. We had her on Ramillies till today; now we've got that fat bitch Chandler instead."

"She seems all right so far," said Vivian vaguely.

"She is, take it from me."

"A friend of yours."

"Good heavens, I don't mingle with charge-nurses." (Vivian was always forgetting, sometimes disastrously, that the hierarchies of the wards held good with equal potency off duty.)

"Matter of fact I don't think she has many friends. One of these reserved people, I dare say. She plays the piano in the old lecture-room sometimes, but only highbrow sort of stuff."

Vivian soon forgot about her, because that night Colonna came to her room and announced that she was going to leave. It was the twenty-ninth of the month, so that meant giving notice in two days' time.

"I came for an experience," she explained, "and I've exhausted it. My people won't mind; they can't make out my staying this long."

"You're honest. I wish I were." For she knew already that she did not want Colonna to go. She would miss in the greyness her ringing peacock colour; miss, too, the illusion of strength and stability given by the background of her hot indiscipline. They had been, though they had not thought much about it, almost perfect foils for one another.

Considering it all, she asked, "Is the experience really all you get? Doesn't the work give you any—any ——" she gave up the search for some other word that would sound less intolerably priggish, and plunged—"any spiritual satisfaction at all?"

"No. Most of the time one just seems to be fighting evolution, pushing back all the junk it's trying to get out of the way. Does it you?"

"Sometimes, I think. Or I wouldn't still be here, I suppose. What else can you do?"

"I was in repertory for a year, you know, before I came here."

"You never told me."

"Didn't I?" Colonna's rare but unbreakable reticence dropped, like a steel safety curtain, over some memory. "You're off duty tomorrow afternoon, aren't you? Let's walk and have tea somewhere out."

"Yes, I'd—no, wait, tomorrow's Saturday." The moving of someone else had fitted her, by this time, into the Verdun schedule. "I promised to go to that sculpture exhibition thing."

"Who the devil with?" asked Colonna, and then began to talk about something else without giving her time to answer.

"I wonder what Matron will say," Vivian reflected, "when you give notice."

Colonna told her. She was a good mimic.

Next day in Verdun an old woman died, and the new charge-nurse, Valentine, called Vivian behind the screens to help her with what was necessary. Vivian began to notice her for the first time, because of the grateful reticence with which she worked. During the last months Vivian had learned to excuse indifference at these offices, preferring it to the sentimentality which some nurses thought fit to assume like a kind of badge ritually pinned to their uniform. There stuck particularly in her head the picture of a pink-cheeked girl

51

dressing a dead baby in flowers and muslin, with the dramatised melancholy of a child dressing a doll for a doll's funeral. "Doesn't he look sweet?" she said proudly, calling Vivian behind the screen to see.

She realised as the day's work went on, why Valentine was liked by people who worked for her. She radiated a kind of impersonal comradeship and enjoyment, and, without any deliberate exercise of charm, invited them to work as to an adventure. She was never in doubt. If she ever made mistakes, Vivian was sure she accepted them as the fortune of war, her self-confidence unshaken. Yet behind all her smooth activity there seemed something detached, poised on action and partly satisfied with it, keeping to itself its other needs.

More than the most acrid criticism, Valentine's mere neighbourhood made Vivian aware of the gulf that still separated her from simple adequacy in her work, still less from any kind of excellence. The thought of Colonna's departure was still depressing her; and suddenly she began to wonder whether she too had exhausted all that this life could give to her, or, more important, she to it. She thought with longing of the moors at home; of the shabby friendly schoolroom, too much a part of life ever to have changed its name; of her father's vague, kind, unsurprised welcome, looking up over the book in which half his mind was still entangled; of being free sometimes with Jan. If she gave notice this month, they might canoe up the Loire again in the summer.

Occupied with these thoughts, she had changed into tweeds for a walk alone before she remembered that this was the afternoon when she had promised to meet Mic. She felt that she had no energy just now for social adjustments; but it was too late to think of putting him off. Her tweeds were old and comfortable, and she would have liked to leave them on, but remembered that Mic was poor and difficult and might think she considered him not worth dressing for. She changed into a newer suit, plain too as all her things were, but thinner and better cut.

Mic, when she met him, had on tweeds the exact analogy

52

of those she had taken off, which made her feel a little foolish and unconsciously scratchy. He was in one of his constrained moods and did little to eke out her shortage of conversation. They exchanged civil commonplaces, while Vivian let her mind wander back to Valentine and the ward. It seemed more natural in his company to retreat into her own thoughts than to affect a conscientious brightness. Mic seemed to have reached some similar conclusion.

He was, at least, a comfortable companion for an exhibition, not expecting her to hang over a catalogue with him nor bursting into comment on everything as soon as it came in sight. The collection was a hotch-potch of good stuff lent by private owners and the prize achievements of local art schools and amateurs.

In front of a surrealist exhibit called "Adventitious Agony" they both looked enigmatic for a long time.

"Well?" inquired Mic.

"Frankly," she said, "I think the indigested contents of the subconscious, and those of the stomach, are about equally significant in visual art."

"Speaking as an expert?" said Mic, laughing. "For all we know, there may be hosts of people on whom this propeller, with the toothbrushes and—er—so on, has exactly the same effect as Delius."

"Make it someone else, will you? I like Delius, in a vague uneducated sort of way."

"Do you? I've got the record of the *Cuckoo*. You must hear it sometime. Look, let's go back to the flat for tea instead of having it out, and I'll play it for you."

"I'd like to," said Vivian, hypnotised, she concluded next moment, by his complete simplicity and unexpectedness. After surrounding himself during the first half-hour with the caution of a Foreign Secretary in a European crisis, he had delivered this invitation as unequivocally as if they had both been twelve years old. His effect on her alternated between strain and an extraordinary restfulness. They talked easily until they reached the shop where he was going to get cakes, when he said with sudden awkwardness, "Going to the flat won't make you late on duty? It's farther away."

It had just occurred to him, thought Vivian, that a convention exists. Unclassified creature, where had he lived? He seemed neither "advanced", provincial, nor very innocent; and, when he forgot himself, assumed a certain charm as if he were used to it. Aloud she said, "No, I've another hour. I should like to see the place, now you've finished it."

She decided that it was remarkably pleasant. He had got a gas-fire, some rough linen curtains and a couple of modern chairs which looked a little bleak but had been designed, she found, by a sound anatomist. There was a solid working table, and bookshelves making an angle round one corner. The room seemed larger and lighter than it really was, but it was so reticent in its display of personality that it would have been difficult to decide at a glance whether it belonged to a woman or a man. She set the table while Mic, in some hidden and, from the sound, very confined space, made tea. It was a comfortable meal.

"I think human beings need some place as an extension of themselves," she said when they were smoking afterwards. "Even children do, if you can remember what it felt like the first time you had a room of your own."

"That was when I went to Cambridge," said Mic. She was on the point of asking him whether he had been one of a large family, and scarcely knew what it was in his face or voice that prevented her.

"Our rooms are almost fascist in their suppression of the individual," she said. "Sometimes I think it's the lack of anywhere you can pretend for five minutes is your own, quite as much as overwork, that makes us so callous about all the patients' non-physical needs."

"You say 'us'?"

"Oh, yes. After six months I notice things much less. The ghastly gloom of the ward services, for instance, and the effect they have."

"I've never known any nurses till now, except one when I

had pneumonia at school. A very kind woman. But I can't associate you with nursing, if you'll forgive my saying so."

"I see you've discovered already that no compliment pleases a nurse more. It's illuminating, as a comment on the industry."

"I hadn't, but I'll bear that in mind."

"Take care you don't get pneumonia again. This is a good place for it—inland and damp."

"I've a very sound instinct of self-preservation. You're used to Jan, aren't you?" He smiled into his cigarette-smoke at a private memory. Vivian found it a little irritating.

"You fence," she said, to change the subject. The hilts of a couple of foils were sticking out from behind the bookcase, in reach of her hand, and she pulled them out.

"Not for ages. Do you?"

"Mother used to teach Jan and me, when we were small. But our style was a bit rakish. Theatrical, you know."

"I see. Jan had a few peculiar mannerisms . . . not like him. He didn't say."

"He wouldn't. He never talks about her." This came so near to something about which she herself never talked, that she got up quickly and made a pass with the foil she held.

"On guard?" said Mic, picking up the other.

"Not after all that tea?"

"There isn't room to move, anyway." He saluted, registering a smart hit on the ceiling. "I don't know why I keep them." He made a feint and a lunge which she parried by a kind of instinct; to her surprise, for she had not touched a foil for years. "You ought to have a jacket on. I haven't got mine. I'll tie a cushion round you, shall I?"

"What, like Tweedledum? And you're not going to need anything of course. On guard."

"You know too much," said Mic after a minute or two.

"Much good it does me." In fact, her technique was impossibly rusty and had never been good, but she did know, with a strange fatality, exactly what Mic was going to do next. Now and again she was quick enough to prevent him from doing it. They fought on, a little short-winded with tea and lapse of training, but deeply engrossed. After a while it brought on Vivian a curious mood. It seemed to her that now for the first time she recognised Mic's narrowed eyes and gentle unconscious smile, that she had stared into them like this long ago, and seen his blade flicker at her like a snake's tongue; and that when she forestalled him she was remembering. The fancy grew on her. Touched—she should have parried that, she had before. No, this was the moment. It was now that she run run in her point, with a longer reach and a stronger arm, six inches down from the left shoulder. He had been wearing something white, and ——

"Yes," said Mic, signalling the hit.

She lowered her foil. An ache of fear and some half-forgotten anguish pierced her.

"Are you ——" Absurd: she had only tapped him. "I thought for a moment I'd hurt you."

"Oh, no." They looked at one another, smiling, confident and intent. "I can't remember where I've seen that done before."

"I invented it." She flirted her foil, a schoolboy's swagger. What was happening to her, she wondered; she was not this kind of person with anyone else.

"Like this?" Instead of demonstrating himself, he took her wrist and made a pass with it.

"No, like that."

"You've a strong wrist," he said.

The illusion of memory, or whatever it was, pressed on her bewilderingly. His eyes on her face and his hand over her wrist had an authority and a challenge; the undertones they moved in were complex and indefinable, like the mood of a dream that remains after its events have been forgotten. She said, "I should have," without knowing why.

"You haven't heard the Delius record yet." He let her go abruptly, and tossed away his foil which he had been holding in his left hand.

"No, I'm looking forward to that." With a little jolt she

returned to normal; straightened with her toe a rug she had heaped up in a lunge; stood her foil neatly against the wall; a polite female visitor.

"I'll just get the gramophone; it's in the other room." He was on his way when she happened to look at the time.

"Oh, Mic, I'm so sorry, I shall have to go. It's my own fault for fooling about. I'll have to run, too. Funny how one's off-duty time always seems to end in the middle of something."

"You must hear it another day," he said, without expressing any conventional regrets for her departure. "I'll run you up in the car; it will save a minute or two."

"That's kind of you. I didn't realise you had one."

"Sort of Heath Robinson one. Every time they patch it up they give it six months, like a chronic heart. But it still does fifty. Lives in the alley just behind."

As they walked round to it she said, "I don't remember if I told you how much I like the flat. We were talking so hard when we came in."

"I thought you did. Anyhow I'm glad you like it. I think I was rather more pleased by what you didn't say."

"What were you nerving yourself for?"

"'Poor man, who looks after you here?'"

"I didn't see anything to justify such rudeness. Did you really think I would?"

"No. Still, it was pleasing actually to hear you not saying it."

"By the way, what were you doing before you came here?"

Mic's mouth straightened. "Starving rats," he said pleasantly.

"*What?*"

"Viner's Breakfast Vitamins. I was in what they courteously called the Research Department. It sounded rather good on paper. I went straight there from Cambridge; I—didn't want to wait about for a job. They were very proud of their Research Department: they used to have sketches of us in their advertisements, holding up test-tubes to the light. Not photographs fortunately; they got film extras for that."

"Where did the rats come in?"

"We used to feed Viner's latest Vitamin to one batch, and starve another batch as a control. Then they could publish the vitamin content, you see. Of course I'd done a certain amount of the same thing at Cambridge, for more varied and useful purposes. But after a time I began to see rats in my sleep—thin ones, with runny eyes and staring coats. You wouldn't know, unless you'd seen it, how unpleasant vitamin deficiency can make an animal look. Even a healthy rat can pall as a matter of fact. . . . Anyhow, when I heard of this job at rather less than half the money. I jumped at it. One needs to feel one's existence has some justification, even if it hasn't. That door will shut, if you slam it hard. Let me."

It was certainly a very old car, but with a marked and pleasing personality, like a mongrel dog's. Mic humoured its eccentricities with apology, but evident affection.

"Well, at least while I was there I got the car, such as it is, and a fairly good gramophone and some records. You're coming again to hear it, aren't you? Delius, Handel, Beethoven, all out of rats with beri-beri and rickets."

Vivian was entertained, till she happened to look round, and saw in his face what seemed the settled bitterness of a much older man.

"Well, the ones that got the vitamins must have enjoyed life. . . . I suppose I came here for some sort of justification too, but I can't claim to have found it. After all," she said in sudden rebellion, "why should we feel we must earn the right to exist? Sometimes I think the happiness—being reconciled, and sufficient in oneself—is the only justification."

Mic took a corner too fast. "The gospel according to Jan," he said.

She was moved, for a moment, to tell him that her mind was not entirely clothed in Jan's cut-down ideas; but though he was smiling, he looked so desperately unhappy that it ceased to matter. She only said, "I doubt whether Jan would claim paternity for it."

They had reached the gates. Collins, coming back on duty

with some friends, saw them, exchanged glances with her group, and hurried on, big with a silent pregnancy of future words. Vivian reflected without emotion that she would have told the whole hospital by this time tomorrow. Mic had noticed nothing; he was unfastening the door, which had stuck.

He had provided her, she found out, with seven minutes to change in. She returned to the ward with a feeling of aeration; of seeing things from different angles and in slightly altered tinges of colour. Although Sister was in charge that evening she felt no anxiety about her work; there was, even a kind of relaxation in it, as of a simple exercise after a complex one that had strained concentration a little.

While they were tidying up the sluice one of the other probationers said, "By the way, Lingard, is it true you're going to leave?"

"No, of course not," said Vivian at once. "Who told you?"

"They were saying it in the dining-room. Just one of these rumours, I suppose. The brainy ones always seem to, like Carteret who used to draw, you know."

"I'm not nearly clever enough to leave." Vivian rubbed an enamel bowl with Vim, remembering suddenly, from a remote distance, the meditations in which she had spent the morning. "I shall just wait till I'm pushed, I expect."

The probationer laughed appreciatively. "Matron will need a few more names on the waiting-list before she pushes a nice quiet girl like you. Now I nearly did get sacked last year. I was out, you see, without late leave, and the boy I was with——"

Nurses," said Sister in the doorway, "you may or may not be aware that the noise of your chattering can be heard half-way up the ward."

Vivian was walking down to the dining-room after duty, feeling less tired than usual, when Colonna caught her shoulder from behind.

"Don't go in to supper. Cut it. I want you to go to a party with me."

"Whose party?" Vivian looked round to see if the Home Sister were watching for defaulters. "Am I invited?"

"Yes, at least she said I could bring whoever I liked. Do come it's going to be awful, I can't think why I was such a bloody fool as to say I'd go." But she sounded pleased.

"Who's giving it."

"Valentine."

"Not Charge-nurse Valentine? Why ever did she ask you?"

"God knows. To rope me into some hell-begotten society or other, I expect. Folk-dancing, or singing glees, you know the things they do. Oh, Lord, is she a Grouper by any chance?"

"I shouldn't think so. All right, I'll come. Can we wear dressing-gowns?"

"I'm going to, anyway. I hope there'll be enough to eat."

"Oh, well," said Vivian comfortably, "I had a good tea."

"Like hell you did. We're going to talk about that."

Evidently Collins had wasted no time.

Valentine had a big room, nearly as big as a Sister's, at the top of the building; part of the old structure, with a huge mansard window from which the lights of half the town and the nearest villages could be seen. It was a good party, with much more than enough to eat, and cocktails as well. There was no one else there nearly so junior as Colonna, let alone herself; the other half-dozen guests were seniors to whom she had hardly spoken. Valentine herself had on a red flowered kimono, and had tied back her dark wavy hair from her forehead with a red ribbon. It made her look surprising young; seniors two or three years younger than oneself always appeared, somehow, to be older on the wards.

Everyone was very gay and silly, but with rather more imagination than at other hospital parties to which she had been. They told, as usual, improper stories, but subtler and more allusive ones. Presently someone—Valentine, as far as she could afterwards remember—suggested charades.

Valentine picked one of the sides, choosing Colonna first; she had a name, of course, for such things.

Vivian, who was on the other side, could never remember later what word it was that Valentine chose. It ended with a dumb-show, fairly heavily burlesqued, of the tomb scene from *Romeo and Juliet*. Valentine was Juliet in a white satin night-gown (she had, Vivian noticed, an immature but charming figure) and Colonna was Romeo, wearing a white silk shirt, a sash, and her own black pyjama trousers—a costume that made her look more than ever like a steel plate of Lord Byron gone blond.

Even the audience enjoyed it. Nurses are easy to excite emotionally, like soldiers and other persons strictly regimented and in too frequent contact with death: and no one noticed that the principals guyed their parts less and less as the scene went on. When, at the end, Romeo took his last embrace, and sealed, very firmly, his dateless bargain on the doors of breath, Vivian thought she saw Juliet stir, for a moment, with un-seasonable life. But she died very well, with a paper-knife, when her turn came. There was loud and prolonged applause. After the other side had been out, Colonna suggested that they should tell ghost stories in the dark.

In the faint glimmer from the window, which after the bright light did not reveal their shapes to one another, they all curled up together on Valentine's bed or on cushions on the floor. Warmed and excited by the cocktails and the play-acting, their personalities spread and preened themselves in the darkness, peopling it with their favourite fantasies. Some-one, she never knew who, gave Vivian a plump shoulder to lean on, and settled her there comfortably; someone else put an arm round her and softly slapped her waist. Neither of them was Colonna. She could hear faint giggles somewhere beyond her in the room. Invisibility, and the fact that half of them were, by regulation, strictly forbidden to know the others, gave to these secret familiarities the illusion of adven-ture. Behind her, against the wall, Vivian could hear someone moving quietly, in search perhaps of more room.

The ghost stories grew sillier and sillier. Everyone had been awake since half-past six, and most were by now unconcealedly half asleep. One by one, with thanks and a weak drowsy joke, they trickled away. Vivian too felt dim and aching with weariness. Her supporting shoulder had gone, and she longed for the cool solitude of her bed. It must be long after lights-out. She would say good-bye to Valentine, collect Colonna and go. She had been so nearly asleep as to have shut her eyes. When she opened them the sky-lit glimmer seemed, after the darkness of her eyelids, much lighter than before. She perceived that round her, on the floor, all the cushions were empty. The bed, too, above her, was no longer a heaped-up frieze: it held only a low indeterminate blur. Rubbing her aching eyes, she could see a faint surface of white silk, traversed by a flowered sleeve. The white silk stirred softly, and Colonna's hand gave her a gentle push. Vivian rose and slipped away, without formality or sound.

Colonna did not give notice, after all, next day. Nor did she ever take Vivian to task for going to tea with Mic.

7

VIVIAN was a little lonely after this, though Colonna wound up her suit with charming politeness; indeed, it was a small pride of hers that she never, so to speak, sent anyone a marmoset. She sloughed her affairs delicately, like the snake its winter skin, leaving the pretty pattern brittle but untorn. Quite often, in an afternoon when Valentine was elsewhere, she came to see Vivian, made her tea, amused her, and paid her improper compliments for art's and old times' sake. But at night the golden dragons prowled no longer; and Vivian, waking as she sometimes did in the first light, would hear down the passage her long soft step and the quiet closing of her door.

Once or twice Valentine asked Vivian up to share their tea or coffee, apparently because she rather than Colonna chose. Vivian found these occasions easy and pleasant; they never behaved embarrassingly and, if they had moods, knew how to keep it to themselves.

For a long time their mutual attraction remained a mystery to Vivian; and a deeper mystery the fact that they never got caught. Perhaps it was because Colonna bore, by the standards of authority, an unsullied reputation. Psychology forms no part of the nursing curriculum, nor did the hospital library contain a single work on the subject. The ruling ranks, settled virgins whose peace of mind was sufficiently disturbed by the direct manifestations of sex, spared themselves the knowledge of its divagations. They had evolved, in many defensive years, an instinct for avoiding discoveries destructive to a rather vulnerable structure of inhibitions. A lipstick a shade too bright; bare legs in the summer; being rung up by a man; on these things the butt-end of Aesculapius's rod was laid. Colonna, though she broke thermometers often—a fairly serious crime—wore clothes that completely covered her body; made-up so discreetly that the Sisters supposed it to be natural; and was never seen with a man at all. Morally, in fact, she was above suspicion. But socially, as she must be well aware, she had assaulted the Decalogue by becoming friendly with a charge-nurse. It was as if a lance-corporal had gone drinking with the Adjutant; an offence beside which, if it were discovered, all subtler considerations of motive or manner would vanish into air.

At all events, Colonna swaggered less, worked much harder, and had dropped altogether the pose of being more interesting than her job. On the ward she and Valentine were both faultlessly correct; apparently without effort.

Now and again, when Colonna was busy, Vivian would arrive before her in Valentine's room, and it was at these times that she found out the little she got to know about her; she would emerge from the façade of rather baroque wit which she and Colonna affected as company manners, and talk with a reserved simplicity. She told Vivian one day that she had intended, first of all, to train as a mental nurse. She had gone to a County Asylum, moved by a strong sense of vocation; and it had been the avoidable, rather than the inevitable horrors of the place that had been too much for her in the end. Finally she had been asked for her resignation, after protesting to one of the Sisters about the treatment of a border-line case. But as her general training accumulated successes, she was tormented by the feeling that it was her duty to go back, take her mental course from the beginning again, force herself into some position of authority and do what she could. It was this which forbade her the easy acceptance of privilege, and kept her apart among the people of her own year.

She talked about the asylum very sparingly; but there had been, a little before she came, a hushed-up episode when a man patient, doing garden work, had eluded the male nurses and got through somehow to the women's side; and during Valentine's time there the dreadful baby had been born. Valentine had been eighteen at the time, fresh from school, and impressionable. Vivian did not find it difficult to imagine how, between these memories and her mind, Colonna's epicene beauty might glitter like a delivering sword.

All this meant one off-duty time a week, or less, of Colonna after a steady four or five. Some of the loose time was filled by examinations, for all the nurses' study-hours came out of their free time. For the rest she had books and the open country, which, after a devastated zone of ribbon-growth, was gratefully near. She had solitude itself—always, after the press of the wards, a luxury eagerly anticipated. It happened also that when Mic suggested things that they might do together, she was generally free.

She became used to finding a note from him in her pigeon-hole. She wondered, when she got the first, why the writing was familiar, till she remembered screwing up her eyes at it on pathological report forms. It was an unexpected hand, quite unlike his sub-toned diffident manner and quiet movements; angular, impatient, and undeliberately picturesque. It resembled no one else's in the hospital and was, as she soon discovered, inconveniently well known. In the end she told him so: having to nerve herself a little first, because Mic was unpredictable. But he only laughed.

"Sorry. I might have thought of that. It can be corrected."

"It's nothing, really," said Vivian, relieved. "Actually, it's rather restful to be a subject of hospital gossip, because then you don't have to listen to it."

She expected no more notes; but Mic's solution, it turned out, was to type the envelopes with one finger while the Senior Pathologist's secretary was at lunch.

After people had stopped saying, "There's a note for you, Lingard," with special smiles, the wind only blew her rare and slender straws—a conversation changing, with a certain grinding of gears, when she came into the common-room; the cessation of jokes, once frequent, about her bookish and solitary ways. It amused her, however, to discover herself, sometimes, half-unconsciously playing up to her reputation. At these moments of dramatisation, the picture at the back of her mind was of a quite fictitious affair with an imaginary man; so remote were the legends from the reality of her tentative, fluctuating contacts with Mic.

These were certain in nothing, except uncertainty. They never had, indeed, anything like a quarrel; that would have implied too much intimacy, a common stock of mutual knowledge. Vivian's difficulties were more like those of Alice with the Cheshire Cat. Because she was conscious of some natural kinship, deeper than emotion or attraction, between them, it was irritating to have all communication switched off, as it generally was once or twice in every few hours they spent together, arbitrarily, abruptly and without discoverable cause. It would happen in the midst of animated, impersonal talk; he would look unexplicitly at her, flick down his eyelashes— she got to know the trick—turn away, finish what he had been saying with a commonplace, sometimes irrelevant, and be unapproachable for five minutes or so. He might emerge, afterwards, as if nothing had happened; on other days, he would be forced and unreal till they said good-bye. Vivian put up with it because he was hardly ever rude, or, when this did happen, seemed quite unaware of it; and because, between his eclipses, he was better company than anyone else.

With a little more wisdom and use of what she knew, she might have found the answer; with a little less, she might have supplied one. But it would almost have defeated Collins, she thought, to see in Mic a nice, shy young man, remembering that he couldn't afford to get married. In the first place Mic was Mic; in the second he was not at all shy; in the third his views on marriage, as they emerged in general discussion, were not particularly sacramental. Moreover, it was at these moments alone that he sometimes behaved as though he disliked her. She noticed that he would go to quite elaborate though unobtrusive lengths to avoid a chance physical touch.

She often wished that she had got Jan to say more about Mic before he went away. He had been ready; but she had been uninterested, even perhaps a little unwilling. Jan had sterilised jealousy in her long ago; but a kind of reluctant envy sometimes stirred in her towards his friends when they were new. In her firmament Jan was fixed, a star whose worth was known and height too surely taken. These new watchers would measure it too; but before them first were discovery and suspense, adventure and experiment and hope.

Jan would have moved on by now, as usual without sending his new address. She wondered, supposing she got it, whether to write to him about Mic. If one required from Jan anything definite and important, he would answer as a rule by return of post. But she felt that he would ask, of himself if not of her, why she should make these efforts; what was the use of a relationship so incomplete that it had to be clarified by other people.

Meanwhile, she continued to see Mic. To interpose a buffer between herself and his uncertainties, she began to consider him as a problem, even, in very defensive moments, as a case. Perhaps he had had some emotional shock which made him distrustful of friendship; perhaps his home life might be—what was the catchword?—maladjusted. (She remembered that Colonna's parents had separated, too late for Colonna, after punctuating her childhood with squalid abusive scenes.) She made up her mind to find out.

Nothing was easier than to get Mic to talk; nothing more difficult than to guide the conversation down the kind of channel she wished to explore. After knowing him for over a month, the only pieces of concrete history she had got out of him were the name of his public school—a third-ranker, not too reactionary—the fact that he had reached Cambridge with a bursary of some sort, worked for a research fellowship which he had failed to get, gone to Viner's laboratory, disliked it, and met Jan at a meeting of some Cambridge scientific society. About Jan he would talk, sometimes, with startling frankness; at other times, refuse to talk about him at all.

One fine Saturday afternoon she determined to forget all about it. They went swimming in an open-air bath outside the town. The sun glittered through light wind; sharp little clouds cleft the sky like racing yachts; the living air braced their skins and washed their minds of complexities, leaving them simple and receptive only of enjoyment. They raced one another, and horse-played childishly.

"Christ, look at that fellow diving," said Mic. "Gets ready like Danilova, and a belly-flopper at the end."

"Let's see you try."

"All right. Coming too?"

"No, I'll watch you. I don't care about water in my ears. Seen too many mastoids."

There seemed no end to the odd cards up Mic's sleeve. He dived beautifully, with the grace of co-ordination perfectly achieved and forgotten; launching himself, from every kind of take-off, into loops and rings and fantastic arcs and sliding into the water like a spear. At first he was enjoying himself too much to notice that everyone else in the bath had suspended activity to watch him; but presently, pausing on the highest board, he saw the upturned faces, came down with a formal dive and swam back to her.

"You can dive, Mic."

He looked a little ashamed of himself. "It's about the only thing I can. I used to do a lot at school to get out of games."

They sunned themselves on the grass at the edge, feeling limber and good-looking and fit to be alive in early June. Vivian had on a new costume, dark and clever and deceptively plain.

"I like you in that," Mic told her suddenly.

Did he, indeed? There was no keeping track of him. Vivian was not unaware that she possessed a well-shaped body, but entirely unprepared for being informed of it by Mic. She found that she was pleased.

He added, "It makes you look like you." It was a compliment typical, she thought, of Mic in Delphic ambiguity.

They went back and had tea, as usual, in his flat. When they had washed up—she had persuaded him, by now, to let her help with this—they talked lazily. Vivian thought what a successful afternoon it had been. So far, Mic had not blacked-out once. She looked at him as he sat smoking, relaxed in pleasant weariness. His hair was drying in a soft childish disorder; he looked young, candid and defenceless. No one knew better than Vivian, by now, how far to trust in such appearances; but they moved her and reminded her how much, in spite of everything, she really liked him. She had been telling him about her home, and the ways in which she and Jan had spent their childhood. The constraints between them seemed trivial inventions, needing only to be brushed aside.

"Tell me, Mic, where do your people live? Let's have a little from you for a change. What's your father, as they say at school?"

Mic ceased to look conspicuously young. He blew a smoking-ring, which he did very neatly.

"I haven't got one."

"I'm sorry. Has he been dead long?"

Aiming carefully, Mic put a second ring plumb through the middle of the first.

"I hope so," he said.

Vivian squeezed the arms of her chair. How obtusely slow she had been! It seemed now that he had been shouting this at her for weeks. But she had never before, to her knowledge, met anyone illegitimate; she would have thought as quickly of his mother being an Eskimo.

She had exposed him from little more than curiosity, and to support her self-esteem. Her scalp tingled. She was too much concerned for him to wonder what her face looked like.

Mic looked round at her. "I'm sorry," he said, with most of the bite gone out of his voice. "I thought Jan would have told you."

Vivian pulled herself together. "I don't suppose it struck him as sufficiently important. It wouldn't me. Though perhaps that's rather a stupid way of expressing it; it must have been important to you."

"I dare say it wouldn't have been, particularly, except that I was brought up by people who didn't approve and never stopped discussing it."

"My *dear*."

"Oh, well, that's a long time ago. Now it's just a nuisance in practical ways. Actually, most people have been rather touchingly good about it. But Jan was the first I met who genuinely wouldn't have minded if it had been himself. Perhaps that—influenced me."

"He wouldn't, as he is. You can't say what another sort of environment would have made of him."

"Would you mind?"

Vivian considered. "When other people did, I expect, like you. But in itself—well, yes, I suppose I should think about my mother."

"Mine doesn't give me much chance. She married someone when I was two, and hasn't seen me since. Probably got a proper decent family by now."

There seemed nothing left to say to that. Nor were helpful little gestures—the pat on the arm, the inarticulate murmur— somehow in the picture with Mic.

"How did you get educated?"

"Somebody put down some money for it. The father, I believe. . . . The people who brought me up always referred to him as 'the father,' so that's how I think of him."

"Why aren't you a revolutionary, Mic? Don't you want to smash the social order? What are you, by the way?"

"Oh, a sort of middle-brow Socialist, I suppose. I want everyone to have enough money, and decent working conditions, and education, as soon as possible. And no more wars. The usual stuff. But getting my knife too deep into the social order would be a bit like blaming myself on to my environment. It may be partly responsible for some things I'd prefer to be different. Doubtless is. But true or not, that's an impossible basis on which to live."

"Yes. It's a basis on which a number of people do live, all the same." Now that the first shock was over, she was glad she had forced it out. It gave her what she had been looking for, the key to Mic. It was all simple, she told herself in relief; his ups and downs, his tacit evasions. He had been wondering if she knew and whether she would mind. She must have hurt

70

him in all sorts of chance ways she could not remember. The sense of danger and conflict he gave her were all explained away. Well, that ground was cleared. Now she could help him. They could have a sensible friendship now.

She discovered herself staring at him as if she were seeing him for the first time, and said quickly, "Heard from Jan lately?"

It turned out, of course, that neither of them had heard from Jan since he went away. "But," said Mic, "there's one thing about Jan as a correspondent, you know where you are. He'll wait a week or two, or a month or two, just as it happens, till he's struck by some thought he feels is communicable to you and nobody else. Then he'll write you twelve pages. You read it once or twice, and lock it up so that if you have the misfortune to survive him you can get it published when he's dead. Then you settle down for another year. And a very good way too. For Jan."

"You are the oddest person, Mic."

"Why, about publishing it when he's dead? Why not, you don't appropriate the wind. If anyone ever thinks he can treat Jan as a treasured possession he—or more probably she—has my sympathy beforehand."

"It wasn't that, altogether." She had been thinking, not for the first time lately, that Mic was a young man singularly capable of keeping his own counsel; and she was puzzled by the deliberate, even provocative way in which he revealed himself to her. It was not as if he were enlisting sympathy, but rather offering some kind of warning. All she knew was that she liked him more than she had before.

They talked a good deal more about Jan. Vivian encouraged it, because it seemed to be taking his mind off what he had told her before. But he broke off in the middle of a sentence and asked her, as though unwilling, "How long have you been so appallingly alike?"

"People have been saying it for about ten years, I suppose. We're not, really, very often."

"Often enough." He was not looking at her. Here it was

71

again. It was her fault; she had strained and upset him and jolted him out of his transient content. It had to come, but she could deal with it better now.

"You said you had a record to play me," she reminded him. She was full of her resolutions. She would be easier with him, less affected by his moods; would bridge the gulfs which his sudden withdrawals so disconcertingly made.

"Oh, yes. You'll like it, I think." He jumped up with a restless jerk, then checked to say, "I'm not making you late, am I?"

"Not for half an hour." How impossible he could be; did he want her to go? "I'll hear it next time, though; you're going out, aren't you?"

"Oh, Lord, no. Do stay." He was so evidently taken aback that she believed him.

He had turned the record over when he suddenly said, "That chair's more comfortable, really. Out of the draught."

"There isn't any draught." Really, she thought impatiently, he was like a cat on hot bricks. Poor Mic, he was thinking already that he had said too much. She would be gentle. "Sit down here," she said, patting the arm of her chair, "and don't prowl about."

Mic clicked on the gramophone and sat down; a little behind her and out of sight, as she had meant him to be. It would give him a chance, she thought, to settle, and her to hear the rest of the record in peace. It was Holst's *Dance of the Earth Spirits*. It happened that Vivian had never heard it before. She forgot Mic and the room in which she sat, straining forward unconsciously towards the sound; enraptured by the wild interlacing of gross and ethereal rhythms.

But that deep underground mutter, pierced with fire—it seemed, more than the composer meant, to dominate the rest; its beat to echo against something in the atmosphere, sultry and overcharged. A nameless unlocated current, it pressed around her, troubling her pure perception of the music, but giving its emotion force. Her eyes shone, she tingled to the play of the half-chained powers. The dance diminished, and faded into air.

"That was exciting," she said.

Mic did not reply. There was, indeed, no reason why he should; yet his quiet had some quality that made her turn. With an arm along the chair-back, he was looking down at her. His eyes went through hers in a perfectly unresponsive stare.

A tight hand seemed to close on Vivian's diaphragm. She looked away; and there was a second, which felt like hours, in which nothing happened at all. Then Mic's voice, close to her, said slowly and, it seemed, quite coolly, "I shouldn't do this." There was a quick, hard pull at her shoulders. He tipped her head back over his arm and kissed her, taking his time over it, on the mouth.

She resisted, in the first moment, out of mere surprise. But by the time she had found out that, held as she was, she had no leverage to escape, she knew too that she lacked the wish. This, then, was Mic: not an image in a dark glass, a code to be translated, but this life on hers, this answering wave. The dance beat through her. She kissed him, passionately, lacing her hands behind his head; she could smell the clean dampness of his hair.

The kiss ended; she heard Mic draw a long, sharp breath as if he had been stabbed. He slipped down beside her and gathered her into a brief, violent embrace. In spite of its furious abruptness his touch was certain, even familiar, and she yielded to it without consenting pause. He kissed her again, this time painfully, and let her go. They opened their eyes on one another, left in deeper darkness by the dazzle of the fusing flame: bewildered strangers.

Mic was smiling remotely; a queer, elated, wondering smile. There was something in it of discovery, of defiance, of release. Vivian saw it, and did not interpret it. She only saw its strangeness, and it made her afraid.

Suddenly, with a bright objective clarity, she saw herself as she had been sitting in the minutes before he kissed her. Her blurred disregarded knowledge of her own body reassembling, the image crystallising as if in a stranger's eyes, she could see her own short beech-brown hair and straight firm jaw; her intent and distant face; her hands, big for a woman's and roughened with soap and antiseptics, clasped in front of her as she sat forward, elbows on knees, in a familiar pose. It was a pose characteristic; but not of herself.

"*Mic!*" She sprang to her feet, away from him. There was no doubt in her mind. He had struggled too hard, against himself and her, to make it plain. That he had tried to warn her and that she had been too vain, too pleased with her own interpretation of him, to understand, was the heaviest notch in the score. What had she, hot steel or cold, that would cut deep enough? She had returned his kiss, and would have returned it again.

"That was a pity," she said. Good; her voice held, stretched and hard. He was still half-lying in the chair, propped on his elbow towards the place where she had been, looking up at her, his smile changing. "It isn't even new—did you think so— except in blatancy." (How easy it was to think of such long words, its ease surprised her.) "But you're rather more aware of yourself than the others. That removes the last excuse."

"What do you mean?" said Mic. He was still a little short of breath.

"Are you asking me to tell you?"

Mic picked himself up out of the chair, and with a mechanical movement shook out the squashed cushion on which they had lain. Then he said, in a small colourless voice, "That may have been true. It isn't any more. You don't give me credit for much decency, do you?"

"No. But I gave you credit for a certain amount of honesty, till now."

Her throat was tightening, her chest grew heavy. With shame and horror she felt the approach of tears—of shock, partly, and nervous strain, with, somewhere behind it all, a bitter sense of loss. She looked away from Mic, in the childish fancy that she was less visible when she could not see.

74

Mic murmured to himself, "Oh, God."

"I'm sorry"—she turned on him savagely—"to upset you. I forgot you're not accustomed to women."

"That didn't sound like you," said Mic quietly.

The fight went out of Vivian; only devastation remained. She sat down in the other chair, and covered her face. She could hear Mic move up to her and stand, afraid to touch her.

"Oh, Mic, how could you?" she sobbed. "We were so nice together."

"We'll be nicer than ever," said Mic unevenly. "Only don't cry."

She shook her head. Mic knelt beside her and tried to dry her eyes with his handkerchief; repeating, as if to a child, "Come on, my dear, don't, please don't; look, it's all right now."

"It will never be all right," said Vivian in a swallowed voice. As she spoke she held up her face for him to dry; it seemed irrelevant, and natural. Presently she stopped crying, and Mic put his handkerchief away.

"Vivian," he said, choosing his words stiffly and carefully, "it's hard to ask you to forgive me, because what you think isn't true. And it's hard to defend myself, because it has been. I'm terribly sorry to have hurt you like this."

What was he saying? She was shaken and dishevelled and unbelievably tired. Her mouth felt bruised. She only wanted to get away.

"It's all right, Mic. Don't mind any more. I'm sure everything happened as it had to. But we'd better not meet again, you know."

He was still kneeling there, quite close, searching her face. The bones of his cheek and chin looked sharp and fine, and she wondered inconsequently whether he got enough to eat. But that would be no concern of hers.

"Will you believe me," he said, "if I say you'll never have anything from me that isn't your own?"

There was a soft untidy strand of hair on his temple that

had got into her eyes when he kissed her. Looking at it she said, "Yes. I'll never have anything from you at all."

She got up, and put on her jacket and hat. She wondered what state her face was in, and would have liked to powder it; but Mic had not taken his eyes off her, and she could not make the squalid little gesture.

She picked up her bathing things. Mic stood and watched her. He did not move or speak. Something, mere social habit perhaps, made it impossible to walk out of the door without a word.

"You have given me some nice times, Mic. Thank you for them. This is my fault too. I ought to have known it wouldn't work. Good-bye."

Mic came out of his stillness, and, with a reflex movement, opened the door for her. He began to speak, and stopped. "Good-bye," he said. She went downstairs, hearing the quiet closing of the door behind her.

— 8 —

THE first thing of which Vivian was conscious next morning was trying not to wake. There was a transitional instant, past sleep but short of waking, like standing sheltered in an open door, to which she clung. It passed quickly. She plodded through the motions of washing and dressing, fixing straps and pins and balancing her cap, thrusting her mind at the daily things which had not altered, trying to think about the ward. But the effort to escape only increased her misery. She tried, instead, to think about what had happened, but could find no materials for thought, only a raw flinching surface that would not be touched.

Breakfast, though she could not eat it, was a relief. She became exceedingly talkative, made a number of jokes, some of which were much admired, and plunged into the concerns of everyone at the table. Once the Home Sister had to speak to them about the noise they were making. She got up disliking everyone to whom she had spoken, and aching as if her mind had been beaten with rubber truncheons. Valentine pointed out to her, on the ward, that she had left the top of a locker dirty.

There was no reason, she told herself, why this should seem so much worse than anything else that had ever happened to her. It was a passing effect of delayed shock. She tried to assemble her old resources against trouble; but one of these had always been Jan, uninvolved in turmoil as a cloud. Mic's achievement was to have struck this resting-place from under her; Jan's name hurt her, like the sunshine and her wet bathing-costume and the sight of her own face in the glass.

She was free in the morning that Sunday, and, changing quickly, hurried out of doors. She walked fast and far, and, lying down when she was tired, on the brackeny fringe of a grass-track, tried to be still. But everything failed her. She could not loosen her mind, nor open it to truth. Her bitter anger against Mic, her condemnation, her longing to see him shamed or cast down, were no refuge but simply the climax of humiliation. She knew, deeply and secretly, that if she had been an impersonal onlooker she would have felt no hostility nor sense of wrong, only concern for him and the wish, if she could, to straighten his confusion. It was herself she wanted to revenge on him, herself for which she could not forgive him.

Returning heavy and unrefreshed, she found that her feet ached already, with the day's work still ahead. As she passed through the Lodge, the porter called after her.

"Note here for you, Nurse Lingard."

She came back, her heart lurching, recognising the hand.

"No," she longed to say, "keep it and throw it away, I don't want it." She took it with a slur of thanks.

"Mr. Freeborn left it." The porter's sandy eyebrows bristled with interest. "You only missed him by a minute or two."

"It doesn't matter, thank you."

She put it in her pocket, and went up to her room. She could still tear it up, now, in its envelope, and go away, her half-dulled wounds untouched. Sitting down on the bed, she opened the envelope with cold clumsy hands.

Mic had written:

"Dear Vivian,

"I let you go yesterday because we were neither of us in a state to improve things by prolonging them. Even now I find I haven't much to say. You know about me, and whether you find me intolerable or not won't depend on my excuses or apologies, but on your temperament and habits of mind. In any case I don't want to excuse anything, except a moment of blind selfishness for which no excuse can exist. Even that I can't repent of as full as decency demands; the results have been too important to me.

"You will wonder, if that's all I have to say, why I

78

couldn't have left you in peace. I would have, for a little longer anyway, if you hadn't said good-bye so finally. You meant it, obviously, at the time, and small wonder. Do you still? I think, myself, that ours isn't the sort of relationship that can cease to exist so easily. Neither of us, I imagine, has ever been much amused by the standard boy-meets-girl manœuvres. We are people first, and belong to our sexes rather incidentally. We liked one another as people, and, as a person, I shall miss you damnably if you go. Does it matter so much that I kissed you once because you looked like Jan? It might, if it could happen again, but it couldn't. Believe that, and sometime I'll tell you why.

"Can't we still pursue a few human interests together? I wouldn't ask if I didn't feel this would be easier for you than for me, since it was I who made a fool of myself, not you. Write to me sometime, and tell me what you think.

"Yours, any way you like,

"Mic."

Vivian lay down on the bed, her face on the cool surface of the letter. She thought, He must be lying, of course, to save my face. How could he not know that I kissed him, and held him, and wanted him?—And still want him, added her restless body; she jerked herself upright again. Or perhaps he thinks I respond like that naturally to any sort of kiss. Or was he really so beside himself he can't remember what did happen? (I kissed you once, he says.) But that isn't the way he writes. She read the letter again. It was very tidy: not a first copy, she thought. Is it really possible that he thinks I'll answer it?

"Because you looked like Jan." She found herself reading and re-reading it; it was, somehow, a relief to see it written down. A sentence among other sentences, it diminished, falling into place in the ground-plan instead of filling the sky. It went over the turn of the page—"I kissed you," on one side, "once because you looked like Jan," on the other. She sat reading the first half, slowly, for a long time; then flipped the page over quickly and read the second.

Looking suddenly at the clock, she found that she had been there for half an hour, had missed dinner, and had five minutes to change and get on duty. The letter she pushed into her pocket. There was no time now, she said to herself, to tear it too small for the corridor maid to read.

Valentine met her at the door of Verdun.

"Oh, there you are, Lingard. Run along quick to Malplaquet. You're extra there today. They've a big bunch of casualties in—something blew up at the power station, I think."

Extra again, thought Vivian wearily, as she walked the long corridor to the men's surgical wards. Never knowing your off-duty. But I forgot, it doesn't matter now.

Malplaquet was one of the oldest wards, a huge stone-floored, iron-raftered place like a railway terminus, and, she found, as busy. There were dressing-trolleys, half-cleared, abandoned in the gangways; the sterilizer, a copper antique like a witch's vat, was belching steam and the senior nurses were running to and from it, cursing one another for putting in unsterile bowls just before the clean ones were due to come out. One of the honorary surgeons was in the ward and the Sister was trying to take in what he said and watch everything that went on around and behind her. Behind one pair of screens a porter was shaving a man's body for operation, while a probationer collected the theatre clothes and blankets with stumbling speed; behind other screens, someone was being laid out. Vivian knew this because under the screens she could see the bedspread thrown on the floor; they were laundered, after a death.

She was swept into it all like a cork into a waterfall: she fetched and carried, washed instruments and bowls, made operation beds; cleared up round the corpse and escorted it to the mortuary; held down a man recovering from an anaes-thetic, who kept begging her to get into bed with him and telling her she reminded him of his mother. Because she was new to the ward, not knowing its routine or the places where things were kept, she was the one spared to take the next case down to the theatre. She helped the porters to lift him on the trolley; a young man, tall and finely proportioned, handsome in a simple physical way, but waxy pale from haemorrhage, for one of his legs had been torn off in ribbons at the thigh. Since he came in he had been perfectly conscious; he thanked Vivian and smiled at her as she settled the pillow under his head.

The trimming and suturing were hopeless from the first, and everyone knew it. They brought the trolley, running, back to the ward for a blood transfusion; but the dressings oozed faster than the donor gave.

His parents should have been there, but he had refused to tell the Sister where they lived: he did not want them worried, he said, unaware that the hospital regulations required they should be present at his death. He gave, however, the address of the girl he was engaged to, because he was to have met her that afternoon. Very politely he asked that, if it would not be troubling the nurses too much, someone should let her know he was all right.

The girl came quickly, fetched from the Sunday School where she had been teaching; wearing neat, cheap Sabbath finery, a tight blue coat, a lace frill, little glass beads. Sister Malplaquet, a towering woman with the feet, figure and terse kindness of a policeman, talked to her at the door. The girl listened, nodding her head stiffly as if at a lesson, and pulling at a little tear in one of her cotton gloves.

She came up to the bed, smiling; her smile became stiff and fixed for a moment when she saw his face, which was already of the colour of death, but she gave no other sign.

"Well, Reg, you silly boy, fancy you getting smashed up like this."

He whispered, "Hullo, Edie. You shouldn't have come all up here. I'll be fine tomorrow. Just a bit knocked out, that's all."

For the rest of the time she sat by his bed, giving him ice to suck, lighting the cigarettes which, since it could make no difference, they allowed him, and meekly going away when the surgeon came. She made mild little jokes about the artificial leg he would have. They were wonderful nowadays, she would never have guessed Ted Barton had one if his mother hadn't told her. He agreed, smiling when he could no longer speak.

Towards evening they both gave up the pretence that he would live, but neither of them had strength remaining for the open gesture of farewell. They held hands, and he turned his eyes towards her and smiled sometimes, to show that he was still aware of her.

The senior nurses did for him the little that could be done; Vivian's semi-skilled labour took her generally elsewhere. She flung herself at her rough impersonal tasks, finishing them with ever-increasing speed and fanatic thoroughness, as if the effort could give out some supporting virtue.

When it was beginning to grow dark he died, quietly, his mind still present and unestranged. The girl got slowly to her feet and stood looking down at him, and at his hand which she still held. Suddenly she threw up her head and screamed, a clear bell-like shriek that echoed in the high roof. The nurses came running to her, thinking, from long habit and discipline, of the decencies first of all. She looked at them with a dim bewildered hostility, as if they had reminded her, out of a distant world, of her customary restraints. "Let me go," she cried, shaking off their hands. "Take me away from here." She broke through them to the door, and they heard, echoing more faintly down the corridors, the noise of her running feet and high clicking heels. The Sister stood staring after her: such a thing was unheard-of, and a great inconvenience, for there were several things needing to be asked about the funeral, and the disposal of his money and clothes.

Vivian helped a staff-nurse with the last offices. She washed the working grime from his hands, square vigorous hands tempered with various skill, the hands of a good engineer. His body was fautless; it would have been accepted by Praxiteles. Vivian remembered that the girl, who looked quiet-living and religious, had probably never seen it.

She stood in the sluice, over the wide china sink, rinsing in endless waters the blood-soaked blankets in which he had died. The tears were streaming down her face so that she could scarcely see. Sister Malplaquet came in behind her and gave her a hard bony tap on the shoulder; whether in sympathy or reproof she never knew.

That night, before she went to sleep, she wrote a letter.

"Dear Mic,
"You are right; let's forget about it. As you say, there are too many other things in the world, better and worse than ourselves.
"I am being moved about, and off-duty is uncertain, so perhaps we'd better not fix anything for this week.
"Vivian."

THE week filled up, like a sack gradually bulging with the slackness and tension of its appointed contents. There was a hospital dance (not attended by Vivian), which provided dining-room topics in all the major and minor keys for the rest of the week. The first-year nurses were examined in physiology. Vivian expended herself, thankfully, in work for this examination during four days' off-duty time and a day off; and was surprised, not so much at finding her name at the top of the list, since the standard set was mediocre, as at noticing that she was not unwilling to receive congratulations on it. One of the staff-nurses nearly died of septicaemia; one of the house physicians became engaged to a Sister, a mystery variously explained according to the temperament of each inquirer; one of the wards was closed for repainting, and the patients inconveniently dispersed elsewhere. Collins was caught by the Night Sister, for the third time, coming in late, and went about telling everyone, with eager pride, what the Matron had said. On Thursday Vivian was moved back to Verdun. On Saturday morning she had a note from Mic, asking her to meet him on Sunday whenever she was free.

She answered it immediately, because she knew that if she gave herself time to hesitate she would refuse. She had begun to be afraid of it, and to put off going to her pigeon-hole, days before it could conceivably have come; so that when it did, expectation was weary, and she found it with a shock almost of surprise. Remarking her own fluency like an onlooker, she wrote over her morning lunch a simple easy acceptance; left it at the Lodge, and spent the morning planning, with hopeless ingenuity, to get it back. In the end, by hanging about persistently, she contrived to get sent on an errand to another ward, and at great risk went back to the Lodge; but her note had gone.

Her off-duty time that Sunday was in the evening. From five in the morning, when she woke, her imagination peopled the hours from six to ten at night with every misery of concealment, embarrassment and shame. It was impossible, in spite of the assurance of their letters, that they should meet on any terms but those of the most agonising constraint. As the time drew near, her longing to escape at any cost was such that she could almost persuade herself she hated him. It did not occur to her that she might, if she wished, simply refrain from keeping the appointment.

During the afternoon the clock seemed not to move at all. The visitors tramped and murmured in the ward, loading the beds with flowers and unsuitable food; they stared at the nurses, when necessity thrust them out of cover, as at rare creatures in a show, or buttonholed them to ask for diagnoses, which they were strictly forbidden to give. The seniors took refuge in the bathroom, where they were cleaning instruments if anyone appeared; Vivian and the other probationer sought the kitchen, cut the patients' bread-and-butter, and made themselves tea. The probationer told stories to illustrate her boy friend's sense of humour; Vivian applauded, and urged her on. But half-past five came at last.

She put on her everyday clothes with a kind of defiant carelessness, knowing that she was only trying to deceive herself, and forget how long she had spent on her face, her hair and hands. Mic was to meet her in their usual place, a quiet square just out of range of the hospital windows. Her hands felt icy cold and damp, her stomach both empty and sick.

Shut up in the ward and her own imaginings, she had scarcely noticed what weather it was, except that it did not rain. Now, coming out of doors, she tasted the heavy hanging sweetness of a summer evening, as it shifted in the first light winds before the dew. The sun was still up, but its light was deepening, seeming to penetrate with its long slant the inwardness of things, so that they themselves grew luminous. A blackbird sang liquidly, and a church bell rang, so far away that it was like a movement of silence. As Vivian walked, her breath came more easily, and her mind was stilled by a premonition of peace.

She turned the corner into the square, and the sun fell full across her eyes, so that for a moment she was blinded. Then Mic, just beside her, said, "Hullo, Vivian."

It was altogether different from her imaginings, the nervous smiling from a distance, wondering, as they walked nearer, what to say. But it became, instantly, inevitable and known, the reality which in these dreams she had forgotten. Mic stood there, smiling. She returned his smile. Immediately she had seen him, she had ceased to be anxious, or to feel any responsibility for their conduct of this meeting. She perceived that he had accepted it for both of them. He looked older but not, as sometimes before, also bitter and defensive. For the first time since she had known him, he seemed self-reconciled, directed and serene; yet it gave her no sense of novelty or change, only of a return to something which had belonged to them always.

"Do you know the 'Hawk and Ring'," he said, "over the top of the Downs? It's a nice pub. I thought we might walk up there and have a drink and something to eat; there'll still be light enough to walk back."

"Yes, I should like that." She had felt that she could not face the flat again, and had wondered many times whether he would know this. Now she could scarcely remember that she had had these fears, or why.

Passing through a loose red rubble of council-houses and villas, they struck a footpath to the hills.

She realised for the first time that the clothes he had on were as familiar to her as her own; that she knew by heart the smooth places on the elbows of his Harris jacket, a loose thread near the shoulder that had been caught on a nail; the pattern punched in his brogues. As a thing dreamed once can appear vividly remembered, it seemed to her that these things had always been the accustomed securities, and the past week an improbable excursion, already almost forgotten.

They talked—in this alone like her expectations—of indifferent things: town-planning, Swedish architecture, the sick staff-nurse, whose blood-cultures as it happened had been in Mic's charge. Yet Vivian did not feel that they were taking shelter or concealing themselves in these things: they were a background, an accompaniment to what was really being said, for which words were instruments too harsh and shrill. A new villa came in sight, with Tudor gables and a machicolated porch supported on Corinthian pillars. Mic said, quite mildly, "Good Lord, deliver us!" and his words had some half-caught significance, tinged with memory.

"What sort of a week have you had?" he asked her. She wanted suddenly to laugh, but only said, "Pretty busy. I've been on Malplaquet, you know."

"That was where the power-station people went, wasn't it? It must have been pretty grim."

"It was, rather." But already that week-old picture seemed years ago; clear, but tiny, gemmed by distance like the image in an inverted glass. "What have you been doing?"

"The usual stuff, and growing some things for Scot-Hallard. It's not my work, of course, but it saves him trouble and amuses me."

"He's always messing about with pathology; the physicians hate it." But she was not much interested in Scot-Hallard's weekly clashes with the Senior Pathologist; she was thinking that all these days, while she had been enclosed in her routine and her own troubles, Mic had been leading a life of which she knew very little, with a complicated routine of which she knew scarcely anything, and troubles of his own. Suddenly she saw her miseries as worse than selfish—a narrowing of bounds, blinkers over her eyes. The last of the houses fell behind; the hills opened, and the sun shone over them.

The path climbed eastward; their shadows shot in arrowy length before them; round them the midges glanced in globes, tiny galaxies limited by their own curve of space. On the skyline, to which their track was making, was a round clump of trees, looking, with the sunlight flat against their sides, like green-gold glass lit from within.

The last slope was steep; they needed their breath, and presently ceased to talk. The steady rhythm of their effort, the steady light, the steady lifting into a rarer and lighter air, loosed the mind from its fretful grasp on body and spirit.

At the top of the hill the grass grew long and green between the open trunks of the trees, and round the edge went the dented, short-turfed rampart of a camp. The town they had left was a vague pool of shadow, cupped by the sunlight on the hills. They climbed the ramp and rested there, Vivian sitting on the top, Mic lying along it, propped on his elbows, beside her. They said nothing at all, but looked into the high air below and around them, self-contented, as if it had been some eminence within themselves that they had scaled.

Mic said at last, "I ought to have asked you, before I brought you all this way, if you were tired. We could have gone in the car somewhere."

He spoke, as he had spoken all along, as if it were pleasant to say something and one thing was as good as another. Vivian answered, "No, I might have been tired in the streets, perhaps, but not here." They might have agreed with the same effect that no other place existed.

"It's only another mile," said Mic. "There's lots of time."

The twinkling, glittering sound of a lark hung overhead. They looked idly for its light-hidden source. A magpie drove by, with long stiff tail and whirling wings.

"One for sorrow," said Vivian, looking after it. "We must find another before we go."

They turned, scanning the shining trees.

"There it goes," Mic leaned across her, pointing. "Over to the left."

"It's the same one again."

"Is it?" said Mic, absently.

She had expected him to defend his magpie, and had been ready to turn and answer; but she did not turn. She sat still, looking up at the branch which the bird had left. Mic was still too, leaning on his arm. His cheek was resting, so lightly that at first she had not felt it, against the curve of her breast.

For a second she held her breath; and knew that she had communicated her knowledge. He made a small sound like a hidden sigh, and she saw as if she watched him that he had closed his eyes.

The shared will born of them in the instant rested and was satisfied. They neither spoke, nor tried to touch one another more closely. Presently Mic moved away, and slipped a little way down the slope, so that his head lay beside her knees. She rested her hand on the grass near his hair.

The lark was still singing, ending the same small jet of sound. Vivian looked about her, at the deepening light, the hills, at Mic lying beside her hand. She knew herself the centre on which the hills revolved, the burning-glass through which alone the sun could warm them, and rejoiced: glorious, apocalyptic error, more true than verity! Wonder filled her, but no astonishment. The life in her, like Mary sitting apart and listening to speech unheard by her careful troubled mind, had foreknown it, and claimed now its acknowledgement. Her mind, rebuked, kept silence, as the one should who has been wrong.

Mic sat up. He stretched enormously, and looked slowly all round the horizon, as if it had been given him.

"Well," he said, "shall we go?"

Their path joined a broad trackway over the top of the Downs, Roman, or older than Rome. They were in the world of high places which from within it seems a separate, continuous world, to which plains and cities are interruptions fugitive and unreal. The skyline hills marched with them, closer neighbours than the valleys between. Curlews cried airily, and tumbled with blunt wings along the wind.

They shouted, and laughed at nothing, and sang. Mic started *The Golden Vanity*; its radiant melancholy matched the light and the air, so that it all seemed to be happening on the blueness just below them; the great-sailed ships becalmed, the yellow-haired boy drifting down, sorrowfully singing like a mermaid, in the lowland sea.

The "Hawk and Ring" stood where the trackway cut a road, a low white house squatting in the cover of some Scotch firs.

"They have that ungodly sort of draught cider you like," said Mic. "Thick and sweet. I still hope sometime to form your taste in beer. This stuff's much more alcoholic, anyway."

"I don't care if it is, I like the taste of it."

"It blows you out."

"If it does I can keep it to myself."

The bar parlour had an oak settle, two cases of stuffed birds and a coloured picture of a soldier leaving home, in excellent spirits, for the Boer War. Mic had a bitter and Vivian her cider, cloudy and golden in a tall glass with a waist. They started drinking while they waited for the supper to be cooked. A foursome of hikers came in, wedged themselves into a corner table, and plied one another with allusive taunts.

Vivian put down her glass. The thick gold of the cider seemed to have invaded the air; she floated in it, faintly swaying, like the cabin-boy in the golden sea. The laughter of the girls broke round her like bubbles, drifting her this way and that. There was Mic, floating too. How sweet he was! Strange that the girls could sit there, absorbed in their fatuous men instead of coming to try and take him away. The nearest one had on shorts and was broad in the beam. Vivian could see her backside through the bars of the chair, looking larger and larger, a pumpkin, a balloon. It was the most exquisitely funny thing she had seen in her life. She began to laugh softly, leaning back against the wall.

One of the men was giving an imitation of someone, egged on by appreciative screams. An especially high note cut through the golden cloud, dispersing it for a moment. Vivian stopped laughing.

"Mic." She put her hand on his arm, and found it solid and stationary. "I believe I'm drunk, what shall I do?"

Mic, who had been thinking his own thoughts, came back to earth. "Nonsense. You couldn't be. Not just on that."

"All right, don't believe me if you don't want to, I don't care." She laughed again, waveringly. "I remember now, I forgot to have any tea." She had eaten practically nothing for lunch either, but was just sober enough not to tell him so.

Mic looked her over, wrinkling his eyes.

"Honestly, I believe you are. Serves you right for drinking that stuff. Don't worry, it isn't terribly obvious. Be all right when . . . Better come out in the air for a minute. It'll soon go off."

She found she could walk well enough not to be noticed by the engrossed guests. From the end of the lamp-smelling passage someone called "Supper's near on ready, sir," and Mic said quickly, "All right, thanks. We shan't be a minute."

They walked through the garden, between clumps of pink and cherry-pie. She hung on to Mic's arm; they seemed still to be floating, but more slowly and securely, in company with the night. The sun had gone down, and half a moon began to be bright as the west grew rusty. At the end of the path a little flight of steps went up and down the stone wall instead of a stile, leading to the field where the fir-trees were.

"Let's go up there," she said.

Mic looked doubtful. "Can you?"

"Of course I can." She felt infinite in faculty, in action like an angel, in apprehension a god.

"Better let me go first," Mic said.

He stood at the bottom, and steadied her down by the elbows. On the last step she stumbled and swayed forward against him. They stood together for a moment, in the deeper twilight of the trees. Vivian caught her breath; her unstable spirits shifted, the tears rushed into her eyes.

"Mic, you are so nice to me."

She felt his hands tighten on her arms: his shadowed face bent over her, unsmiling. She lifted her own.

At the last moment he laughed quickly and let her go.

'Darling, you're awfully drunk. You sit down there."

He put his jacket on the broad bottom step, and settled her on to it. She moved with dreamlike obedience. He sat down on the grass just below her, and lit her a cigarette. His hand was steadier than hers would have been; but that was not saying quite everything.

A bat flickered out from the black boughs above them, and an owl called. Round Vivian the world began to settle. Just beside her glowed the end of Mic's cigarette a long bright spike of red.

"Do you always smoke as fast as that?"

"Yes," said Mic briefly.

Vivian found that she wanted to cry again. She gripped the rough edge of the step, and pressed back her head against the wall. The moon glittered and blurred and ran about the sky.

She fought to keep herself from letting Mic hear. What would he think of her? Try as she might, a throttled sob forced itself out. Through the tears she saw Mic throw his cigarette away. It curved, like a tiny shooting star, into the dimness. Then, without knowing how she got there, she was in his arms, lying across his knees, and he was kissing her. Her tears stopped. They clung together, not hearing the owl when it screamed again.

"I'm not really drunk," she said presently.

"Of course you are. But I can't help it."

"Never mind. You can kiss me again when I'm sober, how will that be?"

Mic did not tell her. A gust of laughter blew out from the inn, a thin joyous sound, distilled by distance. A dry branch rattled to the ground. The sounds, the swaying moon, the sky flowed racing through her; she was embraced by them also and their kisses bewildered her. The dark trees swung into the sky. There was grass under her hair.

"God, how lovely you are."

She had slipped somehow from his knees, and he was lying beside her. Her shirt was open to the waist. When had that happened? She couldn't remember. What did it matter, they had been such fools so long. "Poor Mic," she murmured, stroking his hair; "and you were being so good."

"I still am," Mic said, his voice smothered against her breast.

Vivian was more nearly sober than she had supposed. She understood that it was their past unhappiness, rather than themselves, which was driving them; that they would regret this headlongness afterwards, and that Mic would take the responsibility. Half-intoxicated girls under hedges were not his pattern; whatever heresies he might have followed, he had his own integrities. It was easier to think of this than to remember hers.

"Dear,' she said gently, "we didn't mean it to be like this."

Mic whispered, "I know. Oh, Christ, don't go away," and kissed her mouth.

It was hard to think while he was making love to her. He was without clumsiness, even when he was uncertain or deeply moved. She could not tell whether it came from instinct or experience. It was as if they had remembered and longed for one another for many years. She moved her head a little and said, "I'll come back again."

"You'll never come back." He pressed the words on her lips like kisses. "You've too much sense to come back, if I let you go."

"I love you."

His arm slackened, and he caught his breath. "Oh, God, you're drunk. Don't say it if it isn't true, I—love you so much."

"Of course I love you. You know I do. Look at me."

"Don't. You wouldn't, if ——"

"It's too late for any ifs."

"Kiss me," he said.

She murmured, hardly remembering while she spoke what she was trying to say. "Let's go back to the inn."

"Stay a little. Just let me hold you: I've wanted you so."

"But not like this. It's true, isn't it?" With what seemed an enormous effort she sat up, throwing back her hair. "Mic, I've got a pain with hunger. And you can't keep ham and eggs."

He began a hard little laugh which shaded uncertainly into tenderness. "What a shame. I'm sorry." He helped her to her feet, and stood for a moment with his hands on her waist. She felt suddenly separate, unequal to herself, and lonely. The night wind blew round her ribs in a cool stream.

"We're—not very tidy to meet people," she said.

"Stand still a minute." He brushed her shoulders and began, quite capably, to straighten her clothes. "I'm afraid there's a button off your shirt."

"Only one?"

He took the pin from under his tie and fastened the gap on the inside.

"Mic, darling, you've got half the Downs in your hair. I've got a comb."

He put his arms lightly round her and stooped his head while she combed the pine-needles away. There was something reassuring in these childish services, friendly and secure.

"I haven't behaved very well," he said when she had finished.

"Whose fault was that? Mic, I—won't always be so unkind to you."

He said, almost inaudibly, "We'd better go in."

It seemed almost at once, after he had helped her over the wall, that they were blinking in the lamplight of the inn. She wondered whether she looked as dazed and distant as Mic did; at all events, one of the girls at the hikers' table had a coughing-fit, and her young man had to thump her on the back.

The innkeeper's wife brought in the supper, hoping too impressively that it would not be overdone. She had a long pale face with pale eyes and a sharp nose, and while she was there Mic's pin felt very large. Vivian could not talk to her but Mic thanked her quite convincingly and said that they preferred it well cooked. There was a faint difference in the tone and resonance of his voice, but only if you knew him. They were both leaning back against the oak panelling, and when he spoke she could feel a delicate vibration in the wall.

94

"I can feel your voice in the panels," she said shyly. "Can you feel mine?" She was ashamed to be beside him among all these people; what had happened seemed so near that it must still be visible.

"No." He smiled at her, and she felt safer. "I expect yours is the wrong pitch."

The ham and eggs were sedative. They ate in silence till the hikers' conversation got under way again, only slipping in a word or two when the noise was extra loud.

"I suppose," she considered, "I'd really have sobered more quickly if I'd eaten a meal at once instead of going out."

"The same thing occurred to me," said Mic, "as we were starting."

"And you thought ——?"

"Oh, I told myself some lie or other."

The hikers stopped talking to light a round of cigarettes. After the necessary interval Vivian said, "It's as well you did. We'd never have lasted the evening. Then the whole box of fireworks would have gone off at the last minute, and I'd have been late in."

Mic looked at his watch. "You're free till eleven, as usual, I suppose?"

She remembered something. "Oh, my dear, I'm sorry. Not tonight. Only till ten."

"It's twenty to, now. We'll never do it, even downhill, before half-past. We shouldn't have come so far. But you've always had till eleven before."

". . . So he took it home with him." An anecdote at the other table came to an end, and was received with the homage of stunned silence. Presently someone said, "Well, *really*, Les," and the laughing began.

"I've had late leave before," said Vivian, crumbling her bread. "I didn't ask this time. I thought I ——" She felt alone and naked and knew that she was blushing.

Mic reached for her other hand under the table. "Come on. We'll run for it. Had enough to eat?"

"More than enough, to run on." She returned his grip

gratefully. They got up, feeling four heads turn, as on one pivot, behind them.

While they were waiting for change in the passage, he said, "Doesn't it infuriate you to be dodging rules like a schoolgirl at—what are you—twenty-five?"

"Twenty-six." Their eyes met, exploringly. It was deeply exciting to know so much of one another and so little. "I suppose it's one of the less unreasonable rules; we get up early and one needs to be awake."

She fell silent, realising suddenly how free, till now, her solitude and her few desires had made her. Books, and the country, her thoughts and the placid observation of other people, had been there whenever the chances of work set her free to enjoy them. She had taken for granted, when neighbouring lives were thrown into confusion by the hospital's careless impersonality, that hers would always be tranquil and untouched. By slow degrees the need for seeing Mic had entangled her more and more in anxieties, disappointments and hopes. And now? She felt like someone who had just signed a mortgage; and was aware at once of Mic watching her face.

But, once returned to the night and the growing moon above them, they forgot these questionings and the reason of their speed. They ran, while the moon sailed with them, and the trackway streamed behind like broken water in a dream. The danger in their blood made them tireless. Once, when the track curved, they clambered the low stone wall and cut across a hummocky field, stumbling and laughing. At first she kept level with Mic and sometimes outran him: she liked to hear the little gasp of satisfaction with which he drew level again. When she found herself flagging she forced the pace; it seemed important not to lag behind. Her chest felt sore with hard breathing and her heart beat high in her throat. She looked at Mic jealously to see if he were still running his fastest or easing his speed to hers. He caught her arm and pulled her to a standstill. "Half-time," he said. They leaned for a minute against the wall, too breathless to feel much besides relaxing muscles and labouring lungs. Mic, with his arm along the wall-top and his head tilted back a little, looked impersonally graceful, like the trees, a part of the night.

In a little while they recovered their breath, and smiled. The running, the night and their delight in one another seemed perfectly balanced and poised. She thought, It would be right and good to go to him now. She made a little movement towards him, but remembered the hospital and how late she would be. He took her by both hands and kissed her quickly. "That's just for being beautiful." They ran on.

At the edge of the Downs they paused together, and stood near the rampart, looking at the strewed lights of the town. In the centre, heaped high above the rest, were those of the hospital, dull red and brilliant white.

"They've got two theatres going," Vivian said.

"I hope the Night Sister's busy there when you go in."

He took her hand. His gentleness made her ashamed. Did he bear her no reproach at all for having led him on like a wild thing and then refused him? To him it must have seemed that she was simply afraid. Perhaps, after all, she had been; she was no longer sure.

"Mic." She tightened her fingers on his. "I'll never do this to you again: I promise. Whenever you ask. If you want me any more."

"I love you." He was looking away, across the valley, and the words seemed not addressed to her, but the slow acceptance of a challenge, lonely, and directed elsewhere. With a sudden pang she remembered the fear which had overtaken her for a moment at the inn, and thought for the first time how small her stake was beside his. He had been hurt, in ways beyond her experience, through all the years most capable of pain. The bitter determination with which he had removed himself from the power of other people was written all over him. She thought of the flat and all its little defiant assertions of self-sufficiency. She had seen him watching Jan, whom he loved, like a dangerous enemy. Yet he had delivered himself up to her unarmed.

She felt abased, and liberated by humility. In this moment,

freedom and peace seemed only valuable as things to give in return for what he had given. His mouth was shut in a stubborn recklessness. She came between his eyes and the darkness, and put her arms round his neck.

"I will be good to you, Mic."

He held her, with her forehead against his mouth. She felt an exultation which was beyond emotion or desire, as if she had shaken limits from herself and broken, free, into new space. "Do you trust me?" she said.

"Yes."

She met his eyes; and, closing her own, lifted her lips for him to kiss. Her mind fled, comforted, into the warmth and darkness of her body; but she knew that she had retreated, seeing open before her a height and depth for which she had not been prepared.

– 10 –

THE Matron's office got all the afternoon sun; the ante-room, too, was crossed by a broad beam that haloed the secretary typing in the window, and fell on the fumed-oak centre table with its straight piles of nursing magazines—never, in its progress, picking out a grain of dust. Even in the shaft of it not a mote danced. The air was a thick drowsiness of light and heat, crossed by little threads of activity: the click of the typewriter, the blurred noise of a trolley going by in the outside passage, the shuffling and rustling and broken whispers of the nurses who were strung out in single file from the outer to the inner door.

They twisted and fidgeted, assuring themselves or one another that their caps were straight, their apron-buttons not showing beneath their belts, that there were no ladders in their stockings, or, if they had been out, that they had wiped all the lipstick off. One who had not had time to clean her shoes was polishing them by rubbing each foot in turn against the other calf; another was twisting her cuff round to hide a stain. All their aprons were freshly changed, and stood out round them in a stiff glaze.

Those farthest away from the inner door whispered stealthily together, and gave little sprung giggles which stopped sharply when the door opened to let a nurse out and another in. Sometimes the outgoing nurse would make a stealthy face signifying indignation or relief, but generally they changed over in nervous silence, as though they were already visible from inside. The two or three who were at the head of the queue never talked or giggled; they shifted from foot to foot, or patted their aprons or their hair. One had a broken ther-meter, which she kept pulling through her fingers.

Vivian was, at the moment, fourth. She stood narrowing

her eyes against the sun, which made her blink, looking at an iodine-stain on her apron which the laundry could not remove, and feeling the current of nervous tension twanging through her.

Her apron-strings held back her shoulders, her high round collar kept up her chin, like a scold's bridle; her cap, rigidly pleated, circumscribed the movements of her head. A white stiffened belt, whose constriction she could feel whenever she tried to breathe deeply, gripped her waist from which the clumsy gathered skirt and wide apron hung nearly to her ankles. It was a costume which, except for the fact that it could be laundered, bore little reference to physical function which, in fact, it generally hindered. Its purpose was partly that of a religious habit, a reminder of obedience and renunciation; partly, as such habits generally are, a psychic steriliser, preventing the inconvenient consciousness of personality. In it, all gestures of expression automatically died, leaving only a few of servant-like relaxation, folding the arms, or setting them akimbo.

Vivian put her hand into the bib of her apron and felt the thick double edges of her dress, and the line of linen buttons. The tight stuff strained to waist and shoulder, made her breasts into a hard, shallow curve like a doll's. Her movement felt faintly indecent: it seemed improper, as well as improbable, that there should be a body underneath of which these clothes did not form a permanent part.

Last night, being caught on her way in had made so small an impression on her that in the morning she had forgotten all about it. It had been her own fault; she had walked swinging through the main entrance, hatless, her hair tumbled by the wind and Mic's last kisses at the edge of the town, the pupils of her eyes dilated by excitement and the darkness, so that she had not seen the Night Sister till they were almost colliding. She had to be asked twice why she was late before she took it in, when she replied that she was sorry, she hadn't noticed the time. With something about the office vaguely sounding in her ears she had gone to bed, where she had not slept very much, but for other reasons. When she found her name on Matron's list in the morning, it took her a minute or two to remember why. Now, suddenly, only this place was real: the Downs were a year-old memory, she could not feel Mic in her arms or believe that she had promised to be his lover. She was a nurse who had come in late and had to go (in her off-duty time) to Matron about it. That was all.

She had worked up to second in the queue, with only the thermometer-breaker in front. Whoever was in the office now had been there for some time. She remembered that it was Valentine. Her name had not been on the list, but then she was the charge-nurse. Vivian looked along the line, and found that Colonna had joined it at the other end. She was not speaking to her neighbours, and her face looked set. Vivian felt her own stomach contract with panic. What would become of them? Colonna, no doubt, would dabble with Bloomsbury or the stage, but what would Valentine do? She had been nursing since she was eighteen, and expressed herself too well in it to drift into something else: besides, her people, unlike Colonna's, were not well off. Three-quarters of the responsibility would fall on her. She was years younger than Colonna, and five minutes' observation of their personalities made it obvious who must have taken the initiative: but the hospital would recognise only a charge-nurse and a probationer. Valentine would never get another job.

The office door had opened at last. Valentine came out; Vivian hardly dared to look at her face, but, when she did, saw that it was preoccupied rather than disastrous. As Valentine left she caught sight of Colonna in the queue: she seemed not to have expected her, and, when their eyes met, smiled quickly and shook her head.

After that, her own interview was an anti-climax. She knocked and went in, sped by a *moue* from the thermometer-breaker, who came out, replacement-slip in hand (they were fortunate, compared with a good many other hospitals, in not having, when they broke thermometers, to pay a fine and see the Matron as well). The Matron was a tall, fine woman with a Tudor mouth and scarcely-grey hair; she wore a dove-coloured gabardine dress, eternally immaculate, and organdie veil. When Vivian came in she examined her with interested distaste, as if encountering a depth of human degeneration new in her wide experience. The look was a part of her disciplinary uniform, but one had to encounter it several times before its effect began to wane. She explained to Vivian how what she had done illustrated her disloyalty, her indifference, her lack of direction and purpose. To all of it Vivian made the right answer, which was generally none.

"You are a little older than the other nurses. You should be able to realise that you cannot be an effective member of this profession while your mind is taken up with amusements and outside interests, and with unsuitable friendships with nurses outside your own year. I shall not, of course, expect you to come to me for late leave this week. You may go now, Nurse."

Vivian went. She would have known better than to ask for late leave in any case, and was too much relieved about Valentine to think of anything else. To make finally sure, she hung about in the passage till Colonna came out. Colonna was laughing.

"What did Matron suddenly want you for? Your name wasn't on the list."

"They added it on just before dinner." Colonna choked with laughter: she looked a little hysterical. "It was about you."

"About *me*?" Vivian gasped; then all the complicated emotions she had been throttling down all day detonated, and she laughed till her eyes ran.

"How like hospital, how perfect, it only wanted that!"

This explained the unsuitable friendships. She had thought it meant that she had taken tea with Valentine; but she had not allowed enough for the upward time-lag of hospital gossip. Horizontally, it was a heath-fire; vertically, a time-fuse which sometimes never exploded at all. This was natural; the second- and third-year nurses were forbidden to know the probationers; Sisters were a severely segregated officer caste with their own mess, and of them the juniors, fresh from a modern training, inhabited a different world from the older ones. As for the Matron, anything said to her, even when delivered colloquially by the Assistant Matron, had the status of an official *communiqué*.

"What did she say?" asked Vivian.

"She said that I distracted you. Did I?"

"Very nearly sometimes. I wonder what she wanted Valentine for."

"I don't know, but it's all right. I must go back to the ward, Sister's on." She added over her shoulder, "Better ask the Matron not to tell young Freeborn. He'd be dangerous jealous, I should think."

Vivian spent the rest of her afternoon out of doors, reading *The Tale of Genji*. At first she found concentration an effort, but gradually she worked her way into the atmosphere. The exquisite prince was good for her overcharged state, wandering from amour to amour with the composed sincerity and perfect taste of one assembling the pattern on a lacquer screen. She came back to tea feeling pleasantly exalted, living only in the parts of her life that were decorative and gay.

Hurrying back to the ward with only a minute or two to spare she was held up by Custance, the ear, nose and throat surgeon, strolling with Scot-Hallard in open formation so that it was impossible to edge through. As she walked behind them fretting to get on, she heard Scot-Hallard say "I don't know. The results will be ready tomorrow, but I haven't been up there lately. Freeborn's been looking after it for me. Rather extra for him, of course, but he likes to feel he's doing a bit of original work, I think. He must find the Path. routine rather a grind."

"Freeborn? What, the new Path. boy? You surely don't let him touch stuff like that, do you?"

"Why not? He's got a perfectly good Cambridge degree."

"Has he indeed? What's he doing in this *galére*?"

"No money or influence, I imagine, and not much push." They turned off into one of the theatres.

Vivian ran on to Verdun, not feeling sure whether her dislike of Scot-Hallard had been mitigated or increased. Sister was off duty that evening. While she and Valentine were both working in the clinical room, she said, "Nurse" (even Colonna used the formal address on duty), "why do we fall down flat in front of the Honoraries the way we do? Are we doormats, or are they boots?"

Critcally, Valentine held a test-tube first to the light, and then against a black door-plate. "No albumen there. We train them to be boots. Take equal parts"—she shook a red crystal out of a jar—"of Queen Victoria, the army under Wellington, sex and pot-hunting"—the room became pungent with the fumes of ammonia—"and there we are. Naturally, after it's become routine, they take it as a personal slight if anyone—look, there's a lovely acetone for you." She held up the tube, a rich clematis purple. "That's Mrs. Curtis. Make her some glucose-water, there's a dear."

"All right. But it seems pure totemism. Mr. Scot-Hallard, for instance—I suppose he crawls with his babies and swears at the cat like other people. What does he get out of being treated like something half-way between Hitler and the Archbishop of Canterbury?"

"I don't know," said Valentine, measuring Fehling solution, "what Mr. Scot-Hallard swears at when he isn't in the theatre. But if he crawls with his babies there must be a pretty varied assortment of dust on his trousers, I should think. He isn't married, by the way. Oh, hell, here's Matron coming to do a round." She ran, cramming on her cuffs. Vivian, who had spilt something conspicuous down her apron, found the glucose, concealed herself with it in the kitchen, and thought about Mic.

She had told herself, that morning, she was glad that her next evening off-duty time was not until the following Friday; it had been too sudden an earthquake, the landscape needed time to settle into firm and more permanent contours. But as soon as time and routine began to thrust their meeting backward, she found herself missing him so that, except when she was too tired to think or feel, it was like a constant pain. It had not mattered, so soon after, that she had lost her late leave for the week: but by Tuesday, this forfeiture of an hour began to loom in her mind, an enormous wrong. She tried to push her resentment away and commanded herself not to mind, because she knew it was the beginning of the invasion she had feared.

Mic wrote to ask her when she would be free. He scribbled her something every day, generally on the backs of report forms, from his bench; odd, aimless-seeming discursions about anything that happened to be going on round him at the time, a squabble between two of the physicians, a book he had been reading, or a reproof from the Welshman at the next bench, who knew most of Lenin verbatim, and called Mic a bourgeois intellectual for not believing in economic determinism, and an escapist because he said he didn't know what class he belonged to.

Apart from information such as this, practically all they told her about him was that he had needed to write to her, and she found it difficult to answer them. It seemed incredible that the intervention of a few passages and stairs could do so much. But his Wednesday note finished, "I hope you can. It would be good to talk to you. Presently perhaps I'll be able to write you letters. I've torn up a lot. One reads them over and suddenly feels like a specimen beetle, pinned out on a sheet of paper—it's lack of practice, I suppose. But what's worth keeping will keep till you come. Will you come soon?"

"Yes, I will,' said Vivian aloud.

There was still the greater part of three days to wait. He had asked her when she would be off duty in the evening. He might, of course, as a good many of the nurses' young men did, have asked her to slip out after she came off the ward at nine: but he knew the rules now and would never ask her to take the risk. No doubt, by Scot-Hallard's standards, he lacked push.

She sat, with a blank sheet of paper in front of her, biting the end of her pen and trying to make up her mind whether to say she would come that night. It would be futile, she thought, she would be dirty and tired and stupid, and it would mean staying out late again, unforgivable if she were caught. There was, in fact, every reason against it besides the real one. She began to write promising to come on Friday, and tore it up. She would write later, she said to herself; she was off duty in the morning that day. But when she came back to the ward she had written nothing.

She had just finished tidying the patients' lockers for the afternoon when Valentine came up to her with a slip of paper.

"Oh, Lingard, I was looking for you. Sister wants Miss Bentley's surgical notes for last year. Here's the reference number. I shouldn't waste time going through the shelves yourself. One of the people in the Path. Lab will find them for you." She smiled quickly, and went off with her tray of medicines before Vivian could answer.

Vivian put the paper in front of her apron. As she went for her cuffs she thought, "She's too good for Colonna. I wonder how it will end."

She had fetched notes from the shelves before, and as she was accustomed to the use of reference libraries had done so without assistance: but it was usual to find one of the laboratory assistants, who helped, among their other work, to file them. Sister was off duty, so Valentine must have saved her this from the morning. She climbed through the maze of the technical departments, electric, massage, photographic, avoiding the scurry of the staff who belonged there, and wishing after all that she had not come. It was fluffing and wispy, she thought, to intrude on people at their work, and invited every kind of stupid contretemps. She herself would have felt little but dismay if Mic had appeared unexpectedly in Verdun. Probably she would miss him in any case. By the time she reached the laboratories she had decided to get the notes for herself: but when she got to the door of the pathological department she stopped, knocked once, and went in.

Everything was very quiet and concentrated. Two or three heads looked round at her, in interest or irritation, but not

Mic's. Then she saw him, using a microscope in the window. He had not looked up and was evidently not likely to. In her first glance she received with photographic clearness the outline of his head against the light, the peacefully intent line of his mouth; the bones of his hand just moving as he made a fine adjustment of the screw. Her doubts fell from her, even the need to touch or speak to him. She felt content to have seen him and to have loved him in the stillness of this moment, and was about to turn and catch the eye of one of the others; but before she could move he had looked round, as straight into her face as if she had called his name. He got up and came over to her, seeming in no urgent hurry, but arriving before another man who sat nearer and had risen first.

Since it was evident that she had come on business, he waited to hear it. Though he did not speak or smile or give any sign which the other would have recognised, she knew that he was deeply glad of her coming, and thought how selfish her impulse had been to take her own satisfaction and go away.

She said, as she would have said to any of the rest, "I wonder if you'd mind getting me some surgical notes? The numbers are here."

"Of course." He held the door open and they went through to the place where the notes were kept—a queer labyrinth that had been the X-ray department when X-rays were very new. It had taken on the dusty smell and blanketed quiet of all libraries; Mic shut the door and snuffed out the last sounds.

They looked at one another in an eager, watchful curiosity. They had not met inside the hospital since it had all begun. Uniform made them both look altered, Mic aloof to the point of austerity, Vivian a little schoolgirlish. They waited a moment or two to take in and put aside one another's disguises. Then Vivian put her hands on his white drill sleeves, smoothing them to feel their stiffness, and he caught her quickly into his arms.

"You looked different," she said, "for a minute."

"So you do. Can I take your cap off?"

"If you like, but the rest looks silly without."

"Now I can only see your face. I couldn't remember, this morning, what you looked like. God, it's seemed long."

"I meant to write to you."

"What about?" He looked suddenly anxious.

"Nothing, now."

"I couldn't write to you, either."

"It doesn't matter, does it?"

"No. But I shall want to again tomorrow."

"Do, then. Say anything. I shall know."

"We think that now."

"Don't, darling, it is now."

After a little while he asked, "Was it all right the other night?"

"What, being late? No, they caught me. She didn't say much, I've not been caught before."

"You mustn't be again." His face frightened her. "It isn't worth it."

"Isn't it?" She looked up, hoping he would smile.

"Not if they sack you. What happens then?"

"I see," she said, suddenly sobered. "I hadn't thought."

"Sometime,' Mic said slowly, "we shall have to think about a lot of things."

In the pause that followed she could hear from her breast-pocket the heavy tick of her watch. She turned a little against Mic, so that the sound was covered.

"We know most of them. It doesn't make much difference, does it?"

He slid his hand down from her hair and hid her eyes.

"No. I'm afraid not."

"My late leave's stopped for this week. I'm sorry."

"Never mind. You know, your hair where it starts is just like a baby's."

"It's new there like a baby's, I expect."

"Do you still want to come?" It was a flat, shadeless question. He had talked like that when they first met.

"Yes. I do. I'll come on Friday."

"Two days from now," he said; but he was looking at her as if he must learn her face before one of them should die. She caught her breath, kissed him quickly and moved away.

"Perhaps we'd better find those notes. Sister's off, but I daren't be gone too long."

"That won't take a minute." She could tell by his smile that he knew he had troubled her. "I'll find you the page too, it's confusing till you know."

"Please," she said, "may I have my cap?"

"I'm sorry." He had been dangling it by the ribbon that fixed it behind, and turned it over in his hand, looking at its high starched front and the bonnet-like pleats at the back. "To think of you wearing that."

"I hardly ever notice it now." She put it on.

"Last year's notes, wasn't it?"

He got down the thick volume, flipped over the pages, and stuck a scrap of paper between the right leaves. It took both her arms to hold it.

"What a thing," he said. "I suppose if I carry this down for you there'll be a fuss?"

"Good heavens, yes. It's not bad really, if I hold it this way. Thank you, Mic. Good-bye."

"Till Friday," he said. It was ending; next moment they would have gone. With a sudden, piercing thrill of panic she felt she could not bear it. She slammed down the book on the inkstained deal table, and ran back to him, her cap falling off of itself this time and lying unheeded on the floor. He held her tightly and kissed her, feeling her fear. She could not speak, only gripped him fiercely.

"What is it, my dear?" he said. "What is it?"

"Nothing. I don't know." She slipped her hands over his shoulders, feeling their framework, a clean, reassuring line. Some people's personalities, women's chiefly, seemed spread over the surface of their bodies, skin-deep; other inhabited muscle and sinew; Mic always seemed to live from the bone.

"Why are you afraid?" He spoke with a difficult quiet: she could feel his heart like a runner's. "Is it of me?"

"No. No. Don't leave me." She struggled for words. "Of everything but you, I think. One isn't used to being . . . so much more in danger."

"I know," he said.

She slackened her clasp and looked up, calmed as no assurances of safety and protection could have calmed her.

"I'm sorry, Mic. You've worked through this alone."

"Not entirely."

She sighed, relaxing in his arm.

"Would you go back now, if you could? Tell me truly."

He shook his head.

"We think this has come on us from outside ourselves, but it hasn't. Probably nothing can."

"Maybe. One talks of one thing, and chooses another. But however it came, I'm glad it's here."

"And I," he said. "Whatever happens."

A siren wailed shrilly from a works close by.

"That's two o'clock," said Vivian. "I've been gone nearly a quarter of an hour. Good-bye, Mic. Good-bye. If I try to come back, slam the door."

"Come back quickly. . . . Look, your cap. Let me put it on for you, you've got the book."

"Is it filthy?"

"Do till tomorrow. Just—no, you'd better go. Good-bye."

She dared not look back once she was through the door, but plodded on, farther and farther away, down staircases, along passages, clasping her seven-pound burden and hating its hard angles because they came between her memory and him.

The visitors were streaming in, with their bags and bundles and their wilting flowers done up in brown paper and string. She edged her way through them, aware of them at first as a half-regarded physical nuisance like a dust-storm, till she passed an anxious-faced girl and it occurred to her to wonder what it would be like, if Mic were ill, to sit with him always under the stare of crowds of people; to ask how he was and to be answered, tolerantly, with what was good for her to know. In Verdun, Valentine at the Sister's desk was telling a husband that they would perhaps have decided by the weekend whether there was to be an operation.

"Here are the notes," Vivian said when he had gone. "I'm sorry, I've been longer than I meant."

"It's all right. There's nothing to do. You can help with the trolleys." She saw another strained, question-fraught face bearing down on her, and braced herself again.

Next day, Thursday, was operation day, and a heavy one. Vivian ran for blankets, filled hot-water bottles, mixed salines, heaved the end of beds up on blocks, scrubbed mackintoshes, prevented partly anaesthetised patients from getting out of bed and held bowls under the heads of others, in the intervals doing her routine work as best she might. She took down one case to the theatre, where she stood masked, hooded and robed into the anonymity of a cult priestess while Sir Bethel, like an augur taking the haruspices, paid out fold after fold of intestine, lovingly, on to a sterile towel. She watched, chiefly conscious of a moment's inactivity; the theatre never shocked or sickened her, it was too impersonal—the patient unconscious and almost wholly hidden under the white coverings, the exposed organs detached, as it were, from their context, like the diagrams in an anatomy book. Sir Bethel finished his meticulous work and departed filled with aesthetic joy, leaving the patient blue. Vivian ran back beside the trolley, trying to keep pace with the porters and peer into the blanket-swathed face: collided with someone, and when she found that it was Mic had no time to think about it, after one look to see that she had not made him drop the test-rack he was carrying. But at night-time she was glad of the day, because it was impossible not to sleep.

Friday was a beautiful morning. Vivian jumped out of bed, stretched her back to shake out the stiffness of yesterday, and wondered if Mic was awake. Her sleep had been deep and unbroken, and everything looked easy, direct and clear. She ate a good breakfast, explaining as she did so, to an inquirer recently on Verdun, what Sir Bethel had found in Mrs. Wagstaffe's abdomen. The sun shone on the marmalade dish and made it glow like amber light: a huge cumulus cloud rolled itself majestically across the sky in the window.

The Home Sister got up.

"Nurse Vane to Ramillies. Nurse Lingard to Trafalgar."

Vivian looked round her, at the shaft of sun, the sky, the tall cloud. She had not invented them, they were the same.

"You're lucky going to Trafalgar," said the friend of Mrs. Wagstaffe. "I loved it when I was there."

"Yes."

"You do look fed-up, though. Arranged your off-duty, I suppose."

"Yes, I had."

"Jolly bad luck."

"It's ——" Vivian stopped, driving her fingers into the seat of her chair. It was no use. She could refrain from crying or saying anything, but that meant nothing, it only saved her social pride. It did not alter the fact that she was entirely enclosed in this moment, powerless to escape beyond it; nor change the certainty that she and Mic would need one another increasingly with knowledge and custom, that under the conditions of their life these miseries would continually recur, becoming less rather than more endurable: that she had given herself into the power of things, and would generally be alone.

She went up to her room and tried to write to Mic to tell him: tore up the first draft because it said too much, the second because it said too little; dragged her bed together and went down to chapel, kneeling and standing and picking up her hymn-book when the others did.

> "Prophecy will fade away,
>   Melting in the light of day."

sang the choir. Several other voices had joined in too; the hymn was unusually cheerful for a hospital choice.

> "Love will ever with us stay,
>   Therefore give us love."

The letters danced before Vivian's eyes, and in their place she saw the girl with the glass beads, and heard her scream and her tapping heels.

> *"Faith will vanish into sight,*
> *Hope be emptied in delight ——"*

She shut her book and put it down. The oleograph saints shimmered in the sun, the rows of pleated caps, swimming together, seemed to move like water and slip past her, and she too drifted, subject to time, to the finality of its losses.

Go, lovely rose. The sum of the world's roses will be the same. But tell the free spirit so, not betrayed to transience by desire.

Golden lads and girls all must, as chimney-sweepers, come to dust. Therefore, give us love. For thou, perhaps, on thy return, shalt find thy Darling in an Urne. Therefore, give us love.

They said a prayer for the Diocesan Conference, and went up to the wards.

Trafalgar (men's surgical) was contemporaneous with the Albert Memorial. It was very high, conveyed, in spite of many huge windows, the impression of being always dark, and bristled with odd brackets, pulleys, and knobs whose purpose no one now living could remember. The patients' bathroom contained, besides the bath, shelves of enamel-ware, the testing cabinet and specimen-glasses, and a large brass steriliser heated with a gas-ring. It also contained the off-duty list, but the beds had to be made and there was no time to look at it. She ran round with a red-haired staff-nurse, swinging twelve-stone men up into their pillows, trying to make the clothes look tidy over cradles and splints and pulley-lines, talking to the patients who were fit to talk, and wondering what to say to Mic.

She was putting on her cuffs for prayers when the staff-nurse said to her, "You'll be taking First Pro's off-duty. When are you off today?"

Vivian ran her finger along the list.

"I don't know," she said dully. "I'm supposed to be down for a day off tomorrow, so Sister will give me what she thinks, won't she?"

"If you're down for a day off tomorrow you'll have it, of course, and evening tonight."

Vivian stared at the list till she could no longer see it.

"But I thought—I mean, I'm not due till next week, and if it happened that way on Verdun, Sister used to make you wait three weeks for the next."

"Sister Trafalgar will give it to you."

It was true.

Sister Trafalgar was small and weakly pretty, with pale eyes behind large glasses, faint blonde hair, and a cockney accent, and was a mystery. No Sister in the hospital was more efficient. She never gave any orders, but when she requested this and that in her shy genteel voice it was done, and done her way. She called no one careless, dirty, slovenly, and, in her ward, no one was. She never put the men in their place; and they respected her more than their mothers. She gave Vivian her day off.

"You look quite gaffed," said the red-haired staff-nurse. "After all, it has to come up heads some time or other." Peering in the cracked mirror of the nurses' lobby, she stuck a mouthful of kirbigrips into her hair.

Vivian let out a long, deep breath. "What lovely hair you have," she said. Her voice was deep and warm, and Rodd, the staff-nurse, was for her from that hour. But Vivian hardly realised that she had spoken. She was wondering if Mic knew that a day off included leave of absence for the previous night.

The patients confided to one another, in their few minutes of privacy, that the new nurse was a good sport. It was something to see a bright face, they said.

Mic was waiting in the square. He had persuaded the car to accompany him, and was sitting half-turned towards her, looking about.

"Thank the Lord," he said. "I was afraid they'd stopped you."

"I'm sorry. I was a bit late coming off, and then I had a bath." She slipped in beside him.

"Nice bath-powder you use. I can't believe you're here. This morning I was sure you wouldn't come."

"What time was that?"

"Early. Till about nine."

"Funny, because just then it didn't look as if I would."

"Where shall we go? Do you mind being shaken up in this? You oughtn't to walk after a day in the wards this weather. We've got nearly four hours."

"We've got longer than that."

"What, did she give you late leave after all?"

"No, not exactly. I've suddenly come in for a day off. To-morrow, you know."

"Tomorrow? Lord, what luck, that's Saturday. We'll have half the day. I mean, if you're not doing anything?"

"You know I'm not."

"Aren't you? Everything seems different when you're away. It does still, a bit. Where shall we go? God knows why we're sitting here. What time do you have to be back tonight?"

He did not know. She felt shyer than she had expected, but extraordinarily happy and secure.

"Well—any time. The day off starts from now, you see."

"Oh, good," he began cheerfully. "Then ——" His voice stopped. They both looked into the windscreen, and caught one another's eyes reflected there. "Good," said Mic softly, and started the car.

"Where are we going?" she said, as they left the town.

"God knows. Oh, yes, but so do I. It's just come. I'm taking you to the ballet."

"Mic, darling, you're unhinged. We can't make town under three hours."

"This car takes five, on a good day. But there's a tour in Brancaster this week." He named the company.

115

As there was time, they avoided the macadamised artery with its tea-shacks and filling stations and went by the lanes, which were laced with cow-parsley between great lush hedges tangled in bryony. The evening was warm and cloudy and the fields thick with buttercups, so that the sunlight seemed reversed, swimming upward from the ground.

"We'll have time for some supper before it begins."

They found an inn that was a farm as well, with a clipped yew taller than itself towering in rings against its grey stone face.

"What'll you drink?" said Mic, laughing at her sidelong.

"Beer."

She found that for the first time she rather liked it. The thing was to take long drinks, it got past the bitterness to the flavour. It was a good inn, and they left it unwillingly.

"I hope there'll be seats," he said as they parked the car. "Brancaster is rather on to these things as a rule."

"Upper circle only," said the box-office girl.

"We forgot to look and see what they're doing," she said when they had found the seats.

"Here's the programme." They broke the seal like children diving into a Christmas stocking.

"Oh, Mic, it's *Giselle*."

The lights went down, the music started. They touched one another's hands in the darkness, and looked at the curtain with its flat silly nymphs.

The footlights went on: the curtain lifted on the first act. In the interval they hardly spoke.

Night fell: the water-witches danced by the mere, blown like mist, expiating their brief, too light mortality: and little Giselle floated out to them from her unhouseled grave. The lovers met and danced their brief reunion, their limbs moving in the rhythms of passion and of longing, their faces calm with a secret and dream-like peace.

At last it was over; cockcrow came, the wraiths dissolved; Giselle was drawn into the sepulchre, and the prince left alone in the grey morning. Vivian clung to the last instant, dreading the lights and the noise of applause. There sounded for her, in the last phrases of the music, the lament for Ammon and Osiris, for Lesbia's sparrow, for Lycidas and Adonais, for the flowers of the forest.

The lights and clapping broke, Giselle and her lover took the curtain. Vivian turned, and met Mic's eyes.

Conversation and rustling broke out all round them, and presently two men climbed past them to get a drink. Mic blinked as though he had been asleep, and said, "They're better than I've known them before."

Vivian found the programme slipping from her knees.

"There's something else, of course."

"Yes, I suppose there is. Let's see."

"*Prince Igor*," said Vivian dimly.

"Oh. *Prince Igor*. Yes, they're fond of that."

They held the programme together, looking at the cast, not reading it.

"Do you think," said Mic presently, "that *Igor* is one that grows on you?"

They looked at one another again.

"Well," said Mic "suppose we ——?"

"Yes, we might."

It was scarcely dark outside: the city lights made the sky a deep unearthly blue, but as they got beyond them it greyed and grew luminous. Mic kept the main road this time: its offences were softened, reduced to silhouettes picked out with scattered lights. It saved half an hour.

The dew had laid the smells of dust and petrol, and the field scents blew through to them, clover and great wafts of hay. Trees, and the grass verges of the road, leaped into the beam of the headlights with sudden colour and a hard, metallic clearness of design: moths as they drifted through it waved for an instant vans of fire, and gnats and midges danced like anvil-sparks. Mic and Vivian, scarcely speaking, leaned with their shoulders lightly touching. Mic looked after the car, which could not be treated cavalierly, and Vivian watched his hands through half-shut eyes.

They rounded a bend, and the pale sky was quartered by a towering cube of lights. Vivian, who had not been that way for many months, could not recognise nor remember the huge building which, with its satellites, covered the area of several fields. It was too stripped and hard for a hotel, and too big: bigger than the hospital, and looking, Vivian thought, much more powerful and efficient.

"What on earth's that?" she asked lazily. It was already falling behind them and Mic was where he had been.

"Haven't you seen it before?" His voice, losing some of its sleepy gentleness, was a tone flat. "It's a new chemical warfare experimental station. Been going a month or two now. Scot-Hallard goes there."

"Do they work at night too?"

"So it seems."

Vivian said no more. In her mind scattered experiences linked, with a snap like Childe Roland's closing hills. They came together single and clear, the girl with the glass beads, the chapel hymn, the evocation of *Giselle*. She knew who had been the prophet of their generation, and repeated the words softly, thinking the rattle of the car covered her voice.

"Go on," said Mic.

She put her hand on his knee.

"Listen."

It was the roar of a plane, made deeper by the night, spreading through the sky in pulsing rings of sound. Presently they could see the navigation lights sliding between the stars.

"Yes," said Mic. "Say it."

She said, slowly, accompanied by that throbbing bass,

> " '*But at my back I always hear*
> *Time's winged chariot hurrying near;*
> *And yonder all before us lie*
> *Deserts of vast eternity.*
> *Thy beauty shall no more* ——'

"Mic, I'm sorry. How could I, tonight?"

"Why not? It's always for tonight." He smiled at her, his eyes darkened and made strange by the gloom.

> " 'Thus, though we cannot make our sun
> Stand still, we yet will make him run.' "

The roar of the plane dwindled to a gnat-like drone, to a faint tremor of the air. The car took a bend, throwing them closer together, and they did not move apart again.

They climbed a hill, and saw above the trees the lights of the town to which they were returning, glowing like fixed summer lightning on the sky.

"By the way," Vivian said in a soft blurred voice, "what sort of ballet is *Prince Igor?*"

"Oh, there's a . . . But you said ——"

"I know."

The car protested shrilly as Mic stamped the accelerator down. They said nothing at all for the rest of the way.

They left the car in its dark little garage in the mews, shut the doors on it, and stood with their hands on the bar, half-visible to one another and half-imagined.

Mic took her wrist. "Come on," he said. Laughing, they began to run.

"You can't just—say—Come on," Vivian panted as they rounded the corner. "It isn't—done. It's—won't I—come in for a minute, and—have a drink."

"You can have anything and—everything. Come on."

The light was out on the stairs. She stumbled; Mic pulled her arm over his shoulders and half-lifted her up them. They groped their way breathlessly, smothering their laughter though there was no one to hear.

The door shut with a gentle snap. The room was quite dark; the street-lamp slid across one corner an upward-slanting, pale beam. Vivian only saw it for a second before they reached for one another, and Mic's black silhouette eclipsed it; but in the drowning confusion of themselves, when she could not have said whether her eyes were shut by the night or her own eyelids or Mic's mouth, she could still see the pale light streaming upward and the curtain glowing in metallic lines.

They were still out of breath with the running and the stairs. Mic came to the surface with a little gasp and said, "Do come—in—for a moment, won't you—if you've time—and—have a drink?"

"You're very kind. Perhaps—just for a minute."

They laughed, wandering uncertainly up the scale, and Mic switched on the light. They were dazzled for a minute, not so much by this as what it showed them, the flame of one another's vitality. It was as if neither of them had been alive before.

"Mic, you're ——"

"What?"

"Nothing. I just liked the look of you, that's all."

To herself she had called him beautiful. He had the neutral kind of good looks which in moments of abstraction or constraint passed unnoticed, like an unlit lamp. She had never imagined that he could look like this.

"Why me?" He was staring at her with wide brilliant eyes. "But you're—no, I can't tell you."

He had left sherry and biscuits ready on the table, and a bowl of garden roses. They ate and drank, sitting on the table's edge, looking across their glasses. When they had done Mic jumped down, found a record and started the gramophone. He came back, and pushed the table to the wall.

"Dance with me."

"We can't dance to this." She took the hands he held out to her, swaying to the music. It was Tchaikovski's *Flower Waltz*. They danced, half-drunk with the ballet, half in earnest, half fooling. Mic caught a rose from the table as they went by, and tangled it in her hair. She leaned back against his joined hands, an arm flung out behind her; the snaps of her dress parted at the armpit; he bent, still holding her from falling, and kissed her side.

"Take it off."

When she stood up it slid down of its own accord, and she kicked it away. In this hot June weather it was almost all she wore. Mic said, "Now dance with me," and put his arms round her again. But they did not dance. The gramophone played the rest of the record to itself, and stopped with a discreet click.

She had not thought that he might carry her, for he was slight and she nearly as tall. When he swung her feet quite easily from under her she thought, first, It's all that swimming; then, for a moment, could think no more. A gust of unforeseen fear shook her. She longed, though she would have died rather than do it, to call out, "No, stop, I wasn't ready." The hospital veneer of sophistication cracked away and her ignorance spread in a huge blank before her mind. Their nursing lectures told them nothing. They traced the growth of babies from the first cell, but dismissed their cause with the brevity of a diagnosis. She thought of the elementary psychology, outside their course, which in her brief leisure she had imperfectly assimilated. There were so many things, never adequately explained, which could go wrong. She only remembered that if she and Mic made some mistake they would end by hating one another. It seemed that such things happened. This might be the last moment in which they would be happy together. She clung to him desperately as he carried her the little way, shorter than it had ever looked before, to his own room.

She had not been there since the flat was finished, and there was only a crack of light from the door: it looked a different shape, puzzling with angles and folds of unknown things. She could not see the bed on which he put her down. He moved away, but she would not let him go.

"No, don't put the light on."

"Can't I? I like to look at you."

"There's a lot from the door. Please."

She thought, If I'm going to make his life more difficult than it's been so far, I wish I'd never met him, I wish I'd never been born.

He slipped from her hands, and stood up.

"It's all right. I'm not going to switch it on."

She heard the soft thud and click of his clothes as he threw them away. He crossed the half-lit doorway, sharply black and slim, and lay down beside her. She was no longer afraid: he was familiar like something known in childhood and forgotten, inevitable as herself. But he was troubled: she could feel it in the way he kissed her.

"What is it, tell me."

He did not speak for a moment. Then he said, "Have you had a lover before?"

"No, my darling. Does that matter to you a lot?"

"Yes. It frightens me." He breathed sharply. "How dare I? I'm not fit."

She pulled down his head and kissed him.

"What shall I do? No one else is any good."

He stroked back the hair from her forehead; she made a sound as the rose pulled, and he disentangled it patiently and carefully, only hurting her a little. Some of the petals fell about her face, light and cool, or slid under her, giving up their warm bruised scent.

He dropped the stalk on the floor, and said, in a voice she could scarcely hear, "I can't talk about you. I never shall be able to. But there's a clearness about you, a wholeness, a . . . Not innocence, but better, I can't find words. If I spoil that for you, after—all the rest—it's the end, I've failed in everything that matters, I'd be better dead."

She flung her arms round him, not knowing, till she felt her cheek slippery against his, that tears were sliding from her eyes. She did not feel like someone who might be weeping, but infinite, ancient in wisdom, protective as Hera, a mother of gods and men.

"Is that all? I love you, Mic, I love you."

There was just light enough to see his face stooped over hers. In a moment it would be too near to see, they would be too near to know one another or themselves, not Mic and Vivian any more, but We, a different, narrower, intenser life. The last thing she said was, "We shan't come to any harm."

Indeed, they might both have taken things less anxiously; for they found that, in this as in most other matters, they understood one another very well.

— 11 —

THEY lay in bed discussing who should get the breakfast, chiefly as an excuse not to get up.

"Don't be absurd," Mic said. "It's your day off and I have every Sunday. If you move I shall be really angry." He settled his head back on her shoulder and shut his eyes.

"But you always have your own to get, and I don't." She played about sleepily with his hair till she happened to look at the clock, which indicated that unless something were done at once Mic, at any rate, would get no breakfast at all. She was next the wall and it was tempting to shift responsibility; but she took a deep breath, kissed him, and dived out over the end of the bed before she had time to think again. It felt cold and empty outside, and the thought of thirteen nights in hospital struck leaden on her heart.

"How could you?" said Mic, looking incredulously at the empty place.

In the end she made the coffee while he fried eggs. The kitchen was a sort of cupboard with a gas-ring and a sink, and had almost as little room for two as the bed. The frying-pan was pushed away behind other things, and she wanted badly to ask him what he had for breakfast when he was alone; but Mic was independent about his housekeeping.

"Do you like fried bread with it?"

"Is there time?"

"Won't take a minute, I do too."

They were good fried eggs and she told him so. "I'll have lunch ready when you come home."

"How amazing to come back and find you here. I can't believe it. Will you really be here?"

"Life's unpredictable, but I fancy so."

124

"But look here, there's nothing in the house for lunch. I was going to take you out."

"You can leave all that, it's my turn anyway. Mic, you *will* be late. I'll clear away. Don't be such an ass, I've got all the morning. Look at the time. Yes, I do, I do, good Lord, what do you think? Yes, of *course* I'll be here if I'm alive. All right, but that's the last and I swear it. Quick, run!"

It gave her a pleasant, warm feeling of power and possession to have the flat to herself. Not that much needed to be done, except the bed and the washing-up; the place was very well kept, not finickingly neat but without muddles stuffed away in corners. She found Mic's fountain-pen on the bedroom floor, where it must have fallen out of his coat. He hated using anything else. She would leave it at the hospital for him. She had started out before she noticed anything wrong with her idea of handing it in at the Lodge—"Just give this to Mr. Freeborn, please, he left it behind." She came back, feeling suddenly very raw and clumsy; found an envelope, wrapped the pen in a piece of paper saying, "I'm still here," and stuck it down.

Buying the lunch was consoling. Mic had left her his latch-key to get back again; he was going to get another cut, he said. She pushed open the door with her arms full, and almost walked into a woman who was sitting at the table drinking tea.

"I'm sorry—I ——"

They stiffened at one another, and then she saw that the visitor had on a grubby overall, wore her fringe in curlers, and was, of course, the woman who came at intervals to clean the flat. She must have had an easy morning's work this time. Vivian smiled at her with tardy brightness.

"Good morning. I'm having lunch with Mr. Freeborn, so I came early to get a few things ready."

"Oh, to be sure, Miss." She was about forty, with a red, tightly-buttoned face. Into her beadily appraising stare Vivian's smile sank, leaving no trace. "Would you be wanting any help?"

"No, thank you, I can manage easily." The woman washed

her tea-things noisily, collected outer garments and a sinister-looking American cloth bag, and went, with a look over her shoulder which gave Vivian a feeling in her stomach as if she had eaten something very heavy and indigestible. She walked round the flat to see how much evidence she had left. The bed-room was quite straight; too straight, because Mic would almost certainly have left the bed to be made. Quite certainly he would have left the washing-up. Her compact was on the mantelpiece. Poor woman, she said to herself, firmly reasonable, it's rather too bad. After all, she keeps the flat very clean. I feel sure, if I did for a gentleman, I should hate to have his fancy-friends bursting in on my elevenses. Mic forgot it was her day, of course. It seems neither of us is particularly good at this sort of thing.

She began preparing the lunch, which was more important.

When Mic arrived he said, "You *are* still here!" and took a little while to get over it. Then, "Thanks for the pen, but you shouldn't have bothered. My dear, did Mrs. Gale walk in on you?"

"No, I came in on her. It was all right."

"I'm damned sure it wasn't. Darling, I can't apologise. I didn't remember about her till five minutes before she was due to be here. She lives just outside the hospital, so I took a chance and dashed out to stop her, but of course she'd gone."

"Truly it was all right. We were both awfully tactful."

Mic paid a great many compliments to the lunch, but was a little distrait all the way through it.

"Come out of it, Mic dear. What is it, anyway, not still Mrs. Gale? I forgot about her ten minutes after, and I'm sure she did about me."

"Not her particularly, but just ——"

"Well?"

"Well, what she stands for."

"What does it matter?"

"It can matter, when you get enough of it. I ought to know that, if anyone does. I've lived with it. Now I've let it in on you."

"Don't worry, my dear. It's only because you were a child it seems worse to you. It's all new to me, you know, rather a game."

"It can't be long," Mic said. He got up and went over to the window. "They find me rather useful here in little ways that are really off my beat. If I play for it, one of them—someone like Scot-Hallard, for instance, with a finger in several pies—will give me a leg-up to something we can get married on."

"Did you want to marry me?"

"Vivian!"

"Sweet, don't look like that. I'm sorry. Please. But I thought you didn't believe in it."

"Good God, did you think I'd be satisfied with things as they are?"

"I don't know. I suppose I just accepted it. It's all we can have."

"Well, I don't accept it. I love you, in case I never told you so. Do you suppose I'm content not to offer you any security? What do you think I am?"

"I hadn't thought like that."

It had never occurred to her that she had put Mic under any obligation to offer her security. They had wanted something from one another and got it in fair exchange. Being married was obviously desirable because it would enable them to be together: and it was unfortunate that neither of them had any money, but nobody's fault. They had proved themselves alike in so much, she had taken it for granted that he would share these feelings also. She had reckoned, as now she understood, without his childhood, the years of contempt and his need of compensation.

"I think, my dear," she said at last, "we're both starting life rather late and taking it rather hard. You know, however well-off we were, we'd have been crazy to marry without living like this for a little first. We both have rather angular personalities. It seems the angles fit, but we needed to find out."

"That would have been different. It's feeling that we can't."

"I'm glad, in a way, we can't yet. Not that I wouldn't trust you with every part of my life." Reckless, insane commitment, yet she knew it to be true. "But this leaves us—what Jan would call fluid."

He looked at her in a kind of liberated wonder. "I shall never know you." He held her face between his hands. "Often I think I do, but there's always something more."

They spent the afternoon lying out on the hills, finding a night of four hours' sleep not conducive to anything more strenuous. It was a good time, with hours of being together behind them and in front; they talked in desultory implications, smoked, made easy love and read one another things from *Texts and Pretexts*. In the evening they came back to the flat, not looking much at the clock because it had become unthinkable that this should end.

"You don't mind tonight that it isn't dark," Mic said.

"I'm glad it isn't. You know, Mic, apart from the fact that I love you, it's very restful to see a body that isn't a case and doesn't look as though it could be."

"Did you find so many bodies rather overpowering, coming suddenly at first?"

"Hardly at all. One's mind somehow insulates them, at least, mine did. I suppose it's the only comfortable way to carry on. But I didn't realise how completely one does it till last night. All the men I'd bathed and dressed were as irrelevant as so many tables. Did you think me amazingly silly?"

"Amazing, but not silly."

They dressed, more or less, in order to sit on the bed and look out of the window; Mic in shirt and slacks, Vivian in his dressing-gown, her shoulder half out of a split seam.

"I'm sorry it's so decrepit. I had it at school, I believe."

"I'll mend it for you. It's lasted pretty well if it's ten years old."

"Six, to be exact."

"Only six? How old exactly are you, Mic? I don't believe I know. I've always assumed for some reason that you were Jan's age."

"That was rather flattering of you. Actually, I'm about ten years younger than Jan in development, and four in fact."

"Are you only twenty-five? But then you're a year younger than me. Mic, I can't take this in. When I'm thirty you'll only be twenty-nine."

"Tempted by some fresh little thing of twenty-eight, you think?"

"But you do feel older in so many ways."

"Mostly in ways I'd rather be without."

"How little we know about one another, really. I don't even know how many lovers you've had before me. It's rather exciting, in a way."

"Not very," he said slowly. He looked withdrawn, like someone making a decision. "Do you want to know? One."

"Tell me about her. What was she like?"

Mic got up without looking at her, and rummaged among some papers in a drawer. Presently he came back and put a snapshot into her hand. She saw a fair boy in tennis-flannels, gay and brilliantly vital, laughing into the lens. There was a date on it, five years old.

"You see." He took it back again.

"It's all right, Mic. I guessed, anyway."

"Yes, I suppose so."

"He looks charming. Where is he now?"

"In India. Married." He put the picture in his pocketbook. "It seemed all very natural, at the time."

"Of course. It's a phase a lot of people go through at school."

"We went on to Cambridge together." He looked up quickly at her face.

"How did it end?" she asked lightly.

"Just died a natural death. We both had too much else to think about."

"No women?" She was touched by the kindness he had shown her, and impressed by his imagination. Biology counted for something, she supposed.

"No. At least ——"

"It doesn't matter, my dear."

"I'll finish now I've started. It struck me after Colin had gone that I was twenty-three and hadn't felt anything much about a woman, and I began to wonder. Then I met Jan, and there seemed no more doubt about it."

"But you can't count Jan. The most improbable people lose their heads over him. I can't think why: he never does anything about it. I don't think he knows, half the time."

"I know, but I didn't then. It seemed to me I ought to make up my mind one way or another. Unfortunately I didn't know any girls very well, and it would have hardly been fair if I had. So ——"

"All right. I know what you did. Was she kind to you? People say they are."

"She seemed to think so. . . . I tried to pick one that seemed relatively decent, but it was rather . . . probably my fault. Anyhow I never felt much like another shot. So that's all. Are you revolted?"

"Mic, darling, no. I was wishing I'd been there for you. If you hadn't told me I'd never have known. How could you be so sweet to me, after all that?"

"There isn't anyone but you. There never will be."

"Dear." She had seen his face, and hid his head in her arms so that he should not see she was afraid. Who was she, to be entrusted with this?

It seemed no time at all, after that, till she looked at the clock for the last time and said, "Half-past nine, Mic, dear."

They got ready to go: indeed, their real time together was already over, and for the past half-hour they had been subdued to the expectation of this moment.

"Don't bother to get the car out. It makes so little difference. It's a nice night to walk."

They kissed in a kind of dulled hopelessness, knowing that however much they crowded into it, in another minute it would all be gone. Their life, as they walked through the town, seemed to have ebbed out of them with the fading light. They made conversation between their silences, words that said nothing but were a kindly gesture, as people do before a journey. They were both, Vivian thought, probably a little tired.

"We shan't feel like this in the morning, Mic."

"I suppose you're right. Sleep well."

"I fancy we'll both do that."

"When are you coming back?"

"I've got one evening next week, Wednesday, I think, I'll let you know."

"Only one? My God."

"I know. I might get more next year, when I'm more senior."

"Where's your room?"

She looked at him, appalled. He seemed quite serious.

"Mic, if you love me. You'd probably be arrested." She gave a taut giggle, like the twang of an over-keyed string. "In any case I'd have to leave by the next train. You won't, whatever happens. Swear it. Are you mad?"

"Perhaps not quite. Don't worry. It seems queer I'll never see the place where you sleep."

"Yes; I'd like it better if you'd been there. Look, don't come any farther, dear, we shall meet everyone. I love you. Don't touch me, don't say anything, I'm going now."

In the main hospital corridor she met one of the Verdun pro's.

"Hullo. Got your evening, did you?"

"No. Day off."

"Day off? Some people strike lucky. You weren't due till next week. I say, what do you think, they opened Mrs. Simmonds today and her stomach was almost solid with carcinoma, secondaries in the liver and everything, they couldn't do a thing. Just sewed her up again."

"How awful. She's hardly thirty."

"She doesn't know, of course. Her husband was in the most awful state when they told him."

"Yes. I expect so. Good night."

Her room was almost dark. It looked very chilly and indifferent, and was scattered with odds and ends—bath-powder, face-lotion, and a discarded undergarment—that she had left about in her haste to get ready for Mic. She made a mental note not to do that again. She had been thinking, then, of all the future meetings they would have: now she could see only an infinity of farewells, and dying, in the end, a long way away from one another. Forcing herself to remember how tired she was, she refused to think of anything.

She was just about to put out the light for sleep, when Colonna knocked at her door. Vivian was puzzled, till she remembered there was a charge-nurses' meeting that night.

Colonna had not heard about the day off, and there seemed no need to mention it. They talked vaguely, both in turn making efforts and then letting the conversation sag. She wondered why Colonna had bothered to come: it was unlike her to seek out company for its own sake.

"By the way," Vivian asked in sudden recollection, "what did Matron want Valentine for that time?"

"Haven't you heard? I thought everyone knew now. She's going to be made Sister Gallipoli, when old Packington retires."

"A *Sister*? But—— Well, of course, she's the obvious choice, if they want one of our own. Only ——"

"As you say," said Colonna, "we shall have to be careful."

"Careful!" There seemed no more adequate reply, and Vivian stopped searching for one; her brain was not quick tonight. At last she said, "She won't go back to mental nursing now."

"Oh, yes. She thinks if she takes this for a year first it will give her more pull."

"A year—oh, well, you'll nearly have finished your training by then." Where, she thought, will Mic and I be?

Colonna did not answer for a moment. Vivian noticed that the gold dragons had a few threads frayed out, and one of them had lost an eye.

"Probably it makes very little odds." She spoke in a quiet

unstressed voice, not like her. "A few months, or a few years. Some day she'll leave me. All this is just a passing thing, for her. She happens to need it now, but she won't. She doesn't know it, but I know it."

Vivian stared at her, wordless and helpless, but she seemed unaware of it. She was quite calm, like the bankrupt who knows that every security has been realised. She spoke as one might speak of the death of the soul.

Afterwards, Vivian could not remember how the conversation ended or with what sort of good night Colonna went away, or what thoughts of her own had made her cry herself to sleep.

T
RAFALGAR was taking-in. The wards took it in turns
to admit the new patients, for seven days at a time. This
week the weather was warm and fine; which meant,
besides the emergency operation cases, a steady flood of road
accidents. Six extra beds had been put up already. Sister Trafalgar had been twice to the office to ask for another probationer, but nobody could be spared.

It was a Friday, and Vivian's evening, that week, for seeing
Mic.

She ran about Trafalgar in the July heat, cleaning and lifting and washing, serving meals, bathing the new cases and
getting their beds ready for operation, always against time,
always fifteen or twenty minutes behind schedule, for even on
Trafalgar it had come to that this week. Today one of the probationers had a day off, and no relief had been sent in her place.
Whenever they began to think they were getting abreast of
things, a fresh case came in, or the theatre trolley arrived and
someone had to go down with the case. It all seemed to mount
higher and higher, the heat, the speed, the smells, the pile of
dirty enamel-ware in the sluice, the orange-skins which the
patients were continually leaving on the tops of their lockers,
the shouts and struggling and vomiting of the operation cases,
who had to be watched all the time while the staff tried to cope
with the ordinary work. Vivian's thick twill dress (they wore
the same summer and winter, and were nearly always too hot
or too cold) clung to her, damp with sweat; her back and legs
were a graduated ache, culminating in the feet.

She had set herself a certain amount of work to do before
she went off duty—a little more than was strictly necessary,
because she knew that none of the Sisters except Sister Trafalgar would have given her the evening at all. It was going to

leave the ward terribly short, and the least she could do was to have things straight.

It seemed worse than it really was, she said to herself, because it was five days since she had seen Mic. She counted the diminishing hours—one and a half, one—thinking how all this would disappear. She ought to be thankful, she told herself as she heaved the heavy screens up and down the ward: she had this release to look forward to, but for the patients there would still be the same pain and close heat and squalid sights, and fear of want at home.

Sister was off in the evening too. She was doing all the dressings that could be done early, so as to help the staff-nurse when she had gone. The clock reached five-thirty, and she was still in the thick of it. Vivian was bathing an old man, just admitted, with the dirtiest feet she had ever seen.

"Shall I relieve you?" said the nurse who had just come on duty.

"No, thanks, I'll finish. Sister's doing Ferris by herself: I expect she'd like you to help lift."

As she came through the screens Sister met her with the trolley. "Are you still there, Nurse, my dear? You run along off duty. I made sure you'd gone."

"Thank you, Sister." Vivian cleared up her bowls, washed, got her cuffs on and made for the door.

"Sorry to trouble you, Nurse, but I've been and mucked me pillow up."

Vivian saw that everyone else was tied up with something that could not be left. She cleaned up, changed the bed linen, and washed herself again.

By the time she had changed it was twenty-past six. She had had no time for tea, and could not have eaten in any case. Her face was lifeless, and colourless; she had not the time nor the energy for a clever make-up, and no amount of cosmetics could have taken out the drag of fatigue or put animation into her eyes. She found that the thought of walking half a mile or so to the flat was enough to make her wish she were not going: the discovery did not shock her, because she was not capable of so strong an emotion. Her longing for Mic had become a dull craving for comfort and shelter, the desire a hunted fox might feel for its earth.

I wish to heaven, she thought as she climbed his short flight of stairs, he'd live somewhere on the ground floor.

Mic had heard her coming, and threw open the door before she knocked. He slammed it behind her, laughed, and strained her in the embrace of five days' starvation. His kisses reminded her thoughts that she loved him, but to her dimmed and deadened body they said nothing at all. She yielded obediently, conscious only that his arms were hurting her ribs. In a moment or two he let her go.

"Darling, what's the matter?"

"Nothing is, my dear. I'm just a bit tired, I expect."

He looked into her face.

"But of course there's something. It's obvious. Come on, you'll feel better when it's off your chest."

"Truly, Mic." She heard her voice sharpening. "There isn't anything."

His face suddenly changed. "Vivian, it isn't . . . Come here, let's look at you. It is, isn't it? Listen: you know, don't you, if ——"

His trouble and insistence rubbed the edge of her own fretfulness like something twanging on an exposed nerve.

"Oh, do be *quiet*, Mic. I've told you twice there's nothing whatever the matter. Honestly, if you keep on and on at me like this I'll go mad. I came here to get some peace."

Mic dropped his hands from her shoulders. The responsibility for having hurt him was like an extra weight for her feet to carry. She was too tired to deal with it, much too tired.

"I'm sorry," she said. "Perhaps it would have been kinder of me not to come."

"Perhaps it would," said Mic with a hard mouth.

They looked at one another, not quite able to believe it.

Vivian's irritability flickered down into a grey and exhausted reason. She looked out of the window at the dusty traffic, and the hot and hurrying people in the street.

"You're right," she said quietly. "You ought to be angry. Why should you be the one to get the remains? You give me everything: and I come to you used, when everyone else in the world has finished with me. It isn't the way I wanted it to be."

There was a movement behind her, and his hand came over hers.

"My dear, I ought to be shot."

She turned back to him. Suddenly her chin jerked up: she began to laugh weakly.

"Darling, darling, you've got it wrong." She twisted her arms round his neck. " 'Stood up against a wall and shot' is the expression. You don't read the right books, or else it's lack of practice."

"You sit down." He picked her up and dropped her into a chair, still helplessly laughing.

"Sweet, the difference between me and a broken-down cab-horse is that they have decent manners and don't bite."

"Who's your blasted Sister?"

"Sister's a gentleman. It just happens."

"Let's have these off." Sitting at her feet, he began to unlace her shoes.

"Dear, don't be silly," she said, though what she had wished to say was that she was ashamed to accept such a service of him. He put them aside and threw his arm across her knees.

"You're here. Nothing else matters."

She put her hand on his shoulder. It was strange, she thought, that she would have submitted her body for his sake to any pain demanded of her, yet could not compel it to experience joy.

"I wish I were here, all of me."

"I'll play you some music," he said.

He put on César Franck's *Variations*. She lay back with closed eyes, liberated a little from herself. How happy, she thought, to be bodiless, to know no landscape more substantial than these waters and hills of sound.

137

"Oh, Mic, I feel such a swine. Give me a drink, have you got anything? I'll be all right then."

"You don't have to get tight for me."

"What does it matter? I'll do anything. You've waited nearly a week."

"You may be just as busy tomorrow, and you're not starting with a hangover. Do you like Ravel?"

"Yes." She sat up with a last flicker of will. "But I know what I'd like better. A nearly, but not quite, cold bath. May I?"

'Of course. I might have thought of that." He got up. "Here you are. Soap, towel. Run along, and I'll have some coffee made."

The bathroom was a wedge-shaped space, from which the kitchen had been subtracted with matchboarding. It was just the width of the bath, which had to be entered from one end. She could hear Mic moving in the kitchen, a yard away.

"Don't bump your elbows," he said.

She shouted, over the running of the taps, "Why are old baths with the enamel off always more fun than shiny ones?"

"Probably because you're surprised they have any water."

"Perhaps it reminds me of being little. Or else it's more like water out of doors."

The shock of cold was heavenly. Her feet stopped hurting. She threw the water on her face, splashed and stretched. Something like life began to stir in her. If it would only last long enough.

"Darling," she called.

"Hullo."

"Come and talk to me. We've only got about three hours left."

"I can't leave the coffee."

"Bring me a cup in here."

There was a rattle of utensils that seemed to go on for a long time. After she had decided he was not coming, he appeared with two cups, and sat down on the end of the bath.

138

There were biscuits in the saucers. She had not known that she was hungry.

"My dear, that's perfect." She put the empty cup on the floor. "Your coffee's better than mine."

"It wanted longer to simmer."

"Well, it can't have it. I feel marvellous."

"Don't stay in too long and get cold."

"I haven't finished washing yet. I like your soap, it smells clean. Do you know, Mic, I've bathed six people today and washed nine? I do think I oughtn't to have to wash myself."

Mic turned up, slowly, the sleeves of his blue shirt. Presently she laughed.

"This isn't quite the way I should bathe a patient, Mic."

"My God, I hope not. You have a gorgeous back, do you know?"

"It doesn't seem fair, does it, that you can see it and I can't?"

"Do a lot of the patients make love to you?"

"No. Only coming round from the anaesthetic. It's funny, the women mostly just weep and vomit, but men do the weirdest things. I wonder what you'd do."

He trickled a handful of water down her spine.

"Hold the houseman's hand is what you think, isn't it?"

It was the first time either of them had managed that sort of joke. She hugged him sharply, forgetting her wetness, and soaked him to the skin.

"I'm sorry I haven't got any bath-powder," he said as he finished towelling her.

"Why? Aren't I nice enough without?"

"Here are your things."

"I don't want them. Lend me your dressing-gown instead."

"You'll be late if you leave everything to the last minute."

"I don't care. Mic, why are you so good to me, why are you? Come here to me and let's take that wet shirt off. I'll keep you warm."

"No." He held her wrists away, rather too hard. "You're tired."

"Not any more."

The faint and transient life she had kindled served before it burned away, and with that she was content. But her mind wandered and wavered to and fro: she did not know always where she was, they seemed to be embracing in many times and scenes, by night, by day, in a garden, on a stream. "Are you happy?" she said, and had forgotten what she asked before he kissed her.

The sky in the top of the window was grey and glimmering. Its paleness twisted in a slow, mysterious rhythm before her eyes. Mic was shaking her softly.

"I wasn't asleep."

"You ought to be. That's why I'm taking you home."

"Home. That's funny. What's the time?"

"Nearly ten. Lie still, and I'll bring your things from the bathroom."

"But, dear, it's all right: I've got late leave."

"I'm taking you back and you're going to bed."

"I've gone to bed, haven't I?" She pulled at his arm like a child. "Don't go, I don't want to leave you."

"You mean you don't want to move."

It was true. For a long time, before he roused her, she had not known that he was there.

"All right," she said.

He helped her dress. The cold silk of her frock made her shiver. Kneeling on the bed, she looked out of the window. It was a glorious dusky twilight, full of murmuring and secrecy and adventurous promises. The window was open, but a thick sheet of glass seemed to lie between her and the dew-fallen air and sky. They did not move her.

She leaned her head against the window-frame.

"How little there is of oneself to go round."

"I take too much," he said.

"Never enough, nothing's enough. *You* take too much!" She took the hand with which he was holding her and tightened it against her breast, though it seemed that nothing but a dim kindness would ever stir in her again. "Nothing will give us back this hour we're losing, or these hours I've been half-alive: never, until we die."

"It won't always be like this."

"Neither shall we, young, and able to enjoy, and see things new for ourselves."

He said slowly, looking at the lights on the hillside, "And yonder all before us lie deserts of vast eternity."

"Vast eternity." She tried to recapture the lift of spirit that, long ago, the words had given her, the great space of freedom and of flight. But it was, for her, a desert and a name. She wanted only the hours that they had lost.

– 13 –

I T occurred to Vivian next morning that she had accepted her conditions a little easily. At breakfast, she led the conversation round to the subject of rooms.

"I envy you, Forrester, on the ground floor. No stairs."

"Envy me! Why, good Lord above, mine's the worst room in the hospital. Poky, nearly on top of the road, all the dust and noise, and everything you don't want to be public property you have to do in total darkness. Is it near a pal of yours or something? If so you can have it today, before you change your mind."

"Would you really like to change?"

"*Like* to? Come on to Home Sister now and let's fix it quick."

In Home Sister's office, Vivian explained that downstairs she would be nearer the members of her own set, which happened to be true and produced a good effect. (It was Home Sister, she guessed, who had reported her offences against the caste laws.) Forrester's willingness to change needed no explanation.

The room, as she had been warned, was close, dark and dusty; but the jut of wall that cut off the light also sheltered it from view of the other windows. Beyond lay an asphalt path, some not too difficult railings, and a quiet side-road.

"Of course," said Forrester as they were moving over, "it's not a bad room for going on the tiles." She looked at Vivian with a speculation which she appeared to dismiss. "I did a lot of it at one time, but I had a bad scare and it put me off. I never have the energy these nights anyway; besides, the chief attraction's left the neighbourhood."

Vivian went over the railings about once a week. The danger was too great, and sleep too necessary, to make it oftener; and the strain, she found, fell most heavily on Mic. He would have run a similar risk casually enough himself, but to be the inactive one upset his nerves and his pride.

"You can't go on doing this. It's all wrong. I'd rather do without you than have you this way. Why can't I come to you, if it's as easy as you say?"

Vivian would explain, patiently and repeatedly, knowing his violence to be precisely adjusted to the need he felt of her at the time, "Because the walls are so thin you can hear the person in the next room brushing her teeth. Because it would be suicide. Because it would involve you with no result whatever except to make things ten times worse for me. Would you really rather I didn't any more?"

"Of course, I've told you so."

But before she went away, though nothing had been said, they both knew that she would come. Only once did he ask her on his own account, and then he could not forget it for a moment, and in the resulting tension they nearly quarrelled. He never asked her again, in words: but it was not easy for them to keep these things from one another.

They would start out of a brief forgetfulness, wondering if she had been seen to leave, or whether, in some rare emergency, she might be called up for duty that night. "We won't go on with this," one or other of them would say in such moments, "it isn't worth it." But after they were apart, fear grew dim in memory, and consolation and delight grew clear, and she would come again.

It gave a secret colour to life: the waiting for dark, the old jersey and short skirt to climb in: the dusty and dewy sweetness of night as she raised the window, the sleep in her eyes making everything vaguely different and unreal: the sense of stealth, and kinship with the night-running cats that slid on printless feet from shadow to shadow across the road. For many years after, the smell of dust in the evening made her feel the rusty iron under her hands, hear the ring of her footsteps in the empty streets: remember darting, as if a hunt were following, into Mic's outer door, and the breath driven out of her by his first kiss, compounded of anxiety, desire and self-reproach.

One night, when she was thinking how different all this was from everything she had planned to do or to be, something else came into her mind.

"It's rather a queer thought," she said, "that Jan doesn't know about us. Or have you told him?"

"No, I'd have asked you. I've not written to him since it started: I don't know his address."

"Nor do I. Why should we take Jan for granted like this? Yet we do."

"Had it occurred to you," said Mic reflectively, "that I've seduced the sister of my best friend?"

"Not till you mentioned it."

"It hadn't to me, either."

"That," said Vivian, "may be because it wouldn't occur to Jan." She looked at Mic. "What is it you're making up your mind to say?"

"I'd just made up my mind not to say it, because it probably isn't true. I was only wondering whether Jan would be quite as astonished as we think."

"I can't imagine the Last Trump astonishing Jan."

"That's not what I meant."

Vivian thought it over.

She said, at last, "He was very inefficient over meeting me that day, in a way he isn't, as a rule. Did he say anything to you about me?"

"Practically nothing. That you were supposed to be like him, but you had capacities for life that he lacked, or something of the sort."

"That he lacked? Jan said that about me?"

"He meant it, too, I think."

"He did, if he said it." She fell silent, trying to fit it into the scheme of things. "Mic"—she hesitated—"did he know—that you ——?"

"I never told him. . . . Oh, yes, he knew."

"We're assuming," said Vivian after another pause, "that

144

Jan had a good deal more confidence in us than we had in ourselves."

"He generally has. It's the explanation, partly, of his effect on people. And yet—to exert any influence at all, even that much, is very unlike him. You know his password about letting people alone."

"That was Mother's password. Jan's had a lot from her, I think, that I was too young to get before she died."

"I wish I'd seen your mother. I never got taken to theatres at that age. What did you say her stage name was?"

"Mary Hallows. Her most famous part was in a play called *Marshlight*, before we were born. She was always a kind of fairytale to me; all I know of her as a human being I've had to piece together afterwards. Father's a scholar and not well off, and life in a stage set, on her money, would have killed him I should think. But she managed in some way to live her life without messing up his. They used their own incomes, and she had a flat in town where she threw her parties. I conclude he was happy, though, because he grew old in a year, after she died."

"What did Jan feel about her?"

"It's hard to say." She meant, rather, that it was hard to speak of: indeed, she had never spoken of it before.

"I think the first days, after she died, were the worst I can remember in my life. I was twelve and Jan was fifteen. Everyone was taken up with the funeral, and Father, and I think it was believed by the grown-ups that Jan felt it less than I did. Actually, I'd ceased to cry for Mother after the first night: what was really the matter with me was that every time Jan went out of my sight I thought he'd killed himself. I couldn't tell anyone, so it seemed to me that if he did I should have murdered him." (Funny, I remember an aunt, or someone, saying to me not long ago, "You were so young, I expect your dear mother's death is a little dim to you now.") "She was the only person Jan was ever really involved with. Sometimes I've hoped there won't be another."

Her body and nerves had resisted this unlocking of cellars

longer than her mind, and she was trembling. He kissed her: his comfort seemed to reach back into the past and heal it, as if it had been offered to her then.

"Jan breaks every rule," he said. "Psychologically speaking, he ought to be running about falling in love with deep-bosomed, middle-aged, protective women."

"Mother had a nice figure. But she was never middle-aged, and I don't think protection was a thing that occurred to her very much."

A fire-engine clanged past under the window, shaking the house. "Wonder where it's going," he said idly. "Practice, I expect."

Vivian stiffened in his arm.

"I must go, Mic; if it's a bad fire they may be calling extra nurses up; where did I put my things?"

"Take it easy." He held her down gently: there was always some scare like this. "If it were such a holocaust as all that we'd have seen the glare."

"I suppose so." But in a few minutes she was up again. "It's no good. I shall keep thinking about it now and give you no peace. How long have I been here?"

"About an hour and a quarter."

"Why in God's name do we do it? We won't any more."

"It's madness, I always said so. Kiss me before you go."

"Stop, or I shan't go, and I must."

"I'll come back with you. I can't stand not knowing if you get in all right."

"No. You might be seen with me. It's pointless idiocy to drag you in too."

"Write to me tomorrow to say it's all right."

"You know I will. Don't worry about me, darling, swear you won't. It's absolutely safe, I promise you. I've lost my sweater, where is it, I *must* go."

"Sorry, I was lying on it. Listen, you're never to do this again."

"All right. Good-bye. . . . Oh, my dear, my dear, I know . . ."

Next to days-off, when they could play at living together—and these always seemed too few and far to be quite real—Sundays were the best. She came off duty fresh, and was sure of seeing Mic even if her time were suddenly changed. Sister Trafalgar gave her probationers an extra hour on Sundays, so there was time to explore new places out in the hills, to read and talk, without looking at a watch every ten minutes. "I hope it will be fine on Sunday," they would say; but a wet one was always a warm and secret joy. They still found one another's minds an adventure, and they had enough imagination and physical sympathy to have become, by now, rather accomplished lovers. They used to laugh, sometimes, over their earlier uncertainties and experiments. Now and then they would say to themselves that they had charted one another; but something generally happened soon afterwards to make them humble.

"Darling," said Vivian one day, "can you spare me a handkerchief? I seem to have come without one."

From the living-room, where he was putting some soup on top of the gas-fire, Mic called, "Of course. In the top left drawer, with the ties."

Vivian opened the drawer, and paused for a moment to contemplate it.

"How repulsively tidy you keep your things, Mic. Matron would love to live with you, I feel sure."

"You don't think she'd have me to live with her? That flat of hers looks rather a good one, from the road."

"My drawers are like the Caledonian Market. I wonder if we ought to get married. What do you think?"

"I don't mind so long as you leave my stuff where I put it."

"Aren't you sweet?" She picked out a handkerchief, and smoothed it approvingly. "These are very extravagant, darling. Rats again?"

"No," said Mic, stirring the soup. "I had them given me, as a matter of fact."

"Oh." Vivian looked at the fine linen sideways for a moment, then smiled and tucked it into her dress. She was

147

about to close the drawer again when something else caught her eye. She pulled it out, unrolled it, and said, "My God!"

"What *are* you messing about with in there? Soup's nearly ready."

'But this is serious. My sweet, I do think you ought to have told me you had a velvet tie."

"Oh, that. They were rather hot-dog at Cambridge one term. I only wore it about once, at the sort of party where one would."

"Put it on and let me look."

"You did say you were going to set the table."

"I will presently," said Vivian, laughing to herself. "Don't come in just for a minute." She shut the door.

There was a dark shirt on which the tie looked very effective. Mic's best flannels fitted her fairly well, with a little folding at the waist. She brushed her hair back flat behind her ears, and turned round before the glass, admiring the result. When she emerged Mic had got the table almost laid. His back was turned and he did not see her at first.

"Well, darling?" She lounged in with her hands in her pockets. "All complete except that I couldn't find the green carnation. Nice?"

Mic turned round, looked at her, and carefully put the soup-saucepan down beside the fire.

"Not very," he said. "I should take it off if I were you."

Vivian had slept well the night before; her day's work had been fairly light, and the unusual possession of a little superfluous vitality had gone to her head. In any case dressing-up delighted her: one of her few traces of stage blood. Such danger-signals as she noticed only added to the interest of things.

"Aren't I handsome enough?" she asked, coming nearer. "I was afraid your standard would be too exacting."

Mic stood over her and said, not very loudly, "Are you going to take that off, or am I going to do it for you?"

"Don't lose your temper, dear boy. You know my nerves won't stand it."

She laughed into Mic's eyes, which seemed to have changed from brown to black in a way they had at certain times.

"I mean it," he said. "Take it off."

"After supper I will. Sit down, and I'll pour out your soup for you. Like Ganymede."

Mic caught her by the shoulders.

"Damn you. Come here."

She ducked out of his grip and, slipping up under his arm, kissed him. For a moment nothing happened, then her kiss was returned, at a higher rate of interest than she had bargained for. She laughed while she had breath to laugh, which was not for long.

"And that," said Mic, "will be about enough, I think."

He took hold of her shirt, so unhurriedly that she thought he was going to kiss her again: and with one well-directed jerk split it down from throat to hem. The halves fell back from her shoulders; he pulled the ruin free and threw it away.

"I wish," he said with savage conciseness, "you could see how damned silly you look with only that bloody tie."

It did not occur to Vivian to say anything. Her mouth opened a little. Mic held her at arm's length, studying the effect: then twisted the tie off and threw it after the shirt.

Vivian found her voice.

"*Suaviter in modo*, darling. I thought then you were going to choke me."

"So did I," Mic agreed.

"You expect me to mend that shirt for you, I dare say."

"Shall I tell you what you can do with it?"

"No. Let me go."

"Why? This is your party, isn't it?"

She twisted light-heartedly in his arms; he had never been rough with her. But this time she found she had taken too much for granted. He was a good deal stronger than she thought, and at first it was all rather new and exciting, so she had not the sense, even then, to keep quiet, and presently it ceased to be a joke at all.

"Mic, no!" she said, struggling in earnest this time, though it was unlikely, now, that he would notice the difference. He had wrenched her arm fairly hard as he dragged the shirt off; she could still feel it, and was expecting to be hurt a good deal more: but suddenly she no longer cared whether she was hurt, except for the effect it would have on Mic when he came round. She had sold him for a sensation, she thought as she still fought him: and in a rush of remorseful tenderness she ceased to resist. Let her take what she had asked for, and get it over for both of them. But at once he was still also. Their eyes met in bewildered recognition.

"How much have I hurt you?" he said, looking at her as if she had been concealed from him. "Why didn't you stop me before?"

"Mic. Are you angrier with me than anyone in your life?"

"I haven't much right to be angry at all."

"You have. Why did you let me off, I deserved it."

"What possessed you, anyway?"

"I don't know. To see what would happen, I suppose. And partly . . . it's just I love you so much, I can't help playing up to anything you want."

"I want you and only you, and I thought you knew it."

After that they were wildly happy, though at rather too high a pitch, and the time passed quickly.

"This clock's four minutes fast," Mic said.

"It will be just as bad in four minutes. How I hate this moment more every time. It was all so peaceful and what we needed. We never have time to be quiet."

"I know. I always want you to stay till morning."

"Never mind, I've a day off on Saturday. It seems a year since I slept with you. It's so jerky and scrappy, all this jumping in and out like a tart."

"Don't. I'm sorry."

What had she said, would she never learn? She pulled his averted face back to hers. 'Mic, darling, *please*. Please stop being responsible for everything, honestly. I can't bear it. I never think of it like that, never."

"Why don't you? It's the normal way to think."

"I'm not normal, I suppose."

"Or else?"

"Mic, for God's sake! If you start that again I'll shoot you." He began to say something, and she flung herself on him and shook him, furiously. 'Stop it! I love you, how many times do I have to say it and say it, I love you, can you get that or shall I translate it into something simpler? By God, I could kill you, Mic, sometimes."

"I'll take your word for it." Mic freed himself, needing some force, and held her hands behind her. "How amazing you are." He was laughing as he kissed her: but she felt ashamed of herself.

"What on earth has been the matter with us?" she said as they were walking back. "It's been one continuous nerve-storm, hasn't it? Even the good part, really. We never used to be like that."

"Unnatural sort of life, I suppose. Sometimes I've thought ——"

"What?"

"Nothing."

She did not ask again, because she knew what he had been going to say. She, also, had felt that she would be happier married to Mic on what he had now, even if it meant living in her present clothes for the next few years. But she had heard enough grim stories about the spoiling of young men's careers, and had no intention of putting her weight on his shoulders. Later, when she was fully trained and could be self-supporting, it would be different: in any case, Mic himself was not likely to have marked time till then. Meanwhile he would not ask her, she knew, unless she gave him a lead: and she was not going to give it.

"I'll see you on Saturday," she said, "if we don't meet before."

She would come, as they both knew, some night in the middle of the week: but this formula saved Mic from having to fuss about it.

— 14 —

AT the fag-end of August there was an epidemic of influenza. The medical wards got most of the complications, but the burden fell on the whole hospital because twenty per cent or so of the staff went down. It was a time, too, when a good many people were on holiday. The busiest days of a taking-in week became the normal order of things.

Vivian could not believe, when she dragged herself off duty, that she had ever had the necessary surplus energy to tease Mic. She was grateful enough, now, that he put up with her dullness and was willing, when she had nothing left for him, to look after her and amuse her like a child. He was extraordinarily kind to her: too kind sometimes, for there were moments when she was clogged in a lethargy of weariness and would have been glad to be aroused, but had not the will herself to make the effort. Now and then he would know this: sometimes neither of them knew, and they would struggle against strain and irritability without knowing why. When things were worse nothing mattered except gentleness and rest, and he gave her these.

Curiously, she was often most alive in the middle of the night: she would awaken, then, to a kind of spurious sparkle which would keep her going for an hour or two, then snuff out, and leave everything greyer than before. Once or twice, at such times, she went out of the window to see Mic: but everything had an extravagant, frightening intensity, and she would not do it often because she was so unutterably tired next day. She owed the patients a certain modicum of vitality.

Lying in bed on one of the nights when she might have gone, with her brain running hard and fast like an overturned engine, she took stock of herself. It was time to cease pretending that the hospital was, for her, any longer a testing-ground, an order of discipline, an aesthetic experience, or the means for her service of mankind. It had been, in some degree, all these: now it was simply a power to be placated, because only its consent enabled her to be with Mic.

What remained was honesty, which told her, in a small clear voice like the tick of the watch beside her bed, that such a use of such a community would have to be justified. She must never put in less than if she were there from conviction. It was a thought which remained with her in the morning; and when she was tired and inclined to scamp her work, or to withdraw her mind from what she was doing and think comfortingly about Mic, it often jogged her elbow. If she had tried to forget it, Sister Trafalgar's presence would have reminded her.

It was impossible not to let Mic see that she was tired, but she always worked hard to minimise it: he was too painfully ready to make any of the asserted discomforts of her life his responsibility. His own work was heavy too. It was an airless, scorching August, and it told on both of them. Often they had moods of bitterness, though they managed to keep from turning them on one another.

"By the way," said Mic one evening, "you missed a good chance today of being respectably married to a poisoner."

"A nice one?" said Vivian, catching the ball listlessly.

"Not very. Me. It was hinted in great confidence that if I cared to interest myself in bacterial warfare, I might get a good berth. The thing's in its infancy, you see; a good chance for a pushing man to get in on the ground floor."

"How horrible. What would you have had to do?"

"Cultivate sturdy and resistant bugs that would stand up to being dropped on industrial towns, and into water-supplies, and so on. Anthrax does well, I believe."

"But who asked you? No one at the hospital, surely?"

"I was made to swear secrecy practically in blood, so I suppose I'd better not say. It would have been nice not to be living in sin any more, wouldn't it?"

"I didn't believe that was actually happening."

"Just a few tentative reluctant experiments, in case the other side gets there first."

"It makes things seem near."

"Probably this isn't a very good moment to think about it. You look done up tonight; I'm sorry I told you."

"I've thought a good deal lately, because it struck me the other day that if war comes, my life will just be one endless epidemic, ten times magnified, without this to look forward to. All this time we've spent learning to live will just be so much junk. Your survival-value will be smashing men, and mine patching them up to be smashed again, and emptying bedpans and cleaning away blood and filth quicker and quicker. Neither of us knowing where the other is, and whether alive or dead."

"I'm afraid my survival-value is going to be very slight. My mind's made up about that. You can't spend five or six years watching living cells, at least I can't, and blow people's bodies to pieces as light-heartedly as ever at the end of it. All those microscopic interdependent lives, a corporate state in themselves, obeying a dictator we don't even begin to understand. How do we know a man isn't just a cell of something larger? Big fleas and little fleas, you know. Anyhow, leaving futile speculations out of it, I can't see myself heaving a bayonet through a lump of liver-tissue. If they can use me at my job, all right: if not I suppose they may as well shoot me and save my keep. Does that upset you?"

"No, I'm glad. I wonder if we'd suddenly feel we had to have a baby. They say you do: instinct to perpetuate the race."

"Poor baby. If we do, let's keep it up our sleeve till we see what the race is in for."

"It takes nine months to have a child. Probably neither of us would be alive that long. We're individuals, Mic, a dying species. Why should we mind? I expect God had a lot of enjoyment from dinosaurs, before he thought of something better, and didn't blame them for not being anthropoid apes. Perhaps the future creatures will have a lovely group-soul, but none of their own, like Bergson's animals, and that will do as well."

They reached for one another's hands, thinking beyond the chances of war to the certainties of change and of death.

It was after supper: the sun had gone down, and there began to be a little air to breathe. Mic shivered, and put his jacket on.

"Do you mind if I shut the window?" he said. "It's getting cold."

"Cold? Darling, I think it's tropical." Vivian looked at him, then shut the window quickly herself and felt his forehead with her cheek. "Have you got a thermometer anywhere?"

"Of course not. What for?" But presently he shivered again.

Next night Vivian borrowed a thermometer from the ward, and took it over the railings with her. She found Mic very wide awake in bed, with a temperature of a hundred and one. He ran them up easily, he said; it meant nothing; he would be fit for work again in a couple of days. He urged her to go away quickly and not to hang over him, but he was obviously miserable, and glad that she had come. She gave him hot milk and aspirin, prepared as much of his breakfast as was possible overnight, and slept badly.

Mic proved not to be a good patient. He was disobedient, untruthful about his symptoms, not very sweet-tempered under cross-examination, and used to get up and shave before she came, which infuriated her. At intervals, he would relax into a weary and childishly trustful dependence, from which these self-assertions were the reaction. On the second day she required no information from him to ascertain that he was becoming alarmingly bronchial, and more worried than he wanted either of them to know. She propped him up with all the pillows and cushions she could find, rang up a doctor from the nearest call-box, and arranged to come back, bringing the things most likely to be needed, that night.

In the course of the perpetual readjustments which staff shortage caused, she found herself that day helping in the Private Wing. It was a preserve of senior nurses as a rule, but now there were only just enough of them to run the wards. Vivian was a kind of runner, doing all the small fagging in order to leave the diminished staff free for treatment. There was a spoilt Anglo-Indian widow, thready and arduously preserved, who appropriated her as a personal maid. Vivian, as she threaded a fresh ribbon into her bed-jacket, remembered that Mic, with a temperature, today, of a hundred and three, was doing everything for himself. She imagined him fainting in the passage, lying there indefinitely, and getting pneumonia, if he had not got it already.

At last the day ended and Vivian went to her room. Luckily it was dark earlier now. She made a bundle of the things she had been able to collect, and began to change. In the middle of it someone knocked at the door. She pulled off the skirt she had been hooking on, kicked it under the bed, and said, "Come in."

"I'm glad you're here," Colonna said. She was out of breath. "I thought I'd be too late. Kept on the ward."

"What is it?" Vivian asked impatiently. She would have done much for Colonna, but not now. She felt stupid and bone-weary, her head and back ached; there was one thing ahead, and only just enough of herself left to do it.

"It may not be you at all," Colonna said. "But if by any chance you've been getting out of your window lately, don't do it tonight."

The pain in Vivian's head flared up, as if it had been stirred with a bellows.

"Why not?"

"Because you'll be caught if you do."

Vivian sat down on the edge of the bed. She was only wearing a silk slip, and hugged herself for warmth. Her teeth were chattering.

Colonna explained: "Valentine told me. She says the Assistant Matron saw someone last night, from the end of the road, but she wasn't near enough to see who it was or which window they went in at. So for the next few nights they're going through the rooms to see everyone's there. Valentine thought at first it must be me she'd seen, but the times and places were all wrong, and it struck me it might be you. So I came along to let you know. Cheer up, it's a bad time to burn the candle at both ends, anyway. I don't believe I'll mind a few nights in myself."

Vivian lay down, aching and shivering, on the bed. "What shall I do?" she said. "What shall I do?" She caught a fold of pillow between her teeth, lest she should say it again.

Colonna looked down at her with a face of weariness and pity, mingled with a certain disillusion.

"Wait till you get an evening, I suppose," she said. "And if that's how you feel about it, try not to let him know."

"For God's sake go away." She heard Colonna move, and suddenly it seemed intolerable to be left alone. "He's ill. He'll be awake all night now, thinking I've been caught."

"I'm sorry. I didn't know it was like that." Colonna's voice was flat and tuneless; there were shadows like bruises underneath her eyes. She said, with a faint sight, "I never imagined these things happening to you. You always seemed so apart, and free."

They looked at one another for a moment, thinking of an evening a few months back, and taking, for the first time, the full shock of change. Then Vivian bent and pulled her skirt out from under the bed.

"What's the time?"

Colonna looked at her watch. "Ten past nine."

Vivian was putting her clothes on.

"You're mad," Colonna said.

"No, I'm not. I can do it and be back by ten. They won't start the round before then."

"Someone may have their eye on the window."

"I shall use the door."

"It's your funeral." Colonna paused on her way out. "But I should give them best tonight, if I were you, and take fifteen grains of aspirin. You don't look any too good yourself, to me."

"Don't be a fool," said Vivian, with a force that made her

157

cough. She stopped herself, swallowed hard because her throat was sore, and added, "Thanks for coming, it was good of you. Good night."

To be out before ten was a fairly mild risk, because only people who had seen her in uniform that evening could be certain that she was not off duty. The Matron, she remembered, had not made a round of the ward. But it would only leave her about ten minutes with Mic.

She got out safely, and ran through the town, pausing sometimes because her laboured breathing made her cough till it was no longer possible to breathe at all. Every step jolted a flash of pain across her eyes. She waited a minute or two outside the flat, to straighten herself and quieten down.

The sound of Mic's breathing pleased her less than ever. She could tell, before she took it, that his temperature was up again.

"What did the doctor say?"

"He didn't worry," said Mic huskily. "He just said rest and keep warm."

"Did he say you ought to have a nurse?"

"Good Lord, no. Of course not." She knew that he was lying.

"How much money have you got, Mic? I've got fifteen shillings."

"About two pounds. As a matter of fact, I feel a lot better tonight."

"I'll be off in the afternoon tomorrow. You're not to get out of bed till then. I'll fix everything. And you're to keep this stuff on your back and chest, and if it comes off you're to put it back again. Promise all that."

"All right. Thank you," said Mic gently. She longed for him to argue with her, as he had at first.

"I'll have to go back in half a minute, darling. There's a sort of room-inspection on. Just time to help you get washed first."

"I had a bath today. It didn't take a minute. I felt all right."

"Oh, Mic, I told you. You *must* do as I say. It drives me frantic to think of you doing all these damn fool things when I'm not here."

He took her wrist with sudden force. "Listen. You're not to worry about me. Go back and get some sleep." His cracked voice went up a tone. "You look awful tonight. I ought never to have let you come here. You must be doing fourteen hours a day, counting me."

"I'm all right. I didn't have time to put any make-up on. Nature in the raw, that's all it is."

She straightened his tangled bed. While she was arranging the pillows he slipped his hand up her arm and held it quickly against his face. It was then that she remembered he had had pneumonia, badly, before. She looked at the clock: her time was up.

As she went back the little breezes of the night shocked her heated body like waves of cold water alternating with waves less cold. She knew that he would not sleep: his temperature was too high. She had left him to spend all night alone in the dark, in pain and afraid, and she knew no mastery of life that could make it endurable.

Next morning, when she came on duty, she felt so dazed with fever and sickness that she seemed almost to have ceased to be a person at all. There was a physical machine of limbs and eyes that worked and appeared, somehow, separate from its sensations, which were distractions in the dull brain that pushed it along. She could no longer feel belief in the importance of anything, but remembered, like a learned lesson, that she must keep going long enough to get to Mic in the afternoon.

Sister stopped her as she passed the nurses' duty room.

"Nurse Lingard, I saw you out last evening after duty. I ought to send you to the office; you know that, don't you?"

"Yes, Sister." It all seemed to be happening somewhere else, or in the past.

"I won't say anything this time. But I shall, if it occurs

again. We can't have it, you know: you can't be fit for your work next day. You look half asleep now. It isn't fair to the ward, is it?"

"No, Sister. I'm sorry." It was all true. Everything was true, everything cancelled out. So she could not go tonight. But she had known that she could not go tonight. There was, in this finality, a kind of release.

Mic, when she got there, seemed much the same: or perhaps it was too great an effort to make her mind judge whether he looked better or worse. He had kept his promise, and had not shaved. She roused herself to talk to him and do what was necessary. In the middle of it she felt the approach of a fit of coughing she knew she would not be able to control. She went into the bathroom and shut the door till it was over, and then went back to the lint she was spreading on the table.

"Vivian." Mic's voice, roughened in his chest, was unlike his own and its expression unreadable. "Come here just a minute."

She went through the open door and knelt on the floor beside the bed, partly to hide the fact that she was shaking, partly because it was easier than to stand. She tried to force herself to stop shivering, but could not.

"I thought so," he said, and looked away. He began to speak again, but his voice grated and stopped in the middle of a word, and he pulled her head sharply down into the bed beside him, and held it there. She could feel the muscles of his body harden so that he should not cry. It seemed, to Vivian, a blank wall at the end of all things. She wept without heart, hope or control—probably the kindest service she could have done him, though she was past such calculations.

After a time she raised her face. Everything seemed to have gone out of her. Even to get back to the hospital was like the thought of scaling a mountain. Tonight they would be alone, knowing nothing of one another. She said, simply and literally, "I wish we were dead."

Mic answered her with silence. But it was a silence that leaped between them faster than spoken words. Like a pale light breaking, it came to her that, out of all their vain desires, this was the one that could be fulfilled.

She put her arms round his waist and pressed her head against him—it made the rasp of his breathing sound very loud—and he held her shoulders. Neither of them spoke, but silently their images of rest and refuge met and were joined.

Vivian's eyes went to her bag on the table, and then to the red meter against the wall. Mic was looking at his loose silver on the dressing-table. Their faces shared the same calculation.

Everything could be done in five minutes, Vivian thought. Then she could creep back here again, and never move, never go away, as long as she lived.

Obeying a little movement from Mic, she lifted herself on to the bed and lay down in his arms. They sighed in a tired contentment, though they understood the meaning of what they did: that they were tasting peace with a conscious mind before they sank too deeply into it to know it. There was no hurry now: the clock over there, at whose orders they had lived so long, had nothing more to say to them.

Their embrace tightened: they were both trying, through the blur of sickness, to realise one another for the last time. But their spent perceptions failed them, so that they seemed to be struggling with a wall of glass. Their bodies kissed and strained together, while they themselves, helpless and longing, slipped farther and farther away. Vivian understood, then, how short a part of the journey they would make in one another's company, and her mind turned back, wondering, to the lesser loneliness of which she had been afraid.

Mic had been apart from her in those moments, among his own considerations. He said—it was strange to hear words again between them—"It seems rather rough on Jan. He doesn't know yet we're living together, or anything."

"That's his fault."

The sound of her own voice seemed to waken her, as her own cry had wakened her sometimes from dreams. She looked up into Mic's face. His eyes looked back at her remotely from the dream that she had left, with a faint smile, unstirring. In sudden terror she reached up and shook him by the shoulder.

"Mic! What are we thinking? We've only got 'flu."

Mic sighed; his face lost its distant calm, and took on the lines of conflict and endurance again. He smiled deliberately, and stroked her hair.

"Purely toxic, of course," he said. "I suppose that's how these things happen that you read about in the papers."

"One gets so tired." She felt the weariness in her limbs like a huge added weight, and shifted herself from across Mic lest this should make it harder for him to breathe. Mic sat up—she could feel the effort with which he dragged himself together—and began to talk, quickly and reasonably.

"Now look here. This is all a lot of nonsense. Go straight home, report off sick, go to bed, and don't worry. I'll be perfectly all right here, and if there should be any complications I can go into the hospital. So what's all the fuss about? We only ——" He stopped, out of breath.

Vivian's rebellion and anger had spent themselves. Her mind fell silent.

"Yes," she said. "We may as well let go. Things won't be moved by us. We must leave them to move themselves. I could do that, once."

"Before you met me," said Mic. He spoke in thought, and without bitterness.

"Go to sleep, my dear, nothing we think at the moment is likely to be useful."

They parted quietly, without protesting or clinging to one another.

"You ought to be ashamed of yourself, Nurse Lingard, for going out in this state," said the Home Sister, after her eyebrows had travelled up the thermometer. She meant that by conserving herself Vivian might have managed another hour or two on duty.

In the nurses' sick bay Vivian fell into bed and, unconscious for the moment of anything but rest, slept till midnight; when she woke, was sick, spent an hour in waking nightmares and slept again. She had a letter from Mic next evening, posted she supposed by the milkman or the doctor. It contained cheerful but unconvincing information about himself, contradicted by a general impression that it had been an effort to write at all: and asked for news as soon as possible.

Writing an answer kept Vivian almost happy for an hour or two. Then she remembered that she could not post it. No one saw her except the Home Sister, and Vivian could as usefully have handed her a Mills bomb. Probably it would go straight to the Matron's office, if she accepted it at all. In any case it would ensure a major scandal, and once she and Mic began to be watched, it was only a question of time.

She was allowed no visitors, because of infection. As she dismissed one plan after another she could imagine Mic lying there by himself, listening for the post.

In her search for expedients she had forgotten Colonna, who had a vocational feeling for the illicit and who presently paid her respects at the ground-floor window.

The letter changed hands furtively; they might, thought Vivian with a kind of furious amusement, have been fourth-formers corresponding with the boys' school next door.

"What have you stamped it for?" Colonna asked. "Didn't you know he's in Ramillies side ward? Get back to bed, you blasted fool, what the hell do you suppose I'm going to do if you faint out here? He's all right."

Vivian found the bed somehow, and lay down. "What is it, pneumonia?"

"No, no, bronchitis. His doctor only sent him in because he was living alone."

"Thank God." Vivian began to realise why sick people lost their reserve: it needed too much energy. "How bad is he, do you know?"

"Not very. Sister Ramillies will look after him, she likes a young morsel. You take things gently. That was a pretty dirty colour you went just now." Someone was coming, and she ran for it.

Vivian spent the rest of the day trying to read, without much success. She could only remember Mic and the times when she had been too tired to love him, or had loved him with one eye on the clock, or had left in a hurry with some kindness that had been in her mind unspoken or undone. She admired her own impertinence in entering a social service. She found it impossible to offer Mic's share of her to society and, when society helped itself, bitterly resented it.

She did not sleep well: she knew how it went with chest cases in the night. In the early hours, when the light was beginning to come, it occurred to her that wherever they might be, if one of them should die it would be no one's business to inform the other. It was a thought that lasted her till morning.

Just before breakfast the Assistant Night Sister came to take her temperature. She was in her forties, with limbs that were already setting into elderly angles; but her face had that curious immaturity without freshness, a kind of tired adolescence, into which many nurses become fixed. Vivian was glad to see her instead of the Night Sister, who had no time for sick staff and treated them uniformly as malingerers.

"Is it down?" Vivian asked her.

"You remember you're a patient, now, Miss Curiosity." (It was still up, then, as Vivian had guessed.) "Sleep well?"

"Fairly, thank you. Had a busy night?"

"Never stopped even for a cup of tea. Three acute abdomens in, a man off his head in Trafalgar, and a couple of deaths in Ramillies."

"Who were they?" Vivian asked. My voice sounds just the same, she thought. Her brain felt cold and curiously hollow.

"A diabetic, and a broncho-pneumonia. Quite young, it was a shame."

She gathered up her things to go. Vivian was trying to make her voice come before she got to the door. At the last moment, she forced it out, in a kind of creaking wooden casualness.

"I hear one of the Path. Lab. men's in Ramillies. Freeborn, isn't it? How's he doing?"

"Oh, yes. Poor boy. Nicely educated, too. Queer he doesn't seem to have any people."

"Were they sending for his people?" asked Vivian, feeling sick.

"No, I just noticed there weren't any in the admission book. I'm going to make some tea. I'll send you along a cup in a minute, if you like."

"Is he getting better?" She recognised, in her own sharp thin voice, that of all the querulous sick women she had ever nursed.

As if she had pressed a button, the lines in the night assistant's face shifted from genial gossip to professional caution.

"He's comfortable." She entered Vivian's temperature and pulse in her notebook, and, as an afterthought, asked a few questions about her general condition: including one which, in the stress of hard work and worry, she had quite forgotten lately to ask herself.

"Pardon?" said the night assistant. Vivian was looking out of the window, with a twist of sheet clenched in a forgotten hand. The approaching gleam of a pair of gold-rimmed glasses caught her eye and brought her back again. "Yes," she said. "Perfectly, thank you."

"Well, I must be trotting. I'll send your breakfast along."

Vivian sat up in bed with her arms clasped round her knees, staring at the opposite wall. Her breakfast arrived, grew cold and was taken away. When Colonna tapped on the window, an hour later, she had not moved.

"Catch," said Colonna. "He seems to be getting on all right. You'd better pull your own socks up; don't you sleep, or what?"

Vivian caught the note she had tossed in.

"I'm all right really. Colonna, will you ——" She hesitated, she had only just thought what she would have to say, and had not considered how to say it. But the Home Sister's round was due; there was no time for discreet preliminaries. She explained.

Colonna's face altered. She came a step nearer and leaned through the window.

"My God! Are you sure?"

"How can one be sure? It's probably only because I'm tired, or ill or something. I'd forgotten till today. But I daren't risk it any longer. It's the third week now."

Colonna's curious dark-grey eyes travelled over Vivian in subtle gradations of fascination, repugnance and compassion.

"All right. Next time I do medicines I ought to manage it. Don't worry. I'll fix something."

"I shouldn't let you. It disgusts you, doesn't it? It's risky, too."

"I'll get it today or tomorrow. It'll be all right. You get to sleep, you look as if you need it."

She herself looked in need of it too. "Why should you do this?" said Vivian helplessly. "I wish I didn't have to ask you."

Colonna smiled wearily. "Why shouldn't I? I haven't many responsibilities of my own, you know." Her eyes, searching and a little bewildered, wandered over Vivian's face and body. "Do you hate having to get rid of it like this? Would you have liked to have one, if you could?"

"I don't know," Vivian said. I hadn't thought about it."

"You don't fit into anything. Be good and sleep, I'll look after you." She turned to see if the coast was clear, and slipped away.

Vivian read Mic's letter. It was scrawled in pencil on the backs of opened-out envelopes, as and when he had the chance. Not much of it was about himself. Once he had begun to say something, changed his mind, and made an undergraduate joke about the Sister instead.

She hugged the letter blindly, seeing with her mind's eye the bleak scrubbed wood and brown paint of Ramillies, the curtainless windows, the black iron beds and Sister's heavy stalk over the creaking boards. The nurses would say he was a good patient. He would submit quietly to the mass-produced routine, soon accustoming himself again to being lonely and unimportant; remembering probably what she had told him about understaffing, and not asking even for some of the small things he might have had. She wondered if he was eating anything—the food did not encourage it, unless supplemented privately—and if Sister Ramillies was skinning his bowels with the black draught for which she was notorious. She found that she was nursing his letter in her crossed arms, like a child. Then she remembered.

It was Mic whom this intruding life endangered, who had everything to lose. Little and casually as he spoke of it, she had always known that if anything went wrong nothing she could say or do or pretend would prevent him from marrying her. His own memories had burned him too deeply; his determination not to transmit that suffering was absolute, and it would beat her down. She pictured him, through her fault, impossibly burdened, paying all over again for the miseries of boyhood, with his ambition, his strength and humour, the small graces of his life, his youth. To give him back a little of what he had missed was the only thing she had ever found to do which could not be done as well, or better, by someone else. It was her use for herself; and this competitor would have to return to the non-being from which it had come.

At night Colonna brought her a little rubber-topped phial of thick, brown stuff. After her light was out she fingered it in the darkness; so small a thing, capable of destruction so incalculable; rendered void long trains of consequence; taking out of the lives of God knew what other unborn creatures an enemy, a lover, a betrayer, a guide.

It looked a big dose. She wondered whether it would hurt much or only make her feel ill.

Outside the window the ward lights smouldered under their red shades. She jumped out of bed and, by craning, managed to see the dim glow from the window where Mic would be. It looked remote and impersonal, like a star. If I could touch him for a minute, for an instant, she thought. Her limbs began to ache and shiver, and she went back to bed. On the way she glimpsed herself in the glass, in her dressing-gown, grasping her potion; it looked like a charade, and made her laugh.

" 'Romeo, Romeo! this do I drink to thee.' " She emptied the phial with a flourish, and almost looked over her shoulder; it seemed incredible that Mic should not be there to share the joke. But she was quite alone. She lay staring at the lights and the darkness outside the window, and waiting for the pain.

— 15 —

Vivian went back on duty four days later, in the afternoon.

Colonna had had to get her a second dose of ergot before it took effect. When it did she felt she would have preferred a few grains of morphia; but it did not keep her temperature up, and if it was rather an early discharge even for simple influenza, the hospital was understaffed and had no margin for times like this.

Mic was making good progress: she wrote to tell him how well she felt.

She walked to the wards, feeling heavy-footed and empty in the head. A transparent but quite impenetrable veil lay between her and everything else, including her own past and future. She accepted the fact that she loved Mic as she accepted the fact that two and two made four; the effect of each statement on her emotions was exactly the same. She would have died for him, if the occasion had arisen, because the willingness to do so was a habit, needing too much energy to break, as it would have needed too much energy to change the parting of her hair.

Her place in Trafalgar had been filled, so they sent her to Verdun. A kind of conditioned reflex pushed her ill-co-ordinated limbs through the routine: like the dissecting-room frog, she thought, continuing to swim with its brain removed. She knew in theory all about post-influenzal depression: in practice it was almost impossible to believe she would not always be like this, perfectly flat and uniformly grey, with the cosmos passing over her like a steamroller.

Sister Verdun sent her out to the kitchen to prepare the ward teas. The table where she had to cut the bread-and-butter was very low; the stooping made her head swim, and pain began to come back, so she found a chair.

"I wonder," said Sister Verdun, coming in behind her, "what would have been said at *my* training school if Sister had found me trying to do my work sitting down."

"Yes, Sister," replied the conditioned reflex. Vivian got mechanically to her feet, and went on cutting and buttering. There was a kind of deadness in her stomach, as if it would have liked to be sick but was too tired; and her head seemed to be evaporating, and growing cold in the process. Between her and the bread-and-butter there had begun to form a very finely-spun black veil, which danced about and grew thicker and thicker. Suddenly it was as if the sickness swallowed her heart; the veil became solid, and at once she was struggling with a dreadful non-being, groping for life like something trying to be born. She opened her eyes and found herself on the kitchen floor, with Sister Verdun dabbing water at her in a kind of aggrieved solicitude.

Next day she was sent for to the office, and told that she might take a week of her annual holiday, starting from to-morrow.

Listlessly, feeling little except a reluctance to be disturbed, she looked up a train to her home. She had no money to go elsewhere, and barely sufficient even for the fare. Their first-year pay was twenty pounds a year. She sometimes wondered what happened to nurses who, like Mic, had no family behind them.

She must write to tell her father she was coming. They would sit, in the evenings, with their books, making conversation occasionally because they felt they ought. Of his two children she took after him more; but the circles of their lives did not meet, even enough to cause friction at the circumference. They respected one another's minds, and that was all. Perhaps, though she had never put this quite clearly to herself, she had not forgiven him for being the one who received everyone's pity when Mary Hallows died. That Jan would have rejected pity like prussic acid was beside the issue. She would write, she thought, in the afternoon.

At eleven, she had a note from Mic saying that he was going to be discharged next day, and had been given a week's sick leave.

There was a queer minute or two of breathlessness, in which she experienced no delight, but simply an agonising disturbance, shocking body and mind, which was all her poisoned nerves could substitute for it. She felt, almost, resentment that joy and sensation should be forced on her incompetence. Presently things settled, and she remembered she had no money. Mic would be lucky if he had enough for his own share. The month had turned and their salaries were due, but that in her case came to about thirty shillings. There was her father: but it offended her to lie to him in order that he might subsidise something of which he would disapprove. As she ticked over all these obstacles, she knew that she would go with Mic in the end. Her tired mind was fixed, with the determination of a donkey that has lain down.

She knew that behind this confidence there must be some resource she had not thought of. Presently it came to her. She gambled a trunk call to Jan's college, and found that he had left the Lodge his last address. It was a possibility that had not occurred to her before; they were not in the habit of writing to one another about anything that would not wait. She wrote at once. It was quite likely that he might have some money, if he had not given it all away lately, or left his cheque-book with his washing in the last place but one.

She never knew what to say to Jan. His own letters—three or four a year, on her birthday or when he was abroad—had a virtuosity that paralysed her style: they delighted her, but reduced her to the inferiority of the schoolroom. It was of little consequence, as Jan, given the facts, supplied the marginalia for himself. So her explanation now was very untrimmed ("We've been living together, technically, since June, but this is the first chance we've had to do it actually, so it would be fun if we could") and ended in a postscript dictated by family tradition and knowledge of Jan: "Don't if it leaves you with less than two pounds five, as I have that much myself."

Jan replied next day, by express letter, apologising. He did nothing by halves, and, when he apologised, lay down, strapped himself to the altar-stone, and handed you the knife. That she should have wanted something that he could supply, and been doubtful how to come by it, seemed to have upset him. He sent her twenty pounds (she had asked for five) and his love to Mic. She kept all the money, knowing that he would merely be irritated if she tried to return any. It was useless to speculate on what he had left; if it was less than his fare to Cambridge, he would be certain to enjoy the walk.

It would have been helpful to discuss plans with Mic, but it was unlikely that Sister Ramillies would let her in: and if she did, they might as well advertise themselves on the front page of the *Daily Mail*. She knew he would not want or expect it. There was a little inn on the far side of the Downs, where they had had meals sometimes. She booked a room there for a week, and wrote to Mic to explain. To call for him when he left the hospital would be most dangerous of all, so she arranged that they should meet at the flat.

Everything was as it had been left when Mic was taken away: the bed open, a glass of milk turned sour beside it. It was strange to see dust. He must have kept the woman away for fear of infection. She put things to rights, rather laboriously and with pauses to rest. When it was finished she waited, her spirits suddenly sagging: she felt unequal to the moment of meeting, and turned away from the sight of her own pale face and lifeless hair in the glass.

At last she heard a taxi stop and the downstairs door open. She had forgotten that there were so many stairs, because in the ordinary way they both took them two or three at a time. Half-way up his light careful step stopped altogether. Vivian flung open the upper door and came out on the landing. Mic, who was standing with his hand on the wall, saw her, ran the rest of the way, began to kiss her, and stopped to gasp for breath.

"Oh, Mic, you fool! How *could* you be such an ass!" It was not what she had arranged to say. She held him tightly and felt the sharpening of his shoulders through his clothes. His eyes looked bigger than she remembered them.

"Sorry," he said. But it only seemed to amuse him a little. "Let's go and sit down." He led her in with an arm round her waist and curled up beside her on the bed. His lack of self-consciousness about his own weakness seemed to blow her fretful anticipations away. Her plans and determinations slipped from her; she was no longer in charge. As they kissed again, more efficiently this time, she thought how easy his honesty made it to under-estimate his strength.

"You're not listening," he told her.

"Of course I was." But she had been listening to his voice, not to what he said.

"They had no business to make you take your holiday as sick leave."

"I suppose not. But I'm glad I've got it, aren't you?"

"I've been telling you I'm glad for the last five minutes." His calm continued to surprise her: she had seen him so often in a state of resistance: she had not guessed that this capacity for acceptance could exist behind his rebellions. Perhaps the line between the inevitable and the assailable was more clearly drawn in his mind than in hers. He made no fuss when she confessed to having borrowed from Jan.

"No," he said in answer to her question. "I don't suppose I would have. But you felt it was all right, and anyhow it's done. So let's enjoy it."

To be with him, after so much struggling in solitude, was such a release that she had been reminding herself watchfully how little physical strength he really had.

"I'd better start packing." He swung himself to his feet. "You shouldn't have cleaned this place up, I thought I'd get here first."

"We'll pack together instead." She caught her breath. "Mic, I'm glad you've come back."

"Didn't you think I would?" He caressed her, lightly but

173

provocatively; principally, she knew, by way of a red-herring for the hounds of remembrance.

They took the car through by-ways, cautiously and in shifts. Fortunately she had learned its mannerisms by now. The fresh air, and being free and together, made them both a little lightheaded.

"This is rather fun," said Mic as they changed over. He contemplated his hand, which was still faithfully reproducing the car's vibrations. "I shall never want to convalesce in bed after this, it's too interesting. Do yours do it too?"

"No, it's the other end I feel. Like a sort of low-voltage electric chair."

Half a mile farther on she braked suddenly, restarted, and said, "Oh, damn."

"You lie down in the back for a bit," said Mic. "I'll carry on."

"No, it isn't that. I forgot to stop at Woolworth's and buy the ring."

"The . . . Oh, are we married? I'm glad you reminded me."

"Do you mind?"

"Of course not, it was obvious."

"I thought it would be quieter. You're not angry?"

"Why on earth should I be?"

"I haven't sold your principles or anything? I was so afraid you might think we ought to sort of wave the oriflamme of our unfettered love."

"Unfettered—Christ! When I'm making five hundred we'll buy an oriflamme and a new car. I'd say we were Mormons for the sake of a few hours' peace."

"I said we were Mr. and Mrs. Freeborn, would you rather I'd said Smith?"

"On the whole, no, because they know my name. But about this ring."

"We'll tell them I had to have it cut off on account of my arthritis. That's it. Something cruel it was. You should have heard the way my old man carried on about it. Never had it off for five-and-thirty year. I feel just like that, too. Do you love me?"

"You were driving, I thought you said."

They grew, as they climbed the hills, more and more amused about less and less. They effervesced like something undergoing a chemical reaction. It was impossible to stop, though they both wondered what would happen when they subsided.

"There might be a shop in Kenster," said Mic. It was on their way, a small town consisting chiefly of a cattle-market and three mid-Victorian public houses. Between the Crown and Prince of Wales they found a shop: A. Brewster, Jewellery, Novelties and Gifts. Mic measured her finger with a piece of string.

"Would it come under the heading of Novelties, do you think? Or Gifts?"

"The window-dresser seems doubtful." A card of very yellow rings, labelled "9 ct. Shell, British Made," was propped against the protruding stomach of a plaster kewpie-doll wearing dusty feather drawers. Bridge-markers in the shape of curiously spotted dogs flanked it, like heraldic supporters. Below were many ingenious combinations of electro-plate and coloured glass. Nothing seemed to have been moved for years.

Mic vanished into the penetralia. Presently the kewpie-doll was displaced, and from behind its site a pair of eyes, wearing rimless pince-nez, examined Vivian with fascinated interest. After what seemed a long time the rings disappeared and the eyes followed, reluctantly.

"I'll drive," said Mic when he came out.

"Was it expensive?"

"Only three and six."

"Three and six! Darling, that's extortion. Woolly's are every bit as authentic. Why did you buy it?"

"Well, I felt a bit reckless because I hadn't the bridesmaids' presents to pay for."

When they were out in the country again Mic stopped, and

took the box out of his pocket. It was made, she saw, of paper imitation shagreen.

"Permit me," he said.

Careful! thought Vivian suddenly. She had been perceiving for some time that the allegretto movement was nearly over.

"Shall I say 'Obey'?" she asked. "I don't mind if we leave out the paragraph about procreation."

Mic put the ring on her hand without replying. Its yellowness was faintly browned in places: it had evidently been a Novelty for a number of years. They looked at it, then at one another. She felt the thin metal cutting her as his fingers tightened over hers.

"Vivian. God, I ——"

"So do I, but shut up about it."

She pushed his hand back on the wheel. Their odd physical state had increased their sensitiveness to one another until a moment like this was nearly unbearable. She slid her fingers from under his, and felt his silent consent: but things had got beyond them. He started the car and they drove on in silence, their faces aloof so that a stranger might have thought them enemies, shut away from their outward selves in an inward communication frightening in its completeness, in the impossibility of isolating from one another the slightest current of feeling or of thought. It was too much, and she tried to find words that would break the circuit and end it: she had never in her life felt like this, so unable to determine how much of what seemed herself was her own.

They were too near, she thought, with a strange shudder of the spirit half of delight and half of fear: it was not nature, there were counterpoises and antagonisms set between men and women to divide them, even while they strove for union, and let them keep the shape of their separate souls. With instinctive wisdom they entrenched themselves in their differences, which nature had provided for their security. If people wandered beyond these fronts and met one another in no-man's-land, leaving their weapons behind them, this

176

happened: this insufficiency of the body's surrender, this insatiable mating of the spirit, so lightly invoked in simile and song, so rare and terrifying in consummation.

Mic's face was without expression. Though she would have found it impossible now to drive the car herself, she knew how it felt in his hands and experienced his half-mechanical confidence. She knew what he was thinking—that physical love had become almost irrelevant, but might make them feel better.

"The engine's running well." He said it as though he were talking in his sleep.

"Stop for a minute."

He stopped the car in an empty road, windswept, between half-fallen stone fences. They embraced as though they were trying to break through one another's bodies.

"Hurt?" said Mic on an indrawn breath.

"I wanted it to."

"I know."

He kissed her again: she could feel the saltness of blood in her mouth.

"What can we do?" he said.

"God knows. Be better tonight, perhaps."

"Yes. We might sleep."

"You shall. I promise. Couldn't you sleep?"

"Not much."

"Did you miss me?"

"Yes."

"When, the night before last?"

"Yes."

"I knew.... I'll be there tonight."

"It's beyond that now."

"We'll pretend it isn't, and go to sleep."

The inn where they were going was on the side of a hill, sheltered behind from the north and east, with a great deal of sun and space in front. There was an arbutus hedge, and bushes of berberis in the garden, and the front was washed white. They had liked it first for its name, which was the Live and Let Live.

"I've never seen the bedrooms, have you?" Mic said when they were nearly there. (The lightning-flash had, for the moment, made the emotional air more breathable.)

"No. But ours is the front one. It will have a bed with brass knobs, and a honeycomb quilt with the fringe ironed flat. There'll be two china candlesticks with pink roses on them, and a mahogany-and-marble washstand, and a text over the bed—passion-flowers and 'Thou, God seest me', I expect—and on the other wall a light-brown photograph of Mrs. Swan's father's grave with all the wreaths. Oh, and a feather mattress. Do you hate them?"

"Hate them, I dreamed of them all last week. Do those ward beds *have* to be so hard they need to rub your bottom with methylated spirit every day to keep it from wearing out?"

"Only once a day?" said Vivian, concerned. "They ought to have done you oftener than that, a thin patient like you."

"A *what*?"

"Sorry, darling."

By the time they arrived they were both feeling very cold and stiff-jointed, though they had been driving for less than two hours. They were hungry, too: Mic had had the hospital dinner at twelve, and Vivian some biscuits she had unearthed in the flat. Her spirits had fallen; she wished that they were going to a place of their own, and that her wedding-ring had not brown patches on it, and wondered if the bed would be properly aired. It occurred to her suddenly and sinkingly that perhaps Mic would rather have stayed in town; that he would never tell her so; that she might have let him rest till tomorrow; that he liked to manage things for them and that she had not been able to give him even the illusion of it. Damped with these thoughts, she got out of the car in silence.

"Thank God," said Mic, "you had the sense to fix this up. If you hadn't I should probably have drifted back to the flat, and it needs a rest."

"I hope it will be all right," she said. She took it for granted that he should answer her thoughts and relieve them, but a deeper and watchful part of her was saying, He is surer of himself, less afraid of being dependent: and she felt her own need of him grow frighteningly, and take her by the throat.

The front door was shut, and the place looked blank and unwelcoming, as inns can out of hours. Suddenly, before they could knock, the door opened, letting out a smell of clean warmth and baking bread, and a little light-haired woman in a faded print dress. She had a sweet reedy voice and short-sighted blue eyes, and wrapped them in a welcome full of mild and milky pleasure, like a cow's breath. Was this all their luggage, she had been thinking of them driving over all those hills in all this wind; she did hope they would be comfortable; there was a fire downstairs and two hot-water bottles in their bed and some of those scones in baking the same as they had liked before for their tea, and they'd take an egg with it too, she felt sure. Her soft and maternal eyes never went near Vivian's left hand. Mic thanked her for both of them; Vivian had discovered that if she said anything she would cry.

They had tea by an open coal fire, an unaccustomed joy to both of them. After the table was cleared they sat together in a great horsehair chair, growing heavy-eyed over the flames and melancholy with evening and weariness.

"Hold me tightly," she said. "I feel dark and slipping away."

"It's half-past nine. Let's go to bed."

Vivian's forecast of their room had been fairly accurate, except that it was Mrs. Swan's mother, alive and in bugles, on the wall, and the text was "God is Love." They had unpacked before tea.

"Have you ever thought," said Vivian as she washed by the light of the china candles, "that civilised people undress in separate rooms?"

Mic stretched lazily; he had been quicker and was in bed. "Funny, isn't it? I like you washing. The candle makes a gold line all down you when you're wet and shiny. You're thinner, aren't you?"

"A bit. Does it spoil my chest?"

"I'll let you know. It looks all right. If you'd rather I wasn't here I'll lie on my other side."

"I can't think of anything that would embarrass me more. What do you think is the matter with us? Colette says women should never appear in any stage between their frock and their skin. I know at least one who keeps all her make-up under the pillow so as to do her face before her husband wakes up. Would you love me more if I did those things?"

"Don't talk like that." Mic narrowed his eyes in the candle-light. "I don't like it."

"Why not?"

"Don't call yourself Women. It sounds beastly. . . . Rows of them, all pink and bulging. In frilled drawers."

"Is that how you see them?" She stopped herself from adding "still."

"I don't see them at all as a rule. I did just then."

"Well, what about me?"

His eyes passed over her, loving and familiar, like an embrace.

"You're simply you."

She put down the towel with which she had dried herself, and stooped over him. He looked up at her smiling. She could see a small bright image of herself, picked out by a tiny point of candle, in his eyes. Her heart tightened.

"Mic, don't trust me like this. What am I? You mustn't, why do you?"

"Don't be silly." He seemed amused, as by some childishness. "Obviously, if one loved somebody like this and couldn't trust them, one would go mad. You do look beautiful."

She leaned over him, silent, one hand on the pillow, the other pressed against her heart.

"What's the matter?" He flicked up his eyelids, laughing at her. "Don't you want to—er—give yourself to me?"

"Mic!" She exploded in spite of herself. "You do pick up

180

the most disgusting expressions. Give myself indeed. What *have* you been reading?"

"A book one of the nurses lent me. It was full of things like that. I've been saving them up for you."

"Well, you can go on saving them. Wait a minute, I haven't brushed my hair or put on any cream."

"Not Lady Mary's Secret? It did taste so awful. Like lard."

"You know I only got that because everywhere but Woolworth's was shut. This is the kind you like."

She got her brush and sat on the foot of the bed. The candle threw her shadow on the wall, her chin raised towards her lifted hands, her legs curled away, like the shadow of a mermaid on a rock.

Mic lay watching her, his head tilted on his arm. He said, with a soft breathless laugh, "This girl in the book left the man because he wanted to buy her soul."

She clasped her hands behind her head. She felt straight and shining, weightless, like the candle flames.

"You've never offered me anything for mine."

"How much?"

He had lifted himself on his elbow, and stretched the other hand towards her along the bed. His eyes were wide and still, his mouth faintly smiling.

She put her brush unseeingly down beside her, and heard it slip to the floor. Like water pulled by a moon she seemed to be flowing without her will, out of herself to him and to some ancient fear, darkened with age and secrecy. Leaning, she took his hand. She tried to speak, but shut her mouth again: she had seen, in fancy, her soul passing from her, like a thin blue cloud, between her parted lips.

Suddenly he closed his eyes. Her mind, released, swung back to a trembling equipoise, returning to security with a shadowy and secret regret. Mic had let her go, and thrown himself back on the pillow; she saw the quilt move with the quick rise and fall of his breathing, and, over his head, the text in its cross-cornered frame, with its pink and blue gothic lettering and smug faded flowers.

She gave a little shiver; the nights were beginning to be cold.

Mic opened his eyes. It seemed all in one movement—he could be remarkably dextrous when he wanted—that he leaned out and extinguished the candles, pulled away the arm on which her weight was resting, and flicked aside the bedclothes as she fell. The rough twill sheet, smelling of yellow soap and lavender, closed over her like the sea.

"We're mad." She felt his voice rather than heard it: he was making love with remorseless competence. "For the love of God let's take what we can, and sleep."

They slept like the dead.

It was strange to live for days on end, and never need to consult a clock except for their own convenience. It was proper September weather, with a light frost at night and high glowing afternoons. The first few days, before they had the energy to go far afield, they spent mostly on the hill behind the house; or in the orchard, an elderly unscientific place with lichen on the apple-boughs and the trunks washed white. The apples were little and gnarled-looking like the trees, but sweet and hard.

Mic worked for an hour or two in the mornings. He had technical papers and periodicals and a couple of important new books to keep abreast of, and once he fell into arrears would find it hard to make the time up again. He was apologetic at first, but Vivian was well enough content. She liked lying in the long coarse grass among the windfalls, pretending to read, or looking at the sky through the leaves and crooked branches; or, if he were sufficiently absorbed not to notice it, watching Mic. He worked lying forward on his elbows, or flat with his chin on his arm, heaving himself up sometimes to make marginal cross-references, or pencil structural formulae, like delicate honeycombs, on scraps of paper. Once he swore acidly at a conclusion of which he disapproved: but for the most part his face had that almost frightening purity and peace that come from concentration on impersonal things. Vivian saw with strangely blended sensations. It gave her a simple aesthetic pleasure, like that of watching a ship driving straight forward on its course; and a sense of freedom which passed and repassed into loneliness, in flickering alternations of happiness and pain.

She envied him the cool intellectual roads where she was not equipped to follow: not because she would have dogged his footsteps there, but because they seemed to offer, once mastered, an easier way of being free than her troubled gropings after abstraction. Yet she knew he did not pursue them for freedom's sake, only for the enjoyment of his own capacities and for hard practical use. He seemed without the divisions of which these breathing-spaces made her aware in herself. She put them out of the way, refusing to allow them existence except as undertones of happiness. Use and custom, she said to herself, would come soon enough; she would stabilise, and old habits, like this habit of self-sufficiency, return.

It was pleasant to open her eyes in the morning and reflect that in Verdun at this moment the staff, having rushed through the making of twenty-six beds, were breathlessly lining up for prayers. "Our Father," they would mutter, framing the unnoticed sounds with the accuracy of practice while their minds scrambled over the work they had done, fearful of deficiencies. Over the prayer-book Sister Verdun's eyes would be wandering about the ward registering creased quilts or a bed not pulled out from the wall. Vivian remembered one morning when they had only succeeded in being ready by the skin of their teeth, Sister Verdun had risen and overtaken them before they had time to disperse. "Nurse Kimball, did I see you trying to pray without your cuffs on?" She laughed into Mic's ear, which was beside her mouth, and woke him up.

Vivian loved the moment of opening their eyes—not waked by the banging of the corridor maid, or Mic's alarm—the quiet, with everything taken for granted; the leisured passionless intimacy for which, in their everyday life, they had no time. There was no need, as Mic remarked, to fill the unforgiving minute with eighty seconds' worth of distance run, and be twenty short at the end of it. She had not known, before, how much they needed times like this: it was like finding, after drinking a great deal of good wine, how hungry one had been for bread.

They became with a bewildering speed acclimatised to happiness, as if to have their needs anticipated by one another and every hurtful thing fended off were an element natural for them to live in. Their strength came back quickly, and at once they forgot how sickness had felt. By the middle of the week they were walking as far as, still lazy, they wanted to. It was only sometimes that they remembered it would end.

One hot afternoon they came to a clear brown lake in the middle of a wood. There were blue dragon-flies over it, and a small island in the middle glancing with silver birches.

"I wish we could go on the island," Vivian said. "It's childish how one wants places just because they're inaccessible."

"Inaccessible be damned. It's about fifty yards. Come on." Mic sat down, and began to unlace his shoes.

"But it's deep."

"Beloved, if you've forgotten how to swim I'll tow you."

Tempted, Vivian looked at the lake again. It was clear-surfaced and translucent; the sun slanting through it showed minnows, and a bottom free from weed. They had walked, that day, a little farther than before: she was beginning to be tired, and thought a few minutes' coolness would freshen her for the walk back.

"It's lovely-looking water. Can't they imprison us, or something, for stripping out of doors?"

"No one ever comes here. If they do, wet your hair and stay down and I'll call you Joe."

"All right." She paused with her frock half over her head. "No, but look here, Mic, what about your chest?"

He looked up sharply. "That's nonsense. I've always swum."

"You've just had bronchitis, haven't you, you cuckoo?"

"Oh, I see. Oh, good Lord, I'm over that." He kicked his clothes into a pile and took a running dive.

The water was beautifully warm, and they got to the island only a little short of breath.

"A shame there isn't anywhere to dive properly," she said. "You know, I haven't seen you dive since . . . for months. We must go to the baths again."

"Yes. As a matter of fact, I don't really dive."

"I don't know what you hoped I'd say to that, but I'm not going to."

"I mean, the doctor knocked me off it after I had pneumonia that time."

"Oh, Mic. Why ever did you let me make you?"

"Freud would tell you. I'll race you back."

Before they were half-way Vivian found that she was going to lose badly. Her limbs felt heavier and heavier. She became aware, with protesting surprise, that presently they would refuse to move. She turned on her back, a little unhappy because she could not see Mic from that position.

"Mic!" she called. "Are you feeling all right?"

"Hullo. Fine." His voice sounded alarmingly far away.

"Well, could you . . ." She felt herself sinking, and gave a choked cry of fear.

"Coming. Hold on." She could hear as she struggled the cut splash of the water and his harsh breathing; then she was alone in a cold and breathless gloom, her feet finding nothing, going down. It was only, perhaps, the sixth of a minute. A grip that felt strange to her, hard, urgent and untender, thrust her to the surface. Retaining just enough sense not to cling, she breathed and opened her eyes.

"All right?" Mic's face, under his drenched hair, seemed suddenly to have resolved itself all into straight lines.

"Yes. Just tow me." She filled her lungs with air. The few minutes to the bank seemed a long time. It was suddenly very cold, and when she waded out her body, deprived of the water's support, seemed made of lead. Mic laid her down on the sunny grass and, snatching the garment nearest to his hand, dried her with painful force. He said nothing, only kept his mouth very straight and breathed short and hard. When her skin began to smart she caught his arm.

"Darling, you're flaying me. I'm beautifully warm now. Sorry I was such a rabbit."

"Put your clothes on." He picked up her slip and dragged it, inside out, over her head.

"Dress yourself, Mic, dear, your teeth are chattering."

"I'm not cold." He shook out her dress, pulling it down, as she struggled into it, with a clumsiness that only hindered, and was unlike him. When it was on he still knelt beside her, holding her shoulders. His face looked pinched, and blue about the mouth.

"Dear, do get dressed, you look starved. What's this you've been drying me with? Mic, not your shirt! A handkerchief, anything would have done. Look, spread it out in the sun and get your flannels on and I'll hug you. You *must* get warm."

She sat down in a sunny place and took him in her arms. He was shaking with a fine hard tremor. "You ought to eat something. Is there any of the chocolate left?"

"A little, I think. You have it, I don't want it."

"Darling, what is it? What *do* you feel?"

"I'm all right, I tell you. . . . I might have killed you. What do you expect me to feel?"

"Of course you mightn't. You knew you could get me out."

"You've just had 'flu. Your heart might have gone. I didn't think."

"Well, you've had it too, so might yours."

"Much loss that would have been. Are you feeling all right?"

"Absolutely. Now cheer up."

"Why don't you tell me I'm not fit to live? You must be thinking it. In any case it's true."

Vivian, beginning to feel a little desperate, said the first thing that came into her head.

"Listen, darling, this isn't your fault at all. I had 'flu

186

awfully mildly, really. I'd be as strong as a horse by now, only I took some stuff and it flattened me out a bit. You couldn't know, it was up to me to be sensible."

"What sort of stuff?" He turned his head on her shoulder, looking up into her face.

"Oh, just . . . I probably needn't have, but I thought it might be safer. It worked, anyhow."

Mic opened his mouth to speak, said nothing, and buried his face in the hollow between her arm and her breast. His arms tightened round her till it was hard to breathe. She rubbed his wet hair against her dress, wondering what possession had made her tell him.

"My dear, don't behave as if it were important. It's so awfully small and squalid. Everybody does it all the time."

He did not answer. His face, which ought to have been familiar where it was, felt different with the muscles set. A new thought came to her, like a tentative prick of pain. She bent and put her mouth against his hair.

"Mic, you've never said . . . did you want it? Don't be unhappy, darling. I'll have one later on. Or lots if you like. Anything you want."

Still he did not answer. It's true, then, she thought. Suddenly he flung back his head.

"Anything I want, my God, what do you think? To look after you, to feel I'm the slightest earthly good to you, that you wouldn't be a damn sight better off if you'd never seen me. I give you nothing. No peace, no safety. No comfort even. Now I've risked your life, for fun. And you say do I want you to have children."

"Hush, my dear, you know what nonsense all that is."

"Oh, shut up. I love you. I have to send you back to that stinking hospital, among God knows what filth and danger, to be bullied by those barren bitches of old women. You're ill because of me; and I've half-drowned you on the strength of it. So you apologise to me for not having a baby." His voice cracked. "I'm sorry. I just can't bear it, that's all."

"Darling, *don't*. No, no, Mic, you mustn't. You know

nothing matters; I couldn't be without you. It's only a little while, everything will be all right." She hid his face in her arms, "Why don't I think what I'm saying, why must I be such a fool?"

Helplessly, her eyes wandered round the lake and the clearing. They met with no source of inspiration. A trickle of water from Mic's hair ran coldly between her breasts and down the length of her body. He was still shivering. She looked round again, and saw something move at the end of the lake. Soon there were voices too.

"Mic," she said miserably—it seemed the last straw—"I think there are people coming."

Mic said, "Oh, bloody hell," and turned over quickly on his face, where he pulled a bracken-frond to pieces. She took out a comb and straightened herself a little—her hair, which he had partly dried in the rubbing process, was standing out in elf-locks—trying to think what she would say when they were alone again.

In a moment or two there appeared, along the narrow path that fringed the lake, a company of Girl Guides, rambling, with all their mysterious campaigning gadgets on. At the back was the leader, a bright adolescent in the late thirties, with a solid waist in a shiny leather belt, a well-soaped pink face and eager pale-blue eyes. Vivian saw her throw back her head and give a jolly, inspiring laugh, looking as if she had just received guidance to do so.

"But what's so *wonderful,*" she was saying as her voice came within range, "is that in Nature there's beauty *every-where.* The greatest artists may strike a false note"—her voice became a little self-conscious, as if she were recalling examples —"but Nature never makes a mistake. Look at this lake." She swept a gauntleted hand, following it with her eyes; as, indeed, Vivian was doing also. Next moment she and Mic intersected the visual arc. There was a hollow second of suspension; the gauntlet wavered for a moment, descended in an uncertain curve, and swept with electric eagerness towards the distant shore.

"Look, Daphne! Isn't that a dabchick?"

"Oh, *where*, Miss Curwen?" The cavalcade passed on.

Vivian glanced towards the last spot to which (before the dabchick) Britomart's glove had pointed. Caught on a low spray of bramble was the only one of her garments in which Mic, for reasons of haste rather than modesty, had omitted to clothe her. Both legs hung down gracefully, like something displayed in a shop-window. Her inside contracted in a kind of convulsive crow. Mic turned round to her, supposing that she wept.

"Look at that." She threw herself down beside him, getting the words out between gasps. "Beauty everywhere. Why are we worrying, Mic? Nature never makes a mistake."

Mic looked up. For a second he gazed in doubtful meditation; then he gave a strangled snort, and rolled over on top of her. They laughed till they were warm, and comfortable tears stood in their eyes.

They had a meal soon afterwards, with plenty of scalding tea; got a bus home, made an early night of it, and felt very little the worse.

Vivian was the last to fall asleep. She lay looking at Mic, who was turned towards her. Sleeping, he always looked improbably young and pastoral, his dark hair (he was beginning to fuss about having it cut) tumbled forward, his cheeks a little flushed, his lashes making thick dark shadows. She thought suddenly of the fair boy Colin, for the first time with hostility; he had looked so gay and confident, and had gone lightly away.

There were only three nights left. Then a narrow hospital bed (six objects only belonging to the nurse to be displayed, the furniture not to be moved) all night alone. They would have given her another room—they were always filled as soon as one moved out of them—and she would not be able to climb out and see him. She longed violently for him to wake and speak to her; but he had fallen into his first deep sleep and was very tired. One of his hands was stretched towards her; she moved cautiously nearer so that it just touched her side.

He was sleeping very quietly, his breathing almost inaudible; his mouth was closed in a softer line than it had in waking hours. He looked unbelievably remote, in a peace too distant from life to be called happiness. To know that with a sound or a touch she could wake him made no difference. She remembered a stanza in *Don Juan* about a sleeping lover. "Like death without its terrors," it had ended. Without its ugliness, she thought; but it is not in its disfigurements that death's terror lies.

A tiny strand of water-weed had dried in his hair. She remembered the lake closing over her, going down into a choking darkness where she could not see or hear him any more. She had been horribly frightened; yet she could remember, at the back of her mind, a confused feeling that it might in some unimagined way have been worse. She knew now what she had felt: that if she drowned now she could never see the passage of life remove him from her, she could never be left alone.

Before they had met, some of the happiest moments of her life had been moments of solitude. Solitude now was only a blank screen for longing and hope to project their imaginations on. When she left him, three days from now, it would not only hurt more excruciatingly than any loss she had felt before; it would also make savourless all the other things which had once given life its taste. She lived, now, in flashes of hours and days, separated by empty spaces of time in which she refused life, straining after next day or next week. What would the end be?

Her loneliness grew unbearable. If she kissed him very lightly, she said to herself, he would not wake. She bent towards him, and drew back again, knowing that she had meant to waken him all the time. She was becoming skilled in self-cheating. Why had she told him about the drug she had taken? Not only a second's thought, but instinct even, should have warned her that it must hurt him. Something hidden in her secret self had seized on this unguarded moment for its purposes. His suffering, though she had seemed to feel it as her own, had yet been a reassurance; it had revived her sense of power.

She turned over quickly, and pressed her face against the pillow as if to escape. Disturbed perhaps by the abruptness of her movement, Mic murmured some dreaming nonsense and threw his arm across her waist. His mouth was close to hers; he would have kissed her, she saw, but was still too much asleep to open his eyes and find out where she was. If she kissed him now, she knew that he would wake.

She lay looking at his closed eyes, feeling the warmth of his body beside her, meaningless in its nearness when he himself was so far; and remembered that in four nights' time she would be lying awake, how ready to be contented only with that. Yet still she did not make the tiny gesture that would rouse him. He was not well yet, she said to herself, and needed all his sleep. But she was thinking also of what she had said beside the lake, in the careless candour of sudden need. "I couldn't be without you." How easily she had passed on her spirit this sentence of death. She lay still, refusing to call him to her, because it seemed to her that, if she could refrain, the cup might pass from her after all.

– 16 –

T HERE'S time to go into the flat for half an hour," Mic
said.

"All right," said Vivian listlessly. "You know, we'd
really be much happier if we left at once."

"I expect we would," Mic agreed, flatly, as if to something
about which nothing can be done. They went up to the flat
and sat together on the bed, saying nothing, looking at the
clock, and experiencing all the sensations of having parted
along with the expectation of parting to come.

"A fag-end," said · Vivian unemotionally, after fifteen
minutes of it.

Mic nodded. "No rocket without a stick." They kissed, but
were too spent to feel anything, except a dim sense of not
being there. They had both been awake till after five in the
morning, and would have felt better if (as they had intended)
they had not slept at all.

"It's so silly," Vivian said, trying to rouse herself from the
stupor of depression which was shutting her off from him. "On
any ordinary day we'd have been so glad to get this half-hour.
Let's pretend I've just run in to see you for fifteen minutes."
She jumped up, and came towards him from the door. "Hullo,
darling? Are you surprised to see me? Not busy, I hope?"

"Marvellous. How did you manage it?" He came to meet
her. His face looked finer-drawn, and the shadows under his
eyes darker, when he smiled.

"Where have you been all this long time?" He picked her
up, and sat down with her in the armchair. "Tell me all the
news."

His arms, as they held her, did not succeed in speaking the
same language as his tongue. She clung to him, as she had not,
drowning in the lake.

"Mic, I can't, don't let me go, I'd rather you killed me than leave you now."

"For Christ's sake, stop." He caught back her head and kissed her desperately. Then he paused, steadied himself with a wrench that she could feel, and began stroking her hair.

"It will be better in the morning. Remember, darling, you're very tired."

For Vivian it was the *coup de grâce*. His surrender might have braced her, but under the gesture of consolation her last defences crumbled; she cried in his arms till it was time to go. Once she looked up at him through her tears, and saw in his face, with its disciplined suffering and pity, an older and more stable beauty than she had known there before. But all it did for her was to tighten her clasp and make her tears run faster. His effort, she knew, was made for her sake; he had no other thought now but to make it easier for her: yet he had only increased her helplessness, and made it more intolerable to leave him.

"Don't come to the hospital with me," she said when she had washed her face. "I don't think I can stop while I'm with you, and I have to report to Matron as soon as I arrive."

"If you'd rather." He picked up her handbag from the floor, taking rather long about it. "You look all right. It won't notice if you make up a bit."

"Make up for Matron? Oh, Mic, you are sweet." She shut her hands hard, feeling her eyes beginning to burn again.

"I'll have to take you back," said Mic, looking out of the window, "because of your bag."

"I'll leave it till I come. I shan't want it." There were several things in it that she needed, but she could not bear the thought of unpacking, so many memories lying cold about the room: the crumpled dress she had worn by the lake, her satin nightgown—worn, in honour of its newness, for about half an hour —her ebony brush. She would manage with something or other.

She was ready; the clock, resuming its proper authority, was ready too.

"Darling, we've said everything. Good-bye."

"Good-bye." He tried to kiss her, as he had spoken, gently and restrainedly, but failed. It was impossible that this should be the last. The last of many thousand kisses, she thought (there was time to think); probably Antony, when he said it, had not believed it either, and had slid still incredulous into death. The last. Her mind and body were conditioned to him as they were to daylight, but in a moment he would not be there. The last, and it was over: but she could not believe it till she saw the closed outer door and the empty street.

The Matron was in her office; a slip of evening sun across it, the secretary's typewriter faintly rattling outside, papers on the desk in neat trays and files.

"I've come to report for duty, Matron."

"Yes, Nurse. Are you feeling perfectly well now?"

"Yes, thank you, Matron." (She felt like a puppet without the hand inside it, but she would be well enough when she had slept. She was too tired, she thought with relief, to wake once in the night and look for him.)

"Very well, Nurse. You did not receive the wire I sent to your home this morning?"

"No, Matron." (What wire, what had her father thought? She would have to find some lie for him after all.) "I was away from home today."

"I see. You gave the Secretary your home address. A pity; you should have been in bed this afternoon. I wish you to go on night duty tonight. However, as you have been on holiday you will probably be feeling rested."

"Yes, Matron. Thank you." She went out.

Half-past six: she could lie down till eight, when the night-nurses had their breakfast. She ought, she reflected, to have expected it. She had been at the hospital ten months, and they were eligible for night duty after nine. Her eyes were sticky with sleep, and she felt as if she were carrying her body on a skeleton borrowed from an old woman. Well, she had no ex-cuse for self-pity. If she chose to come to this work in this condition, having expended herself elsewhere, she must take the consequences and do her best to see that no one else suffered. It was the inevitable result of trying to compress two lives into the space allowed for one. Was this what was meant by "leading a double life"? It struck her as feebly amusing: she must remember that this was one of the jokes she could not tell Mic. It was difficult to keep from telling him everything exactly as it drifted through her head. But when she saw him again she would be less tired and, with luck, more intelligent.

When she saw him . . . She paused, half-way up the stairs to her own room, remembering for the first time what night duty entailed. The night-nurses took their free time in the morning, after they left the wards. The hospital, sensibly aware that they were not likely to have their full faculties available for twelve hours' unbroken work and their own concerns, had arranged these in appropriate order. By twelve-thirty they had to be in their rooms; not unreasonably, since it was difficult for two nurses to run a ward, which in the daytime employed six, on less than seven hours' sleep. Once a week, by asking special leave beforehand, they were allowed to go out in the evening instead of the morning, from five-fifteen till eight. Mic was supposed to be free at five; but a busy day, or one of the special jobs that he seemed to be given with increasing frequency, often kept him till after six. There would be that, and an hour or two on Sundays.

Vivian locked herself in, and, throwing off her hat and dress, lay down on the bed. The sun had gone down and everything, indoors and out of the window, was in darkening shades of grey. She lay with a coat thrown over her, staring up at the ceiling. She did not shed any more tears—there seemed nothing left in her to cry with—till the foolish thought came to her that tonight at ten Mic would think of her going to bed, and she would be doing something else. She lay, reaching out to him, with ineffectual memory, slipping into a blackness of being alone; though she knew, when she thought about it a little later, that what she felt could not have had such force if his unhappiness had not followed and kept her company. They had shared these distant moods before.

A spell of night duty lasted three months.

It was a strange life to which she gradually acclimatised herself, dyed in different colours from the daytime world, with its own rhythms, its own emotions and qualities of thought. She suffered in it, as almost everyone did; in health, in power to perceive and even to think, since the mind was perpetually drugged with more or less fatigue, and in the continual pain of longing for Mic which their brief meetings always seemed to sharpen beyond their power to appease. Yet through all this it fascinated her, and she thought sometimes that, if she could have forgotten love or satisfied it, she might have been almost happy.

One woke, heavy-eyed, in the last light; outside the window, a blackbird would be soliloquising on the sunset in low, fluid undertones of inexpressible melancholy. Half-way through breakfast the lights would go on; the little handful of them, bunched in one corner of the huge dining-room, already spoke under their breath as if unseen sleepers surrounded them. They walked to the wards, wondering what changes the lost and unknown day had made there; lit by the yellow corridor lights and by the rusty glimmer of the west through the high windows. The ward on most nights would be quite silent (it was Malplaquet, which looked huger and more vault-like than ever at night); the lights, dimmed with their red shades, lit over the patients just operated on or very ill; the humped white covers of the beds, dyed with the faint reflection, leading in a long perspective to the table at the end and the green lampshade where the Sister sat, waiting to give the senior nurse the day report.

Vivian, if none of the patients needed her, would go into the sluice or clinical room to clean the bedpans or testing things. The work, carried on in quiet and alone, seemed different from the daytime scurry even when, on a busy night, the haste was greater. Perhaps because the air was freer from the tangle of other people's aims and anxieties, her mind felt enlarged and curiously liberated; she was conscious of this even when she was very tired, finding that with much less volition behind them her thoughts travelled more lightly.

The nurses had their midnight meal in two shifts, the seniors going first, so that from twelve to half-past she watched the ward alone. Sometimes she was running errands all through the time, and sometimes had to stand beside the bed of a man who was light-headed or about to die. She would look into the face and listen to the broken life-sounds or wandering speech, feeling, with an awareness impossible in the day, a sense of some permanence behind the ungeared mechanism; that while she tended the body which slumped lower into the filth and squalor of disintegration, an impersonal essence, freeing itself slowly as her own in this stillness was half-freed, shared with her a secret silence.

Her senior was Rodd, the auburn staff-nurse from Trafalgar. She was easy to work for, capable and direct and able to relax when there was no need for strain. Sometimes when there were several bad cases at once, or emergencies came in and had to be got ready for the theatre at a moment's notice, she would become furiously over-wrought and curse Vivian viciously over anything or nothing; but there was a kind of tacit understanding between them that this was to be forgotten as soon as the crisis was over. She was engaged to a warehouse clerk, showed Vivian endless snapshots of his broad, kindly, grinning face, and spent every free minute making her trousseau, which was of the most exotic feminity and had to be kept bunched discreetly in her lap in case any of the patients should be awake. Vivian made her tea and coffee, listened and agreed and admired, feeling her own thoughts move in and out of Rodd's with a curious lack of obstruction, like ghosts through a wall.

If the work were slack they might get several rests in the two or three hours after the midnight round; during a heavy taking-in week they might be working at racing speed for the whole of the night. They made their own tea on the ward, when and if they had the time.

Their fewness, their responsibilities, their freedom from the presence of the Sisters, perhaps the continual necessity for whispering, created a conspiratorial intimacy among the night staff which was impossible during the day. Everyone knew, after the midnight meal, what had happened in all the other wards, and felt a personal concern in it. The hospital seemed to grow, in the night, at the same time larger, more closely a whole, and more visibly dependent on them. It made for solemnity, and for a tacit consciousness of power.

There were times when Vivian felt caught into this life as if into an enchantment, seeing the normal world at the distance of a week-old dream. Once in the early morning when she and Rodd had been silent, in weariness or their own thoughts, for a long while, Rodd suddenly whispered, "It's quiet tonight. It reminds me, somehow; I was on night duty the night the old King was dying. The wind kept blowing all the time, and everything else was as quiet as quiet. I was sitting up at the desk alone, and suddenly the ward looked different, as if it wasn't the shape it really is, but open like a great high passage somehow. The big doors at the end were standing wide apart, perhaps that was why. But it was queer, everything seemed drawn up on either side, sort of waiting. And then the wind stopped. Just like that, cut off in the middle, not a sound. I always remember that. I'm not one to have fancies, as a rule."

But the next night, when she was cleaning the test-tubes in the clinical room, suddenly it all ceased to exist. The snapping of the spell was so sudden, so independent of her own thought, that she knew at once what was happening and, with the glass and polishing-cloth in her hand, went over to the window as if that would help. A street-lamp shone outside, and a distant car whined. She knew that that was the real world; it was not the beginning of night, but the end of day, half-past eleven or so; the crowds from the cinemas had gone home, the streets were emptying, lights snapping out in ground-floor windows; and Mic wanted her.

She knew the mood he would be in, his worst and his rarest

now; when he despaired of himself, his work and his future and despised himself, in a silence harder to cope with than anything he could have said, for ever having allowed himself to take her. She had never learned what to say to him at these times; there was no need any more. He was alone, trying to read perhaps, or lying in the dark staring upwards, with his arm behind his head. The ward was quiet tonight, Rodd sewing and drowsing at the table, none of the patients dangerously ill. Only half an hour, she thought, looking at the mist of her breath on the window; I could have him asleep in half an hour.

The telephone rang in the passage outside. She took the receiver down.

"Malplaquet ward speaking." (Mic, I'd be there if I could. I love you. Don't any more.)

"This is Casualty. We are sending you now a case of strangulated hernia for immediate operation."

"Yes, Nurse." (Oh, my dearest, go to sleep.)

She lit the gas under the steriliser on her way up the ward. He so seldom needed her now like this, absolutely; she might never again, perhaps, be asked to work this miracle which she would not be there to work tonight.

"A strangulated hernia," she told Rodd. "For the theatre at once."

"Damnation, it would be. I did want to finish these camiknicks tonight. Better have him in the end bed. Put the steriliser on as you go."

"I have. The bowls are in."

"Good kid."

The patient came in on the trolley, an old man, childish in his wits, too ill to feel fear or much pain. She got the theatre things and helped Rodd to paint his withered body with iodine, while his rheumy eyes blinked at them vacantly from the pillow; and in his place she kept seeing Mic as she had seen him once, his head on her arm, looking up at her as if she had rolled away the stone from his sepulchre.

("Stay with me, Vivian."

199

"Always, always.")

"Better let me have those teeth of yours, Daddy," said Rodd. "Never do to swallow them. *That's* right."

Then there was the theatre, with little Rosenbaum, the house surgeon on call that night, in high spirits, saying things he hoped would embarrass the nurses, and looking interestedly at the eye-spaces of their masks to see. She had been thinking of Mic, not listening, and when his little black eyes darted into her face she felt naked, and hardened into hostility before she knew it. He looked away, and asked the night-assistant rather brusquely for something that was already there.

In the early morning, a little before it was time to wake the patients and rush at the routine, she went out to look at the men on the balcony, and saw the day beginning to break. The air and the sky were still; there was no colour yet on the earth, but the trees were darkening against the east. Over them the morning star hung, low in the curve of space, seeming nearer than the almost imperceptible dawn; huge and liquid, faintly trembling like a cup too full of light held in a hand. The six men behind her in their iron beds were silently asleep. She knew that Mic too was sleeping. Her solitude was not crossed by any movement of thought or desire. A faint, clear greenish-gold began to lift into the sky from behind the trees; and in the emptiness a bar of cloud, too fine to be visible before, glowed suddenly with the fervency of blown fire.

She thought: This is how all life should be accepted, in desireless wonder, reaching out for nothing and thrusting nothing away, rejoicing in the different essence of each moment as it blazes into the present from the folded future. But she was under no illusions; for a life of such moments one needed a heart without roots, a spirit free in the wind, and empty hands. Once she had had them. She would never know them again. She had committed too much to earth.

IT gave the hours of morning a curious difference, to have arrived at them not by the process of waking, but by living through the night. The patterns of weather were not the same if one had watched the day from the earliest dawn: it was strange, too, when the life around was accelerating, to feel oneself running down. Bone-weariness and the longing for sleep were so incongruous as not to appear, sometimes, for what they were; they disguised themselves in other forms, melancholy, irritability, or a cutting-off from all experience, so that one moved like a shadow in an unreal world.

But the waking for an evening off-duty time was stranger still; to dress and wander out, still drugged and heavy with sleep, into the late sunlight, to meet Mic and struggle to match the developed thoughts and emotions of his evening with her drowsy break of day. It was difficult for them both, at first. That they adjusted in the end was an achievement that was principally his. With a perception that was purely imaginative, since it was quite outside his own experience, he entered somehow into her vague and dreamlike state, understood her complete inadequacy to violent passion of body and of mind, and conducted things with a quiet which she had never expected, or, indeed, desired of him before.

"Don't you mind, Mic? We have so little now, and when I am here all I do is lie and purr like a cat in front of the fire."

"A nice one to stroke, though. No, I only hate for you to be so tired. Sometimes I think you're good for me like this. Peaceful, and stabilising. Something like ——" he hesitated, then quoted, haltingly like something half-forgotten:

> "'O, Shadow, in a sultry land,
>   We gather to thy breast,
>   Whose love ——'"

"Darling. That's a hymn."

"Is it? Will the devil come for me? What a child you are sometimes.

> '*Whose love, enfolding us like night,*
> *Brings quietude and rest.*'

Enfolding us like a night." He relaxed beside her with a little sigh. "If I want you differently, it's generally when you're not there."

Vivian nodded. She too sometimes, when it could do no good, lived at another tempo from this.

"And you're rather often not there, now."

"I'll stay longer on Sunday. What have you been doing?"

"What does it matter?

> '*From all our wanderings we come,*
> *From drifting to and fro* ——'

Lampeter says Scot-Hallard takes up too much of my time. He wants me for some stunt of his own. They've been fighting for my carcass all day. I feel like the dead Patroclus when everyone was bestriding him. Never mind them.

> '*The grander sweep of tides serene*
> *Our spirits yearn to know.*' "

But it was not always, after all, as simple as that.

As the weeks went on she became aware that these changed conditions of living were speeding up a process in their relationship, or, perhaps, simulating a process she had feared: the result was the same. Mic was accepting, quietly, naturally, and inevitably, the responsibility for both of them, and she was consenting more and more that it should be so. He was developing at a speed that frightened her, she felt so unable to match it with any progress of her own. The shock of the lake seemed to have jolted something out of his system: it had been his last capitulation. He helped her, now, through every phase of their companionship, supporting her with his vitality instead of tossing it like a challenge to hers. While she was with him, she seemed to live, to be a person and a force: but after she had left him she would wonder whether she had done anything but give back to him, a little warmed and coloured by her love, the reflection of himself.

It was the morning work, after the anxieties and tensions of the night, that really drained one; the waking and washing and breakfasting of the patients, and running about with screens, all against the clock. It was a strict rule of the hospital that the patients were not to be wakened before six: it looked well in the reports, helped the reputation of the place for progress and reform, and would have been pleasant for the patient too if to carry it out, without increase of staff, had been mechanically possible. When things were very slack it could sometimes be done; otherwise—and it was usually otherwise—the successful night-nurse, liked by authority, was the one who smuggled as many of the washings and treatments as possible into the hours between four and six without being found out. To leave any of the night-nurses' routine for the day staff was unthinkable. They confined their attentions, as far as they could, to patients who were sleepless in any case; but their quietest movements were likely to disturb the others, and there was always the risk of the Night Sister making an early round. If she did, her alternatives were to give them a severe reprimand or confess that the hospital programme was unworkable; so her choice did not admit of much doubt. The net result was a certain amount of added strain, at the time when they could best have done without it.

Sometimes after a heavy night, when she went through the hospital passages to drag herself a mile or two in the open air (she reckoned that, at the rate of three miles an hour, she had already walked more than thirty in the ward) she would long to see Mic without being seen; the effort to carry on anything beyond mere existence seemed too much. It only happened once: he was going up the stairs that led to the laboratories, in a hurry, carrying part of the apparatus for a metabolism test in his hand. Little Rosenbaum, who was just below, looked up and spoke to him, and Mic, leaning out over the rail, answered something with that momentary laugh of his, sharp and vivid like a blade flicked into the light and quickly sheathed again. Then he was gone round the bend of the stairs; they were too far for her to hear what they said. She walked out into the clear autumn sunlight, which felt hostile to her tired eyes, realising that it had made her more, instead of less, empty and forlorn. He had looked so impossibly, unattainably alive; so full of concerns; so sufficient to things without her.

When she met him, a couple of evenings later, he remarked in the course of amusing her with some gossip or other, "But of course, as Rosenbaum, I think it was, said the other evening ——"

She looked up quickly. "You don't go out with Rosenbaum, do you?"

"No. More often I look in on him in the common-room, when he's on call. Anyhow, he says ——"

"But, Mic, do you *like* him?"

Taking a moment to slant his mind round this unforeseen obstruction, Mic considered.

"Well, I enjoy his company. I suppose it amounts to much the same thing." He saw her face and added, "You don't think a lot of him, I expect? I can imagine he isn't at his best in female society."

"He's just squalid."

"Not really. He was awfully good when I was ill: used to lend me books and come and talk to me in his spare time, and he hasn't much. He's extraordinarily interesting about music, too; been everywhere and heard everybody and has rather original ideas."

"He would have." She hated herself but could not stop. She loved music too, but knew her own response to be the simple emotional one of the untrained: she could only express it to him in visual images and other fancies.

"He goes out with fat Collins," she said.

"Yes, I expect he would. Well, he doesn't take me along." Mic looked at her thoughtfully, shifted the cushion behind her head and lit her a cigarette. "Sex in the abstract, of course, sometimes. He's full of esoteric doctrine about it. He doesn't give me the benefit of it very often, though, because I laugh in the wrong places. He puts it down to the psychically sterilising effect of my scientific training." He leaned over and kissed her.

His touch seemed, for a moment, to melt away the shell of possessive fear that was closing her in; but he let her go too quickly, handling her lightly because she seemed unequal to life today.

"All the same," she said, "if you saw me out with him you wouldn't be particularly pleased."

"Of course I shouldn't." The patience in Mic's voice was becoming ever so little tired. "Because, Rosenbaum being what he is, the relationship would be entirely different."

"Would it?"

Silence. She held her breath. She must have been mad. What was he going to say to her? She would take it. Anything that would persuade him to forgive her, if anything would. She looked, hardly daring, at his face.

His expression was purely puzzled, as if he were making up his mind whether her tongue had slipped or his hearing deceived him. Just as she felt she could not bear it for an instant longer, he threw up his head and laughed. She could not believe it. He was not mocking her, even laughing at her. His sense of humour had simply been tickled. His face was like a naughty boy's, full of improper delight.

Was he never going to stop? She sat looking at him, thinking as if he were a stranger what an attractive laugh he had, and feeling afraid.

He seemed, when he sobered down a little, faintly surprised not to find her laughing too.

"Darling," he said shakily, "you did mean that to be funny, didn't you? Because it is, terribly.

Vivian passed her hand across her eyes.

"Yes, of course I did. Don't take any notice of me, my mind's curdled, I think. Mic, I love you."

Mic slid an arm under her and looked into her face, raising one eyebrow a little.

"Yes. Kiss me. It's all I'm good for, anyway."

"That's too funny to laugh at."

But she could feel, in the movement with which he took her into his arms, a gesture of relief, as if he were glad to be done with words.

The next thing he said was, "Look at the time."

Already? She followed his eyes. Yes, there was not a minute, she would be late for breakfast in any case. Though it was the shock of self-discovery that had wakened her with the brutality of a cold plunge, still she was awake and they had been, for the moment, happy. He had answered her brief spark with a flash of his own that had reminded her how foreign to him all these dim smoulderings really were. They had been, for a little while, themselves, and had just been settling into a warm untroubled certainty of one another, something the strength of which would have carried her through the desert stretch ahead. But, as usual, it was time to go. They had had only two hours.

"Oh, Mic, I wish I could stay."

"I wish you could stay for good."

She hid her face on his shoulder, tempted almost beyond her power. Without words, with a look, a movement, she could consent. Until he had more to offer, he would never ask her more plainly than he was asking her now. She shut her eyes, surrendering for a moment to the thought of it. No. If she had lost confidence and strength she had less right than ever to saddle him with her dependence. In her inmost heart she knew, too, that she was afraid of losing herself more wholly than she was already lost.

She said, "It won't be long."

"No." There was a shadow of weariness in his voice. "I suppose not."

"I must go," she said. But she could not force herself to

leave him. The thought of unclasping her hands made her cold with sudden fear. She said, not knowing how or why the words were coming.

"Mic, whatever I do, whatever happens, I love you, I'll always love you, I can never love anyone as I love you, one can't again. You believe me. Say you do."

"Believe you?" he said wonderingly. He tilted her head back to see her face. "I wish you were off this blasted night duty. You wouldn't suddenly ask the Pope if he believed in St. Peter. Or he'd be surprised if you did."

"Are you surprised?"

"Very. Look, you're going to be just incredibly late. Put your things on and I'll run ahead and get out the car."

The night that followed happened to be a quiet one, and she had plenty of time—too long—to think.

Mic was growing up. It was a process so rapid that it could be watched, like the growth of a retarded plant suddenly given a necessary salt. Probably, she thought, his air of diffidence had always been superficial, a trick of manner largely, and the remains of a lack of social security. At school he had been alone a good deal because he could not discuss his people or ask other boys to stay; and at Cambridge, where that need not have mattered, want of money had produced much the same effect. Now, by imperceptible degrees, even the manner was disappearing. He talked about his work with a confidence that verged often on authority; the resident staff, the physicians first and now the surgeons, had begun to notice him and treated him as one of themselves, a thing not usual in his position. The fact that, in view of this and the special work he was often given, he had not quarrelled with the rest of the laboratory staff—though she gathered that there were occasional tensions—argued the use of more than average tact.

She relied on him more and more. The lassitude and continual sub-tone of her present life had destroyed her initiative, and in all their encounters now he managed her, not assuming any dominance but taking for granted that she would wish it; as indeed, when it came to the point she did. It occurred to her that once she would not have left it to him, as she had left it today, to keep an eye on the time. Nor would he have remembered if she had. It was a straw, but a significant one.

If she could have discussed things with persons of greater sophistication they would, she supposed, have laughed at her. These, they would say, were the excellent results of a satisfactory love-affair, and she ought to welcome them. After their uncertain oscillations, Mic was taking up at last his natural inheritance, and she had better make up her mind to hers. But she could not. She could neither reconcile herself to a passive destiny, nor feel her essential being at the mercy of someone else without the sense of sin, and of having given away what should not be given. She recognised Jan's dread of captivity; but she lacked his ruthlessness in self-preservation. Sometimes she envied it.

Her first experience of jealousy had been grotesquely trivial; but it had showed, like a peep-show, what one could become, self-locked, demanding, afraid.

He would weary of her. She brought it into the open for the first time, and looked at it in the grey early light. It might please him to be leaned on for a little while; but he had loved Jan. He had always loved panache, rivalry, an upright carriage of the spirit, a mind that struck sparks from his own, the passion of equals. In honour of these, and still in the faith of them, he treated her now with this unfailing kindness. But he would waken some clear day or other and find that there was only kindness left.

For the rest of the week, as if there were spurs at her back, she flung herself at life; reading the most exacting books she could find; swimming one morning though it was much too cold; doing anything that occurred to her, from moment to moment, to give her mind an existence of its own and stab it awake.

On one of these days she received, from an old friend of her mother's whom she had not known to be living in the county, an invitation to lunch. She should, of course, have refused it out of hand. She could not possibly get back for bed less than three hours late: an insane risk, and one that she would pay for the next night even if she ran it successfully. But she remembered from her childhood Celia Grey's feckless charm, and the circle of bright kaleidoscopic movement that surrounded her. The excursion would be something new, something of her own, something to talk about to Mic on Sunday. She accepted.

When the morning came she wondered whether, after all, it would be worth it, and felt fairly sure that it would not. But she put on her most presentable things, did what she could with her face, and took six grains of caffeine citrate to keep her eyes open.

The place was on a country bus route, and she reached it without trouble. The house was typical of Celia: old and dramatically picturesque, filled with expensive modern fitments, and screaming everywhere for the simplest repairs. The rooms were furnished with a groundwork of homogeneous good taste, overlaid by secondary and tertiary deposits of foreign souvenirs, gala-night presentations and mementoes from old stage sets and dismantled theatres. On the walls of the drawing-room, half a dozen fine Japanese prints, spaced at austere intervals, were jostled by a breathless scrum of photographs, all of them very large, very romantic, and scrawled with very loving dedications.

The place, in the way of places that contained Celia, was full of people. Celia herself was circulating among them like a fork among the ingredients of a *soufflé*. She had altered very little in the years since Vivian had seen her, except that she had had her black grey-streaked hair bleached perfectly white, which suited her. Her steel-sprung figure had set into angles here and there, her mouth had dried a little.

"Well, Vivian, my *darling* child, to think you could come. I was so afraid the Matron wouldn't let you. Some of them are such *peculiar* women. I suppose it's the *lives*, they lead, poor dears. So here you are and how *lovely* you're looking." (This, with Celia, was the equivalent of "How do you do," and Vivian accepted it as such.) "And *how* like Mary. I remember her

209

looking just like that when she played my daughter in *Mrs. Warren*, the first time we played together. Before you were born, Conrad." (This over her shoulder to a satellite young man, fair and handsome but moody-looking, who might equally well have been a lover, a nephew, or one of Celia's innumerable protégés.) "But, my dear, to *think* of a child of Mary's being a *nurse*. But the *rules* and everything and the operations and the *smells*. Donald—has Donald come yet, Conrad? Oh, yes, *there* he is—says they get not to notice it, but when Jan told me—I ran into him in Cornwall a week or two ago and he's even more like Mary than you are, he smiles like Mary, come-hither-but-not-too-hither, *you* know. Why don't you get him married, he simply ought not to be loose. Be *quiet*, Conrad, really I can't cope with you today, you *know* I meant at large, wandering round, that sort of loose. Who's that driving up, it's *never* Charles. Conrad, it *is*, whatever shall we do about Angela? And here's lunch ready. Go and *meet* him, Conrad, and *keep* him a minute. Now where shall we put Vivian? Let's see, there's Donald without anyone. Donald, dear, you and Vivian will look after each other, won't you? Mary Hallows's daughter; but of course, you probably—oh, Angela, darling, I was looking for you. Come here just a minute. . . ."

Vivian was left confronting Scot-Hallard, the surgeon, and wondering how much he enjoyed being presented as Donald to someone who, if unusual circumstances gave her the privilege of addressing him at all, would ordinarily have called him Sir.

He seemed, as they settled down to the meal, to be taking it very easily. One might even have supposed him to be pleased. It was only when he told her he would have recognised the likeness anywhere, that she realised he supposed himself to be meeting her for the first time.

Vivian was enormously amused. It was, after all, natural enough. She had never been near him except in the theatre, where she was shrouded like a member of the Ku-Klux-Klan. When the Honoraries made their rounds in the wards the function of the probationers was like that of St. John the Baptist, to make straight the way and then to disappear.

He had been, he told her, a fervent first-nighter of her mother's all through his student days. He was, after all, the youngest of the honorary staff, probably not past the middle forties.

Stimulated by caffeine, sherry, the aura of Celia and the humour of the situation, Vivian felt herself in increasingly good form. More potent than caffeine was the fact, soon evident, that Scot-Hallard was putting himself at some pains to make an impression. He sent out, from time to time, delicate feelers to ascertain if she was on the stage, and whether she lived in London or in the neighbourhood. Vivian evaded them with equal delicacy, thinking what a good story this would be for Mic.

Her attention wandered for a moment to a snatch of conversation from farther down the table, which revealed the unclassifiable Conrad to be Celia's second husband. When she had recovered a little, and reconsidered them both in the light of it, she became aware that Scot-Hallard was asking her to dine and dance with him.

Evidently the entertainment had gone far enough, and decency demanded that she should let him out as easily as possible.

"It sounds delightful, but alas, I'm on night duty. On Malplaquet. I was hoping to conceal the fact, but I expect I'm not sufficiently practised in crime."

She awaited effects with interest: but his recovery was superb.

"Why, of course. I felt all the time there was something besides the look of your mother. But that appalling uniform . . . one realises now how necessary it is. Never mind, we must fix another time. When you're a creature of daylight again, or on one of your free days. How did you come here? It might cut your risk by half an hour or so if I run you back."

Overhearing his excuses to Celia, she perceived that he was leaving, for her benefit, a good deal earlier than he had meant.

The car saved fully half the time of the journey by bus. He scarcely mentioned the hospital all the way, but talked to her about Stockholm, where he had spent his summer holiday. She ought to go, he said. The Swedes were a delightful people, gay, spontaneous, tolerant and free from shibboleths. She would find them temperamentally sympathetic.

His tact, undoubtedly, was exquisite. He omitted nothing that could obliterate the distance between them, or make her feel like someone with the power to confer obligations rather than receive them. Though she knew it to be a highly-skilled illusion, the sense of exercising power over what was itself powerful gave her its inevitable stimulus, like that of feeling an aeroplane respond to a touch on the stick. But when he looked into her eyes with a mixture of searching scrutiny and tender whimsicality so obviously stylised as a silk hat that she wanted to laugh. She walked in (by miracle uncaught) thinking of Mic and softly smiling. It had been like the promenade deck of the *Queen Mary* after a small yacht in a south-wester. She only got two hours' sleep that day—her brain, when she went to bed, was astonishingly active—but she felt her spirits improved.

By the time Sunday came round she had polished up the story till it was, she thought, a good one. She went to see Mic in the morning. As they were allowed out in the evening on Sunday without special leave she often did both: it was against the rules, but generally safe. Already Sunday morning had almost lost for her its ordinary associations; it was drinking coffee sleepily to the sound of church bells, sitting on the bed with an elbow on the window-sill; smoking, hearing Mic talk and throwing in a lazy word or two, listening to the gramophone and opening her eyes, knowing suddenly that time had passed, to find that the music had stopped and he had not moved because she had fallen asleep with her head on his knees. Sometimes, since autumn drew on, she had not gone back at all.

"Why don't you sleep here?" Mic had said. "I'll be perfectly quiet. I have to read on Sundays anyhow. It will save

212

you two journeys and you're less likely to be caught." She had been sleepy, reluctant to leave him, and easy to persuade.

To make the room quieter he closed and curtained the window, leaving the door ajar; but his movements in the next room never disturbed her. She slept generally for four or five hours, and woke sometimes to find him still working, or, with his technical books put away, reading the *Observer* on the floor on his hands and knees.

Once she opened her eyes to find him curled beside the bed with his head against her pillow and a book slipping sideways on his lap.

"Did I wake you?" he said.

"No. But I was dreaming about you."

"I'm afraid that may have been my fault."

She slid out her arm and put it round him. After the folded warmth of the bed his coat felt rough and cold, and the shape of his shoulders very hard and positive.

"Why didn't you wake me?"

"You don't sleep enough as it is."

His arm let a little current of chilly air down beside her.

"You feel like a warm animal uncurling in its hole."

"That's just what I am like. Come and see."

But she had thought afterwards in the night, when she was growing tired, that he had not fallen in love with her in a state of hibernation.

This morning she was determined to be alive. She made some strong tea, splashed herself with cold water, and ran the last half of the way to get the whip of the October wind.

"You look marvellous," Mic said when she got there. "What have you been up to?"

She kissed him. "Wait till you've heard the story I've got to tell you."

She told it, rather well, over the coffee. He laughed in the right places very creditably, but, she thought, with a certain lack of conviction.

"Darling, you're not getting thoughtful about this, are

you? You know it's purely fantastic. Besides, you said you liked him."

"I said he had a first-class brain and was interesting to work for."

She pulled his hair. "But he isn't the kind of man you'd introduce to your sister, is that it?"

"That's one thing. You probably know all the good stories as well as I do. Of course I know you can look after yourself."

"You know perfectly well I'm as impervious to that type of man as you would be to Mae West. In any case, he was only making a good exit. I shall never hear from him again."

"I don't know, you might. You're rather obviously not the blackmailing kind."

"Darling." She was a little shocked. "He isn't quite as sordid as that."

"Have some more coffee." He poured out two more cups, and there was silence for a minute or two. Then he put his own on one side and said, slowly, "I've often thought of my father as a man like Scot-Hallard."

"But, my dear." Feeling both distressed and helpless, she could only produce a laugh. "That's simply wild. He'd have been hardly twenty then—an innocent straight from school."

"I know that," said Mic curtly. "I'm not suffering from delusions. I mean a man as he is now, with his standards. Except that Scot-Hallard's too damned efficient to get himself landed with a bastard."

"Shut up, darling. I don't like you when you go Somerset Maugham. And I came here meaning to be particularly nice, too."

"Why—conscience-money?"

"Mic, shut *up*. We shall get into a mood. For God's sake let's fence, or something."

"You've hardly kissed me yet."

"I won't either. Honeying and making love over the nasty sty." She pulled out the foils and threw one at him. "Take that, blast you, and use it."

Mic began to say something, changed his mind, pushed a

chair out of the way, and took off his coat. They went at it, without at first any noticeable improvement of temper.

"That's a bloody stage trick," he snapped presently.

"Why not, you're in a bloody stage mood."

She executed a gross flourish straight from *The Prisoner of Zenda*, and succeeded, at the moment of his annoyance, in hitting him very neatly. To lift the foil out of his hand, she thought viciously, would make him look more foolish than anything else: but he knew all about that. He was affecting a rather exaggerated good form: and, being a better fencer in any case and fresher as well, was soon leading by several points.

They had played with the foils two or three times, but she had never had again the curious experience of the first day. Now, as they went on, she found it returning. It brought with it this time not wonder or fear but an angry exultation. She wondered if she could catch him with the same trick as before; she had not used it since. He was grinning at her defiantly. They had each reached the stage of deciding that if they won they might afford to be pleasant afterwards; but it was necessary to win.

As before, the moment came when she knew exactly what to do. She knew, too, that he could not stop her. It was only one hit but it seemed somehow more important than the others. Timing and distance were perfect; the feint succeeded. She was about to lunge when her foot slipped on a rug they had forgotten to move, and she pitched at him, her foil still out. She felt it meet flesh with a heavy jar, and bend in her hand. When she got up (it had brought her down on one knee) Mic was looking past her with a distant stare. There was a triangular tear in his shirt, over the left breast.

"Mic, I am so sorry." Her bad temper had gone like a puff of wind. "We ought not to fool about like this without masks or anything. Suppose it had been your face."

"It's all right," said Mic vaguely. "Did us good."

She went up to him. Suddenly fear went like a sheet of black across her mind.

"Mic! You're bleeding."

"Oh, no. I shouldn't think so."

"But you *are*." She opened his shirt, her hands shaking. It was only a superficial graze—the button had glanced upward —but it was bleeding a good deal. A small, steady trickle ran down his body to his waist.

At the sight of the blood it was as if some lifelong nightmare exploded in her mind. She snatched out her handkerchief and pressed it over the place. In a little while the bleeding stopped: but she still felt icy cold, and weak at the knees.

"Mic, it's silly, but I still feel so frightened I don't know what to do."

He put his arm round her: she was shaking all over. "Funny, wasn't it?" he said. They sat down together on the rug in front of the fire. "How cold your hands are." He held them out to warm. "Better?"

"Yes, much." They leaned back to back, supporting one another's weight, in a posture which custom had found convenient.

"Extraordinary thing," said Mic over his shoulder, "but when you came at me like that I was perfectly certain you were going to kill me. Not surprised, either. As if I remembered it happening before."

She put her hand over his on the rug. "We must have done some queer things in our past lives, Mic, if there's anything in those theories. But they say it's just a trick your mind plays when it doesn't co-ordinate."

"I know. A sort of double-exposure. But I've wondered sometimes if it's possible, in only five months, to get so thoroughly tangled up with another person as I am with you."

"People have always wondered that, haven't they? If it were true I'd owe you a life, I suppose."

"Well, I did my best to kill you last month, so perhaps that will count as a token payment. . . . Have you read Dunne? He says that sometimes we remember the future."

Vivian contracted her fingers quickly over his, and loosened them again. "That sounds awfully far-fetched," she said.

Mic got up, and looked out of the window. "They're coming out of church. It's time you were going to bed."

"I suppose so." She rose, stretching: after the fencing her spurt of energy had petered out all at once. "Good night, darling. Don't let me sleep after five, will you?"

He shut the window, and darkened the room. At the door he took her in his arms and said, "I'm sorry about this morning. I have blind patches here and there I don't seem able to do anything about."

"I ought to know better than to walk on them by now. I'm sorry too."

"They're a lot smaller since you came."

"I'm glad." She felt his arms tighten, and rubbed her cheek against his. "Yes, stay if you want to. I'll sleep all the better when you've gone."

She was asleep before he left her. Next morning she received (in a typed envelope) a letter from Scot-Hallard. It was amusing, well put together, and hoped she would let him know when she had an evening free. It happened that three nights fell due to her in the following week; but she tore the letter finely and threw it away.

— 18 —

F OR most of the next week Vivian lived on credit; she let an almost untasted present slip by her, nourished with anticipation. She could not remember looking forward to anything quite so urgently as, now, to the freedom of three nights and days with which they were rewarded for a month's night duty. In her case it was nearly six weeks, for she had started in the middle of the last month, too late to qualify. The newness of her inverted life had long since worn off, and with this the power to appreciate any strangeness or beauty in it. The thought of sleeping at night, and sufficiently, and of waking in the morning, was delicious; the thought of doing both in Mic's company was so beautiful that it frightened her. She felt that in her diminished state she no longer had the power to attract such happiness to herself; that the moment would know her undeserving, and pass her by. Joy, she thought, is taken by storm, not prayers. She could not assume the arrogance of a claimant, and the knowledge of it chilled her.

It was in this mood, seeking without much hope for anything that would convince her of herself, that she began to think again of Scot-Hallard's unanswered letter. Accustomed as she was to associating sex with a rather complex personal relationship, she had found his approaches almost comically crude, the comic element being supplied by his very evident belief in his own subtlety. But she had intelligence enough to be aware that the entire human being was not to be measured by these manifestations. Scot-Hallard himself was neither crude nor trivial. His admiration had flattered her; his power and vitality had stimulated her: and the fraction of his mind which he thought it appropriate to spend on a woman had suggested new possibilities in her own.

She had dismissed his invitation without a second thought,

because the time he had asked for belonged to Mic: but it occurred to her now that as her holiday did not cover a week-end she would be alone all through Mic's working hours. Scot-Hallard, she recollected, had added a postscript suggesting lunch, or tea, if she could not manage an evening time. It seemed to her that, after all, a brief meeting might make a good *apéritif* for the more important meal of life to follow. So much had to be extracted from it: it had to last so long; it seemed sinful to come to it listless if anything could give her a fillip. Unfair, too, to Mic.

She knew in her heart that she had another motive too, and a more fundamental one. Scot-Hallard had given her an illusion of independence. With him she was sought, and un-seeking; she had left him with indifference, knowing he was not altogether indifferent to her; she desired nothing of him and feared nothing at his hands. In his company, she was free.

On the second and third of her days, Thursday and Friday, Scot-Hallard generally snatched his lunch between work in clinics and the theatre: on the first, Wednesday, he was less busy. By Saturday of the previous week she had made up her mind. She rang up his flat before going on duty: found him in, and, apparently, pleased to hear from her, and arranged to meet him. She had a moment's impression (probably, she thought, conveyed on purpose) that he had decided to put off another engagement.

Once the thing was settled, she found herself thinking about it a good deal. It gave quite a different tinge of colour to her expectations, and it did undoubtedly increase her con-fidence. When she came off duty on Wednesday morning, she thought, she would rest for an hour or two, and for an hour or so after she got back. That would be enough to last her until the evening. In the night, heavenly thought, she would sleep.

On Sunday morning she said to Mic, as they sat on cush-ions by the fire, "I'm going to buy a new frock. What sort would you like me to have?"

Mic contracted his forehead and said, after a few seconds' concentration, "One that buttons down the front."

"*Honestly*, Mic ——"

"Sorry, darling. Green suits you, doesn't it? That Robin Hood thing with the leather tabs on it is the one I like you in."

"I think I'll have a Cossack one, with cartridge-pockets. (They fasten with frogs. Frogs are easy.) Would you like me to be a Cossack?"

"Very much. I always admired their beards. What's the occasion?"

"Next week. Just so I shan't become a habit, my sweet."

"You're not a habit. You're an addiction."

He had begun to learn, lately, to say pretty things.

A new dress was overdue; she had not bought one for the daytime for a year. Ever since Jan had sent her twenty pounds she had played with the idea, and today, looking at other people's new things brought out by the cold, she had made up her mind. She owed Mic something fresh; he had much more taste and observation than he laid claim to and she had had nothing new to speak of since she had known him. Besides, a new dress was imperative if she was not to wear the same one for Scot-Hallard a second time.

She felt very little sense of guilt over not telling Mic about it. Indeed, it was in the nature of a sacrifice, for everything she thought or did gained a new life by being shared with him. But it had been very evident that hearing of the first encounter had not added to his happiness, and to scratch him again would be, it seemed to her, pure egotism. She recalled her own overwrought antipathy to Rosenbaum; she had got over it, but appreciated the tact with which Mic, though he was still seeing him, had refrained from ramming him down her throat until she became reasonable. She would show him the same consideration, and tell him afterwards, at one of those moments when anything can be safely told.

"Shall you be working late on Wednesday?" she asked him.

"No, with luck I'll only get routine stuff. Lampeter never comes on Wednesdays, nor Scot-Hallard either as a rule. I expect I'll be free by five-thirty. But don't get up if you can sleep on."

"I'm going to save some sleep for the night, darling. If I may?"

"You look as though you could do with both," he said, and sent her to bed early.

She woke of her own accord, to find the room quite dark. The wrongness and unexpectedness of it frightened her even before she was fully conscious. As if she had been a little girl at the top of the house, the world seemed suddenly huge, hostile and unknown.

"Mic," she said softly. The door would open, letting in the light, and everything would be safe again.

But there was no answer, and she saw then, by the glimmer from the window, that the door was ajar already and the next room in darkness.

He's in the kitchen or the bathroom, she said to herself; but she knew all the while that she was alone. There was a barrel-organ playing, a long way off, down the street. To the silence, darkness and loneliness it added the melancholy of a requiem. It was an old organ: as she woke it had been finishing *White Wings that Never Grow Weary*, and now it was beginning *Silver Threads Among the Gold*. Its thin lamentation seemed to draw her farther and farther away from life and comfort; alone, as she would be alone when she had died.

"*Mic!*" Her voice was only the emptiness assuring her of her fear.

Why should he not be out, she thought; she was always urging him not to tie himself to the place while she slept. But it was dark. Something had happened. She was in this night alone.

The door downstairs closed. She heard him come upstairs, quietly, and let himself in. She could not call to him. Next minute he came softly into the room and leaned over her.

"Have you been awake long? I just ran out to catch the six-thirty post."

She caught hold of him, silently. The darkness was still on her, more real than his presence: she gripped him more tightly, trying to come back to the world.

221

"What's the matter, darling?" He sat down on the edge of the bed. "Had a bad dream?"

"I woke up and it was dark, and I thought you were gone."

"Gone where? I did come in at five, but you looked so tired I couldn't wake you."

"I wish you had. I feel so horrible."

"Come and toast crumpets while I make the tea. I haven't had mine yet, either, I was reading hard."

They sat to eat it on the hearthrug, but still the same forlornness was over everything. She could not laugh, or talk with her whole mind; everything was changed to a shadow of itself, and in a little while Mic grew quiet too. They pushed the tea-things aside, and sank deeper into themselves and their own imaginings.

After they had not spoken for a long time, Mic said, slowly and without coming nearer, "Will you take off your dressing-gown for a minute?"

Not replying or questioning, she ungirdled it and slipped it away, and sat as she had been, on her heels, looking at the blue flames of the gas-fire. Mic lay with his chin on his hand, making no effort to touch her. At last he said, in the quiet passionless voice of meditation, "You're very beautiful. I shall always remember you like this: kneeling, with the firelight down your side."

She turned towards him; but his eyes were distant and still, as though already he were remembering.

"Mic, dear." She covered herself again and leaned over, feeling afraid. "Don't talk as if I were going to die. It's this mood of mine. Don't take any notice: wake me up."

He sat up, and, putting his arm round her, held her beside him; but neither of them wanted to make love. They sat looking, like solemn and frightened children, into the fire.

"Read to me," she said.

He took the *Oxford Book* at random from the shelves, and turned the pages to and fro. At last he flattened it at John Davidson and began evenly to read.

> *"The boat is chafing at our long delay,*
> *And we must leave too soon*
> *The spicy sea-pinks and the inborne spray,*
> *The tawny sands, the moon.*

> *"Keep us, O Thetis, on our western flight!*
> *Watch from thy pearly throne*
> *Our vessel, plunging deeper into night*
> *To reach a land unknown."*

He closed the book and put it aside.

"What made you read that?" she asked.

"I don't know."

"There must be an angel passing over us. Never mind, we'll be better on Wednesday." She saw that it was nearly time to go, and went to put her things on. But through their farewells, and all through the night that followed, the oppression of strangeness remained.

On Monday morning, feeling (within the limits of night duty) brisk and normal, she bought the new dress. It was dearer than any she had, and she felt reckless and defiant over it, for it was emphatic in its style and would undoubtedly date. There was a rakish little cap to go with it, and as it suited her she bought that too. It would amuse Mic, she thought affectionately: he liked a touch of swagger. The frogs were in the right place and very easy ones. She thought, too, that in its other and fashionable aspect it made her look the kind of person Scot-Hallard seemed to think her.

She undressed, thinking about Mic. She had not been much fun for him on Sunday. Heavy-headed in the morning: asleep for more than six hours: in the evening, a child with sick fancies, only fit to be given nursery tea and comforted by the fire. In the end she had depressed him too. How much longer would he be so patient?

Her mind went back to a conversation a week or two old.

"Mic, I ought to have asked you sooner, would you like to come to the nurses' dance?"

"Are you going?"

"I haven't been to the last few, they used to bore me. But I will if you'd like it. They relieve the night-nurses for an hour."

"Well, we'd get an extra evening together, of a kind, I suppose."

"We couldn't have more than two or three dances, darling. Matron will be there. But I thought you ought to be invited."

He laughed. "Oh, Lord, I have been."

"Who by?"

"I can never remember their names. The tall dark boneless one, and the rather Russell Flint one with chestnut hair."

"Oh. Muir and Haighton."

"And a little fat one covered in scent."

"All those. What did you say?"

"I don't know, something or other."

"They call Muir the Flying Scot, darling. Don't you want to go?"

"Not if I've got to spend the evening looking pleasant with a succession of overheated women breathing down my neck. I never know what to say to them. Do you mind?"

"Of course not. I didn't really want to go, either."

She knew that she had been glad he did not want to go. She was content that he should keep these habits of thought and not perceive that they had become unreal. It seemed incredible that he should not know how acceptable he could be to almost any woman if he wanted. Some day—in a month or two, a year or two—someone might think it worth while to explain this to him: someone more beautiful, perhaps, more expert than herself; with better clothes and more poise; someone less tired.

It was against this moment that she wanted to pick up the scraps of assurance, sophistication and art that a surface flirtation with Scot-Hallard could give her. She was, she supposed, using him rather selfishly; but he must have used so many people that it did not trouble her conscience. Secretly, too, she knew herself flattered that it should be in her power to use him at all. Before she fell asleep she confessed to herself that she was looking forward to the meeting for its own sake.

It did not disappoint her.

They drove over, as she had guessed they would, to lunch in Brancaster. It was a very pleasing little lunch, better, she guessed, than her experience enabled her to appreciate; and as they talked she soon fell, or was conducted, into the Celia Grey atmosphere again. It was quite easy to forget that she had not slept; easy, she found, even to be amusing. She wondered what Scot-Hallard was really like. She was quite well aware that she was talking, not to him, but to a suit of well-cut conversational clothes tailored, like his material ones, by a craftsman to whom fit and finish had become second nature. His pretences at self-revelation—the lightly deprecated indiscretion, the note of emotion suppressed a second too late—were merely the touches that distinguished Savile Row from the Strand.

In their beautifully restrained way the place and the people in it smelt of money. She thought in an odd moment of Mic, remembering that he was unhappy sometimes because he could not give her anything like this. If only, she thought, he could know how little she really cared about it, and then was angry with herself because she knew she was enjoying this excursion into artificiality and her own success; and because her curiosity about Scot-Hallard was increasing. His range of knowledge was enormous, and from time to time, when they wandered upon one of his special enthusiasms—Holbein, for instance, or the sensations of high-altitude flying—something of himself was visible: she was aware of an avid mind and body, greedy for self-extension, intolerant of weakness. She began to understand his delight in the anaesthetised surgical problem on the table, his impatience with the anxious depressed invalid in the ward.

After the meal was over he said, "Well, where now? Which part of the daylight world would you like to revisit, Proserpina, before you go back to the shades?"

She hesitated, smiling and thinking of the clean lift of the long black car over the hills.

"I had been meaning to revisit Morpheus. I'm going out this evening, you see, and I was on duty last night."

"Don't dream of it. Two or three hours' sleep will only make you feel stupid. The open air will brace you up, and you shall have a good strong black coffee and brandy at the end of it. A much better idea."

He was entirely selfish, she reflected; but she had guessed that already. It was the defect of his qualities. She made no more objections. It was weeks since she had seen the country in the afternoon. Since last time the bracken had rusted, the leaves turned; it was a sunny day, pale-blue and clear brown, with the far hills a dark cobalt against the sky. She was enjoying her own mood: little half-tones and nuances, absorbed unconsciously from her mother's world and forgotten in the quiet years after, had crept into her manner and her voice. Between the lines of his conversation Scot-Hallard was saying to her, "It is a pleasure to play this familiar game against such unfamiliar skill." No doubt he knew how to convey this to every woman from whom he hoped to get something; but it was making her feel better pleased with herself than she had for some time.

While they were driving they drifted on to the subject of war. He spoke of its inevitability, sweeping away her arguments in favour of hope. Behind his conventional assumptions of regret she detected an eager and arrogant confidence. She knew he was taking for granted that if it happened he would assume his rightful place: making decisions of which other people were afraid, enduring things under which they broke: using himself to the limit. She acquitted him of the wish for material profit; he was in any case too intelligent to expect even comfort, much less wealth, to survive. He was simply too highly-charged for his age and society; the mere exercise of his skill was not sufficient for him: nothing short of war would give his engines room to open up, and he knew it. Moral affront seemed hardly to the purpose. She wondered how many men like him there were in Europe.

She did not know where he was taking her, except that it

was a good deal farther than she had ever been with Mic. When he began to talk about tea she reminded him that she had an appointment at half-past five. He assured her, with his usual certainty, that he would get her back—"though," he suggested, "if you think it could wait till another day the car is quite without false pride and subject to fallibility."

Vivian did not doubt it. He had put it to her fairly; but she guessed that this proceeded less from scruple than the reluctance of a skilled player to spoil the interest of his game by cheating.

They had tea at a lavish sham-Jacobean roadhouse. Scot-Hallard spent most of the time trying to get it established that they would meet again very shortly, but she was evasive. Her eyelids were becoming heavy, her body tired, and everything increasingly too much trouble. Upstairs in the cloakroom she thickened her make-up to simulate some kind of animation. Yesterday's sleep was twenty hours behind her. As if by a conjuring-trick the black coffee appeared and Scot-Hallard laced it, more than adequately, from a pocket flask. She felt better, but preoccupied. A chance glimpse of a clock had made it clear to her that, unless they could go back a good deal more quickly than they had come, she would be late. She suggested this to Scot-Hallard.

"You're not still determined to go back, are you?"

"But of course I am. We *have* still got time, haven't we?"

"Oh, yes, no doubt, if we make good going. But I was hoping in another half-hour or so we might have forgotten all about it. Stranger things have happened."

"I expect they have," said Vivian. "But not to me." She was beginning, though she would not show it, to be seriously worried. If Mic had to know where she had been, it would have been far better to tell him beforehand.

Long before they got into country that she knew, the sun began to sink. She had not seen sunset for a week, and could not remember what time it was. Her watch was at home: it was too clumsy to wear with formal clothes.

"Turneresque, isn't it—" said Scot-Hallard, and stopped the car on the crest of a hill.

It was too clear-cut for Turner: a sheet of cirrus cloud lit from below, and stretching almost to the zenith. She was longing to hurry on, but felt it would be a little boorish to say so yet. Scot-Hallard touched her arm.

"When are you going to meet me again?"

His voice had changed, and she felt frightened. She had not expected things to reach this pitch the first time. He was looking into her eyes; she tried to harden her own, but she felt she had not succeeded.

"Perhaps next month, if we're both free."

"A month? You dare to talk to me about a month?" His arm went round her, with a confidence so much greater than her own that it got there unresisted. "That was deliberate wickedness. You must be punished for that. Darling" He swept her into an embrace and kissed her.

His strength made her feel like a doll. Her will as well as her limbs were, for the moment, helpless: and during this moment she made a slight, but instinctive response. Next moment she forced herself away from him: but he was looking at her differently, with a new certainty.

She could not make herself ridiculous by being outraged. Any intelligence or honesty should have prepared her for this. He was still holding her, though she would not let him kiss her again. Against his deep chest and strong shoulders she experienced unaccustomed reactions. She was used to Mic's love-making, which was one side of a conversation. This was simply a command. The sensation it gave her of being delicate and frail, something that could easily be broken in half but would not be broken, stirred in her feelings of a primitiveness which, for a few seconds, excited her by their newness. She disengaged herself, feeling shaken.

"Well," she said lightly, "after that, I think the less we spare the horses the better."

"When are you going to meet me?"

"Not for a long time."

228

He leaned towards her. "You can't run away from life like that, my dear."

Vivian's balance returned, and with it her sense of humour and a certain amount of self-disgust. He must imagine I'm a good deal younger than I am, she thought, if he takes that line. Aloud she said, "I'm afraid it's several years since I gave up spelling life with a capital."

He changed direction quickly ."The fact remains that it's very short."

"I don't waste it. That's why I asked you to get me back by five-thirty."

"I see. . . . How serious?"

"Do you define life for yourself entirely in terms of love-affairs? Or do you simply think that's good enough for me?"

"I don't think one way or another. I can see it in your face."

Her retort, which she had thought good, felt suddenly adolescent. She said, "Then I wonder why you're keeping me here?"

"That isn't the only thing I can see. Very well, I'll take you back. You'll find I'm not easily parted from an idea."

The car went on into the dusk. She tried to put what had happened behind her, but found it was still present whether she liked it or not. Scot-Hallard's square head and wiry hair, his broad hands with their scrubbed close-cut nails, had ceased to be simply a visual impression.

The headlights, when he snapped them on, showed her a village twenty miles from home as the church clock struck six.

Scot-Hallard was driving in silence. She sat back and tried to force her tired mind to consider implications. One thing she knew she need not fear from him was any kind of awkwardness in the hospital. The water-tightness of his private and professional lives was a byword. Discretion with him needed no effort, but sprang naturally from his scale of proportions. If he met her on duty he would be as impersonal as his theatre gloves. The most probable event was that he would be too busy to notice her. In any case, she found she could not flog her stumbling brain so far ahead. It was enough, and more than enough, to decide what she was going to say to Mic. She was not likely, now, to be much less than an hour late.

At the thought of beginning the evening with any sort of situation, every weary nerve in her body seemed to cower. She was in no state tonight to fling a foil at his head. Tears, or a thin petulance, felt nearer her mark. It was impossible, she could not make herself face it. She would have to tell him she had overslept. Only for tonight. Tomorrow, when they had been happy for a little while, it would be easy. He would understand if she explained how tired she had been. She rested, in a moment of contentment, on the certainty of his kindness.

She asked Scot-Hallard to put her down at the Post Office. It was non-committal, and three minutes from the flat. They were in the outskirts of the town before she realised that, by the way he was taking her, they would approach it through the High Street. However, it was almost fully dark by now.

She had resolved not to look up; but, as they passed the flat, found it impossible to prevent herself from doing so. She had forgotten the street-lamp outside. It shone full into her up-turned face; and into Mic's, as he stood in the unlighted window looking down.

Before there was time for any sign of recognition, they had passed out of sight. Scot-Hallard, watching the traffic, had not seen anything. She noticed for the first time that her hands and feet were cold. The picture of Mic's silent eyes, encountering hers like a stranger's, stayed with her. She said to herself, trying to make it sound as prosaic and usual as possible, Well, I shall have to see it through now. Better to get it over, after all. He is sure, really, to understand.

Scot-Hallard had stopped. She thanked him with what she hoped was a safe mixture of social gratitude and emotional discretion. He only said, "Au revoir," accompanying it with a look that shouldered her flimsy structure aside and made the wreckage look foolish. She found as she walked to the flat that her limbs were cramped and stiff with driving, and remembered with a shock that she had not attended to her face and hair since Scot-Hallard had kissed her. She tried to tidy herself a little by the reflection in a shop-window. There was no time or place for anything more.

She realised, as she climbed the stairs, that there was nothing in the world she wanted except sleep. She could not imagine, now, what had possessed her to stay out for the afternoon instead of resting. It had taken the evening from Mic as surely as if she had consented to spend it with Scot-Hallard instead. It was this which gave her a feeling of disloyalty: not the fact that Scot-Hallard had kissed her. That was irrelevant. One did not supersede one's right hand by learning to light a cigarette with the left.

As a rule he heard her coming upstairs and would have the door open before she got there; but tonight she found it closed. Her key was in her bag, but for some reason she felt unable to use it. She knocked, and heard the scrape of a chair as he got up. The door opened, the light inside dazzling her for a moment. She saw that he was standing aside politely for her to pass through.

She went in, put down her bag and gloves on the table, and turned to him. He had closed the door and was standing with his fingers on the handle, looking at her.

"I'm sorry I'm late, Mic. Honestly it wasn't my fault. I kept telling him all the afternoon I had to be back."

He said nothing. He made, after Scot-Hallard, a sharp and rather disquieting contrast; like something with a knife-edge balance after the solidity of a monolith: too slim, too highly sensitised, put together with too dangerous a fineness; easy to hurt, frighteningly capable of hurting.

She could not wait for him to speak. She went on, a half-tone higher, "You're not going to be silly about it, are you, darling? You know I wouldn't do it on purpose. Don't you?" She went up to him, and, putting her hand on his arm, made to kiss him.

She felt him stiffen. She had been going to say something more, something light to restore proportion: but when she saw his face she could not speak. That he would be angry she had

231

half-expected; feared that he might be hurt; but nothing could have prepared her for this quiet stare of shocked, incredulous distaste. All her prepared defences vanished. She seemed to contract, as if he had drenched her with icy water.

"Thanks," he said, "but I think I'd rather you washed Scot-Hallard off first, if you don't mind."

She pulled her hand away from his arm and stepped back. Because it was the involuntariness of his movement that had been unbearable, she said, "Don't strike attitudes."

He did not answer.

"I dare say I do look a wreck." She listened to the forced jar of her own voice. "I've been driving in an open car, you know." She took the mirror out of her bag mechanically, looking for him to speak. It could not be real, she thought; she was so tired, it was a trick of her eyes, a trick of the light, that made Mic seem to stand there with a face of helpless and secret shame, like a child that has seen its mother do something it dimly knows to be obscene.

So as not to see his face any more, she looked in the glass at her own. After a moment she lowered it; but Mic's eyes were still there and she looked again. She saw what he had seen; her mouth and eyes sagging with fatigue which her heavy make-up had masked into dissipation: the expression she had been wearing for Scot-Hallard—not one familiar to Mic, with whom she had never flirted—still faintly lingering: the new hat tilted too far: at one corner of her mouth the lipstick blurred in a small, unmistakable smear. She put the glass away.

"I'm sorry. Perhaps you're right. May I use the bathroom?"

"Please do. I think I left a clean towel."

He was still standing there, with his hand on the door, as she went out.

The hot water was comforting, softening her face from the stiffness of stale make-up and lack of sleep. When she picked up the towel, she saw that he had put out, too, the dressing-gown and slippers she kept there, her brush and comb and a fresh cake of soap. They were like a sudden light revealing desolation. For a week she had been living for this evening, and Mic, when he laid out these things as neatly as a lady's-maid, had been smiling to himself, looking forward too. She had wasted it, for some reason she could no longer remember. What had happened? It was only some passing snap of the nerves, a trivial thing; there must be some simple way to get this moment of expected happiness back again.

She brushed her hair back smoothly, left only a little powder on her face, and looked in the glass again. The result was not decorative, but at any rate fairly honest. It will be all right in the end, she thought, it always has been. She went back into the dining-room, and found him setting the table with his usual method and care. The ordinariness of it was reassuring. She came towards him smiling.

"Do I look cleaner?"

He laid down his handful of cutlery and put his hands under her elbows. After a moment's hesitation, he kissed her. She tried to return his kiss, but could not. She seemed to have no part in it, and it frightened her. It was like an experiment in something not quite understood: tentative, watchful, tinged with a kind of reluctant curiosity. She murmured, "Mic—please," and drew away from him.

Suddenly he swore under his breath and pulling her back to him, kissed her furiously, giving her no time or chance to respond. It hurt her physically, but more by what she felt in it of a tormented hostility. It was as if he had struck rather than kissed her. The whole day's strain flooded into her sense of outrage. She wrenched herself out of his arms.

"Was that necessary?" Her voice was shaking a little, but not with tears. "When I've done anything about which you're justified in getting hysterical, Mic, I'll let you know."

"I'm sorry," he said stiffly. "I'm not justified in criticising anything you do. But you looked rather—unlike yourself—when you came in."

"I was dead tired and made up over it. You ought to be used to the look of that by now."

"I'm sorry you're tired. You've been up all day, I expect."

"Yes, I have."

"Would you like some coffee?"

"No, thanks. I've just had some."

"You must have an early night. You'll feel better then."

"I shouldn't wonder. I hardly could feel worse."

Out of a cold solitude Vivian looked up at the unknown young man with whom Mic, departing, had left her. It was terrible that he should be so like Mic. She must not let him see she was afraid.

"In that case it would be almost more convenient if I slept at the hospital, wouldn't it?"

"If you prefer that. Did you enjoy yourself?"

Vivian's self-control gave away.

"For the love of heaven, Mic, make any kind of scene you like except this kind. I ought to have told you I was going: I know that. Black my eye if it makes you feel better. But this sort of thing's impossible and I can't stand it."

"There was no need for you to tell me. Why should you?" His cool tautness suddenly left him. He said, quietly, "Your time's your own. If I've been behaving as if I had a claim on it, I apologise. It will be soon enough to think about that when I can ask you to marry me."

Vivian put her hand up to her head. If only she had slept, she thought, she could deal with this. There was a right thing that could be said. But she could not find it. She could only feel the irritable protest of her weariness at being asked to make the effort. The knowledge that she was about to fail made her desperate: her desperation flooded into anger.

"Mic, we can't labour through all that again. I've tried to tell you I'm not something on hire-purchase. I belong to you now as much as I ever shall however much you marry me and keep me, and you'd better make up your mind to it."

"I've done that," said Mic slowly, "already."

She felt she could have screamed and beaten on the walls of emotion that shut them in as one might on the walls of a cell; flinging her weight in helpless fury at Mic's limitations and his tortured awareness of them, at her own worn-out nerves and defiant fear.

"My dear, we *must* pull ourselves together. It's so futile, such waste. After all, what's really happened? Nothing."

"I suppose not," said Mic wearily. "One should submit these things to reason. It's easy enough to talk about it. I can't do it, that's all. I can only see you coming in at that door." His jaw tightened: she saw that their weak attempt at exorcism was over. "Have you seen any of Scot-Hallard's other women? Because I have."

"His . . . Mic, have you the least idea what you're saying? Do have some self-control. You must be out of your mind."

"I beg your pardon. His women, then. But you evidently have seen them, to give such a good impersonation." He glanced down at her dress.

"Don't be disgusting." She was losing her temper; she felt it going half in fear, half in angry satisfaction. A mixed ferment rose in her: hurt pride: she thought that the dress had cost more than she could afford; the certainty that he would have liked it if she had not worn it for Scot-Hallard first. Her brain seemed to grow hot and light, to expand, and throw off words like steam which smoked away from her before she could examine them "Haven't you enough intelligence to see when you're being simply pathological? I'm wearing a perfectly normal outfit that you can see in every shop and every magazine, and no more make-up than most women put on every day of their lives. Good God, Mic, are you going to raise hell like this every time I show signs of leading an ordinary social life? Because if so let's get the thing clear. I'm not going to spend the rest of my life slopping about in tweeds and an old shirt just because you can't stand the sight of a woman unless she's half got up as a——" She paused, biting her lip.

Mic's face seemed to be uninhabited. "Yes? Please go on. Better to have it clear, as you say."

Where are we going? cried her bruised and terrified mind.

It was like feeling one's clothing caught in a machine: seeing what was coming, struggling impotently to get free.

"I'm sorry, Mic. I'm sorry. I didn't mean that."

"Didn't you? I thought you did. I shouldn't go back on it, it's probably true."

"No. I ought not to have said it."

"It isn't important."

The thing could not have happened, protested her remorse and fear, so easily, with these few seconds' worth of words. There must be some hand-hold that could drag them back again. She groped for it, clumsy with panic.

"Mic, we must stop working up this fever. It's madness, we're neither of us responsible for what we say. Listen. I did flirt with Scot-Hallard, in a trivial way. He kissed me once. That's absolutely all. I don't blame you if you were jealous for a minute. But you know it means nothing. You know really. Don't keep on."

His eyes travelled over her. She saw again that flinching speculation.

"Oh, Scot-Hallard kissed you."

"Of course he did. You knew that as soon as I came in."

"Was it nice?"

"It was amusing, for a second or two. What *does* it matter, to us? Try to keep some sense of proportion."

"Evidently I haven't one . . . God, how could you? A man like Scot-Hallard. How *could* you? It just makes me want to be sick."

"That's morbid. He isn't vicious: too many other uses for his brains. You ought to know that."

"I know enough about Scot-Hallard." She saw that he had gone white. His eyes looked unnaturally large and dark, like the dilated eyes of someone drugged. "He's gross. All he's fit for is hanging around brothels, but he knows his way about too well for that. Seduction's cheaper and more hygienic. I shouldn't think he ever wasted a minute's honesty or kindness on a woman in his life. He's filthy. . . . You know that, and still you go out with him. And without even having the decency to clean him off you, you come back here to me made up like one of his worn-out tarts, with smears of paint where he's mucked you about, and expect me to enjoy it. . . . Go back to him, if he gives you such a damned good time. If that's what you like I don't see what use you can have for me."

"That's more than enough, Mic."

They looked at one another, amazedly remembering the times when they had neither known nor cared where one mind and body ended and the other began. That they could become this. From the friend, the lover—the face seen without eyes in the darkness, the whisper before the kiss, the silence after—had been made this impenetrable thing, this sharpened and hardened instrument of pain.

"Yes. I'm sorry." He sat down on the edge of the table. The incandescence had died down; he looked tired and drawn. "It's what I feel, but I might have expressed it with a little more restraint."

"What does it matter how you express it? If we can do this to one another it's no good going on. We were happy while it lasted, but it's better we know in time. Good-bye."

He got up. "Where are you going?"

"Anywhere. Back to be myself again, if I can."

"Vivian. We ——" Hesitatingly, he came towards her.

"No. Go away from me. Stay away. Mic, if you come near me again and touch me as if I were a new kind of dirt, I'll hit you in the face. Go away, I can't bear any more. For God's sake let me go."

She had been backing away from him: now with a stumbling swerve she snatched open the door and ran down the stairs into the street. As she went she thought she heard the door open again behind her; but the rattle of her own feet drowned it. The street door closed. The lamp threw her lengthening shadow before her; for each of her halting steps it shot forward with a great stride, till its head was hidden in darkness.

It had happened. She was alone.

SHE walked back, through the streets, through the hospital gates, through the passages. Someone said, "Hullo, Lingard, got nights-off?" and she said "Yes," and felt her face move in a smile.

Up in her room her uniform was thrown over a chair, as she had left it in the morning. On the locker was a book that Mic had lent her, with a pencilled note from him marking the page. She pulled it out and began slowly to tear it up. The strips she made were horizontal, and on one of them she read, "I wish you were here. If you were——" Her fingers moved more quickly, tearing the strips into finer and finer pieces.

She undressed, and had a bath. She seemed a shell of physical sensations, the heat of the water, the slipperiness of the soap, the towel's friction, giving entity to a consciousness which, without their definition, would have trickled away, like fluid from a broken glass.

She cleaned her teeth, put out the light, and got into bed. Her mind felt so blank that it vaguely surprised her to find herself unable to sleep. There was no sequent thought in her head: she lay with her eyes wide open, looking upward at a slant of light across the ceiling. As a cracked gramophone record repeats endlessly the same phrase, her brain reproduced over and over what had happened, their voices, their words, Mic's face and the changes of his eyes, ending always with the neat full-stop of the slammed door. She did not think, "If I had said this, if I had thought of that in time." She simply saw and heard, heard and saw. She tried to deaden her mind and be still, thinking of the length of days ahead and wanting to lose a little of their duration now in sleep.

In the early morning she fell into a half-doze, from which

she was wakened by the maids hammering on the day-nurses' doors. She tried to hold the blankness of sleep round her, knowing even before she had gone that something terrible was waiting to spring at her out of the light. But the blankness receded, inexorably, leaving her naked to recollection. When she had dressed she wandered out into the town to get something for breakfast, so as not to have to go into the dining-room. There were two more days and two nights to do nothing in before she went back to work.

On her way in she found a parcel, addressed to her. The writing was Mic's. She felt for a moment a dull wonder that from her life which was over this could emerge into the present; then everything was cut through by an agonising stab of hope. She pulled off the wrapper: it was her gown and slippers, with her afternoon bag of yesterday on the top; all very well folded and packed, the bag wrapped separately. There was no letter, no message of any kind. She took them back to her room and put them away.

In the afternoon, having found that she could not read with any understanding of what was in front of her, she drifted into a cinema. The film was a sea-story, and for a little while she escaped into it. The thought, "If I could only get back to it, there is a whole world of simple things, horses, men working with their muscles, birds flying, ploughland and the sea. Perhaps one day I may find some peace in that." Then the scene shifted to the inside of a cottage, to a hackneyed, sentimental love-scene. At the moment of the kiss the young man turned his back to the lens: the shape of his bent head was a little like Mic's, and he had dark soft hair, through which the girl stroked her fingers. Vivian rose, and went out into the cold cloudy afternoon.

On the second day she felt herself sinking into a stagnation which was worse than suffering, because it seemed less clean. It gave her a loathing of herself: she thought that she was, after all, a temporary vessel for part of the life of the universe, and if she had forgotten how to use it had at least no right to let it rot and stink. With no end in view but to keep up some belief in herself, she dressed in her best walking clothes, put a few touches to her face and hair, and went out.

She was on the outskirts of the town, in a street of scattered houses that trailed away into a lane, when a car stopped beside her and Scot-Hallard's voice said, "I was expecting to meet you today."

He was exactly the same: his strength, his vitality, his air of being a natural ruler of his own terrain and not much concerned with any other. He was the first thing she had seen, since this began, that looked the same as before.

"Were you?" she said. "Why?"

"Possibly because I'm tenacious of an idea." He looked quickly along the road towards the houses. "We can't talk here. Get in." He opened the door. His will, imposed on her unresisting inertia, moved her into the car as if he had picked her up and lifted her in.

"Why did you run away from me?" he said.

"Run? I only continued on my way."

An answer from the property-box; what Mic had called "boy-meets-girl-manœuvres". That was after he first kissed her. Sudden and inescapable, like an animal springing from cover, the memory leaped at her; the wall she had been looking at turning into the ceiling as he pulled her back, then into his face: the feel of his hair, dry on the surface, but still damp from swimming when she held him tightly. . . . This cannot be lived with, she thought: it must be destroyed, something, anything, must take it away. To escape it, she threw her perceptions outward again. Scot-Hallard was saying something. With struggling concentration she got hold of the word "elusive." He was telling her something about herself, and she tried to look intelligent. There was an observation, then, about the art of living. It consisted in something else, which, at the moment of throwing back another memory from the ramparts of her mind, she missed. Refusal of life (she got a whole sentence here) was the only sin against the Holy Ghost. His property-box was much better stocked than hers.

She was like Brünnehilde, he said, encircled by fire and refusing to cross it, waiting for someone to carry her over.

"What do you say," she asked in momentary interest, "to small women? Under about five feet four, I mean? The Sleeping Beauty in the hedge of thorns? Siegfried certainly does suit you better than the Fairy Prince."

He looked, before he had time to conceal it, quite affronted. It occurred to her that he had perhaps, after all, thought up this simile especially for her, and she regretted her ungraciousness. A certain amount of experience, she thought, digested with imagination, could make a man or woman alluring; but too much dulled the edges, gave a stale and handled taste of which a fresher palate could not fail to be aware. Everything he said had the ring of worn coin, his most intimate looks were like stock phrases. He had recovered his assurance in time to laugh and make some retort: the game went on, a ritual, with the predictable regularity of a phallic dance.

("What about me, then?"—"You're simply you." Someone must take the candles away, their light was burning her.)

Scot-Hallard, when she came back, was saying, "I've been trying to analyse your individual flavouring. A very dry sherry—olives—salted almonds none of those is quite right ——"

With a thrust of her mind she overturned the candles and smothered out their intolerable light. "But who," she asked, "is the meal with which you're proposing to follow this *hors d'œuvre*?"

He smiled at her. (She noticed that he had fine teeth, uneven but white and strong.) It was a smile simple in intention, but containing, beside its message, many things: anticipation, calculation; a disenchanted tenderness, and the thin shreds of some faded dream. She understood at that moment that his satisfactions had become cheap and crude because he now preferred them to be so; that he had pursued from woman to woman some expectation long grown weary, and was beginning to know in secret that its failure lay within himself. A

241

still pity filled her: for him, for herself, for the confusion of mortality. Her pasteboard weapons lay idle. She leaned back in the car beside him, her hands loosened in her lap, wondering why she had resented or been scornful of him, a fellow-creature like herself who had missed his way; and thought how trivial the thing was that he asked for, in comparison with what he had to give—all these hours of not being alone with herself, of having no leisure to think or to remember.

He stopped at the first telephone-box they came to. She knew he was ordering tea at his house and giving his man the evening off. She could see his face through the glass, brisk, composed, dispatching a familiar routine. Her hand tightened on her knee: she saw the charwoman with her American cloth bag and her cup of tea, and Mic, taking the stairs in threes and fours, and running to her out of breath. For the first time in these days, she felt the ache of tears behind her eyes. She forced them inward, beneath the smile she was preparing.

— 20 —

Vivian's first thought, when she woke in her own bed next morning, was to remember with relief that she would be on duty that night. It was good to know that in scarcely more than twelve hours she would be doing something whose purpose was unrelated to herself, and which had a slight but undeniable usefulness.

Her feelings about the evening before had a curious dimness and inconsequence. It had all been so like expectation that she might almost as easily have been anticipating as remembering it. But it had left behind, in her thoughts of Scot-Hallard, a kind of weary affection and respect. Mic had been wrong about him; he was kind within his limits, and had a careless instinctive honesty which had relieved the affair of such squalors as might have made it unendurable. He did not try to explain away the fact that he had no idea of marrying her; nor tell her a moving story about the woman who had ruined his life; nor say that she was different, or sympathetic, or that she understood him. But he offered the honours of war with courtesy and a certain amount of charm. The most disconcerting thing had been his elaborate code of manners; she was unused to it and it faintly disgusted her, reminding her of the comic papers in which people addressed one another as "Colonel" or "Miss Smith" in bed.

The small element of primitive female in her had, she supposed, been satisfied. He seemed pleased with her, and genuinely anxious that she should visit him again.

"I know less about you than ever," he said at parting. "You're a peculiarly intact sort of person, aren't you?"

She had smiled and gone away, leaving behind her, like a garment, the personality he had created in her, which seemed irrelevant to herself.

It had filled the evening and rescued her from thought, which was all that she had asked. But now that it was over, she regretted it. Not that she felt herself invaded or possessed —she thought that few experiences she could remember had left less mark on her—but because she knew now that retreat had weakened her. In the half-hour before she met him, some beginning of resolution and courage had been moving in her. Now her will felt drugged, as it had when she crept out of the stuffy cinema, leaving her more sensible than ever of pain.

And now pain was returning. The alienness of the emotional climate she had passed through made her long for Mic with a bitter nostalgia for which nothing offered relief. The numbness of the first shock was over: pain defined her, and kept her alive. Perhaps she felt more because last night, for the first time in weeks, she had slept soundly and long.

She knew that, as she had come to understand love, she would never love anyone else. In time she might settle with someone into some kind of mutual kindness: she would take what offered, since life had somehow to be spent. But in Mic she had struck her balance. It was a thing, once found, for which there was no substitute: and it was not one which nature, out of all her plenty, would be likely to reproduce.

Grief for the loss of it seemed sometimes great enough to fill the world. But behind it was the terror of greater and ultimate loss: the loss of herself.

"Hullo," said Rodd, under the green pool of the lamp. "Had a good binge?"

"Marvellous, thanks. Have you been busy?"

"Busy, we've had everything. That bloody little wet Jacobs, who did your nights-off, let a double hernia get out of bed."

"What happened, did the stitches hold?"

"Yes, they were Scot-Hallard's, thank God. I got sent to Matron, though. Have to watch our step now."

Rodd seemed genuinely glad that she was back again; and

this made her feel unreasonably moved. She remembered all the nights when she had worked with half her thoughts elsewhere, or had only pretended to listen when Rodd talked about her trousseau and her boy. They were busy that night: a patient came in with a perforated stomach ulcer, and little Rosenbaum came up to the ward after the operation to give an intravenous saline. The patient was badly collapsed, and the necessity of self-forgetfulness brought her the first taste of something like peace. When she was clearing away the stained instruments she looked at Rodd, at Rosenbaum's crimped black head bent over the hand-basin, and at the sunken-eyed man propped in his high pillows: and, like the Mariner, blessed them unaware.

During the supper which they had after duty, someone leaned over to her and said, "There's a note in your pigeonhole, Lingard."

"Oh. Thank you." She blinked in a sleepy irritation: she had noticed on the face of her informant a familiar kind of smile.

"Been there since last night. Didn't you know?"

She played for a moment with a wild conjecture that Scot-Hallard had had the madness to write to her in his own hand; but that would have been a sensation out-topping smiles. Suddenly she found she could not eat any more. As soon as the meal was over she got the note and took it into a quiet corner by herself.

She had known. It was from Mic: the shortest letter he had ever sent her.

"I want to ask you to forgive me. If that's possible, will you come on Sunday? I shall wait for you." Half a line was crossed out, then, "I don't suppose there is much you will need me to explain.

"I love you. But perhaps I've no right to love anyone. If you don't come I shall know that is what you have decided, and accept it."

Sunday was today.

She walked unseeingly to her room, with the letter in her

hand, and began to take off her uniform. The release was too great: it seemed to choke her; that or the shame that came with it, to think that, alone as she had not dared to be alone, he should have forced himself to this.

She had not thought of him, except as something that had hurt her, something she had lost. Having used on him every weapon he had ever put into her hands she had left him, to lick her own wounds and hire herself out in exchange for forgetfulness. She reached for her outdoor clothes, no longer coherently thinking; feeling only the need to be there.

She ran a good deal of the way; but when she reached the door at the foot of the stairs it was a second or two before she could make herself turn the handle.

He opened the door of the flat as she reached it. There was a little pause in which neither of them thought of speaking: a moment of acclimatising themselves to not being alone. They looked into one another's faces. Mic's eyes looked as if he had slept less than she: they had a quiet, and what seemed already a habit of private endurance. He said, "I ——" and stopped. She took a step forward: and suddenly they were not separate any more.

The door stood open. Presently, without letting go of her or taking his lips from hers, Mic put an arm out blindly and swung it to.

They had both had words of some kind ready to say, but nothing came. One does not excuse oneself to one's house when one returns weary from travel. Her arms felt the accustomed shape of his waist and shoulders. There had been a moment, two nights before, when Scot-Hallard was being gentle and charming to her and she had almost wept for strangeness; he had been like a foreign landscape reminding her of exile.

They wandered somehow to the window-seat. "I love you," she said. "I was a fool and a beast and a liar." Mic whispered, "Be quiet,' and kissed her again.

They had done too much to one another with words to trust them easily now, and for a time they used none. Vivian

246

tried to cast out the hauntings of fear which seemed, even here, to shadow her. This, if anything, was certainty; this had always been, and would never have to end. Yesterday, in her room alone, she had remembered them like this; Mic stretched along the seat beside her, the fine crispness of his hair against her neck. Which was, and is, and is to come. She folded her hands about his head, in the crossed gesture with which saints in windows fold their symbol or the instrument of their death. His touch with its love and knowledge was like an absolution. The days of wandering were as if they had never been.

They were leaning against the square panes of the window, in a fold of curtain which Mic with a silent laugh had drawn round them. Outside the bells of the churches were ringing, making thick circles of sound in the Sunday air.

"Why do you still love me?" she said.

He answered her in silence. The hard shell of her emptiness had dissolved; she felt like a warm golden stream, flowing under the sun, the banks of its appointed course embracing it.

He stood up, and offered her his hands. She took them, not moving for a moment, though she knew where he was taking her and was glad. They were still, their hands joined, listening to the bells and watching the people stream by with their thick dark clothes and prayer-books in the street below.

Looking down at her, he said, "Next time anything—happens—I expect you'd better simply lie to me. That seems to be all I'm fit for."

Across Vivian's warmth and radiance fell suddenly the chill of a passing wind. He had spoken easily, in the hour's security, but she knew that he had meant what he said.

She pulled him nearer by the hands and rested her face against his sleeve, trying, in these few seconds that she had, to think. She could not think, she could only hide herself for fear. The cruel perversity of it was that she had not thought till now of telling him. It had not occurred to her as being of any immediate importance. It had become no more than an uncomfortable dream for which, when there was time, she would ask him to comfort her.

Now she understood that she had not shed or evaded it, but brought it with her, everything, down to the trace of stale gardenia on the dressing-gown: delicately, inerasably etched into the accomplished past. It was part of the sum of her, of her hands that he held, of her love itself.

Well, he had told her what to do. It was the evident, the accepted wisdom. This was her punishment, the loss of their completeness, the locking of a room within her where he could never come; to be shut away from him, every now and then, into this small and sordid loneliness.

He smiled and pulled at her hands. Now, she thought, it begins from now; being careful, remembering the things I must not say: hiding the gratitude to him for being himself which I dare not even feel.

"What's the matter?" he said.

Already she had hesitated too long: there was an unacknowledged doubt in his voice, a thrust-back fear. She jumped to her feet and clung to him, knowing only the instant, impatient need to be reassured.

He took her in his arms and said, very quietly. "What is it?"

"You love me. Tell me you do. Tell me."

"Yes," he said, looking down into her face. "I love you. More than I ought."

"Mic, I've loved you always, I swear it. There hasn't been a moment when I've stopped loving you, not a single moment, ever."

He was no longer holding her. His arms were round her, but still and forgotten.

"Darling," she said, panic overriding everything, "I'm the same. Nothing of me is any different. It can't be. I love you."

He let her go. She knew, then, that she had told him.

She thought that she would never escape from the silence. It was like the walls of a glass coffin and she dared not break it.

She waited, prepared for anything which in his pain or

248

anger he might say to her. But his face had only a struggling lostness, as if he had been put down without warning in some hostile wilderness.

At last he said, staring at her as if she were a part of his foreign scene, "But you were only away from me three days."

This was worse than anything she had imagined. Finding voice at last, she said, "I suppose it's in the first days, when one isn't acclimatised and thinks one will go mad, that these things do happen, if they happen at all."

"What things? It's true, then. It can't be true. You must mean something else."

She shook her head.

"Who was it?"

She stared at him in silence. It was true; he had questioned sincerely. Scot-Hallard, Rosenbaum, a man she had picked up in the street—all coherence and all certainties were destroyed by the fact that it had happened at all.

"It was Scot-Hallard," she said.

"Oh, yes. Scot-Hallard, of course."

Dear God, she thought, watching his face, why didn't I say a man who picked me up? That I never heard his name or was too drunk to remember it? He has to look at Scot-Hallard every day. He has to take orders from him.

Mic was looking at her, at her disordered hair and loosened shirt. She knew what he was thinking. Something seemed to dry and shrivel inside her; she put up her hand and closed her collar.

"Mic, you must believe I never wanted anything from him, except not to think for a few hours. If I hadn't minded leaving you more than anything in the world, I could never have done it. You must believe me."

He said, as if he had not heard her, "Did you stay the night?"

"No."

"Good. I feel glad you didn't sleep with him. I don't know why."

"He had nothing you'd recognise as being me. Nothing at all. I was like a different person all the time."

"You adapted yourself to his temperament, I feel sure. Or was it mine that needed more adaptation?"

She could see no impulse of cruelty in his face, only the kind of horror in which people speak aloud to reassure themselves of reason.

"My dear, I beg of you. It wasn't a great enough thing to be worth this misery. If I'd drunk myself blind you wouldn't think of it like this. To me it wasn't any more. You must understand. You must forgive me."

"Forgive you?" He looked at her, at first blankly and then as if she had said something which, though irrelevant, had recalled him to himself. "What has that to do with it? You've done nothing wrong."

"What do you mean? I've just told you."

"You're not my property. You say what you did was natural. I believe you. How should I know? It's I who should ask you to forgive me."

"What are you talking about? Mic, please try and see this reasonably. I would, if it had been you."

"Of course you would. Anyone would who was able to. I can't. To know you could want Scot-Hallard. . . . Even if I were dead, if I'd never existed. . . . It's natural you should, most women do, apparently. I just can't think about it, it's unspeakable, it makes me want to kill the lot of us. . . . I told you I wasn't fit for you or anyone. I know why it is that I feel like this. It isn't your fault. I ought to have kept you clear of me."

She knew then what she had done, but would not believe it.

"You've done your best with me," he said. "You see, it was hopeless. I loved you. But I'd gone too far, I suppose."

"Mic, no. You've got to stop thinking that, you must. Say anything else you like to me. It isn't true."

"I expect I'm the best judge of that. . . . I never had any right to you. I ought to have asked myself whether I could stand this kind of thing. I just didn't think of it. God knows why."

"Mic, *please*. It isn't you, it's—don't you see, I've behaved like a bitch. Of course you mind. Any decent man would. Anyone."

"Not quite like this."

For a little while now he had not looked at her. He had moved gradually back till he was a couple of yards away. He went on, with difficulty, looking mostly at the floor, "Didn't you realise—I thought you would have—that the thought of you playing up to Scot-Hallard, like that woman I—God!"

"It wasn't like that." The words passed over him. She had spoken without hope, knowing that in the essentials it had been like. He knew it too. She wished she could have died.

"I thought, after that" (he was still looking down), "I should never . . . but you were so different. That was why I ——"

She finished for him, in a little flat voice like a child reciting, "That was why you loved me."

"You seemed not to be part of it. Unconscious, like . . . The day you came here and we fenced. I suppose I first wanted you then."

"And now you don't want me any more."

"Let's not go into that."

"My dear."

"Please," he said, and stepped backward. Her hands fell.

He was trying to say something more. She waited: it must be something that would release them, awake them from this dream. He looked up at her as if he had slowly forced himself to do it.

"I wonder if you'd mind going now? I think it would be best. I'm sorry: would you mind?"

"Mic, you can't. You can't simply send me away. I can make everything all right, I always have. You know I have, haven't I? How *can* I leave you like this?"

He had gone over to the bookcase in the corner, and was

turning over a textbook that lay on the top of it, looking first at the front cover, then at the back.

"You've been very good to me. Kinder than anyone in my life. I shall never forget that. Perhaps if I could have married you. But you see, I can't even make money. You'll find someone in a little while who's better adapted to life and can make you happy. Good-bye."

Her mind and body both rejected it. She took him by the shoulders and dragged him round to face her.

"Look at me, Mic. Look at me, I said. You can't give in to this. You've no excuse: you know yourself, you can see beyond it. You loved me before I told you this. You still love me. You can't torment us both like this. Neither of us deserves it. Even I don't. Come here. Now kiss me."

He kissed her.

"Satisfied?" he said when it was over. "You asked me. I'm sorry."

"That's all right, Mic. I asked, as you say. It's funny I still love you, isn't it?"

"You'll get over that."

"Probably. I'll go now."

"I think I should." When she was at the door he said, "Remember, I take the entire responsibility for this. You've nothing to reproach yourself with. You've been very good and very patient; but you can't work miracles. No: I want you to go. Please."

She went, and in the thin light of the lamp her shadow fled and hid its face before her.

THE next-door wireless was still playing Noel Coward. Mic flattened his hands over his ears, and focused again on the close print and double columns of the periodical between his elbows.

"The Chemistry of the Colloids. Some Notes on Recent ——" Realising that he had attacked this page four times without getting to the end of the heading, he turned over in search of something else. As soon as he moved his hands the song came through again, rendered by a light baritone with delicate hesitations and a whimsical, ironic melancholy:

> "Reason may sleep for a moment in spring,
> But please let us keep this a—casual thing;
> Something that's sweet to remember ——"

"Christ!" said Mic, and slammed the window down.

"A Comparison of Basophile Changes in Certain Anaemias". Mic took one of his notebooks down from the shelf, found a place and began to read. A thin sweet trickle of sound still infiltrated somehow through the glass. He copied two diagrams, scribbled them through, and reached for another cigarette. It occurred to him, as he lit it, that thirty-odd cigarettes a day were not helping his cough, which had come back after a cold a fortnight ago; but he had struck the match by then, and it did not seem worth while to waste it.

> "Let's look on love as a—plaything"

pleaded the light baritone, smiling through a sigh.

> "All those sweet moments we've known——"

Mic pushed the litter of books on the table into a heap, and got up. It was only ten o'clock, and if he walked till eleven or twelve it sometimes happened that he slept at the end of it. As he shut the street door, the song's last cadences drifted down after him, in a dying fall:

"Let's say good-bye, and—leave it alone."

It was a raw night; the pavements were damp in the middle with mist, and he shivered after the heat of the gas-fire. The fog made his chest feel rough, and he began to cough again. With a faint shrug he turned his collar up and walked on. He had started and it was not worth turning back.

The lights of the High Street swung past him. Swift movement gave the illusion of purpose, of moving towards some attainment of escape. There were a good many people still about, but, closed in himself, he put out no threads of contact; and passed like a shadow, no eye moving after him. He was used to this, and felt dazed for a moment when a girl detached herself from the window of a cheap jeweller's and fell into step beside him.

"You're a nice boy. All alone?"

"Sorry," Mic said, withdrawing his arm quickly from her outstretched hand. "Good night." He heard the girl titter as she fell behind.

Too late he tried to wrench his mind off the worn groove into which, at this reminder, it had slipped with a sickening, accelerated spin. No use. He swung on, past the town, in the first greyness of a hidden moon.

At half-past eleven he decided that he was probably tired enough. His brain and body had settled into an exhausted emptiness which, even if he could not sleep, was almost anaesthetic. He must sleep, though, if he could; his mind had developed, lately, a habit of snapping off, like an interrupted circuit, at moments when he was concentrating hard. Whenever he could nowadays he always put his reports aside to check again, and, if he had to let an urgent one go out immediately, would go over and over it in his mind, imagining slips and errors which, so far, he had not made. A few more nights like last night, and he would begin to make them. Eventually he would make one for Scot-Hallard. Scot-Hallard did not pass errors without comment; and Mic wondered, with a cold feeling, which of several things would happen then. His train of thought was interrupted by another coughing-fit, which hurt.

It was time, he thought, switching on the staircase light to look at his handkerchief, that he put his sputum underneath the microscope again. He was inclined to postpone it, which was, after all, unfair to the people round him. There had been nothing last time. Sometimes he thought that if he found anything it would be a relief; he would be in no doubt then what to do.

Something white on the floor caught his eye. It was a letter, which he must have missed on his way out. Mostly they were mistakes for the shop underneath. But this one was from Colin, to whom he had owed a letter for nearly six months.

Upstairs he smoothed the thin sheets out on the table. The same fifth-form sprawl, running downhill at the end of the lines. ("That's an awfully bad sign of character," Colin had informed him proudly on the first day they met.)

It appeared, after the station scandal, and a bored, but wicked, account of a moonlight picnic, that Colin's wife had at last made up her mind to divorce him, and he was arranging the evidence. (Colin was rather amusing about this.) Afterwards he hoped to get a transfer to Bairanpur. Had Mic heard of the Bairanpur Institute of Tropical Diseases? They were always shouting for pathologists, and, incidentally, paid rather well.

"I wonder what you look like now," it ended. "Have you grown a beard or anything? And do you still quote funeral orations at the most conspicuously unsuitable moments? I always remember *Urne-Burial* up the river that day, and how

I laughed and how bloody cold it was when you threw me in."

Mic remembered it too, very well. "But Man is a Noble Animal, splendid in ashes, and pompous in the grave, solemnising Nativities and Deaths with equal lustre, nor omitting ceremonies of bravery in the infamy of his nature." He had known that day, for the first time certainly, that Colin would forget him.

He remembered that earliest afternoon, near the beginning of the autumn terms; fine September weather; they had shared a study for a week.

"Will you kindly stop your benefit performance, Mansel, and let me do some trig? What the hell *are* you playing the fool like this for, anyway?"

And Colin, sprawled along the edge of the table,

"Because I like watching you laugh."

Silence, and light, in which even the past was altered; a dark wall falling, distances opening of power and value; the shock of beauty, the fear of entertaining awkwardly this unaccustomed guest.

Re-reading the paragraph about the Institute, he discovered with a distant wonder that he exercised, even now, a certain power over Colin's mind. Colin had hinted, not suggested, that he might go out. He played with the idea, and found it beginning to solidify. He had done very little tropical pathology, but enough to make a start on, if he worked. There would at least be an escape from the daily, exhausting effort to be sane when Scot-Hallard came into the laboratory and spoke to him.

He was returning the letter to its envelope when he noticed that this still contained something. It was a glossy clear snapshot, sharply etched by a vertical sun. Colin was standing under a palm tree that made him a crossed background of black swords, dressed in white for polo, his sun-helmet tilted back from his face. Mic looked at it for a minute or two; then slowly took the old one from its drawer and laid them side by side. Yes; in the midst of so much grace and lightness it had all been there. In that gaiety the facetiousness of an arrested mind; this smugness in that endearing vanity. How quickly that dragon-fly inquisitiveness had been satisfied with the second-rate! He had set and thickened; his face was looser on the bone; he looked as if he overdrank a little as a matter of course. He was laughing, like one who must always be amused lest a pause for thought engulf him.

Mic slid the photographs one over the other, and tore them through the middle. Solemnising nativities and deaths —he thought, crookedly smiling—with rather unequal lustre. The light thin flakes of the letter went after them into the basket. He sat staring in front of him, seeing not Colin any longer, but Vivian looking down at the picture, thrusting her tumbled hair out of her eyes. He remembered a little movement of her hand along the bed towards him, accepting everything. Her face had been like Jan's and yet not like: it was as if the rock had been smitten, and given forth a spring of water.

He got up from the table, and returned his books to their places on the shelves. He was tired to death, but it was useless to hope for sleep. If he had had access to drugs, he supposed he would have been taking something by now. Rosenbaum would probably provide it within reason; but so far he had been ashamed to ask. He threw himself down, dressed, on the bed, lit another cigarette, and wondered whether she was with Scot-Hallard tonight; for Scot-Hallard was not likely to be tired of her yet. As if a cinema-projector over which he had no control were playing on his brain, he saw her leaving her room (of which he had always had a clear imaginary picture), leaving the hospital, passing through the streets, into Scot-Hallard's house. He shut his eyes, but the film went on unrolling, through his eyelids, through his skull. . . .

He must have killed Scot-Hallard, by now, in five or six different ways. How long could this violence go on before it destroyed his mind? It was like an ape with an iron bar let loose among instruments of precision. In the morning he repaired the wreckage, always a little less securely.

To distract his eyes from the pictures behind them, he began to blow smoke-rings in elaborate patterns and chains. Presently a deep inhalation made him cough again; so he did not hear the footsteps on the stairs, nor the opening of the door outside.

– 22 –

Vivian had visited Scot-Hallard that evening, for the first time since she had left Mic. He had asked her for some time to promise him her first free night; but she had not, till now, reached the necessary pitch of indifference to herself. She would have been willing enough to make herself useful to anyone who really needed her—it would have given her life a brief appearance of meaning—but with Scot-Hallard it had seemed so certain that any woman out of three or four would do. His invitations were, of course, all conveyed or refused by letter; but one night, when he had remained at the hospital unusually late, they had passed one another on an empty section of the stairs; he had paused for a minute and made as if to speak, and it seemed to her that he remained silent less from caution than from hurt pride. To find him even so far assailable by her had touched her; she had smiled as she passed, and next day, when he wrote asking her again, had accepted.

While she dressed herself she wished, as she wished every day, that she could afford to get herself a new dress, new underclothes, new powder, a new brush and comb, everything new that she had worn or used with Mic. It would have helped a little; but not much, since no one would sell her a new body and she could not throw her memory away.

Gradually, she supposed, a rubble of small things would sift into this great hole in her life, and loosely fill it. Slight purposes, accumulating, would give her a kind of movement.

She was walking through the streets to Scot-Hallard's house when an intolerable blackness seemed to leap like a visible thing upon her mind. She tried to fight it off, reasoning with it, for she had been feeling only the dulled emptiness into which lately she had settled; but it defied reason.

Suddenly she was sure that it was Mic's misery she was receiving, as perhaps unknowingly she had often received it before. It was not a call any longer: there was no answer. In her helplessness, not able to bear more self-reproach, she began to reproach him. It was the fault of his own weakness, he had made no effort, accepted defeat. It should have been in his power to pass this test.

But she found no comfort for herself in these excuses. By the time she reached Scot-Hallard's house the brittle façade of gaiety which, before she set out, she had constructed for herself, had cracked away. There was only a forced brightness, with irritability close behind. She responded to the embrace with which he greeted her deliberately, moved simply by a determination to carry out what she had begun. He offered her a cocktail; they talked with animation but without zest. Like an encroaching dampness there settled into the room the feeling that the party was going to be a failure.

She thought that if she made the conversation impersonal for a little while things might improve; for intellectually he had always the power to interest her. Presently she succeeded in getting him launched on the European situation. He straightened one or two tangled patches in her mind, and passed on, with his usual suppressed gusto, to the approach of war. The Experimental Station, he said, was testing a new and secret gas which seemed in every respect ideal. Unfortunately it was, at the moment, useless because it was unsuitable for dispersal by aircraft, and could not be projected by infantry since, so far, no protection against it had been evolved.

"Thank God for that," Vivian said; but, warmed to his subject, he supposed her to be rejoicing in the efficacy of the gas.

"As a matter of fact," he said, "we have a new mask which I think may possibly do. We've tried it on various animals but the results have been patchy. However, I think presently we shall be ready for a few human experiments. I've had one volunteer: young Freeborn, in the Path. Lab. Courageous, but the boy's a crank."

"I thought he was a pacifist." She listened with surprise to her own voice, which seemed unaltered. "Why did he volunteer?"

"Oh, he imagined it was something for the protection of the civil population, I believe. Wanted an assurance that the experiments were for purely defensive purposes, or some half-baked rubbish. As I told him, to suppose that attack and defence can be kept water-tight in modern war is simply to go about in blinkers. He wouldn't have done in any case. I shouldn't consider myself justified, at this stage, in using a latent tuberculous subject."

Vivian became slowly conscious of a cold dampness over her knee. It was her cocktail, which had tipped sideways in her hand.

"What?" she asked.

Scot-Hallard raised his voice patiently. She remembered how he hated being asked to repeat himself in the theatre.

"I said, you can't separate attack and defence in modern warfare. I told Freeborn so."

"Yes." She passed her fingers over the splash on her dress, feeling its slight stickiness. "I meant, how did you find out—that about him? How did you tell?" Through the damp place she could feel the coldness of her hand against her knee.

"How?" Scot-Hallard's voice was a little bored. "Oh, by looking chiefly. Got all the obvious signs. Take a look at him yourself next time you're up there. The temperament, too—up and down, gets these typical moods of depression. I ignore them, of course. He'll do good work if he lives long enough."

Vivian discovered her handkerchief in her hand, rubbing at the patch on her skirt. She looked at it curiously, having no recollection of taking it out; she was, however, pleased to see it since it gave her something to do till she could speak.

"Did you tell him?" she said.

"My dear Vivian." He was annoyed to the verge of exasperation; no doubt she had irritated him in the first place by spilling her drink. He hated clumsiness. "You'll learn as you go on to take these things less dramatically." Dramatisation was a particular phobia of Scot-Hallard's, as all his students knew. "The boy isn't half-witted. He's educated and has medical knowledge. Of course he knows. Apart from ill-luck it's in his own hands; if he lives reasonably and takes the proper precautions, probably it will never light up at all. As a matter of fact, I did hint the other day that he was letting himself lose too much weight. He got his back up at once, so I let it drop. These people are always difficult."

"And these gas tests. Is he doing any others?"

"Certainly not. He should have had more sense than to suggest it. Heroics, I suppose. Half these pacifists are scared, and the rest are foolhardy."

"If you don't mind," said Vivian, "I think I'll just go to the bathroom and get out this stain with warm water."

"I'll get you a dressing-gown, then you'll be able to take it off."

"It's all right, thank you. It isn't big enough for that."

She stood in the bathroom, among the nile-green enamel and chromium showers, pressing her hands over her face. It had been foolish, she now realised, to go into a place by herself; if once she let her face go she might not be able to put it right again. Scot-Hallard would know if she had been crying. He knew so much about women. He might even remember what they had been talking about before. That seemed the one thing left that she had not done to Mic.

She set her face and made it up again, then remembered the stain on her dress and sponged it over. When she came back Scot-Hallard had shaken her another cocktail. He came behind her chair and offered it to her with a kiss. No doubt he thought they had wasted time enough.

He was trying to make her talk about herself. She listened to her own voice answering, gay and evasive. "You're not drinking your cocktails," he reminded her. "Is it too dry? I'll mix you another."

"No. It's just right." She swallowed it obediently, like a dose of medicine, thinking, He's afraid I'll be no good in bed.

They had supper; she managed to eat something, though

she could not afterwards have said what it was. When they got back into the other room he said, "I hope the frock will recover, because it's extraordinarily effective. Let's hang it over the radiator and complete the cure. Shall we?"

It was fastened at the neck with a painted clasp. Standing behind her, he slipped his arm round her shoulder and loosened it. It was what Mic had done, the first time she had worn it for him. Her hand flew to her throat, and she moved away. She remembered the lift of one eyebrow and a little upward murmur by way of saying "Please"—they had only been lovers for a week—and his smile, as if he could not quite get over his surprise and amusement at finding himself doing this kind of thing. Scot-Hallard was looking surprised too, but not very much amused. She shut the clasp again.

"Donald," she said. "You'll have to forgive me. I'm behaving like a cad, I know. I'm going home."

"I'm sorry." He was looking at her in thought rather than anger. Not to have understood a woman was a scientific defeat; not to have been to bed with her was an inconvenience, easily repaired.

"I came meaning to stay," she said. "I can't explain. Will you forgive me?"

"My dear, that's hardly called for. Your enjoyment is as essential as mine. And there will be other evenings, I hope. You must let me drive you back."

He was behaving charmingly and had evidently reached some conclusion that satisfied him. From the solicitude with which he offered to drive her, she guessed what it was. He knew so much about women; about people so little.

When she found herself in the High Street it did not occur to her that she could have been anywhere else. She looked up, as she had always looked, at the windows to see which room he was in. They were both darkened. She stood unable for a moment to take it in. He had always been there, waiting for her, at the times when she had known that she must go.

It was only a little after half past ten. He never slept so early. Commonsense made it obvious that he was out; but she went up the stairs, hearing the stillness before she knocked. The place is empty, she said to herself, I knew it all along. But in her mind she saw him lying dead, changed from himself, removed from all concern with her; sternly alone, and forbidding, like the dead people she had seen.

She knocked again, and the bare little landing gave the sound back to her. She could not go away. Suddenly she remembered that somewhere in her bag she must still have her key. She had never thought of it till now. At first she could not find it, but presently felt its outline with a pencil and loose coppers in the bottom. She opened the door, and waited for a moment before she had courage to switch on the light. The door from the living-room to the bedroom stood open, so she could see at once that there was no one there. She came to herself, ashamed immediately of her impertinence in invading what was, even in his absence, still part of his privacy and no longer anything to do with her. But she could not leave without looking round, if it were only out of homesickness. Nothing was obviously changed; but everything seemed, somehow, perfunctory; it had the feel that places have which are cared for by people who do not live in them.

She closed the door after her, and stood for a few minutes on the landing, aimlessly. She had suffered before, but not this destructive sense of ruin and of waste. For the first time she comprehended fully how many of her faculties lay unused without her. She felt unlived-in, like this room. But she had wasted more than herself.

It had been enough to know that she had spoiled the lover in him. When he had returned to his weary self-acceptance, it had been as if she had killed a child that had held out its hands to her. She had thought that was all; it would have been sufficient.

She had never thought very greatly of herself; it had seemed a strange and terrible thing that she should have power to kill a love, not conceivable that she had power to kill a man.

His mind might recover from her. He had the honesty that

can look on at passion, and the knowledge of freedom. But there was not time. She knew that now. She saw his face again as she had seen it through the closed door; remote and mask-like, refusing her quietly as the dead refuse. His absence now, even, seemed deliberate, the beginning of that rejection.

She went back to the hospital, undressed and got into bed. Her mind travelled over all those small indications which now, remembered, seemed so plain. Then, suddenly, her mind was silent. She had received a familiar message, changed from its first simplicity and darkened, but not to be mistaken. She wondered how often it had come before, when she had been shut in her own misery and unable to receive it. She lay for a little while, feeling recognition passing into certainty; feeling the darkness also, and afraid. Then she dressed again, and went out.

She could see the lights in the window from a long way off, and her footsteps grew slower. At the landing door she had her hand already raised to knock, when she heard him coughing. It sounded loud, and frighteningly painful. She knocked sharply, but the noise went on. Once she had seen a man haemorrhage from the lungs, and now suddenly and horribly remembered it. Without thinking any more, she got out her key and went in.

At the same moment, everything grew quiet. The light shone slanting from the inner room. The door was half-open; Mic was lying on the bed, propped on one arm, with a cigarette in his hand. She stopped short; she had been prepared for him to look ill, but was confused by his apartness—they seemed separated already by many years of experience—and by the fact, somehow unforeseen, of his not having expected her. There was in his eyes neither welcome nor hostility; rather disbelief, and even a kind of fear, as if she had appeared in answer to some unholy incantation.

"Mic."

He sat up, and, after a moment, said, "What are you doing here?"

"I'm sorry. I meant to knock."

"Yes," he said slowly. "I think you might have."

"I heard you coughing and I—thought you were ill."

"I'm quite well, thanks. I've been smoking too much."

There was a silence.

"What is it?" he said. "Do you want anything?"

She had been prepared for anything except this exclusion. It was as if one of the unnoticed stabilities of life, like the earth's firmness, had given way. Then she looked at him again. The aloofness of his face was willed and set. She knew that after all she had not been mistaken.

"I only came," she said, "to see how you were, and—if there was something I could do."

He gave a thin little smile, and got up. "It was good of you to come. But it's better, really, you know, that we don't meet. It only makes things more difficult. Don't you think so?"

"It needn't," she said.

He had turned away, but faced round and looked at her.

"What does that mean?"

"I'm here. It's all right. You don't have to pretend."

He walked over to the door, and stood half in the darkness of the other room.

"You ought to have known better," he said after a pause, "than to come here."

"I did, but I came. Don't you want me to stay?"

"No."

"Why not?"

He said, speaking into the shadows, "Because I've loved you."

"You don't ask me why I came?"

"Must I? A mistaken sense of responsibility, or pity, I suppose."

"I came because I love you."

"I'm sorry. That makes it all the more necessary that you should go."

"Not to me. Don't worry, Mic. If I only have one thing to give you, that's no reason for not giving you anything."

"You don't understand." His face was turned away.

"No. I've found that. But tell me one thing. Would some other woman—anyone else—do as well?"

He shook his head.

"That's all that matters." She threw her coat over the chair.

"What are you doing?" he said, coming back into the room.

"What do you think?" Unfastening the painted clasp, she pulled her frock over her head.

"I haven't asked you to stay, I believe."

But she saw, as she watched him, that he was pretending to a pride that he had lost.

Letting fall the last of her clothes, she paused for a moment. He came over to her; and she was ashamed to have exacted this from him, when she might have gone to him. She returned his kisses as if they had not frightened her. Suddenly he held her away at arm's length, looked at her, and said, "You've been with him tonight."

It was not the words that shocked her, but the voice with its cynical acceptance. The cold of the room began to penetrate her bare body, so that she shivered in his hands.

"I went to him tonight but I couldn't go on with it. I came here. It's the first time I've been to him since I left you."

"Yes?" She knew that he did not believe her. "Oh, well it doesn't matter very much." He pulled her back to him; she embraced him, closing her eyes.

"Do you wish now that you hadn't come?"

"No."

"Well, it's too late if you do."

She tried to laugh. "Don't talk as if you were seducing me, darling, it's silly."

"Damned silly," he agreed; and suddenly hid his face in her hair.

"Mic, dear." He did not answer.

She drew him closer.

"Don't think about it. Just for a little while don't let's think at all."

He whispered unsteadily, "That's a good idea."

As he lifted her—less easily, she noticed, than before—she knew that she had taken from him something with which he had not meant to part: a forlorn honour, a last defence. But still in her heart she could not believe that she would fail. This was a language in which they had never confused or humiliated one another. So, for a moment, she kept clear before her her separate hope and will. But they were too near, as they had always been; she could not hold herself apart from his passion, it invaded and blinded her, she shared even while she feared it. Her mind struggled with her body to remember that he took her in the bitterness of jealousy and a deliberate, disillusioned sensuality: but her mind ceased to be heard. It was he who made her captive, not she who set him free. She offered herself to his crucifixion, not in forgiveness but in a dark delight. Looking up she saw him smiling with fixed eyes, like someone confronting death. "I love you," she tried to say; but it turned to a wordless sound of abandonment in her throat, and as such he answered it. Once he flinched suddenly, and she knew that she had made some gesture strange to him, and acquired elsewhere. She returned the savage kisses he gave her just after; she returned everything. She was destroyed with him, exulting. Then it was all over; the light was still, watching them; he gave a sigh like all the world's weariness, and hid his face beside her. Awaking to herself, she knew that she had failed.

She stooped over him; and without opening his eyes he turned his head into her breast. But it was a surrender she only witnessed, and did not receive. She wondered that the small circle of her arms could enclose so much solitude. The stillness of his face was deeper than sleep; like the quiet of the dying who sink past the consciousness of pain and acquiesce in this release.

His eyes were still closed, and hers travelled over him, counting all the signs which, stupid with love, she had thought so individually himself, and had taken at their simplest aesthetic value; his clear skin, soft dark hair, and long lashes, the fine down that covered his body, the shape of his finger-nails which she had noticed so often without remembering its significance. Concealed in every life was its proper death, waiting for some failure of the host to take possession. Here it was scarcely concealed, but she had not seen. She would always know that she might have stood between it and him, and had failed.

He opened his eyes and looked up at her, but when he would have spoken she laid her hand across his lips. Everything had been said. He turned back to her as if her refusal were a relief. In a little while she felt him grow heavy with sleep, and laid his head softly on the pillow. Sleep was the only thing, she thought, that she had been able to give him. His arm fell back and she saw that he still carried on his left breast the scar of her foil.

She disengaged herself from him cautiously, and rose without waking him. Even when she covered him with the disordered clothes he did not stir. As she was leaving, she noticed the clock which had always been so important. She wound it, and set the alarm to call him in the morning.

So, she thought as she walked back through the empty streets, there was nothing left to try. She had used everything she had. To do more, she must be more than herself. They were insufficient, and that was all.

But early in the morning, when it was still quite dark, it came to her that there was, after all, something left that neither she nor Mic in their lives had so far tried. It was an unpredictable resource; but it was the last, and she used it. Turning on the light, she found pen and paper, and, working slowly and with difficulty at her unfamiliar task, wrote a letter to Cambridge, sending for Jan.

A LIGHT and early snowfall had laced the hanging branches; against dazzling banks the river slid sluggishly, its green bronze looking much colder than the snow. Jan climbed the willow-pattern curve of Clare Bridge, and scraped a place on the parapet for his elbows.

Overhead was a pale-blue, translucent sky, shading to the zenith like the colour in an egg-shell cup. A few clear-edged silver clouds moved in it smoothly. The sun was shining, making crisp blue shadows on the snow against which its strong whiteness seemed golden.

For a few minutes Jan forgot his thoughts and the errand on which he was setting out. He surrendered himself; the sharp beauty pierced and lightened in him. When he returned after an interval which seemed longer than it was, the clearness remained; it was as if part of him still inhabited the crystalled trees and passed their cold judgement on the rest.

He was a thing without roots, he thought; even the constant and unfailing earth was a mistress with whom he had evaded marriage. He was thirty this year, and had not built a house, or planted a tree, or (as far as he knew) begotten a child. He was as transitory as this snow in all his ways.

He tried to feel his own deficiency; but, now as ever, he could not make it become a feeling, only a thought. Dislike of other people, boredom, intolerance, cruelty, imposed limits to life; he had avoided them. Possession and being possessed, longing, the fear of loss, restricted it also; these he had found sometimes peace, sometimes a subtle excitement, in refusing. He wondered again what had planted this duality in him, that his mind could pass on himself censures that his spirit rejected.

His mind returned to Vivian's letter. He took it out, and unfolded it on the damp stone of the balustrade.

"I thought, perhaps, that if he were to see you again he might realise he was comparatively happy before he met me, and come in time to treat all this as irrelevance. It's an escape rather than a solution, but it's all that I can see. You have always had a good deal of influence on him; I dare say you know that."

He had felt, first of all, only wonder. Through what could she have passed to emerge with all her clarity so destroyed? He could hardly believe that it was Vivian who asked this of him. His respect for Mic, even if he could have sunk his own, made it outrageous. He always felt it something of a disgrace to offer, though to people he recognised as inferiors, retreats he would have rejected for himself; and Mic was his friend.

This, he thought, was the kind of disintegration to which people came through losing their identity in one another. He remembered the irrational feeling of misgiving he had had when Vivian wrote to tell him they were lovers; misgiving that was not for them, since he had hoped for this, but as if something of unknown consequence had happened to himself. It had. He had acknowledged a responsibility.

Once more he read the letter over, though he knew its bald phrases nearly by heart; its lost proportion, its humility and futile sacrifice. He could scarcely remember, now, a state of being in which such offerings were possible. There came upon him slowly a sense, not of shame which was an emotion out of his sphere, but of indemnity, of being concerned in atonement; the kind of guilt in which the Greeks believed.

It was time to go, if he was to catch his train. He did not know what he would say or do when he arrived; he could only make himself a blank cheque for the opportunity to fill in. Life was not so lacking in design that an occasion of symmetry would be refused him. Already it was waiting, contained in the present as these black branches contained next summer's leaves.

. . .

He reached the hospital in the early evening and, since everyone he saw seemed fully occupied, found his way along the corridors to the nurses' home. Here he wandered vaguely, in a maze of narrow identical corridors lined with identical doors, scanning the little white name-cards slotted into them. From behind one he could hear voices and laughter; and was about to knock in search of help when crisp skirts rustled, in crescendo, behind him. It was a Sister, out of breath; the one, Jan supposed, responsible for the Home. He smiled, feeling sorry for her because she seemed to carry her responsibilities uncomfortably (like a badly packed rucksack, he thought) as so many women did.

"Can I help you?" she asked. The inflection was that of the constable who says, "Do you wish to make a statement?" As soon as she spoke the laughter had stopped behind the door.

"That's very good of you," he said, replying to the words. He smiled again, in friendly speculation: the face in its white frilled frame shaped itself a little stiffly, into the unaccustomed lines of a reply. "I seem to have lost my way. It's too bad to take up your time, I can see you're busy."

"No, no, not at all; the building is very confusing. Which ward were you looking for?"

"I was trying to find Miss Lingard's room."

Blankness effaced the struggling smile.

"Nurse is resting. In any case I'm afraid ——" Her voice slanted suddenly to a sharper angle. "Was she expecting you, Mr.—er ——?"

"Lingard," said Jan gently.

This was received, for a moment, with a look that removed him from the police-court to Scotland Yard. Then, uncertainly, the smile returned.

"Why, you must be Nurse Lingard's *brother*. There's quite a likeness, when you come to look at it." She hesitated. Jan produced the smile he used for his grandmother, the Customs, and people who arrested him for taking photographs. "Nurse is sleeping, you see, before duty tonight. Otherwise ——"

"It's rather an urgent family matter. I should be enormously grateful."

The Sister was only thirty-six, though she looked more. "Well," she said, "perhaps, in that case . . . But of course, you know, in the ordinary way ——"

"Of course," said Jan. "I quite understand that. Thank you so much."

She led him to a corridor like the rest, but approached through folding doors, after which they tiptoed. ("These are the night-quarters, so if you wouldn't mind making as *little* noise as possible ——") A few moments later, they met a nurse wearing outdoor clothes. At the sight of her the Sister's head jerked like a pointer's. The nurse stood stock-still for a moment, her face stiffening, then went quietly back into the room from which she had come.

"Nurse Lingard's room is Number Twenty-one," said the Sister. She left him; he heard her tap on the nurse's door, and go in without waiting for an answer.

He walked on, watching the numbers on the doors and wondering how women evolved this power of creating intimate hells for one another. A blend, he supposed, of jealousy with the thwarted protective instinct, growing unmanageable with middle-age. Reflecting that Vivian had lived here for nearly a year, he ceased to find it remarkable that her personal relationships had got beyond her. She was of an age, though, to have some resistance. He felt sorry for the young girls.

A door opened just ahead of him.

"Come in," Vivian whispered. "I thought I recognised your step."

She was wearing a dressing-gown. Her hair was untidy, and her face shocked him a little; it looked forgotten, like a blind person's. She greeted him as if she were listening for something else.

"I came here as soon as I could," he said, forgetting to whisper. She said "S-sh," and, when he took out his pipe which he had felt would help, "Would you mind terribly,

Jan? There'll be the most appalling row if they smell smoke in here."

"Let's go out," he whispered. "We can't possibly talk like this."

"I mustn't. I'm supposed to be in bed. I'm on duty to-night."

The only chair was covered with her clothes; so he settled himself beside her on the edge of the bed. "Don't bother with me," she said. "I'm not fit to talk to and you can't do anything about me, so it's only wasting your time. . . . It was good of you to come so soon. You must have taken the first train after you got my letter."

"I missed the good one, or I'd have been here before."

"It doesn't matter. Mic won't be in till just about now."

There was a pause, from which Vivian suddenly retreated. "They might not have let you see me at all. I ought to have warned you, but I forgot."

She reminded him of a sleepwalker, and he longed to rouse her. "I prevailed with the duenna," he said lightly. "My face was my birth-certificate, as usual. But I still feel rather like Macheath superimposed on Caesar Borgia. I didn't appreciate your staying-power till today. Twenty-four hours here would finish me."

She said, unsmiling, with a weary reasonableness, "After all, I was supposed to be in bed, and the woman isn't a pro-curess."

"I guessed that," Jan remarked, "from little things she let drop in the course of conversation."

Vivian's face relaxed for a moment. "What have you been doing lately?"

He began to tell her. For a few minutes they talked in the old way. But presently her attention drifted away, and her face had again the look of listening. He finished what he was saying, and there was a pause in which neither of them spoke.

"I suppose," he said at last, "you told me everything in your letter that you wanted me to know."

She drew a deep breath, which might have been of resolution or relief.

"Everything you need, I expect. You know Mic."

"I wonder. I used to think I knew you."

"Oh, well." Seeing her dim smile, hushed voice, and circled eyes, the disorder of her hair and dress, he felt it, for a moment, in his heart to be angry with Mic.

She saw him looking at her and said, "Don't take any notice of me. Anyone would look a wreck under these conditions. In any case, whatever happens to me I've asked for. If you're too late getting to the flat, Mic may have gone out again."

Jan considered for a moment. She might rest more easily if he went now, letting her think he agreed. But he found it impossible to break the lifelong habit of truth between them. To spare her a direct refusal, he said, "You know, my dear, if Mic thinks I've come in the capacity of a district visitor I can't think of one good reason why he shouldn't throw me downstairs. It's what I'd do."

He had forgotten to whisper again. There was the creak of a bed on the other side of the thin wall; Vivian said, mechanically, "S-sh." Then, "I'm not asking you to go in that capacity."

He was silent; and, staring past him, she went on, "You must know as well as I do that he only noticed me at all because you weren't there."

It was like a dream, he thought, this whispering in a foreign place of the things one never said awake.

"You're the last thing left," she said, "that hasn't let him down."

Jan found his voice. "I doubt if Mic looks at it like that. I've not known him to suffer much from self-pity as a rule."

"He doesn't. But it is so. It's what gives you a chance."

"What kind of chance?" If I force her to words, he thought, it may stop her.

"Jan," she said, "please make him forget me."

He got up, and, one step taking him across the width of

275

the room, found himself looking into the mirror which hung over the chest of drawers. Behind his own face he could see hers, watching him, and thought suddenly how little was left of the likeness which everyone had found so striking. The Sister, he remembered now, had had to have it pointed out to her.

Her reflected eyes met his in the glass, waiting.

"I'm sorry, Vivian." He spoke, without turning, to her mirrored face. "You're worn out and not yourself, or I don't think you'd ask me. In the first place, it's an insult to Mic. One doesn't offer these bolt-holes to one's equals."

"I don't care what it is if it keeps him alive."

"You may not, but he will. Mic cares a good deal about the terms on which he accepts life."

"Less than he did," she said in a whisper he only just caught.

"Probably he's feeling the strain much as you are. But I think one should only offer people what one feels they'd accept in their clearer moments."

"All this is rather abstract, isn't it?" He heard for the first time the edge of bitterness in her voice.

"I'm sorry," he said again. "It isn't to me." He was silent for a moment, searching for the words that would best reach her. "Look here, Vivian. I'm a pure hedonist, as you know. If I thought Mic was more fully himself as he used to be I'd persuade him of it, as far as I could without—personal dishonesty. But I happen to be convinced of the opposite. You know his history, surely, by now. He had a hellish childhood; he's come out of it, on the whole, with singularly little twist. Of course he's introverted, of course he's got a rooted inferiority complex. He copes with that pretty well. And not unnaturally he attached himself violently to the first person he met who didn't seem to think it a pity he'd been born. It happened to be someone young, attractive, and impressionable, with the inevitable result. If you'd been to a public school, you'd—well, anyway, it seems very understandable to me."

"Oh, I know all that." She spoke with the dull assent of one who has been over the ground many times before.

"Then, why, if you know? Surely you see that if you've meant more to him than most women to most men, it's because he probably feels he's completed himself through you. The thing's done now. You can't make water run uphill. It's a pity this business should have happened so soon; adjustments like that take time, of course. But that's done too, and putting back the clock's no answer. In any case, it can't be done. By him or by me. It's only because I know that, that I'm going to see him at all."

She nodded her head. People are right, she was thinking. What did I hope from him? He isn't to blame. A piece of crystal has its own uses; you don't ask it to oblige you by bending in your hand.

"I think," he said, knowing her to be unreconciled, "one has to accept the hazards of growth for other people as well as oneself."

"Why did you come at all?" she asked.

"I hardly know. Perhaps to keep my conscience quiet, or because it was easier than doing nothing. Chiefly I suppose because I'm fonder of you two than I am of anyone else, and because you met through me."

"We should have met."

He saw that she believed this; and a realisation came to him of the shock that had broken her, the destruction of a happiness so instinctive as to have seemed part of natural law and the structure of life. It was a terror he had known and could understand. He saw, in a sudden clear distance and tranquillity, the experience about which for years, though he lived to the pattern of its results, he had not thought at all. Compared with this, it seemed simple and merciful. He had not thought that he would live to submit it to comparison, even to reason. Was it for this that, unknown to himself, he had come? It gave him a sense of deeper debt to both of them than he had felt before.

"One thing I'll do," he said, feeling his futility, "is to make

Mic get his chest examined, if it hasn't been done. Then at least we'll know that's all right."

"There's nothing yet."

"Better to make sure."

"I am sure."

"How can you be?"

She looked down at her hands folded in her lap, and said without expression, "I was with him the night before I wrote to you. He wouldn't have let me stay."

These were deeper waters than Jan had guessed at. In the pause that followed, many things became clear. He said, "I'll do what I can."

"Which means?"

"It means I'll do anything but lie to him."

"I'd hoped," she said slowly, "that you wouldn't make that reservation."

"My dear, I'm sorry. I can only be what I am. Isn't that what you've found too?"

She nodded without speaking.

"You ought to sleep if you've to be on the wards tonight. I'll be going." He got up, and hesitated for a moment. "If nothing any of us can do is any good," he said, "try not to blame yourself, or me too much. Or Mic. Life's made harder than it need be by the human belief that effort could make us capable of perfection. It's part of the evolutionary instinct, but sometimes it has to be put aside. We're each given some shape, I think, which is the most we can fill. If we can feel we've filled it, sometimes we have to be content."

"I haven't filled mine."

He smiled. "Your life's only begun." It was only afterwards that he wondered why neither of them had found this amusing. "Sleep well."

"Good night, Jan. Thank you for coming." As he turned to the door she rose and, as if moved by some sudden impulse of disquiet, came after him and took his arm. "Even if you can't do anything, Jan, I'm glad you came. It's so long since last time. Don't go away without seeing me again, will you?"

"Of course not. I promise. Sleep if you can." He kissed her, and went out. She stood in the doorway, watching him, till he turned the corner of the corridor.

Jan, as he walked to the High Street, wished that Mic ran to a telephone. He would have liked to announce himself from a decent distance; dwellers in small flats were, after all, singularly defenceless against an unwelcome caller. Once away from Vivian and her distraught hopes, he could see no valid reason why Mic should be even pleased to see him, and several good ones for slamming the door in his face. Besides, there was always the chance of taking Mic somehow off his guard, and he was not likely to receive that with Vivian's indifference.

The flat windows were lit. He opened the street door, considered for a moment, then closed it again softly and knocked. Nothing happened the first time, but after the next attempt he heard the window above him open. There was a moment's stillness, then, "Good God, Jan. Is that you?"

"Hullo," he said, looking up. The leaning face, half in shadow, was only a blur.

"Come on up, you bloody fool; you know that door's never locked."

He came in and groped for the light. Presently Mic switched it on from above. They met on the landing. Jan's first thought was not what he had expected. It was simply, He's grown up.

"Come in," Mic said. He spoke like someone who is trying with a certain curiosity to make up his mind what he feels.

The place was in a reckless litter; Mic had been working, clipping out and filing portions of periodicals that he wanted to keep and discarding the remains where they happened to fall. It was not like what Jan remembered of his methods. He pushed an armful of rubbish off a chair, picked a new paper out of it, and pulled the chair up to the fire. "Why on earth didn't you say you were coming? I might have been out."

"I didn't know I was coming till today."

"Like the Queen's Hall," said Mic, recalling an old joke.

They both smiled, at first spontaneously, then with sudden recollection and constraint.

"Are you working at anything vital?" Jan asked. "If so, I'll read while you finish. Or come tomorrow. Plenty of time."

"Oh, Lord, no. Just the monthly clearance. About as vital as playing patience."

Jan knew the monthly clearances. Mic used, he remembered, to effect them in about half an hour, absently meticulous, while he listened to the gramophone or talked about something else. Following Jan's eyes over the mess, he appeared to be about to say something, but changed his mind. "Cigarette?" he suggested, offering them.

"Thanks," said Jan, "I've got a pipe somewhere." He felt for it, thinking, He's not well, of course. I suppose it's natural for her to have concentrated on that.

"How did you ——" Mic who had just lit himself a cigarette, coughed, apologised, and put it out again. "Road or rail?"

"Rail. Maine's got the car in Ireland."

"Do you ever use your own car at all?"

"Oh, yes, when I really want it. I never use it so much in winter, you know. I'm not a very desirable night-driver, for one thing. Find it too fatally easy to think."

"Thought, its cause and cure." Mic got up, and began stacking the papers on the table. Presently, while Jan was still filling his pipe, he turned, stood still for a minute, and then said quite steadily, "Have you seen Vivian yet?"

"Yes." Jan looked at the bowl critically, and packed on a final layer. "I saw her just before I came here."

"How much did she tell you?"

"How do I know? The elements, I suppose."

He struck a match. It made a little dazzle of flame between them, hiding them from one another.

"Whatever she said," Mic went on evenly, "I'm the one principally to blame."

Jan looked up.

"I shouldn't start cultivating a sense of sin, my dear. You've got trouble enough without that."

Mic said nothing for a moment. Then, "I've found it's better than cultivating a sense of injury. When balance becomes impossible, you have to choose the less dangerous of your aberrations."

It was not an easy remark to follow up. In the ensuing pause, Mic continued to sort armfuls of torn paper from clippings and whole books, and Jan to sort his impressions. The nearest he could get to summarising them was to decide that Mic's personality seemed to have been burned or starved to a skeleton. Such curves and soft places as it had had were gone; the hard framework of support stood stripped, its construction and articulations showing. It was a structure without much elegance, but it had a kind of hard-beaten fineness and was, Jan thought, considering all things, surprisingly straight.

Mic crammed down the last sheaf into the waste-paper basket, and came back to the fire.

"I'm sorry," he said. "I suppose I ought to be apologising to you for making your sister unhappy. Did she ask you to come? God knows I ——" He gave a sudden abrupt laugh. "You're so extraordinarily incongruous in a situation of this kind, somehow. Some people are nature's relatives, some not. Forgive me. You must think I don't take this seriously."

"Must I? I have the use of my faculties."

"I suppose you know we were meaning to get married?"

"I dare say Vivian said so. I can't remember. I imagined you would if the thing lasted; it's more convenient."

Mic laughed again, this time not without amusement.

"Honestly, Jan! Is that the best impersonation of a relative you can put up? I could do it better myself. You ought to have a horsewhip—or a dogwhip is it? Then I could lose my temper and hit you and you could knock me out. Didn't your father ever tell you that sort of thing? I thought that was the great point about having one."

"Simple, wouldn't it be?" said Jan.

Mic lowered himself into his chair and leaned back with a

little grunt of satisfaction, almost of contentment. They looked at one another, in a brief but effectual exchange of understanding; one of those moments when nothing is reached for, but truth passes unhindered. It was strange, Jan thought, that in this man, so in disorder, so scarcely his own master, he should recognise so inevitably the friend he had failed till now to find. But it was so; the needed freedom, the equality, the shared angle of sight. Mic knew it also; Jan could see, in the ease of his face and limbs, the untroubled acceptance of something not discovered, but recognised. It was all good and plain and whole, a moment like bread. This simple and satisfying thing had been shown them when it was, perhaps, already too late. For Jan had no illusions that this by itself could make much difference. Compared with the conflict that was tearing Mic apart it was transient, even superficial. He could not last much longer like this. His growth was like that of a plant in darkness, which, unless light is given in time, soon turns to etiolation and death. Jan knew now that he wanted light not for Mic's sake only but for his own.

"I wonder," he said, "why you're so determined to consider yourself a psychological cripple. I'm all for confronting the worst when it exists; but in this instance, I think out of an overdone honesty you're very largely creating it."

"I might have created the interpretation. But not the experience."

"Don't you think the experience is probably rather normal?"

"Not among properly regulated people."

"How many people do you suppose are properly regulated, to their personal knowledge?"

Mic looked up with a faint smile. He had been about to say, "You, for one," but refrained lest he should be suspected of an irony he did not feel. Instead he said, "If it were only a matter of personal knowledge I could put up with it. Frankly, Jan, while I'm capable of this I don't consider myself fit for any permanent relationship. I couldn't go through it a second time. One has no right simply to put one's mind down the drain. Apart from the—inconvenience to other people."

"I fancy you wouldn't have to again."

"I should expect it even when it seemed least probable. Why not: I could foresee this. Nothing seems incredible after it."

"You might at first. But it might be a risk worth taking."

"No. I'm sorry; but take it from me, it isn't. Still less for her than for me."

"You can't decide whether other people's risks are worth while. Stick to your own and leave hers to her."

"At present it's not even worth it for me. I—well, for obvious reasons I can't tell you everything I feel. You know people enough to have some idea."

"Probably. It's a perfectly normal reaction, and generally I believe a passing one when the cause is removed. As, in this case, it is."

"How do you know it is?"

"I don't, but I'm sure. Aren't you?"

"I'm sure of nothing, now. I tell you, whatever happens it can never be the same."

"Perhaps not. That's very likely. But it needn't prevent you from evolving something different and equally satisfactory. Possibly more."

"Habit," said Mic slowly, "is a very strong thing. And habits of feeling are probably the strongest of the lot. I didn't realise, till this happened. I've thought, once or twice, that perhaps only the impact of some kind of violence—an absolutely clean break into some different kind of thought one couldn't escape. . . ." He took a handful of papers from the mantelpiece and picked out a letter. "I got this today. I'm still thinking it over."

Jan took the sheet, which was typed by an amateur, in an urgent hurry, on an old machine.

"Dear Freeborn," he said, "Here is the information you wanted. If you decide to join us, the sooner the better. The Brigade was badly cut up last week, as you probably know,

283

and every man now may be decisive in saving Madrid. When you ——"

Jan lowered the letter, to find Mic watching his face.

"Surely," he said, "your principles have changed rather radically?"

"I suppose so."

"Or is it just a process of decomposition?" Jan's voice had an edge to it. He was ashamed of himself at once; the fact was that he did not want Mic to go.

Mic blinked, and said, without ill feeling, "You can be most effectively cruel when you choose, can't you? I wonder why you choose so seldom. You hate unexercised faculties."

"Im sorry. I don't think I quite meant it. I was surprised, that's all."

"There's some truth in it. My sense of the value of human life seems to have depended partly on a belief in the usefulness of my own. When your knife's got a chipped blade you might as well use it up for digging up weeds."

"Weeds? You always used to say it was unbiological to divide life up into gradations of value."

"It's the essence of pathology, though," Mic said.

Jan returned to the letter, and finished it.

"Who is this man?" he asked. "I like him."

"A Communist who lives in Fulham. How inconsistent you are."

"Why? He's the kind of man a war like that belongs to; single-minded. He's made the escape from his own ego and seen the hosts of the Lord. Probably he's too much occupied in feeling other people's wrongs to know he's a happy man, but he is. I'd like to meet him."

"Well, that's his address. I shall probably be meeting him myself next week."

"I shouldn't."

"Why not?"

"In the first place I doubt if you'd be much practical use. You're not fit enough."

"Fresh air's a good thing."

"Don't be a damned fool, you know what the conditions are like out there. Do you intend to do the job you enlist for, or not? Because if it's a suicide you're after, you could manage that at home with less annoyance to other people."

"You put things astringently," said Mic with bleak approval. "But—no, I don't think it's suicide, or not necessarily. It's just that if I can only get out of this tangle I'm in, I don't much care whether I die or not. Indifference to death is a good start for soldiering, anyway."

"Belief in your cause is a better one."

"I believe in the cause all right."

"But not as a cause for war."

"There are so many things I don't believe in. One needs to live as though some belief existed."

"I wish ——" said Jan slowly.

"Wish what?"

"Nothing useful." He had wished he could offer something in settlement of this, of which, though Mic seemed to have forgotten it, he was the cause; but it was not the kind of speech he was practised in making.

"You may be right," he said. "I suppose one does sometimes arrive at an impasse where nothing but a break of experience is any use. Out of two choices it's the weaker; but if it's the only choice, of course, it's justifiable."

"I think it is, for me."

Jan knocked out his pipe.

"Still got your car?" he said.

"Sort of. I really shall have to scrap it soon."

"Let's go out."

"What, now?" Mic looked at the clock.

"I feel like it. D'you mind?"

"No, I suppose not. Might be a good idea."

Mic was used to Jan's nocturnal wanderings, though they had generally been conducted on foot. The recollections that stirred in his mind were mixed, but without ennui. Remembering the uncertain duration of these excursions, he threw a meal together before they started.

Jan ate absent-mindedly, but with good appetite; he had had nothing since he left Cambridge, but till now had forgotten the fact. His mind still clung obstinately to the hope of he knew not what suddenly revealed solution; but the time available for revelation seemed brief. Driving always stimulated his ideas, especially in the dark. There was something in the rhythm of it, and the pale stream of the passing world as it slid into the circle of one's headlights and out again, like vanity and time. Even if he arrived at something it would probably be useless to Mic; second-hand answers meant nothing, seven times out of ten. But he could not be content to leave anything untried.

They walked round to the garage, not talking much.

"Seems to get younger every day," said Jan, inspecting the car. "May I?" He climbed into the driver's seat.

"What?" Mic had just returned from hooking back the doors. "You don't mean drive?"

"Yes. Can I?"

"Of course, only ——"

"It's all right. I know about the clutch."

"Well, I suppose if you like."

"I remember all the tricks. Look. I can open the door."

"Oh, all right. You'll have to give yourself plenty of room to pull up, though. The brake-linings are pretty far gone. I didn't mean to use it again till I'd had it done. Costs such a damned lot."

"Don't worry. I'll look after it."

The car started complainingly. Mic shut the garage doors and got in.

"Look here, Jan, honestly, I think I'd better take over. The thing's in a hell of a mess, a lot worse than when you were here. I ought not to be running it at all."

"Of course, if you'd rather." Jan stopped the car again, and, with his sweetest smile, went through faint motions of preparing to move. "I don't want to get on your nerves if you think I can't handle it. But I don't feel like a passenger tonight, somehow. Let's walk instead."

"Oh, carry on. What does it matter? You're probably a damned sight safer than I would be, if it comes to that." Mic settled himself back in his place. Night-walking had acquired a different set of associations for him in the last month; besides, he was tired. Jan with his mind made up to something was more than he felt equal to. "The tyres are worn," he said, yawning, "so look out on the bends."

Jan manœuvred the town, cautiously at first as he felt his way into the car, then with increasing confidence and speed. As the lights slipped past him, he could feel the beginning of the mood of elation and distance that he knew. The perplexities of things receded. He knew himself on the verge of something spacious and delightful. The roads were good, the wind was crisp but not intolerably cold. In this part of the country no snow had fallen. There was a high clear moon.

Jan drove on, in open country now, amusing himself at first with the car's peculiarities, but slowly feeling them sink into the background of his consciousness. Its noises—a rhythmic rattle, a squeak at longer intervals, the loose hoarseness of the engine—smoothed his brain with their monotony. The hedgerows streamed by, a moving funnel of rusty light tipped with darkness. He changed the worn gears carefully as the road began to climb. Relationships, he was thinking, ought to be mapped. They would make lovely patterns, intricate intersecting traceries of sinuous lines, like the tracks of skaters, or of skiers in a snowslope. He began to see it against the black of the windscreen.

"Well?" said Mic.

Jan's map lost its shape and shrivelled into a little formless rag, like cobweb before the broom.

"Did you see that girl in the black Bentley," he said, "when we stopped just now?"

"Too bad. You could have pursued her in a better car. I'm sorry."

"It's all right. I didn't want to pursue her."

"You wouldn't," said Mic wearily. "Sorry I woke you up."

Jan humoured the car up the final steepness that led to the crest of the Downs.

"You don't need to scrap this," he remarked. "It's good for years."

"It seems to like you."

"Is it closing-time yet?"

"Past," said Mic without looking at his watch. The nearest inn was the "Hawk and Ring", and he did not want to go there.

"Never mind. The air up here's nearly as good."

They turned into the Roman road that ran clear along the edge of the Downs for more than seven miles. Jan began to let the engine out, smiling to himself. He had experienced, ever since this morning on the snowy bridge, a curious heightening of life. It had been with him even in Vivian's room: he had been moved and sorry there, but never shaken by doubt. It had given the rightness of necessity to what had happened between himself and Mic. He felt himself encompassed by a clear exaltation and delight. Before him, the headlamps turned the moths and midges that crossed their beam to motes of fire. Suddenly one of their mazes, scattering, made what seemed to Jan the loveliest and most significant pattern he had ever seen. It startled with certainty, it linked and illuminated irreconcilables. He knew all at once what he ought to say to Mic; he knew that it would succeed. He knew, too, the answer to an older question of his own, an answer he had always been seeking.

The light filled him, and the sound of it. Even to his physical eyes light seemed to spring up, leaping to meet him. He heard a shout beside him. It reached him like a sound of triumph: he threw up his head.

"Jan! Look *out*!"

The web dispersed. He saw, and went for the hand-brake as Mic reached desperately for it too. The old car screamed like a stallion, and ground on with dragging but scarcely diminished speed. The huge van ahead seemed to lean over him like a black cliff. Its moon-like lamps swooped apart.

Then the earth smote up at him; a force roared through the air, blasting the universe over sideways; for a great space of thought he was falling, hearing his own voice cry out to him from a long way off.

He seemed to have awaited, for many years before it reached him, the great blow, like the swinging blow of an axe, that drove into his back.

— 24 —

Mic turned over on the road, sucking in his breath with pain, and levered himself up, slowly, on the arm that he could use. The world had come to rest, and he identified with surprise the same patch of road which, a second before, he had seen disintegrated into a leaping chaos. A few yards away was a vague blur, which he recognised as the car on its side; it had skidded when the brakes went on, and struck the van glancing. Mic remembered being hurled out, and imagining, as he hung in the air, the sensations of the impact that was coming and the moment of death. He had landed on his outflung right arm and, by the feel of it, fractured his clavicle with a dislocation of the shoulder. Shock had driven the strength out of him; most of the skin had been stripped off his hand, and gravel ground in; but otherwise he seemed whole.

These discoveries lengthened out the first instant of re-gathered consciousness. He got stumblingly to his knees.

"You went to sleep," he said, startled to hear his own voice; he had not known it was going to say anything. When he had listened curiously to the sound, he became aware of the silence that had followed it. Nursing his dragging arm with the good one, he swayed to his feet.

"Jan!" he called. "Where are you? Are you all right?"

There was a pause, filled with a small and indeterminate, but somehow frightening sound, which stopped abruptly. Mic stumbled towards the car.

"Jan!"

A dark figure crossed the line of the van's headlights, and came towards him.

"Thank God," he said. "I thought ——"

"Are you hurt bad?" It was the vanman, who had climbed

down and seemed, like his van, unhurt. He was a stockily-built cockney; and looked at Mic with a resentment tempered by concern.

"I wasn't doing above ten. Couldn't you of seen there wasn't no room to pass?"

"Yes," said Mic vaguely. "I'm sorry. Jan!"

"The other chap's under the car. I've been trying but I can't shift nothing."

"Where?" Mic started forward, not feeling for a second or two the wrench in his shoulder. The single unbroken lamp of the van gleamed grotesquely into the under parts of the car, sprawled slanting away from it. In the shadow on the other side Jan lay on his face. The car covered the lower half of his body. He was not moving, and made no sound.

"The two of us might shift it," the vanman said.

Mic knelt, and took Jan's wrist. To do it he had to let go of his own arm, which sagged down with a jerk. After a moment of cold sickness he found he was still holding Jan's radial artery; it was pulsating weakly.

"We must get this off him, somehow. I can't use my right arm." Confused by its pain and hindered by its limp encumbrance, he strained at the body of the car. The vanman heaved and grunted; his leather coat ridged itself across his broad shoulders. The mass felt settled like a granite boulder.

"Could you take down the door, do you think?"

"Not the way it's jammed now. Have to be cut away, that would."

"Well, we can't leave him here," said Mic, as if the statement must produce some effect.

"I've got a rope. Maybe I could tow it off of him."

"Good God, no, you'd drag him too." Mic looked round him. There was a kind of shelter in the moment's necessity, in crisis and expedient. "How long's the rope, a good long one? Well, look, run it round that tree on the far side of the road. Fix it to the top side of the car, and get into reverse if your bus will move. That should right it. If you could only ease it up a bit I might—oh, hell; can you sling up my arm with something or other? I can't do anything like this."

Taking his crispness for the voice of habitual authority, the vanman did as he was bid without discussion. He rigged a sling out of his bandana and Mic's tie, with what seemed endless fumbling. Mic gritted his teeth more for the loss of time than for the pain. The arm ought to have been strapped to his side, but there were no more minutes to waste.

In the van they found two ropes which, joined, made just length enough. The vanman fixed them, and climbed into his seat. "There's a front wheel half buckled," he said, "but I think she'll shift that much." The engine started; the rope grew taut. Presently, with a broken sound like scrap-iron, the car began to move.

Mic stood with his left hand and right foot braced against Jan's side. The car was just clear; but the rope was creaking, and he thought suddenly that it might break and let the thing crash back again. One quick heave now would get Jan beyond it; something in the look of his back and the way he was lying prevented Mic from making it. Instead he got down on his knees and, as the car lifted, slid his own shoulders between. Jan lay still.

With a sudden shattering noise the car fell back on to its chassis, and lurched drunkenly forward at the end of the rope. The van stopped.

"Did the trick," said the driver, returning. He looked at Jan, rubbing the back of his head uncomfortably. "I've got some sacks in the van he could lie on fairly soft." Bending, he put his hands under Jan's armpits to lift.

"Stop!" Mic lurched forward, his loosely-secured arm swinging as he moved. When he could speak again, he said, "Don't lift him. We'll have to get the ambulance. If you could just help me roll him on his back without twisting him. . . . There ought to be a pad for the lumbar flexure. My coat might ——" He tried to remove it. "Oh, God damn this arm."

In the end the vanman produced a folded sack, and turned Jan while Mic steadied him in a cold sweat. The man was powerfully made and, apart from mechanics, terrifyingly clumsy, but at last took in what was required. Finally they managed it. Jan lay with upturned face, a trickle of blood coming from a graze on his forehead. His eyes were closed. He looked, as usual, perfectly calm, and in command of his part of the situation.

Mic took him by the shoulder and called his name. His mind repudiated what he saw, as the stomach rejects food it lacks the strength to assimilate. Jan would get up in a moment, and explain that it had all been a mistake. While one part of his brain repeated this, the other half saw with a cold clearness the anatomical structures over which the buckled metal of the door had lain, what was likely to have happened to them, and the result.

"There's an A.A. box at the bottom of the hill," he said.

"That's right," said the man. "Have to walk it. No room to turn. Flat tyre and wheel buckled, too." He paused. "Came at me like he couldn't see nothing there." He looked appraisingly at Mic, who seemed sober, and a sense of his own wrongs rose in him. "I'll be finding myself on the dole over this, you'll see. My firm don't like accidents. Wife and five kids. I wasn't doing above ten."

"My brakes were defective," Mic said. "Tell your firm I'll admit it. Better hurry on and get that ambulance."

Jan felt very chilly to touch. Mic groped in the back of the car for a rug to put over him. He tucked it round as best he could. The vanman's footsteps receded and died away. Mic sat down beside Jan, nursing his arm. The activity that had supported the last few minutes sank into stillness. There was nothing but a great cold, the wind, and the thin wailing of the wires. A nightjar sounded. Mic's mind came out of its trance of action, into the cold, the silence and the wind.

If he had refused to take out the car. If he had refused to let Jan drive it. If he had not said it was past closing-time. If he had watched what Jan was doing, as he would have watched anyone else. If, even when he saw what was going to happen, he could have shaken off an instant sooner the blind faith which Jan evoked in the teeth of reason and of natural law. It all lay such a little way back in the past. It seemed fantastic that one could not reach out a hand and make the small needed alteration. But it was done; all those fluid alternatives were set, like cooled steel, into this fact.

Today he and Jan had met. They were at the beginning. There was no logic in it, no shape.

He was aware of some difference in the shadows beside him; and looked down into Jan's open eyes.

"Is that you, Mic?"

"Yes. How are you feeling?"

"I'm sorry I did that."

"It's all right. Don't move." Mic put a hand warningly on his shoulder.

"I wasn't going to. What's the matter with your arm?"

"Glenoid dislocation chiefly. They'll slip that back in half a minute. Got much pain?"

"Hardly any. Just a backache, and I feel sick. A lorry, wasn't it? Where's the man?"

"Not hurt. He's gone to get help."

"How long's he been gone?"

"Five or ten minutes."

"Has he? Funny. I thought it had only just happened. Was your car insured?"

"Yes," said Mic untruthfully. "Don't worry about anything."

"What's that light?"

"Just the headlight on the van."

"It keeps dimming and going up again."

"Probably pass off in a minute. Are you cold?"

"Not really. I never feel the cold very much. No, don't take that off, I don't want it."

"All right, only keep still."

The moon came out from behind a huddle of driving cloud, seeming to sail on a strong trade-wind across a starred gulf of sky. Jan turned his face towards it. Its whiteness made a still glitter in his eyes; he lay unstirring until its smooth traverse ended in another cloud.

"It won't come," he said.

"What won't?"

"I was going to tell you something. But I can't remember now what it was."

"Never mind. It'll come back later on."

"Perhaps."

A hunting owl went over them with its dark silent stir. Soon afterwards there was the brief cry, shrill and hard like glass, of some small creature being killed.

"I told him to ring up for the ambulance," Mic said. "You'll be more comfortable in that. Properly warmed, and everything."

"I always wondered what they were like inside."

There was silence again. The wind was rising.

"I'm sorry about driving," Jan said. "I ought not to at night. I knew that really."

"I shouldn't have let you. The car wasn't fit to be on the road."

"I knew that too. Nothing would have stopped me, though. I don't know why."

He finished with a gasp, and his lips looked blue. "Don't talk so much," Mic said. He was trying to calculate whether the man could have reached the telephone yet.

A scudder of small clouds came over, lightening and darkening as they netted the light of the hidden moon. It was getting steadily colder, and Mic's dislocated arm felt like ice enclosing protesting nerves. Jan was quiet for several minutes. His voice hardly carried against the wind when he spoke again.

"I wish I could remember what it was I wanted to tell you. But I knew it would go."

"Leave it till the morning."

A pause again. Mic was reminded of he knew not what; it was like the fantastication in a dream of something well-known. He found himself listening for a whistle. Then he

295

remembered. It was like seeing someone off by train; the clock crawling through the last minutes, the futility of one's remarks increasing with the last-minute effort to be significant. A remembered picture came to him of Jan standing in strong sunlight, checked in a moment of suspended movement: "No, don't come to the station; it's so dim."

"Are you warmer now?" he asked.

"Fine, thanks."

Hope you have a good journey. Well . . . it's been nice having you. The train's late starting, surely, isn't it? Don't forget to write to me.

"Mic."

"Yes?"

"My back's broken."

A gust of wind came over like a wave, and licked the rug from Jan's shoulders. Mic caught it and held it down with his left hand and his knee.

"What makes you think that?"

"I felt it go. And my legs won't move."

Mic slid his hand under the rug and touched Jan's knee.

"Can you feel that?"

"Feel what?"

"Nothing. Never mind. Sometimes if you have a bad jar it numbs you temporarily."

"I dare say."

"They don't make anything of spinal fractures nowadays. Just put them in a plaster jacket. You'll be walking in a few weeks."

"Yes," said Jan, like one unwilling to be argumentative. "I expect I shall."

He closed his eyes. Mic knew he was conscious because now he looked tired. As if simplified by the body's extremity, his face seemed to have shed a decade of experience and maturity. It moved behind Mic's mind the image of another sleeping face; but, concerned with the present, he let the vague thought go.

From time to time he could hear the passage of cars along

the distant main road. Every second or third sounded like the ambulance till it passed. Jan's head lay on the naked road and he dared not lift it to his knees. Drawing cautiously away, he got somehow out of his coat and, returning, eased it under as best he could.

"I told you ——" Jan began, opening his eyes; but his voice drifted off as if he were no longer interested. "Thanks," he said.

His forehead was still bleeding a little. Mic got out his handkerchief and held it over the place.

"Don't look so worried." There was a tenuous amusement in Jan's voice. "You'll see bloodier heads in Spain."

"Damn Spain. You don't suppose I'd go till you're better, do you?"

"Won't you? That's good. You haven't a cigarette?"

"Of course. Oh, but the petrol; it's all over the shop. I'm so sorry, Jan. I'll give you one in the ambulance."

"It's all right. I didn't really want it."

He shut his eyes again. Gradually his face was smoothed, as if by sleep.

Don't come to the station. Messing about. You could be doing something. Mic sat still, his back to the wind, nursing his aching arm.

He was surprised when at last the ambulance came. It was like time breaking in on eternity. They could hear the bell, clearing the high-road, a long way off. Jan turned his head.

"Ambulance coming," Mic said.

"I know. This is the first time I ever tried to make myself useful. Apparently not my function."

The lights of the ambulance turned the bend, swinging a long shadow round the wreckage in the road.

There was a smooth sound of brakes. The ambulance men, cheerfully capable and interested, ran up with their stretcher.

"It's his back," Mic said. "Possibility of a fracture."

"Right, sir. We'll watch after that."

They rolled the stretcher under Jan with skilled smoothness, and were about to cover him again when the man who

297

knelt lowest took his hand away and held it out in the light of the headlamps.

"Here," he said, "half a minute. What about this?"

Jan looked round at the palm's wet redness. "I don't know," he said. "I can't feel anything."

"Run back and get the dressing-box, Fred."

They got it, found scissors and slit Jan's clothes away. When the stuff had parted Mic shut his eyes for a second, then watched while they did what could be done. The darkness, the cold and the wind's edge were in his heart and bones. Jan glanced at the proceedings and then away, as if a momentary interest had been satisfied, or a foregone conclusion confirmed.

In the ambulance they let him have Mic's cigarette.

By the time Mic's arm had been splinted to his body (he had become so used by then to the pain that its partial cessation was like a shock of pleasure) they were purring in through the hospital gates. The night-porter came out and helped to unslot Jan's stretcher from its supports and to slide it on the trolley; casually efficient, exchanging gossip with the ambulance-men over his shoulder. They wheeled it into the little ante-room beside the out-patients' theatre, changed the blankets belonging to the ambulance for older ones, belonging to the hospital, and left him with the porter and Mic. It was a tiny cell-like place, just holding a cupboard and examination-couch; the stretcher nearly filled it.

On the journey Jan had become increasingly quiet. Now, under the unshaded light, his head might have been cut, with the reticence and precision of some archaic craftsman, out of one hard pale-brown stone. His colourless face seemed to shade into his hair, bleached hemp-fair by many latitudes of sun. His eyes did not wander, like those of the other injured men that Mic had seen.

"Who's on casualty call?" Mic asked the porter.

"Mr. Rosenbaum. But he's in the other theatre."

"Will he be long?"

"Couldn't say, Mr. Freeborn. He's only just opened up."

298

"But ——" The violence that had been on Mic's tongue died away. Everyone knew that casualties sometimes had to wait. The resident staff was hopelessly insufficient. He pictured little Rosenbaum in the theatre, his fads about his mask and gloves, his pleasantries which, recounted after, had seemed so funny. Now Mic could only think of them in terms of the extra seconds they took. He looked at Jan again. His own impatience seemed an intrusion in the presence of so much leisure. To release it he got up from the couch where he had been sitting, and wandered outside. The ambulance-men had stopped a little way off to fold their blankets up.

"Well," said the one who had travelled inside, "we got him in, anyhow. Never reckoned we would."

"Nice-looking chap, too," said the driver. "I'll need to fill-up before we go in; only about a gallon left. Looked pretty mucky, didn't he?"

"Pelvis fractured. See it through the skin. Cuts their guts to bits, that does. Wonder to me he didn't pip out on the way."

"Poor bleeder. Didn't make much fuss."

"They don't feel nothing, not with the spine gone." He handed a packet of Tenners. "What was that you was asking me about your Pool coupon when the call came through?"

"Stoke and the Arsenal."

"Ah. You want to watch Stoke. I reckon that last home match ——" They had gathered up the folded blankets, and passed out of hearing.

Mic stood still for a moment, looking after them, then went back into the little ante-room. A nurse had come in by the other door, and was trying to take Jan's pulse, moving her fingers over his wrist because she could not feel it. He turned his head as Mic came in.

"Hullo. Have they fixed your arm?"

"Not yet. I was just walking about." He saw that there was beginning to be a blueness round Jan's eyes, and turned away.

"Don't go."

Mic said "All right," and lowered himself mechanically on to the couch: then his mind became motionless in a half-dulled wonder. Had Jan said that? He himself seemed to be denying it. He was not looking at Mic; his half-shut eyes were steady, not flickering, like the eyes of the very sick and hurt, in search of reassurance or rescue.

"Stay here with me."

"Yes," said Mic half under his breath, "I ——"

"*Well*," said the nurse, putting her watch away and suddenly recognising Mic. "Whatever have *you* been up to?"

Mic heard her the second time. He answered something, looking at Jan's face, composed like something carved in a calm forgotten age. But he had said it; he had said it in the end.

"What's the matter with your arm?" asked the nurse. "Feel like a fracture?"

"No; it's nothing really." Mic got up, and stood near the stretcher-head. He could not be sure any longer that Jan was conscious; his eyelids had fallen lower.

"Mic?" It was Jan's voice, though it seemed to have come from another room with a closed door between, so that one only just heard it. Mic leaned down a little and touched his sun-baked hair. It felt shockingly young and warm, and shone in the light.

"I'm here."

The Night-Assistant's head poked briskly round the door.

"Are you with this patient?" she asked.

Presently Mic realised that she and the nurse were both looking at him.

"Yes," he said.

"Well, would you just come outside and give me a few particulars?"

Mic closed his hand over one of the stretcher-poles.

"Would you mind if ——"

"Run along," murmured Jan.

Mic let go of the stretcher and went out to the waiting-hall. It was a huge pillared place, with rows of benches, for the out-patients, stretching away into darkness. A solitary bulb burned over the Sister's desk. The distant walls, half-lost in darkness, echoed like a cave.

The Night-Assistant settled herself at the desk and drew the admission-book towards her; a tome three inches thick and an arm wide, ruled in blue and red. She had taken over since Mic's illness and they had never met. She was thin and sallow, with prominent eyes and teeth; very spruce and consciously methodical.

"We shall be admitting you too for tonight, I expect. May I have your name and address?"

Mic gave them, too quickly, and had to repeat them again.

"Age?"

"Twenty-five."

"Are you married?"

"No."

"Well, where does your nearest relative live?"

Mic knew this dialogue by heart; he had rehearsed it in Ramillies.

"I have none."

"We must have *some* address. It needn't be a *near* relation."

"I have no relatives at all. If you'd just let Dr. Lampeter know where I am in the morning." His piece said, he turned back towards the closed door.

"Well, your landla —— Oh, you're on the *staff* here." Her voice trailed faintly upward; but the pathological assistants were fairly small beer.

"Yes. If you'll excuse me, I ——"

The desk telephone rang.

"Yes, Mr. Rosenbaum. . . . Yes. . . . Yes, a good deal. . . . Very poor. . . . Yes." She put back the receiver and brushed past Mic to the ante-room door. "Nurse, give that patient an ampoule of coramine and get him wheeled through into the theatre." Returning, she blotted the admission-book carefully and ran her finger down to the next line.

"Funny my not having seen you in the labs, but I don't go

up there very often. I expect they'll discharge you in the morning. Now what was the other patient's—your friend's name?"

"Jan Lingard."

"John Lingard," she repeated precisely, writing it down.

"J-a-n," said Mic, his voice rising a little. He wanted suddenly to snatch the book out of her hand, to hit her over the head with it, to kill her. His hand was shaking, and he steadied it on the edge of the desk.

Looking annoyed—for the correction spoiled the neatness of the page—the Night-Assistant altered the line.

"Address?" she said. Mic gave it.

"How old, about, is he, have you any idea?"

"He'll—he'd be thirty next month."

Little Rosenbaum, still wearing his theatre gown and cap, crossed the hall with his scampering trot and disappeared through the door beyond.

"Would you just wait here, please?" The Night-Assistant got up and bustled after him.

Mic waited. In a few minutes the other nurse came out and hurried across the hall, her feet awaking responses from walls lost in darkness, got something from a cupboard and hurried back again. The door closed behind her. There was a long hollow silence, into which footsteps in a distant corridor dropped and dwindled, tiny, distinct and menacing.

Under the theatre door a crack of brilliant light showed; the shadows of feet came and went across it. Mic had only been in the place once, but suddenly he saw it all clearly and in minute detail; the position of the instrument-cabinets and sterilisers, the anaesthetic apparatus (they would not be needing that), the great Zeiss lamp over the table, with its diffused primrose-pale effulgence. He could picture Rosenbaum sucking his cheeks, as he did when he was pensive. ". . . And such a beautiful body. Beautiful, beautiful," he used to say afterwards, with lingering melancholy.

Jan stripped well. A skin tanned like thick brown silk, over sleek hard curves of muscle; open shoulders, narrow waist;

302

the down of his chest and belly golden with sun. On the table under the soft shadeless glare of the Zeiss, what remained of him would satisfy Rosenbaum's standards.

"Stay with me," he had said, perhaps for the second time in his life, perhaps for the first. But little Rosenbaum, considering the *lachrymae rerum* over the ligatures and artery-forceps, would discover no protest in his eyes. It's all right: I didn't really want it.

The Night-Assistant came smartly out, walked past Mic, picked up the desk-telephone and dialled a number.

"Casualty speaking. We are sending you a patient with fractured spine, crushed pelvis and ruptured right kidney. Will you prepare for a blood-transfusion at once, please." She took a form from the desk, and got up.

A blood-transfusion, thought Mic. Christ, why can't they leave him in peace!

'Tell Rosenbaum," he said, "that his blood-group's two. It will save time." (It had always amused Jan to be experimented on. His own group was incompatible, so he could not do even that.)

The nurse's teeth closed like a rabbit's over her lower lip.

"Well, I expect Mr. Rosenbaum would want a test taken."

"I have taken it. Did you think I was guessing it, you fool. . . . I beg your pardon."

"Not at all." Both lips closed firmly over the teeth, she departed.

The theatre doors swung back. A great shaft of light stabbed the gloom and ribbed the long tiers of the benches. Out of it they brought Jan, a vermilion streak of mercuro-chrome across his temple, his face still.

Mic went up to the trolley. His eyes were half-open, but they did not move. Mic touched his arm through the blanket.

"Jan."

With a little contraction of the lids his eyes quickened, and met Mic's in the focus of sight. His lips moved, soundlessly.

"What is it?" Mic asked.

Jan drew in a thin breath and whispered, "Will **you** ——"

"*Just* a moment, please." It was the Night-Assistant, with a white card in her hand. "We haven't got all this patient's particulars."

"For God's ——" Mic checked himself, and stood for a moment silent. Jan's lips moved again; but Mic perceived that this time it was a smile that he was attempting. The porter was ready at the trolley's head.

Mic let his hand fall. "All right," he said. "Good night, Jan."

He never knew whether Jan replied: the trolley was already on its way.

The Night-Assistant had her book open again, and was unscrewing her pen.

"We haven't got the address of Mr. Lingard's relatives. Do you know it?"

Derbyshire, thought Mic dimly. The trolley, the other nurse beside it holding the case-sheet, vanished through the door at the end of the hall. Their father lives in Derbyshire. Near . . . There was a pause in his mind. Like someone returning fom a long journey to a place grown strange, he said,

"Yes, of course. His sister's a nurse here."

— 25 —

COLONNA put back the last scoured bedpan on the rack and, to avoid thought, picked up a tattered Western magazine she had found in the ward. There was, for the moment, a lull in the work, so she sat down on the edge of the steriliser to read it. She preferred it to sharing the table in the ward with the night-nurse in charge, who was a couple of months junior to herself. Colonna was well overdue for this position; but she had been caught coming in late the month before. Pratt, the "first," was plodding, humourless, and pointedly in earnest; disapproved of Colonna from the bowels outward, and did nothing to smooth the situation. It had, however, this in its favour, that it allowed little opportunity to meditate.

The Western was called *The Two-Gun Dude*, and promised well. Cowboys of the classic kind were a fairyland which Colonna had never outgrown. In their company she dismissed life with its painful compromises, and became her private picture of herself. Flicking open the thumbed pages, and skipping the preliminaries with the ease of practice, she was the Dude in less than a couple of minutes. Clean-limbed, with sinews of steel and whipcord, she toted his silver-mounted guns, knotted his silk bandana, canted his elegant ten-gallon hat, confounded his hairy rivals, shot up his enemies, and kissed his pale-pink, incidental girl.

But tonight even this exorcism failed, as every other was failing.

She had given herself, in her own mind, two years to keep Valentine. Three, perhaps; perhaps four; but two at the least. There was security in the thought of years, even of brief years. But it was happening now. She did not know why. She had no experience to point her. She had always been the one to go away.

Doubling back the gaudy paper cover, she read doggedly on.

" 'So you figgered to frame me, Red.' The Dude's blue eyes were colder than the steel. With a sound that was half curse, half scream, Red Santander hurled forward; but the Dude's guns had leaped to his lean fingers. 'Waal,' he drawled ——"

At the beginning of next year she would be twenty-seven. In a few years more her pose, her tricks of manner, her clothes, all her assumptions would have become ridiculous. She had not acquired any resources against growing old. A few months ago she had believed that she had. She had acquired Valentine. Secure in her, she had begun to let her other securities slip imperceptibly away. Now, with her going, everything had gone. She was not the Dude any more, not a glittering outlaw, but a tired woman, a rather humdrum case, conforming to the textbooks.

It was not too late. It was never too late. She would buy a new suit, throw up her head, stop pleading with Valentine and begging her for this and that; find another girl, a prettier one, and make her jealous; leave her, forget her.

" 'Waal,' he drawled, 'I guess this is where you and me ——' "

"Oh, *there* you are, Nurse Kimball. I've been looking for you *everywhere*." Nurse Pratt, with her elbows sticking out at the angle characteristic of her, had come into the sluice. Colonna suppressed her instinctive movement to conceal the book, and tossed it casually aside. "I thought you might have heard the telephone."

"Well, I didn't. I was purging the mind with pity and terror, as a change from giving enemas. Anything coming in?"

"A patient is being admitted with a fractured spine, crushed pelvis and ruptured right kidney ——"

"*Sacré bleu.* I thought tonight was too peaceful."

"—and he's to have a transfusion immediately."

"A transfusion! That will be Rosenbaum, I suppose. I wish he'd cultivate a lower boiling-point. Getting a poor devil of a donor out of bed at midnight and bleeding a pint out of him for a man who won't live twelve hours whatever happens. We'll put him in the side-ward, of course?"

"Certainly," said Pratt with dignity. Secretly she found her precedence even less comfortable than Colonna, but was determined not to let it appear. "Will you be getting on with it? Don't forget the boards and the binder and the sandbags and the cradle. And put the transfusion things on to boil. I shall go down now and get a meal, so as to be ready when the case comes up. You'll be sure to keep an eye on the ward, won't you?"

"Of course not," said Colonna, exasperated. "I shall bolt myself in the lavatory and sit there till you come back."

Nurse Pratt stiffened her shoulders, tucked in her chin, and departed. Colonna tiptoed about the preparations, smiling sardonically. She guessed that Pratt was uncertain of the setting—a fairly complex one—for a blood-transfusion, and must be congratulating herself on passing the buck without loss of face.

The case had not arrived when Pratt came back, and Colonna left in her turn for the second meal. In the passage she met Vivian, on her way to the dining-room too. Suddenly she remembered that Vivian had been another of her failures. She had, till now, long ceased to regret this and, indeed, enjoyed the ease of their friendship, but tonight she forgot it and the pleasant recollections that went with it. Only the thought of defeat remained.

Vivian looked, as she generally did nowadays, deadly tired and devitalised. They greeted one another with indifferent smiles.

"Had good nights-off?" asked Colonna, for the sake of saying something.

"Yes, thanks," she answered listlessly. Awake all last night with the boy, Colonna thought, feeling a dull resentment directed she hardly knew where. "Been busy?" Vivian asked with the same perfunctoriness.

"Not yet, but by hell we're going to be. What do you think we've got coming in?" She explained.

"Too bad," said Vivian wearily.

"I wish," Colonna remarked as they walked towards the dining-room, "that old Beth would tell Rosenbaum where he gets off. A transfusion, I ask you."

Vivian said unemotionally, "I expect it's a young man. Rosenbaum always panics when young people die. I suppose it seems to bring it nearer."

The casual bitterness in her voice penetrated Colonna's self-absorption, and shocked her a little.

"Are you taking iron, or anything?" she asked. "You ought to be. Most people need some sort of a tonic on nights. Your ward's pretty full, too, isn't it?"

"Yes. Extra beds in the middle. They tried to get us to take another case just now, but we hadn't room. It was only a clavicle, or a dislocation or something."

"Well, *we* haven't anywhere."

"I expect," said Vivian without interest, "they put him up in Casualty somewhere. Or sent him home. After all, his wife could look after him with a little thing like that."

The Night Sister came hurrying—she was always in a hurry—along the corridor towards them.

"She looks in a hell of a flap," remarked Colonna idly. "Found someone's room empty, I expect."

"Nurse Lingard. Will you just come in here for a moment?"

Colonna walked on, wondering what Vivian could have done. She had obeyed with a harried vagueness unlike conscious guilt, but it must be something serious from Sister's sickbed manner. Only the worst kind of trouble started with that. Perhaps the Matron had found out about young Freeborn. That—she felt unable to work up much feeling about it—would mean dismissal, for Vivian. He would get off, of course; the man always did.

One would miss Vivian, probably, more than one expected. She was self-centred but not self-blinkered; and she saw things, if not always straight, at least first-hand. That was rare enough, hereabouts, to be valued. This kind of training ——

Her feet stopped; and her mind, checking too, said "This kind of training" over again, and clicked to a standstill. She had come to a junction with another corridor, and, a little way along it, Valentine and Macklin, the senior house physician, were saying good night. They were dressed for the evening and had evidently just come in. Macklin had his back half-turned, but Valentine stood facing one of the big corridor lights, and there was nothing in her face that Colonna missed.

Just round the corner was a small staircase, leading circuitously to the nurses' home. Colonna turned up it, glancing mechanically at her watch to make sure that she did not outstay the half-hour allotted for the meal. When she reached her room she sat down on the edge of her bed, dry-eyed, dry-brained, everything in her hard and dry. There was no palliative for what had happened, nothing at all even to take the edge off it. Valentine had seen her that morning, and had not told her that she was going out. She had not even said anything about the new dress she was wearing.

Colonna's was the simple emotional finality of a child, for whom the moment's experience colours all the future and tinges even eternity.

This one instant seemed to contain the gradual losses of a decade: the loss of pride, the loss of youth, the dawning on the imagination of what loneliness can be in middle-age.

At the end of the half-hour she tidied her uniform, and went back to the ward again. The transfusion in the side-ward was still going on. In the Sister's sitting-room the donor, a plump sleepy young woman with her lipstick put on in a hurry, was sipping tea, her function discharged. A first-year probationer, borrowed from elsewhere, was taking nervous charge of the main ward.

"You might as well be getting back now," Colonna told her. "Tell Nurse Pratt on your way that I've come."

"Please, Nurse, I think I was to stay and help in the ward and you were going to 'special' the case. I *think* that's what Sister said."

"Oh, very well. Have you had your meal yet?"

"Well, no, I hadn't time really to go down."

"Go now, then. And tell Nurse Pratt I'm here."

"Yes, Nurse. Thank you."

Colonna made a round of the ward, attending to a few obvious necessities overlooked by the probationer's inexperience; then returned to the Sister's desk and, in a blind craving for distraction, fiddled with the papers and oddments scattered over it. In a small tin box, among the nibs, drawing-pins, and odd bone buttons from the surgeons' coats, the key of the poison-cupboard lived. She fingered it over, thinking of things she had said to Valentine; they had only been threats at the time, but after all, she thought, that emptiness was less to be feared which destroyed even the consciousness of itself. Into Leslie, too, it would burn her final and ineluctable seal. Pratt came out for a moment in search of something, and she slipped the key quickly into her pocket. But they were still hard at it in the side-ward; she could see their shadows crossing and recrossing the lighted door. It seemed a pity that, instead of an ineffectual pint of blood, she could not hand them in a waxed phial the life she was weighing so distastefully in her hand. The imagination of it pleased her; in spite of all she had seen in hospital, death, to Colonna, was still essentially the supreme dramatic climax.

Pratt had pushed the trolley of instruments out from the side-ward into the passage. In a few minutes they would be ready to leave the patient to her. His case-sheet was lying on the desk; she picked it up and stared at it vaguely, her eye lighting first on the age at the top corner. Twenty-nine. Only two years older than herself. For a man, at the beginning of things. That was another part of the injustice she had always resented. Her mind encountered the strongly-planted, confident shape of Macklin: she recoiled with a small physical movement which made the key in her pocket jingle against a couple of loose coppers. She picked up the case-sheet again.

Dully questioning what had arrested her, she read the name over twice before she took it in. She was still staring at it, wondering if a coincidence was possible, when Pratt trotted up to the table to give her her instructions. Colonna asked no questions; if she had been down to the dining-room she would know all about it and more, and had no wish to be asked by Pratt where she had spent the time.

"Nurse Lingard will be here to sit with him for a little while," Pratt said, her whisper husky with chastened importance. "But I don't think you ought to *leave* him at all. He's a very difficult patient. He practically refused to have the transfusion; kept saying it was a waste or something like that. Mr. Rosenbaum was very good with him. Explained everything almost as if he were talking to another doctor. (He's still in there now; you'd better hurry along as soon as he comes out.) In the end we told him the blood had been taken from the donor already, and that seemed to quieten him down."

"And had it?"

"Oh, yes. I don't think Mr. Rosenbaum would have said so if it hadn't: he seemed to take it all quite seriously—a bit silly I thought, considering how collapsed he was. You expect them to wander a bit, I mean. I don't like having these private patients in a general ward, it makes things awkward, really."

"Well," said Colonna, picking up a pulse chart, "you're very unlikely to have him after tonight."

Pratt pursed her lips. One did not make these observations about the relatives of members of the staff. "They won't be able to plaster him, of course," she said. "So be sure, won't you, not to let him *move*?"

"I put you a binder and sandbags ready. Didn't you fix them properly?" Colonna picked up her pen and notebook and went out.

Rosenbaum was just leaving when she got to the side-ward door. He had been washing his hands, and was still holding the towel and screwing it absently into a ball. He stood in the doorway with a kind of discomposed look, like an actor who has been given the wrong cue. Colonna heard a voice say, with a quiet not so much suggestive of weakness as of a careful courtesy, "You mustn't worry." This was a favourite valediction of Rosenbaum's; but it was not Rosenbaum who had spoken.

He left without looking at Colonna; in any case, they had always disliked one another cordially.

There was still a good deal of litter left in the room from the transfusion, and Colonna set about clearing it up. The red shade had been taken from the light over the bed, and thrown over a chair; she collected and replaced it—easily, for she was tall enough to reach the bracket without a chair. A gap at the bottom of the shade dropped a pool of yellow light on the face of the white-lipped young man lying, pillowless, on the bed. He had shut his eyes, probably because the glare worried him. She pinned the shade together and closed the chink.

So this is Vivian's brother, she thought; her mind partly rousing itself from the daze of misery which had, for a moment, obscured everything but the routine task lying next her hand. Surely Vivian had said that they were alike. How vague people were about their own appearances. Poor Vivian, she was very fond of him. Colonna repeated this to herself, trying to make it mean something; but it was only words in her mind. She could not believe in her heart that after what had happened Vivian, the hospital, the universe itself could remain real and unchanged.

Routine, however, remained, distantly connecting with sanity. She pushed the trolley into the main ward for the probationer to clean, tidied up, filled a feeding-cup with lemon water, made out a half-hourly pulse chart, and slipped her hand under the clothes to take his pulse. He opened his eyes. She saw that they were nearly the same colour as Vivian's, but with less brown in them and more green.

"Again?" he said.

"Just every half-hour." Mechanically Colonna assumed her professional voice. She picked up the chart and marked the first point of the graph.

"Does that give them a line on the next case?" His voice had got a little stronger, and sounded faintly interested.

"No, it's just to see how you're getting along."

"I shouldn't worry, then. You're busy, aren't you?"

"Not really. I'm just here to look after you."

"I see." He was silent while she put the chart away, and then said, "I hope I shan't need to keep you very long. About how long does it take, as a rule?"

Colonna selected the correct response, mechanically, as she would have put her hand in her pocket for her surgical scissors. Situations like this were always having to be met.

"That depends. It's difficult to say how long bones will take to unite. They'll know better when they've X-rayed you a few times."

His greenish eyes flicked up at her face. Defensively she added, "Really, only a surgeon could give you an opinion."

"I did ask him. But he thought I was afraid."

Colonna opened her mouth. The words she had expected to find in it were absent, and she closed it again.

He seemed to consider for a moment, then asked, curiously, "Or is that part of professional etiquette?"

She could think of nothing. Behind his almost motionless face another face seemed to stir, having a different and secret vitality of its own.

"It's preferable, I think, to know." He said it like a reflection rather than a request.

Colonna pulled herself together. "I don't expect Mr. Rosenbaum knew himself. It's very hard to tell exactly. Would you like a drink?"

"Thank you. I believe I am thirsty."

She held the feeding-cup for him. He choked a little over it, and apologised. "It's all right," she said. "It's just practice. You'll soon get used to drinking on your back."

"Thank you," he said when she had wiped his mouth for

him. "I'll be able to do it myself next time. I can use my hands, you know, quite well."

"You must keep very quiet just at first."

"At first?" His pale lips twitched at the corners. Avoiding his eyes, she put the cup back on the locker and folded the napkin away.

"By the way, who gave me the blood for the transfusion?"

"A Miss Pomfret. One of our regular donors."

"That round girl in blue who passed the door?"

"Yes, that would have been Miss Pomfret, I expect."

"And how much of me is Miss Pomfret?"

"About a pint."

"Mic would laugh at that."

She did not contradict him.

Rousing himself—he had been abstracted for a moment—he said, "You might thank her from me. Tell her I—enjoyed her blood very much. Or what does one say?"

"I'll tell her next time she comes."

"Why do you suppose they gave it me?"

"To make you stronger."

"God Almighty," he murmured, and relapsed into silence.

Colonna settled herself in the chair, her notebook in her lap. What would he answer, she wondered, if she were to ask him, "What do you expect of death, behind all this reason?" All she was sure of was that the question would neither shock nor dismay him; that he would answer as simply as if she had asked him about the weather, would speak the truth and would tell her nothing. She would hear the words; they would beckon her like the sound of verse in an unknown language, magical and meaningless: solitude speaking to loneliness, a gulf too great for translation to bridge.

She hoped he would die easily. He would live longer than he supposed; for another night, perhaps for two. The transfusion had done wonders and, by the look of him, his constitution had been like iron. Thinking of him, she began for the first time to taste death with the senses of the imagination; the losing of touch and sight, knowledge and experience, the inexorably advancing dark. It had been in her mind till now a situation, never an experience. She sat silent, the footlights of her private theatre suddenly, chillingly extinguished.

He had turned his eyes away from her, silent with himself. For him, she thought, there was no imagining; it was now, and here. For him there was no afterthought, no compromise, no excuse.

The Night Sister, her torch and notebook in her hand, came gingerly round the door.

Colonna rose. The Sister was short and stout, pasty from her subterranean life, and had the air of always being oppressed with secrets too great to bear. She crooked a conspiratorial finger, and Colonna followed her out into the passage.

"How does he seem, Nurse?"

"His condition has improved a good deal, Sister." She quoted his rates of pulse and respiration.

"That's right, Nurse. Is he taking anything by mouth?"

"Taking fluids quite well, Sister."

"*That's* right, Nurse. I just wanted to make sure he was all ready before I sent Nurse Lingard to sit with him. You want to keep an eye on him, Nurse." Her voice dropped a couple of tones. "Nurse Lingard's only in her first year and there might be a change at any moment, you can't never tell."

"Yes, Sister."

"We've sent for his father, but he lives up in the North of England. He can't be here before tomorrow morning. I hope he won't be gone before then. Poor boy; clever, too, from what I hear. Oh, and Mr. Rosenbaum particularly says, will you have him waked if his condition gets worse."

"Yes, Sister."

"It's been a great shock to Nurse Lingard. About half an hour, I told her she could stay, but you don't want to have her here too long, if it seems to be upsetting him. I shouldn't like him to go before his father comes, not if we can help it."

"Yes, Sister."

The Sister put her hand on the knob of the side-ward door;

315

and, as if the action had pressed a switch in her face, its expression changed to a soothing, solicitous cheerfulness. Colonna followed her in. He had got an arm out of bed, and was reaching it cautiously towards the cup on the locker. The Sister, her starched skirts rustling, bustled across the ward and forestalled him. Over the cup she darted at Colonna her routine look which said, "You must have been neglecting him to make him do that." During this momentary pre-occupation she tipped the cup too sharply, and he choked again.

"I'm so sorry," he said as if he were getting used to the sound of it. "I was trying to practise."

"Now you mustn't go trying anything like that, there's a good boy." She wagged her finger at him. "You've got Nurse here to do everything for you."

"I know. Thank you. But I've always been used to doing things for myself. I'd rather, really, as it doesn't make any difference."

"Well, I never, difference indeed. You've got to save up every bit of strength to mend that back of yours. Hasn't he, Nurse?"

Colonna formed her face into a convenional pattern.

"It's very good of you"—he formed the words rather slowly and carefully, as if to be sure of getting himself understood—"to take such care of me. But I'm sure you'll understand that I don't want to make this a needlessly long business. It takes up your time. And I don't care for loose ends. Besides, I think it's—probably an experience you should come to with your perceptions still awake. So you see——?"

His voice had struggled a little unevenly with so long a speech, but he finished with a faint sound of satisfaction, like one who knows he has succeeded in making himself clear.

The Night Sister clicked her tongue against her upper plate; a gently reproving, encouraging sound.

"Now, you don't want to *worry*. We're all out to get you better just as quick as ever we can. And the way you can help us best is by lying quiet and doing just what Nurse here tells you, and not trying to move or worrying or anything like that. I'm sending your sister to sit with you for a little while; but you mustn't go talking or getting excited. Now you *do* see, don't you?"

"Yes," he said. "I see. Thank you. Good night."

The Sister went out, beckoning Colonna with an eyebrow.

"You want to watch him, Nurse. He's not a good patient, not a good patient at all. These clever men, they're often the worst. They worry about themselves, and they won't be *told* anything. You be careful and keep that binder very firm. Matron would never forgive me if anything was to happen, particularly before his father comes."

"Yes, Sister."

Colonna went back into the side-ward. He greeted her with the kind of look which shares a joke too obvious to need underlining with a smile.

"I'm just going to turn back the clothes a bit," she said, "and see if your sandbags are all right."

When a spinal case could not be plastered, it was kept splinted with a strong roller towel, the ends of which were made fast under narrow sandbags laid closely against the patient's sides. Colonna saw that everything was firmly in place and that the haemorrhage had, for the moment, stopped.

"What's that arrangement for?" he asked her, interested.

"To keep you from moving your back."

"What would happen if I did?"

"You'd be likely to damage your spinal cord."

"More than now?"

"Probably a good deal more."

"You mean it would ——?"

Colonna hesitated, suddenly cautious. "It would be pretty serious. So we must be careful, as Sister said." She picked up the cup. "Would you like to hold this, if I just steady it?"

He took it, managing very well. "Thank you. You remind me, do you know, of a man at Cambridge."

"What sort of man?" asked Colonna, automatically pleased.

"Terrible. But very good-looking."

She laughed; then, remembering, said, "You're talking too much. You really must rest now."

"Yes." He was quiet for a little while; and she saw, when the false vitality of motion had left his face, that he looked more exhausted than before. Suddenly he said, in a stronger voice, "The Sister seems to hold you responsible for my—behaviour."

"They do, in hospital, you know."

"It's hard," he said, "to get used to that kind of thing."

"Yes, I can imagine that." She saw that it was time to take his pulse again. It was weaker and more rapid than before. "You must keep quieter," she said, and sat down with her notebook in front of her.

She thought that he was dozing, till he said, slowly, "You set an almost mystical value on life here, don't you?"

"I don't know. It's just our job."

"Almost as if it were an end, instead of a means."

"Well, it's the only thing we've expert knowledge of, and that not much. Probably it's better we shouldn't meddle outside."

"Mic Freeborn has ideas about life too—you know him?"

"A little."

"My own are different, I think."

Colonna missed the last sentence. She had been listening to a step approaching along the flagged passage between the wards.

"I think," she said, "this is Vivian coming to see you."

"Yes, I promised I'd see Vivian."

"I'm afraid she mustn't stay very long, tonight."

"No. She's on duty, isn't she?"

"Well, yes, and — —"

"Besides, she's not very fit. People find these interviews upsetting."

"How can you"—Colonna's mental uniform suddenly fell from her—"talk like this, as if you were discussing someone else?"

"I am. This mess under the sheet, I can't even feel it, you know."

The outer door of the ward swung to, and closed again. Colonna slipped out, and met Vivian in the passage. She only said, "Will he know me?"

'Oh, yes. The transfusion made a lot of difference.'

She said, in a perfectly level voice, "Rosenbaum shouldn't have done that to him."

Colonna moved back towards the door, and stopped. "I'm supposed not to leave him," she said. "I'm going into the other side-ward. Just see that he keeps still. I shall hear if you want me."

"Thank you, Colonna." She went in.

The man in the other side-ward was asleep. A convalescent, he needed no lamp at night, and would probably wake if she switched it on. She sat there in the dark, near the open door, where she could hear if Pratt or the Night Sister were coming.

The door of the next side-ward was ajar too, so she could hear, through it, the desultory murmur of their voices, broken with silences. The man in the bed beside her snored a little; the rhythmic sound wove itself into the pauses, becoming less and less audible as her accustomed ears ignored it. After five minutes or so he turned over on his side, and the noise stopped. The place was very quiet, so that once, when they raised their voices above a whisper, she heard what they said.

"Don't, Jan. You know it was all through me, from the beginning."

"You? No. We just lived it."

"But if I hadn't ——"

"This didn't happen; it was, always. Mic knows. Or he will, when he has time."

"Time? Mic will never . . . I've taken everything from Mic now. Everything he ever had."

"Oh, no. He isn't a person to whom that can be done."

I ought to turn her out, Colonna thought mechanically. Talking to an ill patient like that. She got to her feet without noticing, stood for a moment, and sat down again. Their voices sank lower, and she did not hear any more.

The half-hour was nearly over when she heard Pratt coming down the main ward. There was no sound from the other room. She slipped from her place and knocked softly. It was Jan who said "Come in."

"I'm sorry. But nurse is doing a round."

"She'll tell me to go," Vivian said. Colonna could tell from her voice that she had been weeping. There was a pressed-down place on the sheet where her face had been.

"Go by yourself," he said. "It feels better. You'll be all right when you start working again."

It had taken a great deal out of him. Colonna wondered what Pratt would say.

Vivian got up. "Yes," she said dully; then, recalling something, "Jan, Mic's down in Casualty. Someone said he wanted to come and see you, but they wouldn't let him."

"Why on earth not?"

"He's not a relative, you see."

"But ——" he was speaking with much more effort now, "no one told me. Wouldn't they have—asked me if I wanted him?"

"You see," Colonna explained, "it's only relatives when— as a rule. But perhaps if I said you'd asked for him ——"

"Would they?" His face altered for a moment, then was quiet again. "No. Mic's had enough. There's no point, we've done all that. Tell them to—give him something to make him sleep."

They heard Pratt's footsteps passing from the ward into the passage.

"You'd better be going," he said.

She stood, her will helpless, her hand on the black iron foot of the bed.

"Jan, I wish I could have ——"

"I'm glad you came. It was good to speak the truth for a minute. Everything's all right, Vivian. Good-bye."

"Good-bye." She turned away quickly and went out.

"That's right, Nurse," said Pratt in the corridor. "Better not stay too long tonight. You'll be able to look in again to-morrow when you come off duty."

Colonna took her patient's pulse—she had a good deal of difficulty in counting it—and marked up the chart.

"Well," said Jan, "I think that's everything." He shut his eyes. She thought his consciousness was slipping; but realised, after a time, that he was asleep.

Colonna sat with her hands folded over the notebook in front of her, absorbed in the newness of her own thoughts.

At four o'clock the probationer brought her in a tray of tea. She managed the crockery without noise, but suddenly, his voice quite wakeful, he said, "Wouldn't you rather be having it with the others? This is very dull for you. Have you been sitting here all this time?"

"Yes, but it's all right. Just routine."

"I don't like to think I'm wasting your time like this. Can you sleep if you want to?"

"Well, no, hardly. Would you like a cup of tea? I've lots here."

She filled the feeding-up and helped him to drink. When she had finished her own meal he said, more diffidently than he had spoken before, "I wonder if you'd mind doing something for me?"

Mistaking the reason for his hesitation, she said, "Of course not. That's what I'm here for."

"You've been awfully good. But I feel, now, that I'd rather like to be by myself for a little while. Do you mind?"

"But I ——" As she spoke he turned his face a little to look at her. She could see that he was wondering whether she would think him discourteous, not whether she would refuse. That had not occurred to him. She was suddenly unable to finish what she had begun to say.

He added, as an afterthought, "You can tell the Sister that I said it would be all right."

She rose to her feet, still silent. She could have found an answer to most things, but not to this native unnoticed

321

arrogance. It unnerved her to see the security of a lifetime poised so carelessly within reach of her overturning hand. "Well," she said, slowly, "you see——"

"It isn't for that. That wouldn't be fair to you."

She had no idea what he meant, but could not say so. There was a silence.

"There's something I want to remember. So would you—as there isn't much time? You've been so sweet about everything." He smiled deliberately, into her eyes.

Suddenly she thought, with unbearable certainty, This is the first time he has needed to coax a woman. "Yes," she said; "of course, that's perfectly . . ." Unable to finish, she went outside and hid herself in the darkness of the next ward. It was a good many years, it occurred to her, since she had cried about anything except her own disappointments and desires.

She had ceased for a little while to listen to the sounds that went on round her, even the instinctive watchfulness of her work suspended. The arrival of Pratt, on her next round, took her entirely by surprise. The first thing she was aware of was the dazzle of a torch across her eyes. She jumped up from the stool she had been sitting on, out of its range.

"Nurse *Kimball*!" The convalescent was still asleep; Pratt's sense of outrage could only vent itself in a hiss, like compressed steam. "Whatever are you doing here? Why aren't you with your patient?"

"I know perfectly well what I'm doing, thank you, Pratt. I specialled cases long before you." Attack was the only form of defence in which Colonna was practised. She was wondering if her face showed, and if Pratt had noticed it. "I went out because he asked me to. I can hear him quite well from here."

"*Hear* him!" It took Pratt a moment or two to recover even such voice as the situation allowed. "You can hear if he haemorrhages, I suppose! Are you absolutely out of your senses, Kimball? To leave a patient because he *asks* you to—a patient in that condition!"

"He knows his condition. That's why he asked to be left alone."

"What did you say to him?" The increased pressure behind Pratt's whisper raised it nearly an octave.

"Nothing, you fool!" The blindness of mounting anger was, on the whole, a relief. Against the dim light of the doorway Pratt's cap, shoulders and elbows stuck out at rigid angles. Colonna added, viciously, "If you're incapable of following adult mental processes I'm sorry; but there's nothing I can do about it."

The outline of Pratt's cap quivered. "Next time Sister comes round," she said, "I shall tell her I can't be responsible for running this ward unless she sends me someone more competent."

Colonna drew a long breath. The tears were drying quickly on her flushed face. "You've got a bloody nerve, Pratt, to think you can speak to me like that." Her voice rose from a whisper to an undertone. The sleeping man grunted and turned over noisily in bed. She moved out towards the doorway, pouring a shrill sibilance as she went. "Competent my foot. You're as much use on a ward yourself as a hen with its head cut off, and you know damned well it's only a fluke you're not doing second to me."

They stopped, a little shaken. A preceding fortnight of underground hostilities made the surface explosion more, rather than less, devastating. They had said these things to one another by hints and implications a dozen times; so that open directness became shocking, like the sudden use of a prohibited weapon in war. The mattress behind creaked as the patient rolled over in search of the more comfortable position he had left. Pratt edged out after Colonna. Her starched apron-bib creaked audibly with the spasmodic rise and fall of her chest.

"Everyone knows Matron wouldn't give you a ward because she thought you weren't fit to look after one. And I'm not surprised."

"Anyhow"—Colonna's half-controlled voice slipped on and

323

off the vocal tones—"I'd sooner have you as first than second. I have to run everything in any case, and at least the cleaning gets done."

"How—how *dare* you speak to me like that when I'm in charge?" Pratt had reached the verge of hysteria, but the darkness supported her. "I shall go to Matron first thing in the morning. I shall give in my notice if you're not moved. I've never been spoken to like it in my life and I——"

"Oh, shut it, you ——'s," murmured the patient, imperfectly awake. The noise had made him dream of his domestic troubles. Still muttering, he lifted the top pillow and bumped it down over his ears.

Pratt backed out into the passage. "You'll have the whole ward awake in a minute," she whispered, very softly.

"*You* were talking," breathed Colonna. They found they had neither of them, at the moment, anything else to say, and tried to conceal from one another their feelings of foolishness and dejection.

"Well," said Pratt, by way of a rearguard action, "you'd better get back to your patient, Nurse. His father can't be here till nearly midday tomorrow. And you know what Sister said."

"Oh, anything," said Colonna sullenly. There was a heaviness in her like a dull pain. She did not realise, till she turned to go in, how near they had both been, at the end, to the open door. He was looking at her as she closed it.

"I'm so sorry," he said, "to have got you into trouble." Afterwards the humour of this seemed to strike him, for he turned his head away and she saw him smile.

"I'm sorry," she said, "for everything. I'm going to sit very quietly in that corner and soon you'll forget I'm there."

"It doesn't matter." She perceived, now, a flat gentleness in his voice that hurt her more than her own sensations. Something had gone out of it. "Nothing would come, anyway. I ought not to have expected it."

"Perhaps if you were to sleep again."

"There'll be time for that."

324

She took his pulse—more even, but weaker than before—entered it, and went over to her chair.

"There's something else," he said.

"Yes?"

"I shouldn't have overheard. But was anything said about my father coming here?"

"Yes. He's coming to see you tomorrow morning."

"Vivian didn't tell me she'd asked him to come."

"It was the hospital. They—often do, you know. They'd have his address on her records, I expect."

"Why haven't I been told?"

"Well . . ." Her voice trailed away. She had become so used to his quiet that she took it for granted, thinking, if she thought at all, that his weakness enforced it. This clipped hardness seemed to belong to someone else; though, in fact, Jan in his travels had not always been able to rely on charm to get what he required.

"Tell them at once, please, that I don't want the message sent."

"I think it's gone." She knew that it had; but so effectively had he imposed his illusion of authority that it was fear, not kindness or caution, that kept her from saying so.

"Gone? Do you suppose these people realise that I'm of age?"

"You were too ill to be worried. They just assumed you'd want to see him, I suppose."

"Why the hell should they assume anything of the kind?"

"Keep him quiet," said Colonna's two years of training. Not that he had spoken loudly; she knew that it would have used less effort if he had. Her voice, in habit-formed reaction, grew mild and maternal.

"Sister will be talking to him, you know, before he comes in here. Perhaps, if you've quarrelled, she could say something first that would help."

"Quarrelled?" He said it with a kind of dubious astonishment, like someone savouring a new joke in very bad taste; and fell silent, either in weariness or in a hopelessness of

325

getting himself understood. But in a few minutes he went on, forcing his voice a little, "We simply have nothing to say to each other. We never have had. How long is he going to be here?"

"It depends, I suppose, on—on how you get on."

"You mean he's going to *wait*?"

"He'll want to stay for the present, I expect."

"But this is quite fantastic. You've sent for my father, without consulting me, in order to let him sit here on the edge of a chair waiting indefinitely for me to die?"

"It doesn't mean that. People often come and——"

"You know perfectly well that's what it means. Surely someone could have asked me whether I wanted to spend my last hours making conversation to an almost total stranger?" This left him a little out of breath. He added, when he had recovered it, "And they wouldn't let Mic come in."

"I'm sorry. You see most people—it's just always done."

"Presently I shan't even be able to talk to him. What will he do all that time? Read the *Tatler*?"

"If you really don't want to see him," said Colonna at last, "perhaps Sister could send him away. But wouldn't he feel rather ——?"

"No. One can't do that sort of thing."

"He won't be in here all the time."

"What will they do if he isn't at home? Broadcast, I—suppose?"

"He was at home. He's on his way, I believe."

"What, on the milk train? They got him up in the night? Really, this—this is too bad."

"He would probably prefer it," she suggested.

"Poor soul. I can see him sitting among the milk cans, wondering how long it will last and what he'd better talk about. You say they always do this?"

"In a place like this . . . a great many people, you know, aren't equal to being alone."

"I see. I hadn't thought of that. . . . I'm sorry, I've been unreasonable."

326

"No. Too reasonable, perhaps. But you ought to be resting now."

"Why?"

"You'll use yourself up."

"That's my own affair."

"Not altogether, here."

"I keep forgetting." His mouth was dry, and she helped him to another drink. He thanked her and said, "I used to think sickness only meant pain, dirt—things that one knows about."

"Most people seem to find those quite unexpected. What more can it be?"

"It's not belonging to yourself."

As if a light had been flashed in them, Colonna's eyes contracted, and she turned them away.

"Is that such a bad thing?"

"Yes." She heard the remnants of passion in his voice. "It's ——" He paused. She saw a look cross his face that might at first have been fear, but was changed to something more like wonder.

"It's death, I suppose," he said.

She wandered away to the uncurtained window and stared out, unseeing, at the few lights left burning in the town below. After an interval she did not measure, she looked at her watch and found that it was time to take his pulse again. If he was sleeping, she thought, she would let it go. It was a long time since he had stirred. But she found him awake, though he did not immediately notice her. She felt a longing to recall him, a craving for some contact, however slight, with his mind; not the hope of establishing a personal relationship, but the need to recapture an experience, as one longs for the repetition of music, or to climb a remembered hill again.

"Are you unhappy?" she said.

He stared at her for a moment as if he were bringing her into focus, then smiled.

"No. I was resting. You wanted me to rest."

"You sound better."

"Perhaps I am."

But she saw, when she looked, that he was beginning to bleed again. Presently she would have to get Pratt to help her with the dressings. She straightened the clothes.

"You've never belonged to another person, have you?" She had not meant to say it; but some compulsion in her brought it out.

He did not answer at once. "I think," he said at last, "that it's better to take death in one piece."

After that she left him undisturbed, and presently he slept again, more deeply than before. Opening her notebook, she added to what she had already written, "Has been somewhat restless, but has slept for short periods. Fluids taken well."

The handle of the door turned softly, and the pink sleepy face of the probationer looked in.

"Please, Nurse, Nurse Pratt says we're just going to do Barton, and could you come for a minute and help lift?"

Colonna raised her eyebrows. "Nurse Pratt was particularly anxious for me not to leave this patient."

"She said it would only take a minute. He's so heavy, you know, he really needs three. If you're not too busy." Her amateurishly-pleated cap disappeared again. She was in awe of Colonna.

Colonna straightened her long limbs, cramped from the chair, stretched, and looked under the cradle at the sandbags and drainage-tube. Everything was in order. She replaced the coverings softly, and looked up to find him awake, his eyes smiling at her.

"She sent for this time, didn't she?"

"Yes, but I don't have to go. Are you comfortable?"

"Yes. Do you know—I am." She hesitated by the bed, making a needless adjustment of the cradle. "The other nurse heard her, too," he said. "So it isn't your responsibility."

"I'd better go, I suppose. She'll drop the man, or something. I shall only be gone a minute. You'll be all right?"

"I shall do very well. Don't be angry with me."

"Angry? You've—you're a very good patient." She turned away quickly to the door; but when she had opened it she came back again. "There's nothing you want before I go?"

"No. Thank you. Nothing now."

"I'll be back before you know it."

"Yes."

In the main ward the screens were round the bed of a hernia patient of sixteen stone.

"I thought," said Pratt, "that as you'd already left your patient for more than half an hour, another minute wouldn't hurt." She slid her hands under Burton's broad buttocks.

"All right"—Colonna clasped her wrist from the other side—"if you can't manage it between you. It's only knack. You have to teach the pro's to lift *some* time or other, you know. Keep your head forward, Barton. Ready—up!"

"Thank you, Nurse," said Pratt distantly. "We shan't need you any more. You can go back to your patient now."

"May I really?"

For Pratt's benefit she drawled, and strolled casually away. But when she was outside the screens she hurried, and crossed the passage nearly at a run.

As soon as she was over the threshold she knew: and knew, then, that she had always known.

His eyes were open, and his mouth set; but his face had no look of resistance or dismay, rather of an intent and eager concentration. The spent traces of a striving which might have been of the body or the mind, only made more complete the alienness of death, the absolute having done with effort, with direction, with desire. She looked down at him, confused with doubts and discoveries of herself, bewildered by what she felt; turning to him as though, if she asked him, he would clarify it all; but he was no longer concerned with her.

The door was still open behind her. She went over on tiptoe, and shut it without sound. Returning to the bed, she folded back the clothes and lifted the cradle. The linen towel that had fixed his waist, loosened from its sandbags, lay crumpled under his left hand. Against his right arm, the mattress was still dented with the thrust of his elbow.

She did not pause, but, as swiftly as if this purpose had brought her, smoothed out the towel, rolled its ends in the sandbags, and laid them closely against his sides. Nothing else had been disturbed. She covered him again, and, seeing that his head was turned a little towards the left, set it straight. When it was done she was still for a moment, looking down at his face between her hands: searching it for she knew not what tacit confidence, or acknowledgement, or even irony. But there was nothing, or nothing related to any thought or emotion that she knew; only the fixity of a forgotten aim, the intentness of an amazement quenched and over.

"*Dead?*" said Pratt. She pushed back her chair so that it squeaked on the polished floor. "What do you mean? When did he go? Why ever did you leave him just now? I told Nurse to tell you not to come unless everything was all right. It was up to you. It's your responsibility. You're senior to me."

"I'll take it," said Colonna slowly. "You needn't worry. I'm leaving the hospital in any case."

"I must ring up Night Sister. I don't know *what* she'll say."

"I've rung her already. Oh, by the way, you'd better take this key. I took it by mistake for the stationery one."

"And Mr. Rosenbaum not called after he specially said. I can't *understand* how anyone who took the least interest in a patient ——"

She rustled down the ward, Colonna keeping pace with a long silent stride. Her advantage of inches always irritated Pratt at close quarters. Near the door she turned to hiss over her shoulder, "And you'd better not start the Offices till I'm there to help you. I want to be sure of having him look nice when his father comes."

T HE whole thing is," said Evans, "that you won't look
at things class-consciously." He swivelled round on
his stool. "When you reduced a thing to its simple
economic factors ——"

"Yes," said Mic. "I know. Look here, I'm sorry, but I'm
afraid I'll have to turn these cultures over to you. I've been
through everything I can manage left-handed."

"O.K. If Mister Scot-Hallard can bear up. I know he likes
his actinomycoses to get a university education."

"These are the treated ones and that's the control. I've put
down some notes about them—can you read the writing?"

"Looks better than usual, to me. Well, as I was saying, it
all boils down to the economic factor in the end. Take this
smash of yours, for instance. If the State—seen the police yet,
by the way?"

"Yes, this morning."

"Spot of bother, I suppose?"

"The blood-counts are here. I've done those. And there
was one for grouping lying about, so I did that too. Have you
got the slip anywhere? It's a two."

"Oh, you wasted your time doing that one. That ought to
have been thrown away. Some mess of Solly Rosenbaum's,
took it for a transfusion and found it had been done already,
or something. Chap's dead, anyway. Any others? . . . I say,
Freeborn? That the lot?"

"Yes. That's all."

Mic reached for a box of paper-clips, and began to attach
a pile of specimen-slips to their reports.

"Here," said Evans, "I can do that for you in half a
minute. Gets on my nerves to see you fumbling about with
one hand."

"Don't look, then."

"What you like, of course. Arm hurting?"

"No, thanks."

Evans returned to his microscope.

Mic worked through the reports, stacked them, and reached over for some finished notes that had to be sorted for filing. The second sheet he came to was headed, "Jan Lingard. Male. 29. Ward: Trafalgar." Then a long screed in Rosenbaum's twirled writing, and at the end, in red "Died, 5.15 A.M." Mic remembered the quarter striking as he lay awake on one of the Casualty examination-couches. It had sounded exactly like all the others. He filed the notes and picked up the next—"Gladys Simmonds. Female." His mind, slackening in weariness, suddenly refused it all. Nothing had happened. He had had a bad night, one of the nights when coughing kept him half-awake and made him dream. Jan was at Cambridge, and owed him a letter.

He reached for another file, and, in moving, jolted his sling against the edge of the bench. With the small, dulled echo of pain, suddenly everything was present again; the wind, the moon, the lopsided beam of the headlight; the guard's unheard whistle. But the train had gone. There was left the empty platform, the grey light in the roof, the stale advertisements; paper blowing about, incompetent passengers asking porters the way.

"Well, Freeborn." Dr. Esmond Lampeter paused behind him, shrugging his scrawny shoulders into a clean white coat and fastening it, as usual, by a single button in the wrong hole. He had a face like a cleanly and intelligent vulture; his predatory nose supported a pair of spectacles, dwarfed by its size, which he was continually straightening, a gesture which showed the back of his right hand, glazed by an X-ray burn thirty years old. "This is the last place where I thought of looking for you. Just been making inquiries which of the wards I'd find you in. Never thought of you struggling up here."

"I haven't done a great deal, sir. I just wanted to keep the

332

special stuff going. My notes are a bit unintelligible, I'm afraid, to anyone else."

"Shouldn't be, my boy. Never be indispensable, it's good art and bad science. What if you'd been killed, hm? Leaving me to decode that scrawl of yours, wasting my time. . . . Sorry to hear about the young fellow with you. Know him well?"

"Yes, sir. Fairly well."

"Hm, sorry about that. Well, you get away home and take it easy. Looks a touch of delayed shock about you, pretty sure to be."

"I'd sooner be here, sir, if there's anything you can use me for. I feel all right."

"No difficulty about that, if you feel up to it. I'm getting out some cancer statistics that want checking with the notes. Long job, I'm afraid, knock off when you've had enough."

He went to his desk behind the glass screen, and came back with some figures he had annotated in his beautiful Greek-formed script. Mic left him with regret; the man's benevolent impersonality, like the wash of air over a wide plain, gave one the sense of freedom from oneself. He got down a thick volume of notes and tried to concentrate on it; but he ached all over with stiffened bruises he had not felt until today, and in his mind he kept seeing Jan's profile under a cotton sheet in the mortuary, with its feel of stale and hackneyed death. There should have been fire for Jan; an olive-wood pyre, or a raft of pine burning on the water, releasing his restless limbs into light ashes and warm rising air. How would he endure the enclosing boards, the earth's weight, the smug encumbrance of the stone? The thought became a horror to him, till its violence jerked some compensating balance into play; and suddenly he seemed to see Jan, arrested for a moment in going about his affairs, turning in the sunlight to smile at his childishness.

He spread out Lampeter's figures on the bench in front of him, and forced himself to attend. Everything was in order and exquisitely clear; it was true enough that if Lampeter himself were to drop dead tomorrow, his successor would find his unfinished work as intelligible as a text-book. Mic, in his checking, worked over the columns and delicate annotations with a kind of abstract love. He began to grasp the novel plan of the statistics; a few minor additions, even, suggested themselves to him, and he noted them on a rough pad of his own, in the straggling, back-sloped lettering of his left hand. Once, at a useful idea, he found himself smiling in pleasure and paused amazedly: till he reflected that here, in this clearness, was all of Jan with which, henceforward, he need be concerned.

"Morning, Freeborn. Have you—Hullo. What have you been doing to yourself this time?"

It was Scot-Hallard, freshly arrived, looking brisk and hearty from his walk through the morning's frost. He peeled off his overcoat as he spoke. He often came on foot when it was fine. His heavy shoulder, intervening between Mic and the nearest window, seemed to block out all the light. The swing doors were still flapping behind him, and the wind of his brisk passage disarranged the papers on the bench. He looked at Mic and his sling with irritation, as at an instrument-trolley short of a pair of forceps.

"It's only a collar-bone, sir." Mic straightened his notes mechanically. Scot-Hallard leaned a square hand, with wiry black hair growing upward to the wrist, against the edge of the bench. His clothes seemed, in spite of their excellent fit, to be strained a little by the force they enclosed. The cold had congealed his breath in a little fringe of droplets along the bottom of his moustache. Mic moved back an inch or two in a vague physical distaste; not giving much thought to the feeling, but obeying it like a habit which other pre-occupations push into the background. "Had you come about the biopsy results? I've got them here, they're both squamous epitheliomata."

"Thought so. How are the cultures going?"

"I'm afraid I've had to pass those on, sir. I thought they were a bit delicate to fiddle with like this. Evans has them, and the results up to date. I explained what you wanted done."

"Yes, yes. Pity. All right. I'm sending up a cervix I want pickled in section for the nurses' gynaecology course—oh, but I suppose you can't do that with one hand either." He looked impatiently over Mic's head at the other benches. "Oh, well, tell someone about it, will you? Can't stop now." He slung his coat over his arm and strode off, setting the papers fluttering again.

Mic re-arranged them, settling his arm into a more comfortable position against the edge of the bench. Dimly he recalled that Scot-Hallard's approach had often been enough to disorganise his mental processes for ten minutes afterwards; wondered at it ,and got on with what he had been doing.

Behind the screen Lampeter straightened his glasses, removed them, polished them with the piece of greyish chamois he kept in his drawer, and focused them on Scot-Hallard as he barged the swing doors open with his shoulder and disappeared. Somewhere in the innocent scientific Eden of the Senior Pathologist's mind, an unregenerate Adam muttered; observing, for the hundredth time, that Scot-Hallard used the place as if it belonged to him. Surely, in heaven's name, thought Lampeter, there were enough semi-skilled assistants about to deal with the surgeons' routine tests? It was like Scot-Hallard to appropriate Freeborn. Only the best was good enough for him, whether he could use it or not. And wasting the lad's time—wasting Lampeter's, in effect—over this actino experiment which, if he read his current literature more carefully, he might know had aborted in Germany a couple of years ago. Well, he had not asked Lampeter's advice in the matter, and Lampeter had no intention of tendering it unsolicited. He decided, however, that later on he would lend young Freeborn the relevant paper, casually, among a pile of others: his German would be perfectly adequate. Unless, indeed, he had read it already; he kept remarkably well abreast of things. Lampeter became conscious of a mild enjoyment, and reproved himself.

Well, he reflected, scratching a sparse eyebrow with the butt of his pen, in a few months now there would be no more

335

Scot-Hallards for him. He hoped that freedom from these petty annoyances would not impair his flexibility, an asset important now as never before. A pity, he thought, to be leaving a lad like Freeborn behind to be made a hack of. He had the right of way of going about things, and his heart was in it; witness the way he had crawled up to his bench this morning, as soon as he was discharged. It was what one would have done oneself at that age; but the moderns, most of them, were soft. His sense of proportion, too, was sound; he had been in no doubt which part of his work to turn over to Evans.

With sudden resolution, Lampeter unlocked the bottom drawer of his desk, straightened his glasses which the abrupt movement had displaced, and took out a file. After all, why not? He had short-listed Steadman very reluctantly. He was overfond of rushing into print, and for pot-hunters Lampeter had very little time. Young Freeborn would provide more work for less noise. Scot-Hallard might not be pleased; but Scot-Hallard was not, after all, quite the pathologist he esteemed himself to be. Scot-Hallard could manage with Evans very well.

Thumbing the neat file over, he reached a leaf containing a list of names; scored one out with fine parallel pen-strokes, and inserted "?, Freeborn" in its stead.

Mic worked on till after dark. Lampeter, who thought he looked ill, stopped on his way out to tell him to go home; but in the end he persuaded someone to let him stay on and finish a test that would not be ready till after six. He had only dozed for a couple of odd half-hours in the night, and was feeling rather sick, aching and heavy-headed, but adequate to this kind of work, which he could have done in his sleep. He filled in the time with filing, and any trivial arrears that came in his way. As weariness grew on him, his reluctance increased to leave this sheltering frame of small activities and entrust himself to solitude. Since, however, the moment had to come, he would not let himself linger beyond the end of what he could usefully do, but tidied up and went away down the

336

deserted yellow-lit corridors, turning them, as he snapped off the switches, into caves of echoing darkness behind him.

When he was out of the gates he began walking mechanically down the blind alley where he generally parked the car, then remembered and went back to the main road. It seemed a long way to the flat; he found that he had wrenched his ankle the night before, not badly enough to be noticed at the time; now it had grown stiff and nagged a little with each step. The night had become very cold, and the air felt heavy as if with the promise of snow. A few tiny flakes were floating in the air, so small and light that they seemed to rise and be blown away again before they could touch the ground.

The flat, unlived-in for twenty-four hours, struck chilly as he let himself in. He had forgotten that the table would still be littered with the last meal he and Jan had eaten together. Bread-and-cheese and beer and celery. Jan had arranged the celery-tops in a feather fan on his side-plate. Mic remembered his brown hand touching the pale leaves as he talked. The cold had kept them crisp; they might just have been bitten off.

Mic cleared up after a fashion; then realised he was empty with hunger, and ate such oddments as the shelves provided. He could not cut bread or spread butter, so the meal was primitive. Pushing the remnants out of sight, he went over to the window and stretched himself in the armchair, putting off the moment when he would have to struggle with his clothes.

The yellow of the electric light kept turning to brown in his aching eyes, so he switched it off. At first only the lighted places in the street were visible, but presently he could see the hard black edges of the roof-tops against the transparent darkness of the sky. The moon had not risen yet.

As, in the effort of limping home, the last of his energy drained away, purpose with its consolations had left him, and nothing remained but the certainty of loss. He did not argue with it or retreat from it or cover its face with the fantasies of hope. His was a mind not skilled in mitigations; neither his studies nor his experience had encouraged them. The species topped their curve and were devoured by their successors; mind foundered in the body's disease; and no compensation was offered. Forgetful and expectant, life moved on. There was no relief, no ivory tower of withdrawal, only the hard peace of adaptation and truth.

Jan also while he lived had made himself no promises, loved no legends, built himself no cities of refuge in the mind. He had had neither the need nor the time. For him the real had been wonderful, sharp-tasting and new as to a child. If anything of him had outlasted the astonishment of death, it must be this which was most his own. Living, as dead, he would be out of call; eager, concerned with his journey, casting no glances behind.

> "*If by miracle can be*
> *This livelong minute true to thee* ——"

Once, a long time ago, as they talked of someone else, he had quoted that to Jan. A reproach had been in his heart; but Jan had only looked up in the quick pleasure with which people greet the neat expression of a dear personal truth. For him it had been a simple statement of the dimension in which he lived. In the minute of miracle his truth was absolute; when that ended, what mattered was to be ready for the next. Mic, who was accustomed to accepting facts on their own terms, had accepted Jan also, as one accepts, along with the uses of fire, the knowledge that it will burn. The burn hurt, but inflicted no sense of wrong.

In this stillness of his mind and the deep exhaustion of the body, a peace fell on him greater than any he had known before. Life ceased to consist in duration; Jan, who would not return, was indestructible, contained in the achieved miracle of being, the instant wholeness that was all of immortality he had known or desired. Mic remembered his face just before the car crashed, full of something unknown beside which death seemed a casual irrelevance.

Very pleasant hast thou been unto me. Mic closed his eyes,

pain silenced him by completion. Against the brilliant blackness of a gable an arc of the moon was rising. O Jonathan, thou wast slain in thine high places.

There was quiet in the street, in the room about him, in his body and mind. Time and place faded in the vagueness of approaching sleep.

He was not awakened at once by the knocking on the door. It blended itself with some dream, so that when he opened his eyes he was not sure what it was that had roused him. He shivered; he was very cold, and so stiff that he could hardly rise from the chair. The moon was high, full in his face. It must be nearly midnight. He had better get to bed. Then the knock came again; a slight, un-urgent sound, the knock it seemed of someone with time on their hands and no great sense of conviction in their errand. Feeling too dull and dazed for speculation, he went over to the door, switching the light on as he passed.

It dazzled him, so that for a moment the unmoving profile in the shadows seemed to be Jan's. Even this caused him no violent feeling, only a stunned suspension of reason. Then he saw that it was Vivian; she stood there, silent, like a sleepwalker, blinking in the sudden light.

"Come in," he said. It was a little strange to find himself speaking; he had been, and still felt, so much alone.

He tried to rouse himself, to wonder why she had come. He could feel nothing, only a dim resentment at being recalled to things, and a half-deadened shock of pain because for a moment she had been like Jan. Her eyes, he saw, had wandered to his sling. So that was it, he thought, a little stupid still with weariness and sleep: she had come to look after him, to ask if he wanted helping with his things, to get him a meal perhaps; she had always wanted to be kind to him. What could one say?

She wandered into the room. She was bareheaded, and in her hair were a few thin flakes of snow that melted to dewdrops as he looked. Her eyes encountered his and passed through them, moving on to the furniture and walls.

He closed the door behind her, but did not at once follow her in. It had come to him that perhaps she wanted to reproach herself with all this, to take the blame; and he did not know how he would answer, or bear with it. He wished he had had time to think and to prepare himself. It was important not to be unkind.

She pulled off the worn fur gloves she was wearing, and laid them down on the table; then picked them up again, hesitantly, as if unsure whether it had been good manners, like a child visiting.

"Mic," she said in a light strengthless voice, "may I stay here for a little while?"

"Of course," he answered, wondering; then came forward quickly and dragged up a chair. He had suddenly noticed her pallor and the blind darkness of her eyes, and thought she was about to faint. "Sit down, my dear," he said, and steadied her into the chair with his hand on her arm.

"Thank you." She ran her fingers lightly along the table's edge, as if to test its substance, seeming scarcely aware of what she did; then, recollecting herself, put her hands together in her lap. "I shall be all right now. You mustn't bother with me any more." She looked up at him; dimly, as if it were an effort to see him. "Go to bed, Mic, dear, you look so tired. I shall be gone when you wake up. I only want to stay for a minute or two."

Mic looked down at her hands. The fingers were blanched with cold, the nails bluish, as if the blood had stopped; they were like the hands of a dead woman. He went over and lit the gas-fire, then knelt down by her and put his good hand over them. "You're awfully cold." He tried to rub them; they felt like marble. "I can't do it properly, I've only got one hand."

"They don't feel cold." She looked down at them, as if she were surprised to see them there.

"The fire will be warm in a minute. You must have something hot to drink. I've got some milk left, I think."

"Thank you," she said again mechanically; then straightened herself, and turned to look at him. "No, Mic, you mustn't worry with me. I don't need anything. It's good of you to let me be here."

"That's foolish," he said gently. He went into the kitchen, and tipping out what was left in the milk-bottle into a saucepan, brought it back to the small gas-ring on the top of the fire.

"That will be nice." She slid from her chair to the rug, holding out her hands to the glow. "I'll take it off when it boils. I won't forget about it."

He fetched a glass and some biscuits and put them down on the table. "You don't want me to go, do you?" he asked, feeling nothing clearly.

"You mustn't feel you have to stay." She spoke still in the same vague voice, light and without substance. "Go into the other room and forget about me. Go to bed, dear. I shouldn't have come here, I know."

"Where else should you come?" he said.

"No. There wasn't anywhere else. I'll go again soon. You're not angry with me. I thought you might be, I didn't know."

"Angry?" he said, groping through slow memory to comprehension. "No. That—isn't anything. I'd forgotten."

She was shivering. He knelt and put his arm round her shoulders.

"How did you get out of the hospital?" he asked.

"I have a few nights off. Till after the——" She controlled herself with a moment's rigidity, and went on without a change of tone, "They think I'm with my father. He's staying the night here. I've been with him most of the day. I told him tonight I had to go back."

The saucepan hissed. Mic put it down by the fire and came back to her. She went on, as if he had not moved, "I couldn't go on being alone."

He bent his head overs hers. His heart hurt him with a physical pain. It had been a statement, without personal appeal; the declaration of an ultimate surrender of the spirit. It

341

was a defeat to which he had been so near that he could feel, almost, the taste of it on her lips. He seemed to pass out of himself, without desire of his own or thought of the future or of the past; feeling only her need and his compassion. It would have been nothing for him to have died for her.

"You're not alone," he said.

She turned her head against him, silently. For a moment her body remained hard with the control she had imposed on herself; then, making no sound, she loosened in his arm, and he felt her tears.

He held her near to him, thinking only to lend her some sense of security; not remembering the nights when the longing to hold her had been like a sword in him, and had kept him waking till the morning. The faint unforgotten scent of her hair was under his mouth, and he could feel, crushed to him as she clung, the lifted softness of her breasts; but it was only as if a child in terror of the dark had run into his arms to be hidden.

He had lied to her too as if to a child, for she would always be alone and he also, though he knew, with a certainty detached from his perception of the present, that they would return to one another, and would pass and repass through one another's flesh and thoughts and spirit, and would seem often to be a single body and sometimes a single mind. But the fact of essential human solitude was, it seemed to him, for the people able to know and to endure it to reserve to themselves.

When her crying lost its first urgency of release, he poured the milk out into the glass and held it up to her. "It's still rather hot. Don't drink it too quickly."

"You must have some too," she said. In some cloudy way she seemed to attach importance to this, and he drank a little to please her.

"Now you must lie down," he told her, when he had taken the empty glass away: and, as this made little impression on her, "You'll have to get some sleep, you know."

She looked up quickly; he felt her fingers clench them-

342

selves on the lapel of his coat. "It's all right," he said. "I'm not going away."

He found her a spare pair of pyjamas and put them to warm by the fire. She undressed mechanically, stopping sometimes to watch him as he moved about the room putting things straight for the night. He was trying to ease his coat off in the bedroom by himself, when she appeared in her drifting way and helped him out of his clothes with practised, impersonal efficiency, tied up his sling and pinned it to his pyjama jacket, then drifted out again. He found her, when he was ready, sitting and staring into the red of the fire.

"Come along." He turned it out, and she blinked and looked up at him. "You're going to sleep now." He remembered as he spoke the extent of his own weariness, which for a time he had forgotten.

She slipped into the bed and lay at the far edge of it, making herself narrow against the wall. "I won't knock your arm," she whispered as he put the light out. "Good night."

Mic lay down. Sleep and fatigue pressed like dark heavy hands on his brain; he wanted nothing but to slide into silence under their weight, to loose himself from his bruised body and flagging mind. He could lie easily, as if he were alone, for she had drawn herself into so little room that even in that small space she hardly touched him. She was quite still, even her breathing made no sound. But he knew in the dark that her eyes were open. Presently, with a tiny, secret movement, he felt her put her finger-tips on the stuff of his sleeve.

She lay, as she had always lain, on his left side. Without speaking he reached out for her, and drew her into the hollow of his arm. She came with a long sigh, her head slipping to his shoulder; he kissed her forehead.

It seemed then that she lay with the heaviness of sleep; but in a little while when his own eyelids were dropping, her voice stirred, hardly moving the darkness.

"Mic, I only wanted you to know, this is what I shall remember you by, always, after I've gone away. More than all the rest. Always."

He made a sleepy questioning sound, the words only half penetrating his mind. "You're not going away."

"Yes. I've no right. I've nothing for you, Mic. I'm beaten."

"So are we all," he said, "in one way or another. Different ways, sometimes. That's the use of being two."

"You say that, my dear. You're kinder than I thought anyone could be. But we know that isn't enough."

He laid his cheek against her hair. "I love you," he said. "I've never ceased to love you."

The words sounded strange in his own ears, for he was emptied of emotion, almost of thought. It was as if his spirit had spoken in a stillness within him.

For a moment she was quite still; then he felt and half saw the lifting of her head as she tried to look into his face. He stooped and kissed her on the lips. They stayed so for a little while; it was a long, strange kiss, without physical passion but curiously intent; they were too spent to know what they found in it, a communion or the taste of their private dedications.

Suddenly, as if a spell had been lifted, Mic looked up and said, in his ordinary voice, "Good Lord, I forgot to open the curtains. We shan't get any air." He slid out of bed and drew them back, letting in a faint not-darkness which seemed like light.

She opened the clothes to receive him back again. "Was it cold out there?"

"Feels like a frost."

"What a shame," she murmured drowsily. "Here." She folded the warmth of her body against him, and almost at once they were asleep.

Vivian opened her eyes in the early light, dimly aware that some slight sound from Mic had aroused her; he had coughed, perhaps, or groaned at a sudden movement in his sleep. Whatever it was, it had not waked him. He lay with his face turned upward; at some time while they slept he had taken away the arm that had been around her, and crossed it, in subconscious defence, over the other that was slung to his chest. It was the posture of an effigy, calm and self-contained. Perhaps it was the watchfulness of his body, guarding its injury and forbidding him quite to relax, that had so dispelled the casual, almost childish abandonment in which he used to sleep, which had so often given her the sense of pathos, and, hardly realised, of her own power. In the grey glimmer of dawn she could see the contours of his face. There were changes of stress about the mouth and eyes, an indefinable shifting of shadows; traces of ill-health were there, but she noticed them, with a faint surprise, after the rest. It was the face, she saw, of a man and a possessor of himself. She knew, without joy or sorrow but in a motionless certainty, that he was the possessor of her self also.

Henceforward their relationship was fixed, she the lover, he the beloved. She believed that he would never abuse it, never perhaps wholly know it; he had a natural humility and he had his own need of her, not final like hers but implicit in him and real. She too would hide the truth a little; for there is a kind of courtesy in such things that love lends, sometimes, when pride has been destroyed.

But she would know always; it would always be she who would want the kiss to last longer, though she might be the first to leave hold; she for whom the times of absence would be empty, though she would often tell him how well she filled them; she who stood to lose everything in losing him, he who would have a little of the stuff of happiness in reserve.

In the secret battle which had underlain their love, of which she, only, had been aware with the mind, she was now and finally the loser. There were several ways in which she might partly have evaded the knowledge she brought to this moment. Half-truths might have sheltered her; that poverty had fought against her; that her work had demanded more of her than was just or than her life could afford; even that she was a woman and had the fluid of submission in her blood-stream. But she knew that she could not surrender on any of these terms without dishonour. Mic had been right long ago: true or not true, that was not a basis on which life could be lived. There was an integrity which, illuminating

345

defeat, could reflect in it the image of victory; and, embracing this, she acknowledged to herself that none of these things had settled her course. Like water she had found her own level; this was as it was, only because she had fought in the conscious craving for self-certainty and power, he in the simple instinctive reaching of his spirit for the good.

The sounds of the birds, dispersed and broken, was beginning, and the footsteps of the earliest workers rang at intervals, clear in the quiet and firm with their morning purpose, along the road. She turned softly on her side, in a position from which, without having to move again, she could lie and watch him; keeping her face pressed close to the pillow so that she might seem to be sleeping when he opened his eyes.

THE END